Praise for JAMAICA KINCAID'S
At the Bottom of the River

"Of a handful of internationally known West Indian writers, only Kincaid so precisely conveys the dual texture of the smaller islands: the translucent overlay of colonial British culture upon people and places so absolutely alien to England. Gently, she peels back the fragile tissues of religion, vocabulary and manners to expose the vibrant life beneath the imported, imposed customs."
                    —Elaine Kendall, *Los Angeles Times Book Review*

"Jamaica Kincaid's first book of short stories . . . plunges us into the strange, magical, shifting world of childhood in the West Indies . . . These pieces are . . . full of brilliant colors, magical symbols, secret feelings and tropical scenery."
                    —Roxana Robinson, *The Philadelphia Inquirer*

"She is a consummate balancer of feeling and craft. She takes no short or long cuts, breathes no windy pomposities: she contents herself with being direct . . . So lush, composed, direct, odd, sharp, and brilliantly lit are Kincaid's word paintings that the reader's presuppositions are cut in two by her seemingly soft edges."
                    —Jacqueline Austin, *Voice Literary Supplement*

"What Kincaid has to tell us, she tells, with her singsong style, in a series of images that are as sweet and mysterious as the secrets that children whisper in your ear."
                    —Suzanne Freeman, *Ms.*

JAMAICA KINCAID
At the Bottom of the River

JAMAICA KINCAID was born in St. John's, Antigua. Her books include *Annie John*, *A Small Place*, *Lucy*, *The Autobiography of My Mother*, *My Brother*, *My Favorite Plant* (editor), and *My Garden (Book):*. She lives with her family in Vermont, and she teaches at Harvard University.

Also by JAMAICA KINCAID

Annie John

A Small Place

Lucy

The Autobiography of My Mother

My Brother

My Favorite Plant (editor)

My Garden (Book):

At the Bottom of the River

JAMAICA KINCAID

AT THE BOTTOM

OF THE RIVER

Farrar, Straus and Giroux • New York

Farrar, Straus and Giroux
18 West 18th Street, New York 10011

Distributed in Canada by Douglas & McIntyre Ltd.
Printed in the United States of America
First published in 1983 by Farrar, Straus and Giroux
First Farrar, Straus and Giroux paperback edition, 2000

Grateful acknowledgment is made to *The New Yorker* for
the following stories, which first appeared in its
pages: "Girl," "In the Night," "At Last,"
"Wingless," "Holidays," "The Letter from Home,"
and "At the Bottom of the River," and to
The Paris Review for "What I Have Been
Doing Lately."
The excerpt at the beginning of
"Wingless" is from *The Water Babies*
by Charles Kingsley.

The Library of Congress has cataloged the hardcover edition as follows:
Kincaid, Jamaica.
  At the bottom of the river / Jamaica Kincaid.
    p. cm.
  Contents: Girl—In the night—At last—[etc.]
  ISBN-13: 978-0-374-10660-7
  ISBN-10: 0-374-10660-6
  I. Title.
PS3561.I425A93
813'.54

                                        83–16445

Paperback ISBN-13: 978-0-374-52734-1
Paperback ISBN-10: 0-374-52734-2

www.fsgbooks.com

12   14   15   13   11

For my mother, Annie, with love, and

for Mr. Shawn, with gratitude and love

Contents

❧

GIRL · 3

IN THE NIGHT · 6

AT LAST · 13

WINGLESS · 20

HOLIDAYS · 29

THE LETTER FROM HOME · 37

WHAT I HAVE BEEN DOING LATELY · 40

BLACKNESS · 46

MY MOTHER · 53

AT THE BOTTOM OF THE RIVER · 62

At the Bottom of the River

→ also, shows it is a one-sided
conversation, sense of desperation
and urgency
Structure shows that these are not
seperate, but all related things in order
to be a woman. They have to be
applied together.

GIRL

Wash the white clothes on Monday and put them on the stone heap; wash the color clothes on Tuesday and put them on the clothesline to dry; don't walk barehead in the hot sun; cook pumpkin fritters in very hot sweet oil; soak your little cloths right after you take them off; when buying cotton to make yourself a nice blouse, be sure that it doesn't have gum on it, because that way it won't hold up well after a wash; soak salt fish overnight before you cook it; is it true that you sing benna in Sunday school?; always eat your food in such a way that it won't turn someone else's stomach; on Sundays try to walk like a lady and not like the slut you are so bent on becoming; don't sing benna in Sunday school; you mustn't speak to wharf-rat boys, not even to give directions; don't eat fruits on the *expects the worst from her* →

street—flies will follow you; *but I don't sing benna on Sundays at all and never in Sunday school*; this is how to sew on a button; this is how to make a buttonhole for the button you have just sewed on; this is how to hem a dress when you see the hem coming down and so to prevent yourself from looking like the slut I know you are so bent on becoming; this is how you iron your father's khaki shirt so that it ← *sew for dad* doesn't have a crease; this is how you iron your father's khaki pants so that they don't have a crease; this is how you grow okra—far from the house, because okra tree harbors red ants; when you are growing dasheen, make sure it gets plenty of water or else it makes your throat itch when you are eating it; this is how you sweep a corner; this is how you sweep ← *clean* a whole house; this is how you sweep a yard; this is how you smile to someone you don't like too much; ← *smile* this is how you smile to someone you don't like at all; this is how you smile to someone you like completely; this is how you set a table for tea; this is how you set a table for dinner; this is how you set a table for dinner with an important guest; this is how you set a table for lunch; this is how you set a table for breakfast; this is how to behave in the presence of ← *behave* men who don't know you very well, and this way they won't recognize immediately the slut I have warned you against becoming; be sure to wash every day, even if it is with your own spit; don't squat *rules/directions on how to be a girl* [handwritten]

down to play marbles—you are not a boy, you know; don't pick people's flowers—you might catch some- thing; don't throw stones at blackbirds, because it might not be a blackbird at all; this is how to make a bread pudding; this is how to make doukona; this is how to make pepper pot; this is how to make a good medicine for a cold; this is how to make a good medicine to throw away a child before it even be- comes a child; this is how to catch a fish; this is how to throw back a fish you don't like, and that way something bad won't fall on you; this is how to bully a man; this is how a man bullies you; this is how to love a man, and if this doesn't work there are other ways, and if they don't work don't feel too bad about giving up; this is how to spit up in the air if you feel like it, and this is how to move quick so that it doesn't fall on you; this is how to make ends meet; always squeeze bread to make sure it's fresh; *but what if the baker won't let me feel the bread?*; you mean to say that after all you are really going to be the kind of woman who the baker won't let near the bread?

cook ← [handwritten]

abortion [handwritten]

love ← [handwritten]

mother to daughter? [handwritten]
rules passed through generations values [handwritten]
does she approve of this structure or is [handwritten]
she just trying to help her survive [handwritten]
→ either way its perpetuating it [handwritten]

IN THE NIGHT

In the night, way into the middle of the night, when the night isn't divided like a sweet drink into little sips, when there is no just before midnight, midnight, or just after midnight, when the night is round in some places, flat in some places, and in some places like a deep hole, blue at the edge, black inside, the night-soil men come.

They come and go, walking on the damp ground in straw shoes. Their feet in the straw shoes make a scratchy sound. They say nothing.

The night-soil men can see a bird walking in trees. It isn't a bird. It is a woman who has removed her skin and is on her way to drink the blood of her secret enemies. It is a woman who has left her skin in a corner of a house made out of wood. It is a woman who is reasonable and admires honeybees in the hibiscus. It is a woman who, as a joke, brays like a donkey when he is thirsty.

There is the sound of a cricket, there is the sound of a church bell, there is the sound of this house creaking, that house creaking, and the other house creaking as they settle into the ground. There is the sound of a radio in the distance—a fisherman listening to merengue music. There is the sound of a man groaning in his sleep; there is the sound of a woman disgusted at the man groaning. There is the sound of the man stabbing the woman, the sound of her blood as it hits the floor, the sound of Mr. Straffee, the undertaker, taking her body away. There is the sound of her spirit back from the dead, looking at the man who used to groan; he is running a fever forever. There is the sound of a woman writing a letter; there is the sound of her pen nib on the white writing paper; there is the sound of the kerosene lamp dimming; there is the sound of her head aching.

The rain falls on the tin roofs, on the leaves in the trees, on the stones in the yard, on sand, on the ground. The night is wet in some places, warm in some places.

There is Mr. Gishard, standing under a cedar tree which is in full bloom, wearing that nice white suit, which is as fresh as the day he was buried in it. The white suit came from England in a brown package: "To: Mr. John Gishard," and so on and so on. Mr.

Gishard is standing under the tree, wearing his nice
suit and holding a glass full of rum in his hand—the
same glass full of rum that he had in his hand shortly
before he died—and looking at the house in which he
used to live. The people who now live in the house
walk through the door backward when they see Mr.
Gishard standing under the tree, wearing his nice
white suit. Mr. Gishard misses his accordion; you
can tell by the way he keeps tapping his foot.

꿎

In my dream I can hear a baby being born. I can
see its face, a pointy little face—so nice. I can see its
hands—so nice, again. Its eyes are closed. It's breathing, the little baby. It's breathing. It's bleating, the
little baby. It's bleating. The baby and I are now
walking to pasture. The baby is eating green grass
with its soft and pink lips. My mother is shaking
me by the shoulders. My mother says, "Little Miss,
Little Miss." I say to my mother, "But it's still
night." My mother says, "Yes, but you have wet
your bed again." And my mother, who is still young,
and still beautiful, and still has pink lips, removes
my wet nightgown, removes my wet sheets from my
bed. My mother can change everything. In my dream
I am in the night.

"What are the lights in the mountains?"

"The lights in the mountains? Oh, it's a jablesse."

"A jablesse! But why? What's a jablesse?"

"It's a person who can turn into anything. But you can tell they aren't real because of their eyes. Their eyes shine like lamps, so bright that you can't look. That's how you can tell it's a jablesse. They like to go up in the mountains and gallivant. Take good care when you see a beautiful woman. A jablesse always tries to look like a beautiful woman."

No one has ever said to me, "My father, a night-soil man, is very nice and very kind. When he passes a dog, he gives a pat and not a kick. He likes all the parts of a fish but especially the head. He goes to church quite regularly and is always glad when the minister calls out, 'A Mighty Fortress Is Our God,' his favorite hymn. He would like to wear pink shirts and pink pants but knows that this color isn't very becoming to a man, so instead he wears navy blue and brown, colors he does not like at all. He met my mother on what masquerades as a bus around here, a long time ago, and he still likes to whistle. Once, while running to catch a bus, he fell and broke his ankle and had to spend a week in hospital. This made him miserable, but he cheered up quite a bit when he saw my mother and me, standing over his white cot, holding bunches of yellow roses and smiling down at him. Then he said, 'Oh, my. Oh, my.' What he likes to do most, my father the night-soil man, is to sit on a big stone under a mahogany tree

and watch small children playing play-cricket while
he eats the intestines of animals stuffed with blood
and rice and drinks ginger beer. He has told me this
many times: 'My dear, what I like to do most,' and
so on. He is always reading botany books and knows
a lot about rubber plantations and rubber trees; but
this is an interest I can't explain, since the only
rubber tree he has ever seen is a specially raised one
in the botanic gardens. He sees to it that my school
shoes fit comfortably. I love my father the night-soil
man. My mother loves my father the night-soil man.
Everybody loves him and waves to him whenever
they see him. He is very handsome, you know, and
I have seen women look at him twice. On special days
he wears a brown felt hat, which he orders from
England, and brown leather shoes, which he also
orders from England. On ordinary days he goes
barehead. When he calls me, I say, 'Yes, sir.' On
my mother's birthday he always buys her some nice
cloth for a new dress as a present. He makes us
happy, my father the night-soil man, and has
promised that one day he will take us to see
something he has read about called the circus."

In the night, the flowers close up and thicken. The
hibiscus flowers, the flamboyant flowers, the bache-
lor's buttons, the irises, the marigolds, the whitehead-
bush flowers, the lilies, the flowers on the daggerbush,

the flowers on the turtleberry bush, the flowers on the soursop tree, the flowers on the sugar-apple tree, the flowers on the mango tree, the flowers on the guava tree, the flowers on the cedar tree, the flowers on the stinking-toe tree, the flowers on the dumps tree, the flowers on the papaw tree, the flowers everywhere close up and thicken. The flowers are vexed.

Someone is making a basket, someone is making a girl a dress or a boy a shirt, someone is making her husband a soup with cassava so that he can take it to the cane field tomorrow, someone is making his wife a beautiful mahogany chest, someone is sprinkling a colorless powder outside a closed door so that someone else's child will be stillborn, someone is praying that a bad child who is living prosperously abroad will be good and send a package filled with new clothes, someone is sleeping.

Now I am a girl, but one day I will marry a woman—a red-skin woman with black bramblebush hair and brown eyes, who wears skirts that are so big I can easily bury my head in them. I would like to marry this woman and live with her in a mud hut near the sea. In the mud hut will be two chairs and one table, a lamp that burns kerosene, a medicine chest, a pot, one bed, two pillows, two sheets, one looking glass, two cups, two saucers, two dinner plates, two forks, two drinking-water glasses, one

china pot, two fishing strings, two straw hats to
ward the hot sun off our heads, two trunks for things
we have very little use for, one basket, one book of
plain paper, one box filled with twelve crayons of
different colors, one loaf of bread wrapped in a
piece of brown paper, one coal pot, one picture of
two women standing on a jetty, one picture of the
same two women embracing, one picture of the same
two women waving goodbye, one box of matches.
Every day this red-skin woman and I will eat bread
and milk for breakfast, hide in bushes and throw
hardened cow dung at people we don't like, climb
coconut trees, pick coconuts, eat and drink the food
and water from the coconuts we have picked, throw
stones in the sea, put on John Bull masks and
frighten defenseless little children on their way home
from school, go fishing and catch only our favorite
fishes to roast and have for dinner, steal green figs to
eat for dinner with the roast fish. Every day we
would do this. Every night I would sing this woman
a song; the words I don't know yet, but the tune is
in my head. This woman I would like to marry
knows many things, but to me she will only tell about
things that would never dream of making me cry;
and every night, over and over, she will tell me something that begins, "Before you were born." I will
marry a woman like this, and every night, every
night, I will be completely happy.

AT LAST

THE HOUSE

I lived in this house with you: the wood shingles, unpainted, weather-beaten, fraying; the piano, a piece of furniture now, collecting dust; the bed in which all the children were born; a bowl of flowers, alive, then dead; a bowl of fruit, but then all eaten. (What was that light?) My hairbrush is full of dead hair. Where are the letters that brought the bad news? Where are they? These glasses commemorate a coronation. What are you now? A young woman. But what are you really? A young woman. I know how hard that is. If only everything would talk. The floorboards made a nice pattern when the sun came in. (Was that the light again?) At night, after cleaning the soot from the lampshade, I lighted the lamp and, before preparing for bed, planned another day. So many things I forgot, though. I hid something under the bed, but then I forgot, and it spawned a feathery white moss, so beautiful; it stank, and that's how I remembered it was there. Now I am looking at you; your lips are soft and parted.

Are they?

I saw the cat open its jaws wide and I saw the roof of its mouth, which was pink with black shading, and its teeth looked white and sharp and dangerous. I had no shells from the sea, which was minutes away. This beautifully carved shelf: you can touch it now. Why did I not let you eat with your bare hands when you wanted to?

Why were all the doors closed so tight shut?

But they weren't closed.

I saw them closed.

What passed between us then? You asked me if it was always the way it is now. But I don't know. I wasn't always here. I wasn't here in the beginning. We held hands once and were beautiful. But what followed? Sleepless nights, oh, sleepless nights. A baby was born on Thursday and was almost eaten, eyes first, by red ants, on Friday. (But the light, where does it come from, the light?) I've walked the length of this room so many times, by now I have traveled a desert.

With me?

With you. Speak in a whisper. I like the way your lips purse when you whisper. You are a woman. Stand over there near the dead flowers. I can see your reflection in the glass bowl. You are soft and curved like an arch. Your limbs are large and un-knotted, your feet unsnared. (It's the light again, now in flashes.)

Was it like a carcass? Did you feed on it?

Yes.

Or was it like a skeleton? Did you live in it?

Yes, that too. We prayed. But what did we pray for? We prayed to be saved. We prayed to be blessed. We prayed for long and happy lives for our children. And always we prayed to see the morning light. Were we saved? I don't know. To this day I don't know. We filled the rooms; I filled the rooms. Eggs boiled violently in that pot. When the hurricane came, we hid in this corner until the wind passed; the rain that time, the rain that time. The foundation of this house shook and the earth washed away. My skin grew hot and damp; then I shivered with excitement.

What did you say to me? What did I not hear?

The mattress was stuffed with coconut fiber. It was our first mattress. It made our skin raw. It harbored bedbugs. I used to stand here, at this window, look-ing out at the shadows of people passing—and they were real people—and I would run my hand over the pattern of ridges in the cover belonging to the kettle. I used to stand over here too, in front of this mirror, and I would run my hands across the stitches in a new tablecloth. And again I would stand here, in front of the cold stove, and run my fingers through a small bag of green coffee beans. In this cage lived a hummingbird. He died after a few days, homesick for the jungle. I tried to take everything one day at a time, just as it was coming up.

And then?

I felt sick. Always I felt sick. I sat in this rocking chair with you on my lap. Let me calm her, I thought, let me calm her. But in my breast my milk soured.

So I was loved?

Yes. You wore your clothes wrapped tight around your body, keeping your warmth to yourself. What greed! But how could you know? A yellow liquid left a stain here.

Is that blood?

Yes, but who bled? That picture of an asphalt lake. He visited an asphalt lake once. He loved me then. I was beautiful. I built a fire. The coals glowed so. Bitter. Bitter. Bitter. There was music, there was dancing. Again and again we touched, and again and again we were beautiful. I could see that. I could see some things. I cried. I could not see everything. What illness was it that caused the worm to crawl out of his leg the day he died? Someone laughed

here. I heard that, and just then I was made happy.
Look. You were dry and warm and solid and small.
I was soft and curved like an arch. I wore blue, bird
blue, and at night I would shine in the dark.

The children?

They weren't here yet, the children. I could hear
their hearts beating, but they weren't here yet. They
were beautiful, but not the way you are. Sometimes
I appeared as a man. Sometimes I appeared as a
hoofed animal, stroking my own brown, shiny back.
Then I left no corner unturned. Nothing frightened
me. A blind bird dashed its head against this closed
window. I heard that. I crossed the open sea alone
at night on a steamer. What was my name—I mean
the name my mother gave to me—and where did I
come from? My skin is now coarse. What pity. What
sorrow. I have made a list. I have measured everything. I have not lied.

But the light. What of the light?
Splintered. Died.

THE YARD

A mountain. A valley. The shade. The sun.

A streak of yellow rapidly conquering a streak of
green. Blending and separating. Children are so
quick: quick to laugh, quick to brand, quick to scorn,
quick to lay claim to the open space.

The thud of small feet running, running. A girl's

shriek—snaps in two. Tumbling, tumbling, the sound of a noon bell. Dry? Wet? Warm? Cold? Nothing is measured here.

An old treasure rudely broken. See how the amber color fades from its rim. Now it is the home of something dark and moist. An ant walking on a sheet of tin laid bare to the sun—crumbles. But what is an ant? Secreting, secreting; always secreting. The skin of an orange—removed as if it had been a decorous and much-valued belt. A frog, beaded and creased, moldy and throbbing—no more than a single leap in a single day.

(But at last, at last, to whom will this view belong? Will the hen, stripped of its flesh, its feathers scattered perhaps to the four corners of the earth, its bones molten and sterilized, one day speak? And what will it say? I was a hen? I had twelve chicks? One of my chicks, named Beryl, took a fall?)

Many secrets are alive here. A sharp blow delivered quicker than an eye blink. A sparrow's eggs. A pirate's trunk. A fisherman's catch. A tree, bearing fruits. A bullying boy's marbles. All that used to be is alive here.

Someone has piled up stones, making a small enclosure for a child's garden, and planted a child's flowers, bluebells. Yes, but a child is too quick, and the bluebells fall to the cool earth, dying and living in perpetuity.

Unusually large berries, red, gold, and indigo, sliced open and embedded in soft mud. The duck's bill, hard and sharp and shiny; the duck itself, driven and ruthless. The heat, in waves, coiling and uncoiling until everything seeks shelter in the shade.

Sensing the danger, the spotted beetle pauses, then retraces its primitive crawl. Red fluid rock was deposited here, and now the soil is rich in minerals. On the vines, the ripening vegetables.

But what is a beetle? What is one fly? What is one day? What is anything after it is dead and gone? Another beetle will pause, sensing the danger. Another day, identical to this day . . . then the rain, beating the underbrush hard, causing the turtle to bury its head even more carefully. The stillness comes and the stillness goes. The sun. The moon.

Still the sounds of voices, muted and then clear, emptying and filling up, saying:

"What was the song they used to sing and made fists and pretended to be Romans?"

WINGLESS

The small children are reading from a book filled with simple words and sentences.

" 'Once upon a time there was a little chimney-sweep, whose name was Tom.' "

" 'He cried half his time, and laughed the other half.' "

" 'You would have been giddy, perhaps, at looking down: but Tom was not.' "

" 'You, of course, would have been very cold sitting there on a September night, without the least bit of clothes on your wet back; but Tom was a water-baby, and therefore felt cold no more than a fish.' "

The children have already learned to write their names in beautiful penmanship. They have already

learned how many farthings make a penny, how many
pennies make a shilling, how many shillings make a
pound, how many days in April, how many stone in
a ton. Now they singsong here and tumble there,
tearing skirts with swift movements. Must Dulcie
really cry after thirteen of her play chums have sat
on her? There, Dulcie, there. I myself have been
kissed by many rude boys with small, damp lips, on
their way to boys' drill. I myself have humped girls
under my mother's house. But I swim in a shaft of
light, upside down, and I can see myself clearly,
through and through, from every angle. Perhaps I
stand on the brink of a great discovery, and perhaps
after I have made my great discovery I will be sent
home in chains. Then again, perhaps my life is as
predictable as an insect's and I am in my pupa stage.
How low can I sink, then? That woman over there,
that large-bottomed woman, is important to me. It's
for her that I save up my sixpences instead of spending for sweets. Is this a love like no other? And what
pain have I caused her? And does she love me? My
needs are great, I can see. But there are the children
again (of which I am one), shrieking, whether in
pain or pleasure I cannot tell. The children, who are
beautiful in groupings of three, and who only last
night pleaded with their mothers to sing softly to
them, are today maiming each other. The children

at the end of the day have sour necks, frayed hair,
dirt under their fingernails, scuffed shoes, torn cloth-
ing. And why? First they must be children.

I shall grow up to be a tall, graceful, and altogether beautiful woman, and I shall impose on large
numbers of people my will and also, for my own
amusement, great pain. But now. I shall try to see
clearly. I shall try to tell differences. I shall try to
distinguish the subtle gradations of color in fine cloth,
of fingernail length, of manners. That woman over
there. Is she cruel? Does she love me? And if not,
can I make her? I am not yet tall, beautiful, graceful,
and able to impose my will. Now I swim in a shaft
of light and can see myself clearly. The schoolhouse
is yellow and stands among big green-leaved trees.
Inside are our desks and a woman who wears spec-
tacles, playing the piano. Is a girl who can sing
"Gaily the troubadour plucked his guitar" in a pleasing way worthy of being my best friend? There is the
same girl, unwashed and glistening, setting traps for
talking birds. Is she to be one of my temptations?
Oh, this must be a love like no other. But how can
my limbs that hate be the same limbs that love?
How can the same limbs that make me blind make
me see? I am defenseless and small. I shall try to
see clearly. I shall try to separate and divide things
as if they were sums, as if they were drygoods on

the grocer's shelves. Is this my mother? Is she here to embarrass me? What shall I say about her behind her back, when she isn't there, long after she has gone? In her smile lies her goodness. Will I always remember that? Am I horrid? And if so, will I always be that way? Not getting my own way causes me to fret so, I clench my fist. My charm is limited, and I haven't learned to smile yet. I have picked many flowers and then deliberately torn them to shreds, petal by petal. I am so unhappy, my face is so wet, and still I can stand up and walk and tell lies in the face of terrible punishments. I can see the great danger in what I am—a defenseless and pitiful child. Here is a list of what I must do. So is my life to be like an apprenticeship in dressmaking, a thorny path to carefully follow or avoid? Inside, standing around the spectacled woman playing the piano, the children are singing a song in harmony. The children's voices: pinks, blues, yellows, violets, all suspended. All is soft, all is embracing, all is comforting. And yet I myself, at my age, have suffered so. My tears, big, have run down my cheeks in uneven lines—my tears, big, and my hands too small to hold them. My tears have been the result of my disappointments. My disappointments stand up and grow ever taller. They will not be lost to me. There they are. Let me pin tags on them. Let me have them

registered, like newly domesticated animals. Let me
cherish my disappointments, fold them up, tuck them
away, close to my breast, because they are so
important to me.

But again I swim in a shaft of light, upside down,
and I can see myself clearly, through and through,
from every angle. Over there, I stand on the brink of
a great discovery, and it is possible that like an
ancient piece of history my presence will leave room
for theories. But who will say? For days my body
has been collecting water, but still I won't cry. What
is that to me? I am not yet a woman with a terrible
and unwanted burden. I am not yet a dog with a cruel
and unloving master. I am not yet a tree growing on
barren and bitter land. I am not yet the shape of
darkness in a dungeon.

Where? What? Why? How then? Oh, that!

I am primitive and wingless.

❧

"Don't eat the strings on bananas—they will wrap
around your heart and kill you."

"Oh. Is that true?"

"No."

"Is that something to tell children?"

"No. But it's so funny. You should see how you
look trying to remove all the strings from the
bananas with your monkey fingernails. Frightened?"

"Frightened. Very frightened."

❧

Today, keeping a safe distance, I followed the woman I love when she walked on a carpet of pond lilies. As she walked, she ate some black nuts, pond-lily black nuts. She walked for a long time, saying what must be wonderful things to herself. Then in the middle of the pond she stopped, because a man had stood up suddenly in front of her. I could see that he wore clothes made of tree bark and sticks in his ears. He said things to her and I couldn't make them out, but he said them to her so forcefully that drops of brown water sprang from his mouth. The woman I love put her hands over her ears, shielding herself from the things he said. Then he put wind in his cheeks and blew himself up until in the bright sun he looked like a boil, and the woman I love put her hands over her eyes, shielding herself from the way he looked. Then, instead of removing her cutlass from the folds of her big and beautiful skirt and cutting the man in two at the waist, she only smiled —a red, red smile—and like a fly he dropped dead.

❧

The sea, the shimmering pink-colored sand, the swimmers with hats, two people walking arm in arm, talking in each other's face, dots of water landing on noses, the sea spray on ankles, on over-developed calves, the blue, the green, the black, so deep, so smooth, a great and swift undercurrent,

glassy, the white wavelets, a storm so blinding that
the salt got in our eyes, the sea turning inside out,
shaking everything up like a bottle with sediment, a
boat with two people heaving a brown package
overboard, the mystery, the sharp teeth of that
yellow spotted eel, the wriggle, the smooth lines,
open mouths, families of great noisy birds, families
of great noisy people, families of biting flies, the
sea, following me home, snapping at my heels, all
the way to the door, the sea, the woman.

"I have frightened you? Again, you are frightened of me?"

"You have frightened me. I am very frightened
of you."

"Oh, you should see your face. I wish you could
see your face. How you make me laugh."

🍃

And what are my fears? What large cows! When
I see them coming, shall I run and hide face down in
the gutter? Are they really cows? Can I stand in
a field of tall grass and see nothing for miles and
miles? On the other hand, the sky, which is big and
blue as always, has its limits. This afternoon the
wind is loud as in a hurricane. There isn't enough
light. There is a noise—I can't tell where it is coming from. A big box has stamped on it "Handle
Carefully." I have been in a big white building with

curving corridors. I have passed a dead person.
There is the woman I love, who is so much bigger
than me.

❦

That mosquito . . . now a stain on the wall. That
lizard, running up and down, up and down . . . now
so still. That ant, bloated and sluggish, a purseful of
eggs in its jaws . . . now so still. That blue-and-green
bird, head held aloft, singing . . . now so still. That
land crab, moving slowly, softly, even beautifully,
sideways . . . but now so still. That cricket, standing
on a tree stem, so ugly, so revolting, I am made so
unhappy . . . now so still. That mongoose, now asleep
in its hole, now stealing the sleeping chickens, moving
so quickly, its eyes like two grains of light . . . now
so still. That fly, moving so contentedly from tea bun
to tea bun . . . now so still. That butterfly, moving
contentedly from beautiful plant to beautiful plant
in the early-morning sun . . . now so still. That tad-
pole, swimming playfully in the shallow water . . .
now so still.

I shall cast a shadow and I shall remain unaware.

My hands, brown on this side, pink on this side,
now indiscriminately dangerous, now vagabond and
prodigal, now cruel and careless, now without remorse or forgiveness, but now innocently slipping
into a dress with braided sleeves, now holding an

ice-cream cone, now reaching up with longing, now clasped in prayer, now feeling for reassurance, now pleading my desires, now pleasing, and now, even now, so still in bed, in sleep.

HOLIDAYS

I sit on the porch facing the mountains. I sit on a wicker couch looking out the window at a field of day lilies. I walk into a room where someone—an artist, maybe—has stored some empty canvases. I drink a glass of water. I put the empty glass, from which I have just drunk the water, on a table. I notice two flies, one sitting on top of the other, flying around the room. I scratch my scalp, I scratch my thighs. I lift my arms up and stretch them above my head. I sigh. I spin on my heels once. I walk around the dining-room table three times. I see a book lying on the dining-room table, and I pick it up. The book is called *An Illustrated Encyclopedia of Butterflies and Moths*. I leaf through the book, looking only at the pictures, which are bright and beautiful. From my looking through the book, the word "thorax" sticks in my mind. "Thorax," I say, "thorax, thorax," I don't know how many times. I bend over and touch my toes. I stay in that position until I count to one hundred. As I count, I pretend to be counting off balls on a ball frame. As I count the balls, I pretend that they are the colors red, green, blue, and yellow. I walk over to the fireplace. Standing in front of the fireplace, I try to write my name in the dead ashes with my big toe. I cannot write my name in the dead ashes with my big toe. My big toe, now dirty, I try to clean by rubbing it vigorously on a clean royal-blue rug. The royal-blue rug now has a dark spot, and my big toe has a strong burning sensation. Oh, sensation. I am filled with sensation. I feel—oh, how I feel. I feel, I feel, I feel. I have no words right now for how I feel. I take a walk down the road in my bare feet. I feel the stones on the road, hard and sharp against my soft, almost pink soles. Also, I feel the hot sun beating down on my bare neck. It is midday. Did I say that? Must I say that? Oh me, oh my. The road on which I walk barefoot leads to the store—the village store. Should I go to the village store or should I not go to the village store? I can if I want. If I go to the village store, I can buy a peach. The peach will be warm from sitting in a box in the sun. The peach will not taste sweet and the peach will not taste sour. I will know that I am eating a peach only by looking at it. I will not go to the store. I will sit on the porch facing the mountains.

I sit on the porch facing the mountains. The porch is airy and spacious. I am the only person sitting on the porch. I look at myself. I can see myself. That is, I can see my chest, my abdomen, my legs, and my arms. I cannot see my hair, my ears, my face, or my collarbone. I can feel them, though. My nose is moist with sweat. Locking my fingers, I put my hands on my head. I see a bee, a large bumblebee, flying around aimlessly. I remove my hands from resting on my head, because my arms are tired. But also I have just remembered a superstition: if you sit with your hands on your head, you will kill your mother. I have many superstitions. I believe all of them. Should I read a book? Should I make myself something to drink? But what? And hot or cold? Should I write a letter? I should write a letter. I will write a letter. "Dear So-and-So, I am . . . and then I got the brilliant idea . . . I was very amusing . . . I had enough, I said . . . I saw what I came to see, I thought . . . I am laughing all the way to the poorhouse. I grinned . . . I just don't know anymore. I remain, etc." I like my letter. Perhaps I shall keep my letter to myself. I fold up the letter I have just written and put it between the pages of the book I am trying to read. The book is lying in my lap. I look around me, trying to find something on which to focus my eyes. I see ten ants. I count them as they wrestle with a speck of food. I am not fascinated by that. I see my toes moving up and down as if they were tapping out a beat. Why are my toes tapping? I am fascinated by that. A song is going through my mind. It goes, "There was a man from British Guiana, Who used to play a piana. His foot slipped, His trousers ripped . . ." I see, I see. Yes. Now. Suddenly I am tired. I am yawning. Perhaps I will take a nap. Perhaps I will take a long nap. Perhaps I will take a nice long nap. Perhaps, while taking my nap, I will have a dream, a dream in which I am not sitting on the porch facing the mountains.

🙢

"I have the most sensible small suitcase in New York.

"I have the most sensible small car in New York.

"I will put my sensible small suitcase in my sensible small car and drive on a sensible and scenic road to the country.

"In the country, I live in a sensible house.

"I am a sensible man.

"It is summer.

"Look at that sunset. Too orange.

"These pebbles. Not pebbly enough.

"A house with interesting angles.

"For dinner I will eat scallops. I love the taste of scallops.

"These are my chums—the two boys and the girl. My chums are the most beautiful chums. The two boys know lumberjacks in Canada, and the girl is fragile. After dinner, my chums and I will play cards, and while playing cards we will tell each other jokes —such funny jokes—but later, thinking back, we will be so pained, so unsettled."

❦

The deerflies, stinging and nesting in wet, matted hair; broken bottles at the bottom of the swimming hole; mosquitoes; a family of skunks eating the family garbage; a family of skunks spraying the family dog; washing the family dog with cans of tomato juice to remove the smell of the skunks; a not-too-fast-moving woodchuck crossing the road; running over the not-too-fast-moving woodchuck; the camera forgotten, exposed in the hot sun; the prism in the camera broken, because the camera has been forgotten, exposed in the hot sun; spraining a finger while trying to catch a cricket ball; spraining a finger while trying to catch a softball; stepping on dry brambles while walking on the newly cut hayfields; the hem of a skirt caught in a barbed-wire fence; the great sunstroke, the great pain, the not at all great day spent in bed.

❦

Inside, the house is still. Outside, the blind man takes a walk. It is midday, and the blind man casts

a short, fat shadow as he takes a walk. The blind
man is a young man, twenty-seven. The blind man
has been blind for only ten years. The blind man
was infatuated with the driver of his school bus, a
woman. No. The blind man was in love with the
driver of his school bus, a woman. The blind man
saw the driver of his school bus, a woman, kissing a
man. The blind man killed the driver of his school
bus, a woman, and then tried to kill himself. He did
not die, so now he is just a blind man. The blind man
is pale and sickly-looking. He doesn't return a greeting. Everybody knows this, and they stay away from
him. Not even the dog pays any attention to his
comings and goings.

∾

"But things are so funny here."

"But where? But how?"

"We are going to the May fair, but it's July. They
are dancing a May dance around a Maypole, but
it's July. They are crowning a May queen, but it's
July. At Christmas, just before our big dinner, we
take a long swim in the warm seawater. After that,
we do not bathe, and in the heat the salt dries on
our bodies in little rings."

"Aren't things funny here?"

"Yes, things are funny here."

∾

The two boys are fishing in Michigan, catching fish with live frogs. The two boys do not need a comfortable bed and a nice pillow at night, or newly baked bread for breakfast, or roasted beef on Sundays, or hymns in a cathedral, or small-ankled children wearing white caps, or boxes of fruit from the tropics, or nice greetings and sad partings, or light bulbs, or the tremor of fast motor vehicles, or key chains, or a run-down phonograph, or rubbish baskets, or meek and self-sacrificing women, or inkwells, or shaving kits. The two boys have visited the Mark Twain museum in Missouri and taken photographs. The two boys have done many things and taken photographs. Here are the two boys milking two cows in Wyoming. Here are the two boys seated on the hood of their car just after changing the tire. Here are the two boys dressed up as gentlemen. Here are the two boys dressed up as gentlemen and looking for large-breasted women.

✑

That man, a handsome man; that woman, a beautiful woman; those children, such gay children; great laughter; wild and sour berries; wild and sweet berries; pink and blue-black berries; fields with purple flowers, blue flowers, yellow flowers; a long road; a long and curved road; a car with a collapsible top; big laughs; big laughing in the bushes;

no, not the bushes—the barn; no, not the barn—the house; no, not the house—the trees; no, not the trees, no; big laughing all the same; a crushed straw hat that now fits lopsided; milk from a farm; eggs from a farm; a farm; in the mountains, no clear reception on the radio; no radio; no clothes; no free-floating anxiety; no anxiety; no automatic-lighting stoves; a walk to the store; a walk; from afar, the sound of great laughing; the piano; from afar, someone playing the piano; late-morning sleepiness; many, many brown birds; a big blue-breasted bird; a smaller red-breasted bird; food roasted on sticks; ducks; wild ducks; a pond; so many wide smiles; no high heels; buying many funny postcards; sending many funny postcards; taking the rapids; and still, great laughter.

THE LETTER

FROM HOME

Ι milked the cows, I churned the butter, I stored the cheese, I baked the bread, I brewed the tea, I washed the clothes, I dressed the children; the cat meowed, the dog barked, the horse neighed, the mouse squeaked, the fly buzzed, the goldfish living in a bowl stretched its jaws; the door banged shut, the stairs creaked, the fridge hummed, the curtains billowed up, the pot boiled, the gas hissed through the stove, the tree branches heavy with snow crashed against the roof; my heart beat loudly *thud! thud!*, tiny beads of water gathered on my nose, my hair went limp, my waist grew folds, I shed my skin; lips have trembled, tears have flowed, cheeks have puffed, stomachs have twisted with pain; I went to the country, the car broke down, I walked back; the boat sailed, the waves broke, the horizon tipped,

the jetty grew small, the air stung, some heads
bobbed, some handkerchiefs fluttered; the drawers
didn't close, the faucets dripped, the paint peeled, the
walls cracked, the books tilted over, the rug no
longer lay out flat; I ate my food, I chewed each
mouthful thirty-two times, I swallowed carefully, my
toe healed; there was a night, it was dark, there was
a moon, it was full, there was a bed, it held sleep;
there was movement, it was quick, there was a being,
it stood still, there was a space, it was full, then there
was nothing; a man came to the door and asked,
"Are the children ready yet? Will they bear their
mother's name? I suppose you have forgotten that
my birthday falls on Monday after next? Will you
come to visit me in hospital?"; I stood up, I sat
down, I stood up again; the clock slowed down, the
post came late, the afternoon turned cool; the cat
licked his coat, tore the chair to shreds, slept in a
drawer that didn't close; I entered a room, I felt my
skin shiver, then dissolve, I lighted a candle, I saw
something move, I recognized the shadow to be my
own hand, I felt myself to be one thing; the wind was
hard, the house swayed, the angiosperms prospered,
the mammal-like reptiles vanished (Is the Heaven
to be above? Is the Hell below? Does the Lamb still
lie meek? Does the Lion roar? Will the streams all
run clear? Will we kiss each other deeply later?);
in the peninsula some ancient ships are still anchored,

in the field the ox stands still, in the village the
leopard stalks its prey; the buildings are to be tall,
the structures are to be sound, the stairs are to be
winding, in the rooms sometimes there is to be a
glow; the hats remain on the hat stand, the coats
hang dead from the pegs, the hyacinths look as if
they will bloom—I know their fragrance will be
overpowering; the earth spins on its axis, the axis
is imaginary, the valleys correspond to the mountains, the mountains correspond to the sea, the sea
corresponds to the dry land, the dry land corresponds to the snake whose limbs are now reduced;
I saw a man, He was in a shroud, I sat in a rowboat,
He whistled sweetly to me, I narrowed my eyes, He
beckoned to me, Come now; I turned and rowed
away, as if I didn't know what I was doing.

WHAT I

HAVE BEEN

DOING LATELY

What I have been doing lately: I was lying in bed and the doorbell rang. I ran downstairs. Quick. I opened the door. There was no one there. I stepped outside. Either it was drizzling or there was a lot of dust in the air and the dust was damp. I stuck out my tongue and the drizzle or the damp dust tasted like government school ink. I looked north. I looked south. I decided to start walking north. While walking north, I noticed that I was barefoot. While walking north, I looked up and saw the planet Venus. I said, "It must be almost morning." I saw a monkey in a tree. The tree had no

leaves. I said, "Ah, a monkey. Just look at that.
A monkey." I walked for I don't know how long
before I came up to a big body of water. I wanted to
get across it but I couldn't swim. I wanted to get
across it but it would take me years to build a boat.
I wanted to get across it but it would take me I didn't
know how long to build a bridge. Years passed and
then one day, feeling like it, I got into my boat and
rowed across. When I got to the other side, it was
noon and my shadow was small and fell beneath
me. I set out on a path that stretched out straight
ahead. I passed a house, and a dog was sitting on
the verandah but it looked the other way when it
saw me coming. I passed a boy tossing a ball in the
air but the boy looked the other way when he saw
me coming. I walked and I walked but I couldn't tell
if I walked a long time because my feet didn't feel
as if they would drop off. I turned around to see
what I had left behind me but nothing was familiar.
Instead of the straight path, I saw hills. Instead of
the boy with his ball, I saw tall flowering trees. I
looked up and the sky was without clouds and seemed
near, as if it were the ceiling in my house and, if I
stood on a chair, I could touch it with the tips of my
fingers. I turned around and looked ahead of me
again. A deep hole had opened up before me. I
looked in. The hole was deep and dark and I
couldn't see the bottom. I thought, What's down

there?, so on purpose I fell in. I fell and I fell, over and over, as if I were an old suitcase. On the sides of the deep hole I could see things written, but perhaps it was in a foreign language be- cause I couldn't read them. Still I fell, for I don't know how long. As I fell I began to see that I didn't like the way falling made me feel. Falling made me feel sick and I missed all the people I had loved. I said, I don't want to fall anymore, and I reversed myself. I was standing again on the edge of the deep hole. I looked at the deep hole and I said, You can close up now, and it did. I walked some more without knowing distance. I only knew that I passed through days and nights, I only knew that I passed through rain and shine, light and darkness. I was never thirsty and I felt no pain. Looking at the horizon, I made a joke for myself: I said, "The earth has thin lips," and I laughed.

Looking at the horizon again, I saw a lone figure coming toward me, but I wasn't frightened because I was sure it was my mother. As I got closer to the figure, I could see that it wasn't my mother, but still I wasn't frightened because I could see that it was a woman.

When this woman got closer to me, she looked at me hard and then she threw up her hands. She must have seen me somewhere before because she said,

"It's you. Just look at that. It's you. And just what have you been doing lately?"

I could have said, "I have been praying not to grow any taller."

I could have said, "I have been listening carefully to my mother's words, so as to make a good imitation of a dutiful daughter."

I could have said, "A pack of dogs, tired from chasing each other all over town, slept in the moonlight."

Instead, I said, What I have been doing lately: I was lying in bed on my back, my hands drawn up, my fingers interlaced lightly at the nape of my neck. Someone rang the doorbell. I went downstairs and opened the door but there was no one there. I stepped outside. Either it was drizzling or there was a lot of dust in the air and the dust was damp. I stuck out my tongue and the drizzle or the damp dust tasted like government school ink. I looked north and I looked south. I started walking north. While walking north, I wanted to move fast, so I removed the shoes from my feet. While walking north, I looked up and saw the planet Venus and I said, "If the sun went out, it would be eight minutes before I would know it." I saw a monkey sitting in a tree that had no leaves and I said, "A monkey. Just look at that. A monkey." I picked up a stone and

I threw it at the monkey. The monkey, seeing the
stone, quickly moved out of its way. Three times I
threw a stone at the monkey and three times it
moved away. The fourth time I threw the stone, the
monkey caught it and threw it back at me. The stone
struck me on my forehead over my right eye, making
a deep gash. The gash healed immediately but now
the skin on my forehead felt false to me. I walked
for I don't know how long before I came to a big
body of water. I wanted to get across, so when the
boat came I paid my fare. When I got to the other
side, I saw a lot of people sitting on the beach and
they were having a picnic. They were the most
beautiful people I had ever seen. Everything about
them was black and shiny. Their skin was black and
shiny. Their shoes were black and shiny. Their hair
was black and shiny. The clothes they wore were
black and shiny. I could hear them laughing and
chatting and I said, I would like to be with these
people, so I started to walk toward them, but when
I got up close to them I saw that they weren't at
a picnic and they weren't beautiful and they weren't
chatting and laughing. All around me was black
mud and the people all looked as if they had been
made up out of the black mud. I looked up and saw
that the sky seemed far away and nothing I could
stand on would make me able to touch it with my
fingertips. I thought, If only I could get out of this,

so I started to walk. I must have walked for a long time because my feet hurt and felt as if they would drop off. I thought, If only just around the bend I would see my house and inside my house I would find my bed, freshly made at that, and in the kitchen I would find my mother or anyone else that I loved making me a custard. I thought, If only it was a Sunday and I was sitting in a church and I had just heard someone sing a psalm. I felt very sad so I sat down. I felt so sad that I rested my head on my own knees and smoothed my own head. I felt so sad I couldn't imagine feeling any other way again. I said, I don't like this. I don't want to do this anymore. And I went back to lying in bed, just before the doorbell rang.

BLACKNESS

Conflicts who she is

How soft is the blackness as it falls. It falls
in silence and yet it is deafening, for no
other sound except the blackness falling can be heard.
The blackness falls like soot from a lamp with an
untrimmed wick. The blackness is visible and yet it
is invisible, for I see that I cannot see it. The blackness fills up a small room, a large field, an island, my
own being. The blackness cannot bring me joy but
often I am made glad in it. The blackness cannot be
separated from me but often I can stand outside
it. The blackness is not the air, though I breathe it.
The blackness is not the earth, though I walk on it.
The blackness is not water or food, though I drink
and eat it. The blackness is not my blood, though it
flows through my veins. The blackness enters my
many-tiered spaces and soon the significant word and

event recede and eventually vanish: in this way I am annihilated and my form becomes formless and I am absorbed into a vastness of free-flowing matter. In the blackness, then, I have been erased. I can no longer say my own name. I can no longer point to myself and say "I." In the blackness my voice is silent. First, then, I have been my individual self, carefully banishing randomness from my existence, then I am swallowed up in the blackness so that I am one with it...

There are the small flashes of joy that are present in my daily life: the upturned face to the open sky, the red ball tumbling from small hand to small hand, as small voices muffle laughter; the sliver of orange on the horizon, a remnant of the sun setting. There is the wide stillness, trembling and waiting to be violently shattered by impatient demands.

("May I now have my bread without the crust?"

"But I long ago stopped liking my bread without the crust!")

All manner of feelings are locked up within my human breast and all manner of events summon them out. How frightened I became once on looking down to see an oddly shaped, ash-colored object that I did not recognize at once to be a small part of my own foot. And how powerful I then found that moment, so that I was not at one with myself and I felt myself separate, like a brittle sub-

stance dashed and shattered, each separate part
without knowledge of the other separate parts. I
then clung fast to a common and familiar object (my
lamp, as it stood unlit on the clean surface of my
mantelpiece), until I felt myself steadied, no longer
alone at sea in a small rowboat, the waves cruel and
unruly. What is my nature, then? For in isolation I
am all purpose and industry and determination and
prudence, as if I were the single survivor of a species
whose evolutionary history can be traced to the most
ancient of ancients; in isolation I ruthlessly plow the
deep silences, seeking my opportunities like a miner
seeking veins of treasure. In what shallow glimmering space shall I find what glimmering glory? The
stark, stony mountainous surface is turned to green,
rolling meadow, and a spring of clear water, its
origins a mystery, its purpose and beauty constant,
draws all manner of troubled existence seeking
solace. And again and again, the heart—buried
deeply as ever in the human breast, its four chambers exposed to love and joy and pain and the small
shafts that fall with desperation in between.

❦

I sat at a narrow table, my head, heavy with sleep,
resting on my hands. I dreamed of bands of men
who walked aimlessly, their guns and cannons slack-
ened at their sides, the chambers emptied of bullets
and shells. They had fought in a field from time to

time and from time to time they grew tired of it. They walked up the path that led to my house and as they walked they passed between the sun and the earth; as they passed between the sun and the earth they blotted out the daylight and night fell immediately and permanently. No longer could I see the blooming trefoils, their overpowering perfume a constant giddy delight to me; no longer could I see the domesticated animals feeding in the pasture; no longer could I see the beasts, hunter and prey, leading a guarded existence; no longer could I see the smith moving cautiously in a swirl of hot sparks or bent over anvil and bellows. The bands of men marched through my house in silence. On their way, their breath scorched some flowers I had placed on a dresser, with their bare hands they destroyed the marble columns that strengthened the foundations of my house. They left my house, in silence again, and they walked across a field, opposite to the way they had come, still passing between the sun and the earth. I stood at a window and watched their backs until they were just a small spot on the horizon.

❦

I see my child arise slowly from her bed. I see her cross the room and stand in front of the mirror. She looks closely at her straight, unmarred body. Her skin is without color, and when passing through a small beam of light, she is made transparent. Her eyes are ruby, revolving orbs, and they burn like coals caught suddenly in a gust of wind. This is my child! When her jaws were too weak, I first chewed her food, then fed it to her in small mouthfuls. This is my child! I must carry a cool liquid in my flattened breasts to quench her parched throat. This is my child sitting in the shade, her head thrown back in rapture, prolonging some moment of joy I have created for her.

My child is pitiless to the hunchback boy; her mouth twists open in a cruel smile, her teeth becoming pointed and sparkling, the roof of her mouth bony and ridged, her young hands suddenly withered and gnarled as she reaches out to caress his hump. Squirming away from her forceful, heated gaze, he seeks shelter in a grove of trees, but her arms, which she can command to grow to incredible lengths, seek him out and tug at the long silk-like hairs that lie flattened on his back. She calls his name softly and the sound of her voice shatters his eardrum. Deaf, he can no longer heed warnings of danger and his sense of direction is destroyed. Still, my child has built for him a dwelling hut on the edge of a steep cliff so that she may watch him day after day flatten himself against a fate of which he knows and yet cannot truly know until the moment it consumes him.

My child haunts the dwelling places of the useless-winged cormorants, so enamored is she of great beauty and ancestral history. She traces each thing from its meager happenstance beginnings in cool and slimy marsh, to its great glory and dominance of air or land or sea, to its odd remains entombed in mysterious alluviums. She loves the thing untouched by lore, she loves the thing that is not cultivated, and yet she loves the thing built up, bit carefully placed upon bit, its very beauty eclipsing the deed it is meant to commemorate. She sits idly on a shore, staring hard at the sea beneath the sea and at the sea beneath even that. She hears the sounds within the sounds, common as that is to open spaces. She feels the specter, first cold, then briefly warm, then cold again as it passes from atmosphere to atmosphere. Having observed the many differing physical existences feed on each other, she is beyond despair or the spiritual vacuum.

Oh, look at my child as she stands boldly now, one foot in the dark, the other in the light. Moving from pool to pool, she absorbs each special sensation for and of itself. My child rushes from death to death, so familiar a state is it to her. Though I have summoned her into a fleeting existence, one that is perilous and subject to the violence of chance, she embraces time as it passes in numbing sameness, bearing in its wake a multitude of great sadnesses.

❧

I hear the silent voice; it stands opposite the blackness and yet it does not oppose the blackness, for conflict is not a part of its nature. I shrug off my mantle of hatred. In love I move toward the silent voice. I shrug off my mantle of despair. In love, again, I move ever toward the silent voice. I stand inside the silent voice. The silent voice enfolds me. The silent voice enfolds me so completely that even in memory the blackness is erased. I live in silence. The silence is without boundaries. The pastures are unfenced, the lions roam the continents, the continents are not separated. Across the flat lands cuts the river, its flow undammed. The mountains no longer rupture. Within the silent voice, no mysterious depths separate me; no vision is so distant that longing is stirred up in me. I hear the silent voice—how softly now it falls, and all of existence is caught up in it. Living in the silent voice, I am no longer "I." Living in the silent voice, I am at last at peace. Living in the silent voice, I am at last erased.

MY MOTHER

Immediately on wishing my mother dead and seeing the pain it caused her, I was sorry and cried so many tears that all the earth around me was drenched. Standing before my mother, I begged her forgiveness, and I begged so earnestly that she took pity on me, kissing my face and placing my head on her bosom to rest. Placing her arms around me, she drew my head closer and closer to her bosom, until finally I suffocated. I lay on her bosom, breathless, for a time uncountable, until one day, for a reason she has kept to herself, she shook me out and stood me under a tree and I started to breathe again. I cast a sharp glance at her and said to myself, "So." Instantly I grew my own bosoms, small mounds at first, leaving a small, soft place between them, where, if ever necessary, I could rest

my own head. Between my mother and me now were
the tears I had cried, and I gathered up some stones
and banked them in so that they formed a small
pond. The water in the pond was thick and black
and poisonous, so that only unnamable invertebrates
could live in it. My mother and I now watched each
other carefully, always making sure to shower the
other with words and deeds of love and affection.

❦

I was sitting on my mother's bed trying to get a
good look at myself. It was a large bed and it stood
in the middle of a large, completely dark room. The
room was completely dark because all the windows
had been boarded up and all the crevices stuffed with
black cloth. My mother lit some candles and the room
burst into a pink-like, yellow-like glow. Looming
over us, much larger than ourselves, were our
shadows. We sat mesmerized because our shadows
had made a place between themselves, as if they
were making room for someone else. Nothing filled
up the space between them, and the shadow of my
mother sighed. The shadow of my mother danced
around the room to a tune that my own shadow sang,
and then they stopped. All along, our shadows had
grown thick and thin, long and short, had fallen at
every angle, as if they were controlled by the light of
day. Suddenly my mother got up and blew out the

candles and our shadows vanished. I continued to sit
on the bed, trying to get a good look at myself.

❦

My mother removed her clothes and covered
thoroughly her skin with a thick gold-colored oil,
which had recently been rendered in a hot pan from
the livers of reptiles with pouched throats. She grew
plates of metal-colored scales on her back, and light,
when it collided with this surface, would shatter and
collapse into tiny points. Her teeth now arranged
themselves into rows that reached all the way back
to her long white throat. She uncoiled her hair from
her head and then removed her hair altogether.
Taking her head into her large palms, she flattened
it so that her eyes, which were by now ablaze, sat
on top of her head and spun like two revolving
balls. Then, making two lines on the soles of each
foot, she divided her feet into crossroads. Silently,
she had instructed me to follow her example, and
now I too traveled along on my white underbelly,
my tongue darting and flickering in the hot air.
"Look," said my mother.

❦

My mother and I were standing on the seabed side
by side, my arms laced loosely around her waist, my
head resting securely on her shoulder, as if I needed
the support. To make sure she believed in my frail-

ness, I sighed occasionally—long soft sighs, the kind
of sigh she had long ago taught me could evoke
sympathy. In fact, how I really felt was invincible.
I was no longer a child but I was not yet a woman.
My skin had just blackened and cracked and fallen
away and my new impregnable carapace had taken
full hold. My nose had flattened; my hair curled in
and stood out straight from my head simultaneously;
my many rows of teeth in their retractable trays
were in place. My mother and I wordlessly made an
arrangement—I sent out my beautiful sighs, she received them; I leaned ever more heavily on her for
support, she offered her shoulder, which shortly grew
to the size of a thick plank. A long time passed, at
the end of which I had hoped to see my mother
permanently cemented to the seabed. My mother
reached out to pass a hand over my head, a pacifying
gesture, but I laughed and, with great agility,
stepped aside. I let out a horrible roar, then a self-
pitying whine. I had grown big, but my mother was
bigger, and that would always be so. We walked to
the Garden of Fruits and there ate to our hearts'
satisfaction. We departed through the southwesterly
gate, leaving as always, in our trail, small colonies of
worms.

❦

With my mother, I crossed, unwillingly, the valley.
We saw a lamb grazing and when it heard our foot-

steps it paused and looked up at us. The lamb looked cross and miserable. I said to my mother, "The lamb is cross and miserable. So would I be, too, if I had to live in a climate not suited to my nature." My mother and I now entered the cave. It was the dark and cold cave. I felt something growing under my feet and I bent down to eat it. I stayed that way for years, bent over eating whatever I found growing under my feet. Eventually, I grew a special lens that would allow me to see in the darkest of darkness; eventually, I grew a special coat that kept me warm in the coldest of coldness. One day I saw my mother sitting on a rock. She said, "What a strange expression you have on your face. So cross, so miserable, as if you were living in a climate not suited to your nature." Laughing, she vanished. I dug a deep, deep hole. I built a beautiful house, a floorless house, over the deep, deep hole. I put in lattice windows, most favored of windows by my mother, so perfect for looking out at people passing by without her being observed. I painted the house itself yellow, the windows green, colors I knew would please her. Standing just outside the door, I asked her to inspect the house. I said, "Take a look. Tell me if it's to your satisfaction." Laughing out of the corner of a mouth I could not see, she stepped inside. I stood just outside the door, listening carefully, hoping to hear her land with a thud at the bottom of the deep, deep hole. Instead, she walked up and down in every direction, even pounding her heel on the air. Coming outside to greet me, she said, "It is an excellent house. I would be honored to live in it," and then vanished. I filled up the hole and burnt the house to the ground.

❦

My mother has grown to an enormous height. I have grown to an enormous height also, but my mother's height is three times mine. Sometimes I cannot see from her breasts on up, so lost is she in the atmosphere. One day, seeing her sitting on the seashore, her hand reaching out in the deep to caress the belly of a striped fish as he swam through a place where two seas met, I glowed red with anger. For a while then I lived alone on the island where there were eight full moons and I adorned the face of each moon with expressions I had seen on my mother's face. All the expressions favored me. I soon grew tired of living in this way and returned to my mother's side. I remained, though glowing red with anger, and my mother and I built houses on opposite banks of the dead pond. The dead pond lay between us; in it, only small invertebrates with poisonous lances lived. My mother behaved toward them as if she had suddenly found herself in the same room with relatives we had long since risen above. I cherished their presence and gave them names. Still

I missed my mother's close company and cried constantly for her, but at the end of each day when I saw her return to her house, incredible and great deeds in her wake, each of them singing loudly her praises, I glowed and glowed again, red with anger. Eventually, I wore myself out and sank into a deep, deep sleep, the only dreamless sleep I have ever had.

꧂

One day my mother packed my things in a grip and, taking me by the hand, walked me to the jetty, placed me on board a boat, in care of the captain. My mother, while caressing my chin and cheeks, said some words of comfort to me because we had never been apart before. She kissed me on the forehead and turned and walked away. I cried so much my chest heaved up and down, my whole body shook at the sight of her back turned toward me, as if I had never seen her back turned toward me before. I started to make plans to get off the boat, but when I saw that the boat was encased in a large green bottle, as if it were about to decorate a mantelpiece, I fell asleep, until I reached my destination, the new island. When the boat stopped, I got off and I saw a woman with feet exactly like mine, especially around the arch of the instep. Even though the face was completely different from what I was used to, I recognized this woman as my mother. We greeted each other at first with great caution and politeness,

but as we walked along, our steps became one, and as
we talked, our voices became one voice, and we were
in complete union in every other way. What peace
came over me then, for I could not see where she left
off and I began, or where I left off and she began.

❦

My mother and I walk through the rooms of her
house. Every crack in the floor holds a significant
event: here, an apparently healthy young man suddenly dropped dead; here a young woman defied her
father and, while riding her bicycle to the forbidden
lovers' meeting place, fell down a precipice, remaining a cripple for the rest of a very long life. My
mother and I find this a beautiful house. The rooms
are large and empty, opening on to each other, waiting for people and things to fill them up. Our white
muslin skirts billow up around our ankles, our hair
hangs straight down our backs as our arms hang
straight at our sides. I fit perfectly in the crook of
my mother's arm, on the curve of her back, in the
hollow of her stomach. We eat from the same bowl,
drink from the same cup; when we sleep, our heads
rest on the same pillow. As we walk through the
rooms, we merge and separate, merge and separate;
soon we shall enter the final stage of our evolution.

❦

The fishermen are coming in from sea; their catch
is bountiful, my mother has seen to that. As the

waves plop, plop against each other, the fishermen are happy that the sea is calm. My mother points out the fishermen to me, their contentment is a source of my contentment. I am sitting in my mother's enormous lap. Sometimes I sit on a mat she has made for me from her hair. The lime trees are weighed down with limes—I have already perfumed myself with their blossoms. A hummingbird has nested on my stomach, a sign of my fertileness. My mother and I live in a bower made from flowers whose petals are imperishable. There is the silvery blue of the sea, crisscrossed with sharp darts of light, there is the warm rain falling on the clumps of castor bush, there is the small lamb bounding across the pasture, there is the soft ground welcoming the soles of my pink feet. It is in this way my mother and I have lived for a long time now.

AT THE BOTTOM

OF THE RIVER

*T*his, then, is the terrain. The steepest mountains, thickly covered, where huge, sharp
rocks might pose the greatest danger and where only
the bravest, surest, most deeply arched of human
feet will venture, where a large stream might flow,
and, flowing perilously, having only a deep ambition
to see itself mighty and powerful, bends and curves
and dips in many directions, making a welcome and
easy path for each idle rill and babbling brook, each
trickle of rain fallen on land that lies sloping; and
that stream, at last swelled to a great, fast, flowing
body of water, falls over a ledge with a roar, a loud-
ness that is more than the opposite of complete
silence, then rushes over dry, flat land in imperfect
curves—curves as if made by a small boy playfully
dragging a toy behind him—then hugs closely to the

paths made, ruthlessly conquering the flat plain, the
steep ridge, the grassy bed; all day, all day, a stream
might flow so, and then it winds its way to a gorge in
the earth, a basin of measurable depth and breadth,
and so collects itself in a pool: now comes the gloam-
ing, for day will end, and the stream, its flow stilled
and gathered up, so that trees growing firmly on its
banks, their barks white, their trunks bent, their
branches covered with leaves and reaching up, up,
are reflected in the depths, awaits the eye, the hand,
the foot that shall then give all this a meaning.

But what shall that be? For now here is a man
who lives in a world bereft of its very nature. He lies
on his bed as if alone in a small room, waiting and
waiting and waiting. For what does he wait? He is
not yet complete, so he cannot conceive of what it
is he waits for. He cannot conceive of the fields of
wheat, their kernels ripe and almost bursting, and
how happy the sight will make someone. He cannot
conceive of the union of opposites, or, for that
matter, their very existence. He cannot conceive
of flocks of birds in migratory flight, or that night
will follow day and season follow season in a seemingly endless cycle, and the beauty and the pleasure
and the purpose that might come from all this. He
cannot conceive of the wind that ravages the coast-
line, casting asunder men and cargo, temporarily
interrupting the smooth flow of commerce. He can-

not conceive of the individual who, on looking up
from some dreary, everyday task, is struck just then
by the completeness of the above and the below and
his own spirit resting in between; or how that same
individual, suddenly rounding a corner, catches his
own reflection, transparent and suspended in a pane
of glass, and so smiles to himself with shy admira-
tion. He cannot conceive of the woman and the child
at play—an image so often regarded as a symbol of
human contentment; or how calamity will attract the
cold and disinterested gaze of children. He cannot
conceive of a Sunday: the peal of church bells, the
sound of seraphic voices in harmony, the closeness
of congregation, the soothing words of praise and
the much longed for presence of an unearthly glory.
He cannot conceive of how emotions, varying in color
and intensity, will rapidly heighten, reach an unbear-
able pitch, then finally explode in the silence of the
evening air. He cannot conceive of the chance invention that changes again and again and forever the
great turbulence that is human history. Not for him
can thought crash over thought in random and
violent succession, leaving his brain suffused in con-
tradiction. He sits in nothing, this man: not in a full
space, not in emptiness, not in darkness, not in light
or glimmer of. He sits in nothing, in nothing, in
nothing.

Look! A man steps out of bed, a good half hour
after his wife, and washes himself. He sits down on
a chair and at a table that he made with his own
hands (the tips of his fingers are stained a thin chocolate brown from nicotine). His wife places before
him a bowl of porridge, some cheese, some bread that
has been buttered, two boiled eggs, a large cup of
tea. He eats. The goats, the sheep, the cows are
driven to pasture. A dog barks. His child now enters
the room. Walking over, she bends to kiss his hand,
which is resting on his knee, and he, waiting for her
head to come up, kisses her on the forehead with lips
he has purposely moistened. "Sir, it is wet," she says.
And he laughs at her as she dries her forehead with
the back of her hand. Now, clasping his wife to him,
he bids her goodbye, opens the door, and stops. For
what does he stop? What does he see? He sees
before him himself, standing in sawdust, measuring
a hole, just dug, in the ground, putting decorative
grooves in a bannister, erecting columns, carving the
head of a cherub over a door, lighting a cigarette,
pursing his lips, holding newly planed wood at an
angle and looking at it with one eye closed; standing
with both hands in his pockets, the thumbs out, and
rocking back and forth on his heels, he surveys a
small accomplishment—a last nail driven in just so.
Crossing and recrossing the threshold, he watches
the sun, a violent red, set on the horizon, he hears

the birds fly home, he sees the insects dancing in the
last warmth of the day's light, he hears himself sing
out loud:

> *Now the day is over,*
> *Night is drawing nigh;*
> *Shadows of the evening*
> *Steal across the sky.*

All this he sees (and hears). And who is this man,
really? So solitary, his eyes sometimes aglow, his
heart beating at an abnormal rate with a joy he cannot identify or explain. What is the virtue in him?
And then again, what can it matter? For tomorrow
the oak will be felled, the trestle will break, the
cow's hooves will be made into glue.

But so he stands, forever, crossing and recrossing
the threshold, his head lifted up, held aloft and stiff
with vanity; then his eyes shift and he sees and he
sees, and he is weighed down. First lifted up, then
weighed down—always he is so. Shall he seek comfort now? And in what? He seeks out the living
fossils. There is the shell of the pearly nautilus lying
amidst colored chalk and powdered ink and India
rubber in an old tin can, in memory of a day spent
blissfully at the sea. The flatworm is now a para-
site. Reflect. There is the earth, its surface apparently stilled, its atmosphere hospitable. And yet here
stand pile upon pile of rocks of an enormous size,

riven and worn down from the pressure of the great
seas, now receded. And here the large veins of gold,
the bubbling sulfurous fountains, the mountains covered with hot lava; at the bottom of some caves lies
the black dust, and below that rich clay sediment, and
trapped between the layers are filaments of winged
beasts and remnants of invertebrates. "And where
shall I be?" asks this man. Then he says, "My body,
my soul." But quickly he averts his eyes and feels
himself now, hands pressed tightly against his chest.
He is standing on the threshold once again, and,
looking up, he sees his wife holding out toward him
his brown felt hat (he had forgotten it); his child
crossing the street, joining the throng of children on
their way to school, a mixture of broken sentences,
mispronounced words, laughter, budding malice, and
energy abundant. He looks at the house he has built
with his own hands, the books he has read standing
on shelves, the fruit-bearing trees that he nursed
from seedlings, the larder filled with food that he
has provided. He shifts the weight of his body from
one foot to the other, in uncertainty but also weighing, weighing . . . He imagines that in one hand he
holds emptiness and yearning and in the other desire
fulfilled. He thinks of tenderness and love and faith
and hope and, yes, goodness. He contemplates the
beauty in the common thing: the sun rising up out of
the huge, shimmering expanse of water that is the

sea; it rises up each day as if made anew, as if for the first time. "Sing again. Sing now," he says in his heart, for he feels the cool breeze at the back of his neck. But again and again he feels the futility in all that. For stretching out before him is a silence so dreadful, a vastness, its length and breadth and depth immeasurable. Nothing.

The branches were dead; a fly hung dead on the branches, its fragile body fluttering in the wind as if it were remnants of a beautiful gown; a beetle had fed on the body of the fly but now lay dead, too. Death on death on death. Dead lay everything. The ground stretching out from the river no longer a verdant pasture but parched and cracked with tiny fissures running up and down and into each other; and, seen from high above, the fissures presented beauty: not a pleasure to the eye but beauty all the same; still, dead, dead it was. Dead lay everything that had lived and dead also lay everything that would live. All had had or would have its season. And what should it matter that its season lasted five billion years or five minutes? There it is now, dead, vanished into darkness, banished from life. First living briefly, then dead in eternity. How vainly I struggle against this. Toil, toil, night and day. Here a house is built. Here a monument is erected to commemorate something called a good deed, or even in remembrance of a woman with exceptional qualities, and all that she loved and all that she did. Here are some children, and immeasurable is the love and special attention lavished on them. Vanished now is the house. Vanished now is the monument. Silent now are the children. I recall the house, I recall the monument, I summon up the children from the eternity of darkness, and sometimes, briefly, they appear, though always slightly shrouded, always as if they had emerged from mounds of ashes, chipped, tarnished, in fragments, or large parts missing: the ribbons, for instance, gone from the children's hair. These children whom I loved best—better than the monument, better than the house—once were so beautiful that they were thought unearthly. Dead is the past. Dead shall the future be. And what stands before my eyes, as soon as I turn my back, dead is that, too. Shall I shed tears? Sorrow is bound to death. Grief is bound to death. Each moment is not as fragile and fleeting as I once thought. Each moment is hard and lasting and so holds much that I must mourn for. And so what a bitter thing to say to me: that life is the intrusion, that to embrace a thing as beauty is the intrusion, that to believe a thing true and therefore undeniable, that is the intrusion; and, yes, false are all appearances. What a bitter thing to say to me, I who for time uncountable have always seen myself as newly born, filled with a

truth and a beauty that could not be denied, living
in a world of light that I called eternal, a world that
can know no end. I now know regret. And that, too,
is bound to death. And what do I regret? Surely not
that I stand in the knowledge of the presence of
death. For knowledge is a good thing; you have said
that. What I regret is that in the face of death and
all that it is and all that it shall be I stand powerless,
that in the face of death my will, to which everything
I have ever known bends, stands as if it were nothing
more than a string caught in the early-morning wind.

Now! There lived a small creature, and it lived
as both male and female inside a mound that it made
on the ground, its body wholly covered with short
fur, broadly striped, in the colors field-yellow and
field-blue. It hunted a honeybee once, and when the
bee, in bee anger and fright, stung the creature on
the corner of the mouth, the pain was so unbearably
delicious that never did this creature hunt a honeybee
again. It walked over and over the wide space that
surrounded the mound in which it lived. As it walked
over and over the wide ground that surrounded the
mound in which it lived, it watched its own feet sink
into the grass and heard the ever so slight sound
the grass made as it gave way to the pressure, and as
it saw and heard, it felt a pleasure unbearably
delicious, and, each time, the pleasure unbearably
delicious was new to this creature. It lived so, bank-

ing up each unbearably delicious pleasure in deep,
dark memory unspeakable, hoping to perhaps one
day throw the memories into a dungeon, or burn
them on an ancient pyre, or banish them to land
barren, but now it kept them in this way. Then all its
unbearably delicious pleasure it kept free, each thing
taken, time in, time out, as if it were new, just born.
It lived so in a length of time that may be measured
to be no less than the blink of an eye, or no more
than one hundred millenniums. This creature lived
inside and outside its mound, remembering and
forgetting, pain and pleasure so equally balanced,
each assigned to what it judged a natural conclusion,
yet one day it did vanish, leaving no sign of its existence, except for a small spot, which glowed faintly
in the darkness that surrounded it. I divined this, and
how natural to me that has become. I divined this,
and it is not a specter but something that stood here.
I show it to you. I yearn to build a monument to it,
something of dust, since I now know—and so soon,
so soon—what dust really is.

"Death is natural," you said to me, in such a flat,
matter-of-fact way, and then you laughed—a laugh
so piercing that I felt my eardrums shred, I felt
myself mocked. Yet I can see that a tree is natural,
that the sea is natural, that the twitter of a twittering
bird is natural to a twittering bird. I can see with my
own eyes the tree; it stands with limbs spread wide

and laden with ripe fruit, its roots planted firmly in
the rich soil, and that seems natural to me. I can
see with my own eyes the sea, now with a neap tide,
its surface smooth and calm; then in the next moment
comes a breeze, soft, and small ripples turn into
wavelets conquering wavelets, and that seems natural
to me again. And the twittering bird twitters away,
and that bears a special irritation, though not the
irritation of the sting of the evening fly, and that
special irritation is mostly ignored, and what could
be more natural than that? But death bears no relation to the tree, the sea, the twittering bird. How
much more like the earth spinning on its invisible axis
death is, and so I might want to reach out with my
hand and make the earth stand still, as if it were a
bicycle standing on its handlebars upside down, the
wheels spun in passing by a pair of idle hands, then
stilled in passing by yet another pair of idle hands.
Inevitable to life is death and not inevitable to death
is life. Inevitable. How the word weighs on my
tongue. I glean this: a worm winds its way between
furrow and furrow in a garden, its miserable form
shuddering, dreading the sharp open beak of any
common bird winging its way overhead; the bird,
then taking to the open air, spreads its wings in
majestic flight, and how noble and triumphant is this
bird in flight; but look now, there comes a boy on
horseback, his body taut and eager, his hand holding

bow and arrow, his aim pointed and definite, and in this way is the bird made dead. The worm, the bird, the boy. And what of the boy? His ends are number-less. I glean again the death in life.

✌

Is life, then, a violent burst of light, like flint struck sharply in the dark? If so, I must continually strive to exist between the day and the day. I see myself as I was as a child. How much I was loved and how much I loved. No small turn of my head, no wrinkle on my brow, no parting of my lips is lost to me. How much I loved myself and how much I was loved by my mother. My mother made up elaborate tales of the origins of ordinary food, just so that I would eat it. My mother sat on some stone steps, her volumi-nous skirt draped in folds and falling down between her parted legs, and I, playing some distance away, glanced over my shoulder and saw her face—a face that was to me of such wondrous beauty: the lips like a moon in its first and last quarter, a nose with a bony bridge and wide nostrils that flared out and trembled visibly in excitement, ears the lobes of which were large and soft and silk-like; and what pleasure it gave me to press them between my thumb and forefinger. How I worshipped this beauty, and in my childish heart I would always say to it, "Yes, yes, yes." And, glancing over my shoulder, yet again I would silently send to her words of love and adoration, and I would receive from her, in turn and in silence, words of love and adoration. Once, I stood on a platform with three dozen girls, arranged in rows of twelve, all wearing identical white linen dresses with corded sashes of green tied around the waist, all with faces the color of stones found lying on the beach of volcanic islands, singing with the utmost earnestness, in as nearly perfect a harmony as could be managed, minds blank of interpretation:

> *In our deep vaulted cell*
> *The charm we'll prepare*
> *Too dreadful a practice*
> *For this open air.*

Time and time again, I am filled up with all that I thought life might be—glorious moment upon glorious moment of contentment and joy and love running into each other and forming an extraordinary chain: a hymn sung in rounds. Oh, the fields in which I have walked and gazed and gazed at the small cuplike flowers, in wanton hues of red and gold and blue, swaying in the day breeze, and from which I had no trouble tearing myself away, since their end was unknown to me.

☙

I walked to the mouth of the river, and it was then still in the old place near the lime-tree grove. The water was clear and still. I looked in, and at the

bottom of the river I could see a house, and it was a
house of only one room, with an A-shaped roof. The
house was made of rough, heavy planks of unpainted
wood, and the roof was of galvanized iron and was
painted red. The house had four windows on each of
its four sides, and one door. Though the door and
the windows were all open, I could not see anything
inside and I had no desire to see what was inside.
All around the house was a wide stretch of green—
green grass freshly mowed a uniform length. The
green, green grass of uniform length extended from
the house for a distance I could not measure or know
just from looking at it. Beyond the green, green
grass were lots of pebbles, and they were a white-
gray, as if they had been in water for many years
and then placed in the sun to dry. They, too, were of
a uniform size, and as they lay together they seemed
to form a direct contrast to the grass. Then, at the
line where the grass ended and the pebbles began,
there were flowers: yellow and blue irises, red
poppies, daffodils, marigolds. They grew as if wild,
intertwined, as if no hand had ever offered guidance
or restraint. There were no other living things in
the water—no birds, no vertebrates or invertebrates, no fragile insects—and even though the water
flowed in the natural way of a river, none of the
things that I could see at the bottom moved. The
grass, in little wisps, didn't bend slightly; the petals

of the flowers didn't tremble. Everything was so
true, though—that is, true to itself—and I had no
doubt that the things I saw were themselves and
not resemblances or representatives. The grass was
the grass, and it was the grass without qualification.
The green of the grass was green, and I knew it to
be so and not partially green, or a kind of green, but
green, and the green from which all other greens
might come. And it was so with everything else that
lay so still at the bottom of the river. It all lay there
not like a picture but like a true thing and a different
kind of true thing: one that I had never known
before. Then I noticed something new: it was the
way everything lit up. It was as if the sun shone not
from where I stood but from a place way beyond and
beneath the ground of the grass and the pebbles. How
strange the light was, how it filled up everything, and
yet nothing cast a shadow. I looked and looked at
what was before me in wonderment and curiosity.
What should this mean to me? And what should I
do on knowing its meaning? A woman now appeared
at the one door. She wore no clothes. Her hair
was long and so very black, and it stood out in a
straight line away from her head, as if she had com-
manded it to be that way. I could not see her face. I
could see her feet, and I saw that her insteps were
high, as if she had been used to climbing high mountains. Her skin was the color of brown clay, and she

looked like a statue, liquid and gleaming, just before
it is to be put in a kiln. She walked toward the place
where the grass ended and the pebbles began. Perhaps it was a great distance, it took such a long time,
and yet she never tired. When she got to the place
where the green grass ended and the pebbles began,
she stopped, then raised her right hand to her forehead, as if to guard her eyes against a far-off glare.
She stood on tiptoe, her body swaying from side
to side, and she looked at something that was far,
far away from where she stood. I got down on my
knees and I looked, too. It was a long time before
I could see what it was that she saw.

I saw a world in which the sun and the moon shone
at the same time. They appeared in a way I had
never seen before: the sun was The Sun, a creation
of Benevolence and Purpose and not a star among
many stars, with a predictable cycle and a predictable
end; the moon, too, was The Moon, and it was the
creation of Beauty and Purpose and not a body
subject to a theory of planetary evolution. The sun
and the moon shone uniformly onto everything. Together, they made up the light, and the light fell on
everything, and everything seemed transparent, as if
the light went through each thing, so that nothing
could be hidden. The light shone and shone and fell
and fell, but there were no shadows. In this world,
on this terrain, there was no day and there was no

night. And there were no seasons, and so no storms
or cold from which to take shelter. And in this world
were many things blessed with unquestionable truth
and purpose and beauty. There were steep mountains, there were valleys, there were seas, there were
plains of grass, there were deserts, there were rivers,
there were forests, there were vertebrates and invertebrates, there were mammals, there were reptiles, there were creatures of the dry land and the
water, and there were birds. And they lived in this
world not yet divided, not yet examined, not yet
numbered, and not yet dead. I looked at this world
as it revealed itself to me—how new, how new—
and I longed to go there.

I stood above the land and the sea and looked back
up at myself as I stood on the bank of the mouth of
the river. I saw that my face was round in shape,
that my irises took up almost all the space in my eyes,
and that my eyes were brown, with yellow-colored
and black-colored flecks; that my mouth was large
and closed; that my nose, too, was large and my
nostrils broken circles; my arms were long, my hands
large, the veins pushing up against my skin; my legs
were long, and, judging from the shape of them, I
was used to running long distances. I saw that my
hair grew out long from my head and in a disorderly
way, as if I were a strange tree, with many branches.
I saw my skin, and it was red. It was the red of

flames when a fire is properly fed, the red of flames
when a fire burns alone in a darkened place, and not
the red of flames when a fire is burning in a cozy
room. I saw myself clearly, as if I were looking
through a pane of glass.

I stood above the land and the sea, and I felt that
I was not myself as I had once known myself to be:
I was not made up of flesh and blood and muscles
and bones and tissue and cells and vital organs but
was made up of my will, and over my will I had complete dominion. I entered the sea then. The sea was
without color, and it was without anything that I
had known before. It was still, having no currents.
It was as warm as freshly spilled blood, and I moved
through it as if I had always done so, as if it were
a perfectly natural element to me. I moved through
deep caverns, but they were without darkness and
sudden shifts and turns. I stepped over great ridges
and huge bulges of stones, I stooped down and
touched the deepest bottom; I stretched myself out
and covered end to end a vast crystal plane. Nothing
lived here. No plant grew here, no huge sharp-
toothed creature with an ancestral memory of hunter
and prey searching furiously for food, no sudden
shift of wind to disturb the water. How good this
water was. How good that I should know no fear.
I sat on the edge of a basin. I felt myself swing my
feet back and forth in a carefree manner, as if I

were a child who had just spent the whole day head
bent over sums but now sat in a garden filled with
flowers in bloom colored vermillion and gold, the
sounds of birds chirping, goats bleating, home from
the pasture, the smell of vanilla from the kitchen,
which should surely mean pudding with dinner, eyes
darting here and there but resting on nothing in
particular, a mind conscious of nothing—not happiness, not contentment, and not the memory of night,
which soon would come.

I stood up on the edge of the basin and felt myself
move. But what self? For I had no feet, or hands, or
head, or heart. It was as if those things—my feet,
my hands, my head, my heart—having once been
there, were now stripped away, as if I had been
dipped again and again, over and over, in a large vat
filled with some precious elements and were now reduced to something I yet had no name for. I had no
name for the thing I had become, so new was it to
me, except that I did not exist in pain or pleasure,
east or west or north or south, or up or down, or
past or present or future, or real or not real. I stood
as if I were a prism, many-sided and transparent,
refracting and reflecting light as it reached me, light
that never could be destroyed. And how beautiful I
became. Yet this beauty was not in the way of an
ancient city seen after many centuries in ruins, or a
woman who has just brushed her hair, or a man who

searches for a treasure, or a child who cries immediately on being born, or an apple just picked standing
alone on a gleaming white plate, or tiny beads of
water left over from a sudden downpour of rain,
perhaps—hanging delicately from the bare limbs of
trees—or the sound the hummingbird makes with
its wings as it propels itself through the earthly air.

Yet what was that light in which I stood? How
singly then will the heart desire and pursue the small
glowing thing resting in the distance, surrounded by
darkness; how, then, if on conquering the distance
the heart embraces the small glowing thing until
heart and glowing thing are indistinguishable and in
this way the darkness is made less? For now a door
might suddenly be pushed open and the morning light
might rush in, revealing to me creation and a force
whose nature is implacable, unmindful of any of the
individual needs of existence, and without knowledge
of future or past. I might then come to believe in a
being whose impartiality I cannot now or ever fully
understand and accept. I ask, When shall I, too, be
extinguished, so that I cannot be recognized even
from my bones? I covet the rocks and the mountains
their silence. And so, emerging from my pit, the one
I sealed up securely, the one to which I have con-
signed all my deeds that I care not to reveal—
emerging from this pit, I step into a room and I see

that the lamp is lit. In the light of the lamp, I see some books, I see a chair, I see a table, I see a pen; I see a bowl of ripe fruit, a bottle of milk, a flute made of wood, the clothes that I will wear. And as I see these things in the light of the lamp, all perishable and transient, how bound up I know I am to all that is human endeavor, to all that is past and to all that shall be, to all that shall be lost and leave no trace. I claim these things then—mine— and now feel myself grow solid and complete, my name filling up my mouth.

MACADAM DREAMS

L'espérance-macadam

MACADAM DREAMS

Gisèle Pineau

Translated by C. Dickson

University of Nebraska Press, Lincoln and London

Publication of this translation was assisted by grants from the French Ministry of Culture – National Center for the Book and the National Endowment for the Arts. ❦

Cet ouvrage, publié dans le cadre d'un programme d'aide à la publication, bénéficie du soutien du Ministère des Affaires étrangères et du Service Culturel de l'Ambassade de France aux Etats-Unis.

This work, published as part of a program of aid for publication, received support from the French Ministry of Foreign Affairs and the Cultural Services of the French Embassy in the United States.
This title was originally published in French as *L'espérance-macadam* © 1995, 1996, Éditions Stock. Translation © 2003 by the University of Nebraska Press. All rights reserved ∞ Manufactured in the United States of America. Library of Congress Cataloging-in-Publication Data Pineau, Gisèle. [Espérance-macadam. English] Macadam dreams / Gisèle Pineau ; translated by C. Dickson. p. cm. ISBN 0-8032-3730-8 (cloth : alk. paper) – ISBN 0-8032-8773-9 (pbk. : alk. paper) I. Dickson, C. II. Title. PQ3949.2.P573E8413 2003 843′.914 – dc21 2002043039

MACADAM DREAMS

I

Nothing worthwhile was left. Only garbage. Not even a board standing, or a sheet of tin roofing in place. Ruins of shanties. Memories of the paths that ran through the heart of Savane. Not a birdsong or the hint of a feather in the broken arms of the trees that had fallen to their knees. But a few belongings hung in the sky. A mattress atop a miraculous straight pole, amidst all the others, bent, decapitated, flung to the ground. Pieces of material clung to the roots of the fallen trees, fluttered in the wind, seeking to take wing after the nearly pageless notebooks flying swiftly away. Notebooks bearing Angela's handwriting, which held the secret of her mama Rosette's fairy tales. And the air was laden with odors. Smells of life and death interlaced. Incense and putrefaction. Treacherous, deceitful fragrances redolent with the life of Savane. The smell of amours and of women in heat, the smell of Sonel's warm bread, the musky smell of young goats, the rancid smell of Sister Beloved's coconut oil. The sweet smelling dreams of growing rich, the hope of bearing a child . . . And also, the reek of mouths bitter with jealousy, spitting out prayers to the followers of Satan.

Nothing but garbage . . . Cyclone had smashed and trampled everything. Nothing worth patching up. Nothing good enough to salvage. Would just have to plow it all under, that and the secrets, the shame, the sinfulness of Savane in one fell swoop. Just had to make a clean sweep and bury it all.

Surely some way to get the paradise that had lived in Joab's dreams back on its feet. Plant new flowers and bushes, happy-cabins. Open the sky back up to the birds that had vanished. Dredge the river. Lay new roads. Haul away the old stoves, the fans with broken blades, and the washing machine drums full of holes. Had to loosen grief's moorings, snuff out the cries that echoed in the silence left by Cyclone's great winds. Don't despair, Eliette kept telling herself.

Everything started on that crazy Sunday . . .

Up until then, the only thing on this earth that Eliette sought after was the peace of her cabin. Not get her life mixed up in the turmoil of Savane. Not let her mind color the sounds, build cathedrals of pain in her heart. Eyes and ears shut, she struggled to keep the sorrow of others at bay. Life outside was a clatter of hard luck and 'God have pity on us brothers!' Sorrow always tried to catch up with her in the midst of hearty laughter and the strong beating of the tambourka. So much suffering all around . . . Blood splattered in the grass on the path. A blue tongue sticking out from the flowers of the mango tree. Gray eyes tied at the end of a rope. A small mangled body under Nèfles Bridge. Hortense hacked to pieces with the cutlass. And those children who'd gone off into the mountains and never come back. And how many other painful recollections . . .

That Sunday had turned her world topsy-turvy, undermined everything she believed in.

For a time, Eliette had prayed for God to give reason to her belly. She was thirty-five years old, had just married Renélien, her first husband. Fortunetellers had been recommended to ensure that a child would result from their conjugated prayers. They had all promised that unfaltering patience followed by a string of novenas and I-believe-in-Gods would bring favorable results. After the death of Renélien, a Haitian woman had convinced her that she was too old to continue cherishing the hope that a child would spring from her body. Yet the woman insisted that she could clearly see her with a child . . .

A child, a girl, the Haitian woman swore. A relative that I would take in, a niece pulled out of God knows what magic hat . . . I smiled inwardly. I told her that I knew of no remaining family, but that there was a god who punished imposters. She said that no one ever questioned the dead who worked for her. She cried me impudent and said that I would see soon enough. I paid two thousand francs for her visions. I'd been had, disillusioned one-two days. And then I ended up laughing at my foolishness. Laughing alone.

After that, I married Hector, but that didn't pan out either, I was already forty-five. So I stopped trying to find out why I was deprived. I even stopped asking the Good Lord why such flagrant injustices existed. I got gray hair while Savane sunk into agony, sweated blood, burned with jealousy and meanness. And even if I wasn't able to blot out all the sounds of life and death, I didn't want to see or hear anything. Just let me live in peace in my cabin.

Before that Sunday, a bunch of fears, scattered visions, rocky memories were shut up in my soul. My mama's voice always rose to cover other sounds that drifted up from way deep down. She told of how, when I was eight, the Cyclone of 1928 had dismembered Guadeloupe, had thrown that rafter right smack into the center of my belly. With the years and the foolish wanderings of the mind, I would find myself more often than not with furrowed brow and squinted eyes, trying to bring back the night of those high winds, the night that had pushed my mama Séraphine into a variety of madness that had not yet been denounced, that pain-filled night. Memories burrowed down into long-ago time floated up one after the other, without showing their faces. Pieces of sheet iron whistling past in the blackness of a cyclone. Sails, linen galore whirling around. Raging twister winds. Tidal wave. Fallen coconut trees. Screams and rains piling up together . . .

That Sunday came with no fanfare. An ordinary Sunday dawning behind a full-moon night.

In the old days, when her mind happened upon a clear path, my mama used to say, 'You born, you die, and between the two, you pack your bags with whatever comes along. Little nothings that you weigh on the end of your little finger. Crumbled mountains that bear down upon you the rest of your life. Colors fathered by God knows what crafty devil. And even if you see the sun all high and mighty, don't go thinking it's any more than a break in the clouds. Know that every day that comes will leave its silt. You might have feather-light mornings when you sing out Glory be to God! But when the evening dampness falls, a right angry cyclone might decide to cart off your cabin and wreak havoc in the garden of your dreams. Liette, preserve yourself! Don't laugh too heartily, don't cry too hard. Think about them bags you packing day after day . . . For sure, your eyes would go bad if you counted the pinheads crucifying your days. Maybe you'll look for a light that went out in your past. But when you get to the end of the line, there's no more time for fondling memories and regrets, you'll leave all that on the banks . . .'

If luck came my way in the days when Savane set life's course, I didn't recognize it. How many times? . . . I'm not sure. Sometimes, I regretted not having let the Haitian fortuneteller talk more, regretted having laughed spitefully. Every time misfortune took root in a cabin in Savane, I'd find a terrorized damozel that could have been my daughter. I thought that maybe the child the Haitian woman had seen would come from one of the cabins in Savane, because we blacks were all related: brothers and sisters, uncles and aunts, nephews and nieces . . .

One day I was given a little girl in a breadbasket. It scared me. By the time I weighed the pros and the cons, another woman had snatched her up. It was just after the death of Renélien. My manless belly already bore nothing but gas and wind.

Before that Sunday, I didn't want to take on anyone's sorrow. Just pass what was left of my life far from the world's knocks and bumps. And pray for my body and the souls of the sinners all around. Pray that nothing came to stir up my heart or hasten my last tour of duty. That Sunday, standing resolutely in the midst of my loneliness, it had been ages since I'd sought the favors of a male. I had known the abysses of love, but hadn't had a taste of what maternity was like. Married twice. I really believe they loved me, my men, before departing. But all they did was wear down the cleft I have between my legs. Like me, they spent a long time hoping for the child. They saw how disappointed I was. Saw me cry with rage because of the blood that ran thick at every new moon. They were fine men. I might have seen the world through rose-colored glasses with them. But since the child did not come, I grew whimsical. So, depending upon our ups and downs, we each took and gave what we could. Love ebbed and flowed with no blows, no yelling or cursing. But there were days when the silence hurt, when words turned to dagger blades. At times, I couldn't control my moods. One after the other, Renélien and Hector had promised me a family. And I waited, with empty belly and idle hands. I waited for so many years . . . Watched my life going by, swept along like the big rocks and the small leaves in the river under Nèfles Bridge. Hoped for a new break in the clouds.

At times the blue sky suddenly stabbed into the grief with a laugh so rough that years stiffened with old dreams fell away. Forget for a moment the longing of the past. Believe that a myriad of hopeful days still lay ahead. And consider yourself saved, not see the faces of the surrounding demons anymore . . . Eyes closed, suck on a piece of cane. Let the sugar run through your body, mingle with your blood. Become sweet. Walk past people and things and suddenly take all of life as something infinitely sweet, a stick of candy.

That Sunday, I had just come out of church. Squinting my eyes, I glanced at the sun, which was already high in the sky. As usual, those children – the survivors of the mountain brotherhood of Rastas and some others that smoked city ganja and rocks of crack – lay on the four stone benches in front of the church. The poor souls, they had no idea how to change directions now or even think about tomorrow with a clear mind. Five of them were asleep there . . .

Moses and Eddy were among them. In the old days those two walked nice and straight, one behind the other, on their way to school. They were from Ti-Ghetto. Took a bad turn. Went astray in the hills of Ravine-Guinée. They'd come close to dying. Were recovering by laying their lives down on the benches in front of the church, as if they were offering their bodies up in sacrifice, living lambs amid the stray dogs that scavenged about in the streets of the town. Packs of weary she-dogs with their flaccid dugs dangling. And male dogs that didn't even know how to yap anymore, only scheme for their bellies: the leftovers of stale food, an old dug-up bone. Grapple over the carrion by the roadside. And flee from hunger, kicks in the rear end, and stray buckshot. I knew those children.

Some of them had become cellophane in their mama's eyes. They had completely scratched them off their lists, down to their very names, their first baby teeth, all the laughter and tears combined. Cut all ties.

At night they slept on tables in the marketplace, in canoes on the beach, or in culverts. If it started raining, they'd run and hide themselves under the verandas at the low end of town. In the morning folks swiped them out with their brooms. And Moses, who thought he was a prophet ever since he'd come back from the mountain, always shouting, 'You're all as good as dead! Two–legged zombies! The day coming when Babylon will be destroyed forever! Cower, you blind, lost souls, slaves chained to the realm of darkness! The time's already been set and you still walking in the dust . . . You're just a bunch of little birds that been pecking at the crumbs of Babylon for four hundred years!' People said they'd drunk too much pure Ital tea and that they sought neither bread nor job because they fed on an herb that gave them light, opened the gates to paradise, and beat the drums of love and the dream country in Africa that had been founded across the seas. They stank. The filth on their skin was a mixture of red and black dirt. Their hair, reddened from the sun, stuck up in a riot and let out a kind of silent, tragic and magnificent, yet desperate roar. They wore rags with no backwards or forwards, stiff with grime. You couldn't stare at them too long. They cursed and promised hellfire, damnation, and thrashings from the devil. In the old days, as children, they cursed and swore only in play. But they had grown up, gone in quest of paradise on earth and the meaning of life, following in the footsteps of Sister Beloved. That's how they and I had gotten to the point of not looking at one another anymore. We didn't want to recognize each other. And so, turning our eyes away, each stood firmly in his particular form of dignity. When Cyclone came through Ti-Ghetto, Moses' younger brothers were already running after false suns . . .

8 Nobody knows how, but Savane was cut in two after the death of my stepfather Joab. Right behind my house, Ti-Ghetto sprung up. At times, when rifles got to talking too much, people said, 'It's Chicago over that way! Call Eliot Ness!' On the other side, before you went over Nèfles Bridge, sprawled Quartier-Mélo. Together, that was Savane . . . And in there were cabins where miserable lives ran their course, closed up under the tin roofing and the boards. Damozels that had stopped counting their brood. Mamas with no feelings. Only half-budded young black women that had walked straight for a long time, the dread of the whip keeping them tied to the dreams and the fears of their battered mamas. Alas, once they were left at school, they became female, savvy, and wicked. Skirts hitched up, certain that their bottoms and their titties would deliver them from poverty, lay the earth's riches and the seven wonders of the world at their feet, they filed out of the light in a long line. Laughing. There was no lack of mouths to pass the word on and lead them further down the path that so many other damozels had cursed. And even there, lost smack in the thick of the dark woods, they still thought they would find their way back. But at the foot of each and every tree were fifty just like them. After a little while, bobbed-bounced in life's roll, they were broken without even knowing it. And, imagining themselves stepping onto the pier of some Eldorado, they squared their fool shoulders, buoyed by their notorious glory, their only beauty – in short, all of youth's cockiness. And so they surrendered their virginity and allowed its web, threads, and hidden seams to be torn. Men took them, in the same way that they swallowed rum, squinching at the burning pleasure. Then cast them off, with a sprouting seed. And the cycle of calabash bellies began. With a hope

at the end of each pregnancy. The hope that this time the man that rammed the hot poker into their body would stay hooked, ardent, generous, at least for a small spell of eternity. When they began to want a little peace, when they hoped to never see a man's face again, there were already four-five children underfoot. Empty bellies and schoolbags. Patience and clenched jaws of the poor at the ticket windows of the welfare office.

I had no descendants, but I know that those women dreamt of model kids, of whole entire families displayed like gold jewelry in a Syrian's shop window . . . 'Hey, sweetie, till you got the whole matching set – necklace, earrings, bracelet, broach, and ring – just tell yourself there's a missing link in the chain leading up to paradise!' But those dreams weren't within their reach; they couldn't place orders and take them down from the hooks like articles from the Redoute catalog – a size eight dress, an electric coffee maker, a latex girdle. The first time that their belly let its fruit fall, they thought maybe it was enough to provide a roof and food for the newborn. They expected everything to just drop into their laps miraculously with a puff of strong wind: bread and butter and chocolate, note paper, sneakers, honors. To their mind, it would simply be a matter of reaching out their hand to harvest the bright future and the job that brought money orders and a concrete cabin in its wake.

In Savane, some mamas were deaf, dumb, and blind. Wambling women with half their screws loose, running after fate and claiming their due. Poor, bewildered creatures. Women with pressed hair. Misbegotten sapodilla flesh, perpetually vaunting. Madonnas with patent leather pumps and purses on I-believe-in-God Sundays, but damned foulmouthed, fearing neither God nor man on No Jesus Christ days. Nights, women possessed with the echoing of drums in their bodies danced drunkenly, fell to their knees, grinding their hips before big strapping fellars astride fevered *tambour-kas*. There were the not-so-mean ones too. Like Hortense, the poor soul . . . And Rosette, with all of her dreams and the tales she told to make her life easier. Like Esabelle, who loved gold and ended in torment . . . I heard it all, I saw it all, but I didn't get mixed up in it . . . I never let the sound of the ka steal into my veins, carry me off into that sink seething with all the misery of Savane.

The break in the clouds didn't last long.

I opened my parasol. Because of the sun and those children that just crept into my thoughts of their own accord, like worms get into the pods of pigeon peas. The malady had come with age: thoughts played at turning visions around and around again, ruminating over the same conversations, churning up memories. That Sunday after mass, I just wanted to go back to my cabin and my little cat, brown some meat, cook up some rice, eat, burp, and set my exhausted body down in the rocker.

When sleep crept up on me at nap time, the sneaky thoughts and the old ragged dreams that hung in my mind flickered out, went off to lie down someplace too, a place behind my head. I no longer saw the years going by. My memory didn't come and shake its rattle filled with useless chatter. And those who were dead, whom I had known in their glory or their misery, didn't connive to trip me up anymore. I no longer saw the living all around me either, the people of Savane, the nations of Ti-Ghetto and Quartier-Mélo, those who flung open the door to the devils locked in their bodies. I didn't see my crazy mama anymore, sitting on her little bench, reliving Cyclone '28, which she called the Beast. When she said, 'Eliette, my girl, let me tell you about the Passage of the Beast . . . ,' her face shriveled up like gray paper, her voice suddenly came out choppily between the driving gusts of a furious wind that arose simply from evoking that terrifying night.

I didn't see the baby in the breadbasket anymore either.

I crossed the square. Greeted Désilia. Just a little wave so that she'd understand I had no time for her. When I've taken Communion, I don't like to open my mouth to exchange limp words with the creatures from Ravine-Guinée, who eat the herb soup of fortunetellers and then go and suck on the body of Christ. Désilia didn't come after me like she usually does. She was deep in conversation with Bethsabée. They both had a delighted smile on their face that was downright pitiful. I knew that look of Désilia's, the one she would get when someone told her a new story. She'd never had any men in her life. According to her, no black man had ever mounted her. So she worked up an easy fever when she snagged a living bit of someone else's existence. She hooked on to your arm and wouldn't let go until you'd told her everything. You were hopelessly surrounded by her questions. They closed in on you. Her tongue became snakelike. Her voice sharp, cutting. 'And then, and then, é ka i fé? É ka yo di? É alos? And so, who told you this? And how? And why? And the mama? And the papa? É ka yo fé? . . .' She loved ugly rumors, Désilia did. That Sunday she'd come upon something that really stirred her blood.

A fine Sunday. I looked both ways to cross the street. And there I saw a crowd of people that had left the church before the last hymns were sung. The police car was parked by the town hall, right in front of the unfinished building that had been looking for next-of-kin for at least three winter seasons. The eleven o'clock sun was straddling the rain-streaked roof beams. I didn't want to see any more. So that another vision wouldn't come and take its seat in my mind, get chummy with the thoughts of the gray eyes, of the blue tongue, of the children lying on the bench, of Cyclone '28.

I lifted my head. The building blocked out the sky. Its walls gaped open. Hoping for doors and windows, gray plank casing wept dry dribbles of cement. It was dark inside, so dark on this bright day. I tried to find something else to look at. At times I just didn't know where to let my eyes fall. That's how, without really meaning to, I met the depths of Rosan's eyes. It was worse than a red-hot iron. Singed, I quickly turned away so that the vision wouldn't have time to burn me even worse, be branded into my mind.

Rosan sitting in the police car.

I walked past Violette's shop, she was old, like I was, and sold everything that had anything to do with sewing – ribbons, thread, and lace collars that you just couldn't find anymore.

Rosan sitting in the police car. My whole body was shaking. Rosan . . .

Then a batch of thoughts came bolting down the street and there were even some that started chasing after me. I wanted to step up my pace. If I'd been young, I would have run all the way to Savane to get away from that street in Ravine-Guinée where thoughts crept out like crabs from their holes and crawled up on me. Me, Eliette Florentine.

Rosan sitting in the police car.

As I went past Seoud's place, I saw a face in the window, the little round face of a blue-skinned Negress. With eyes that had already known their lot of suffering, but that still knew how to smile all the same, and dream high too. It wasn't Rosette, Rosan's wife, but it looked like her. It could have been Angela too, Rosette's daughter: mother and daughter were carbon copies. So that's how everything started linking together in my mind. The thoughts were all holding hands and I let them in. My mama Séraphine said that it was all because of Cyclone '28, which had left a great whirlwind in my head. The smallest thing could take me back through the years and, oh joy, I'd suddenly find myself fifty years earlier in my mama's kitchen. Or else at the first dance I'd been forced to go to – I was thirty – with my nose under my escort's arm, who smelled of patchouli and lavender. Whenever I heard just any old person whistling at just any old thing, I always thought of all those fellars trying to pick everything that was blossoming in me. That was back in the days when my titties stood up all by themselves, in the days when my fate was dreamt about, but not yet written. Those black men sure knew how to whistle. And play the banjo, and even the violin, and pluck the bass, and give real pretty serenades that came sliding through the woods and right up under the sheet metal roof as easy as pie to reach my ears. It was to my ears alone that the unique music was addressed. I married late, at thirty-five. I'd never really wanted to have anything to do with men. They trailed after me. For a long time . . .

I'd let my body go stale. Maybe that's why I didn't have any children. Sometimes, after I was already a widow, I'd close my eyes and let my body slip into youthful dreams. Renélien came to take me as he had on our marriage night. Renélien, he was my first. I really should have been the widow of only one man. He'd made me swear on the Holy Virgin that I wouldn't take another after him. I didn't listen, because of the child that I still hoped for. He never forgave me for having opened the door to someone else. With Hector, things didn't work out as well as his eyes had promised. Luckily, he got sick and died soon after our marriage. When I first met him, Hector strutted his fifty years proudly. He was a docker and a bit of a doctor in the art of the French language, the kind I'd always loved. Huge arms, buttocks firm and round in his pants, chest wider than my open window, and the power that emanated from his bellowing voice – all of those things he put on display had pulled the wool over my eyes. I was almost forty-five, not bad-looking or withered at all. I'd said to myself, 'Eliette, my girl! Now that iron will confer a child upon you. Alas, Hector beat out two-three bars, sang one-two verses, and then declared himself 'perpetually inoperative' due to something beyond the forces of logic and his deceptive eloquence rolled into one. His being stricken so suddenly wasn't a natural thing. You should have seen it, even when his head was already nearing thirteenth heaven and started to shake out the rhythm, his affair was still kneeling. Since the culprit surely wasn't far off, the priest came to bless my cabin and sprinkle holy water to keep out the spirits that tormented him. An old woman apothecary from the main market in La Pointe spelled out some recipes for me, treatments for all ills, with ginger, bwa-bandé, celery root, star anise. Someone else taught me how to open the Bible on the dresser in my bedroom, at the page in the Epistle of James that says, 'For what is your life? It is even a vapor that appeareth for a little time, and then vanisheth away.' Every blessed morning I repeated, 'For what is your life, Renélien? It is even a vapor that appeareth for a little time, and then vanisheth away.' I burned candles for three days and three nights. Nothing worked. In spite of all the remedies, Hector remained inoperative in action. In the end the poor soul began to shrivel up from the inside, ever so slowly. It was like a tree whose roots were being attacked by invisible vermin. He suddenly shed all his leaves all at once and then, one by one, lost all the other traits that had made me believe he was filled with an animal-like vigor. In the beginning of his illness he swore to me in his fine French that the calamity had taken him completely by surprise. He wanted to cry out to all the women he'd ever known, just so they could testify to his exploits and his great and defunct virility.

I could have been a good mama to any child. I fed Hector his dinner with a teaspoon and he sucked water out of a baby bottle, keeping his eyes fixed on mine, accepting that he was utterly at my mercy. When the end drew near, he didn't even weigh a hundred pounds. I carried him in my arms from the bed to the rocker, from the living room into the bedroom. The mass of his muscles melted away, and his swaggering pride shrank back under the cold wings of death, he was husbanding his strength. Couldn't expose him to drafts or shake out the sheets too hard or even sigh with weariness. Trembling at the thought of being snuffed out like a candle and fading away, not from sickness but by accident, he feared any wind that heralded the Apocalypse. He wasn't really in his second childhood, because he kept his wits about him, but I took care of him like a baby, and he didn't complain. He understood his sad plight when he rejoined Renélien, to whom I'd made the promise never to remarry. I know that he was furious with me for having gotten him mixed up in that malediction, that he's still furious, especially since he has so many things to regret . . . Was never able to give me a taste of his vigor or the length of his capacity. Wanted to live with his musculature to a ripe old age, Hector did. Hoped to travel, take an airplane, go on ocean cruises . . . Since then, not a living male has come into my cabin, not even come to sit down on the edge of my bed. And I was alone in the world when that Sunday suddenly came unhinged.

Eliette had to make a detour by way of Rue Siméon-Poche to get to a bakery. Rosan's name was laid out flat in front of the counter. There were five or six of them thrashing him right there on the floor, and then throwing him around, and separating the 'Ro' from the 'san', and calling up the name of Rosette and the kids, and repeating, 'Ain't it a pity! Ain't it a pity!' Eliette pulled two long furrows up onto her brow so that those who knew they were neighbors wouldn't come asking her any whys and hows.

The bread was dry, just the way she liked it. It would do her three days. She was alone in her cabin. Alone with her little black cat, who had just a few white hairs on the ends of his two front paws. Rosan sitting in the police car, his eyes not saying a thing. Not shame, or innocence, or injustice. Had some misfortune come to Rosette? No, Eliette would have heard. Their cabins were so close they almost touched. How many years had it been since she'd seen the folks from Ravine-Guinée carry on like that? Rosan . . . No, not that man, he was no murderer. Maybe he'd been caught stealing. But he hadn't killed . . .

Eliette pushed the thoughts out of her mind, asked the Lord not to send her more hardships to bear, more visions to endure. She didn't want to let anyone's grief get her all worked up again, not anyone's in the whole world. Only live a little longer, just because she was afraid of dying. She was in no hurry to join the deceased. Was past being interested in the young people, who wasted the time that life had allotted them. 'Kill, steal, murder! Do whatever you like!' she sometimes said to them with silent cries that crept into reproachful glances.

The bread was dry, just the way she liked it. Brown her meat, and then cook up some rice.

Rosan sitting in the police car. No, his eyes didn't say a thing.

In the old days, we called this place Savane Mulet. When my step-father Joab set his cabin down, there was nothing here. He and my mama Séraphine were alone for a heap of years, tramping down the Guinea grass and clearing paths to get here or there. Just the two of them, running into lost souls with broken wings, wounded by the first shafts of dawn. Whenever the folks from Ravine-Guinée wanted to suggest the remoteness of a place, they'd say, 'It's out at the other end of Savane Mulet!'

The river ran nearby. Carrying her basin of wash on her head, my mama used to sing real loud as she crossed the savanna that bore frangipani, dragon trees, silk-cotton trees, and ilang-ilangs. She didn't like the place and said that she-devils came from afar to sleep there and rub their bodies up against the high branches of the trees in Savane that scented the night hours with their diabolical fragrance. At the stroke of midnight – the witching hour – the menfolk would follow the strong perfume and fall giddy-happy into the traps laid with silken spider webs. The beautiful temptresses had only to stick out their cloven foot and send the poor men tumbling down the side of a cliff at Anse-Bertrand. The jagged rocks, the sea, and the voracious sharks would tear the bodies apart in no time.

Mama Séraphine always took it for granted that behind the lush foliage lurked the languorous shadows of one-two maleficent creatures. Joab was forever telling her that she shouldn't tremble like a leaf here-there anywhere she put her foot down. 'Actually, Savane is the Good Lord's paradise!' he said. But Séraphine thought she was in hell. Wherever her eyes fell, the Beast had spawned young that were proliferating. The great-wind Cyclone never stopped blowing. Imagining herself already taken by the storm, she sang out loud and clear, like a soldier facing the canons. Alas, in the end her voice grew hoarse with terror. So then the poor woman would gather her skirts, push me out in front of her, and we ran with three hundred armies at our backs: bloodthirsty she-devils, squadrons of dragons, *soucoug-*

nans sansculottes, flying grognards, and still others, unnamable, ineffable, come straight from Africa or the bowels of the earth to wage battle, throw us in irons and onto the auction block. On the other side of the savanna, wild guavas, coco plums, medlars, and brush cherries grew in a small grove. We didn't even enjoy eating the fruit. The collywobbles twisted our insides. We just grabbed a few in passing, breaking the branches, with our hearts almost leaping out of our chests from feeling like some demon was hot on our heels. Cracking sounds, mingled with strange voices that sometimes teased and sometimes wailed, made us weak in the knees. Many times my mama cursed Joab for having buried her alive in Savane Mulet. So very far from God's eyes, she would say. But there was no place else to go, and it wasn't with the money from the coconut sherbet she sold on Sundays that she could build a cabin in the navel of Ravine-Guinée. So the poor woman washed her laundry ridden with anxiety, because even the river leapt over the rocks in an unnatural fashion. There, the rocks weren't round and smooth like elsewhere in Guadeloupe, but long, like arms and legs. My mama mumbled that they were probably the broken-dismembered-petrified bodies of apostate angels, from back when the Good Lord had done his spring-cleaning in heaven and cast the followers of Satan down to earth.

The stories had turned some heads in Savane, but they died out along with Séraphine. Some old bodies from Ravine-Guinée thought about them every now and again, hunkered down in their rockers. They shook and rattled with a fury with those fleeting memories. A cold shudder ran through their bones. They stuttered. But, in truth, those who still tried to find words for the old magic of Savane Mulet were few and far between. Little by little, throughout the sixties, the evil spirits were driven back to the other side of the river. And suddenly the multitudes populated Savane. They came from everywhere, blocked off plots of land, planted horrid cabins . . . Folks that had been thrown out of all corners of Guadeloupe. Families that landed without a word, holding back even their names. One-eyed Negresses, with stitch-marked faces clumsily patched back together, countless kids hanging from their skirts, a one-room cabin unloaded from a truck to shelter the heads of their posterity. Yes, multitudes, raining down on Savane like the grasshoppers on the vast lands of Pharaoh. Zombies of the new age.

In the beginning they set their cabins down among the trees, marked off territories where nature had nothing to plant or harvest. But when land started running short, they brandished their cutlasses and slashed at the frangipanis, the silk-cotton trees, and the ilang-ilangs. They opened up paths that ran everywhere between the sheet metal fences, as many as there are lines in the hand. And then the mayor built Nèfles Bridge so that they could spread deeper into the countryside. But there was always some obstacle cropping up to bar the way of those who tried to take root on the other side of the bridge, brave the *soucougnans*. The spirits settled in the four corners of that territory weren't driven back until Beloved and the tribe of Rastas came. Until then people were satisfied to simply make a trash heap of it and the river. And then other nations came from the English and Spanish lands of the Caribbean Sea. One day the little grove where the coco plums clustered turned into Quartier-Mélo – it had to do with a French gendarme who was looking for clues about a cabin that had been burned down. As he searched through the ashes and bits of burned wood marked with criminal fingerprints, he kept sighing, 'Quel méli-mélo! Quel mélo!' What a hodgepodge! What a melodrama! The natives of Ravine-Guinée whispered that Savane was no longer simply at God's back but in the devil's own bedroom, and that all the exiled demons were to be found there, dealing cards against honest folks, giving a flick of the finger to life's dominoes, and preparing the route to ruin. My stepfather Joab went off to meet his death at l'Anse-Laborde in '36 and didn't have time to see the face of his paradise change.

It was after my second marriage in '65 that I started feeling cramped in Savane Mulet. There weren't so many she-devils about anymore, but there was constant coming and going on the paths. Cartfuls of boards and tin roofing, floozies in heat walking around in brassieres stuck full of rusty safety pins, cutlasses slashing out after arms and legs, shops run by men, by women, perorations-correlations lacking all consideration, loose kids fleeing from the whip of a good upbringing. And cabins, so many cabins, leaning one on the other, stuck-close behind my place. It had become Ti-Ghetto.

Renélien came from Mahault; he owned a bus.

He wanted us to stay in Savane Mulet, so he sold all his possessions to build our cabin on the site of Joab's old shack, which was leaning to one side. He loved to see the faces of the people that neighbored there. Renélien knew them all, better than I did. He wasn't scared of strangers. English from Dominica and Haitians, the Spanish heirs to the New World . . . All of them mourned his death. Especially since after him no bus went out as far as Savane. They let people off in the village of Ravine-Guinée, had to take to your feet to climb up the rest of the way. Hector, my second, wasn't the same, he might have had a nice life in Savane, but his great inoperability dominated his thoughts. And then, what with his sickness, he didn't see the people around us. So not many can recall him. When widowhood struck me the second time, I felt like I was being sucked into cruel solitude. And that's why my cabin let all the sounds in the neighborhood come in without permission. Quarrels, screams, tears, laughter, drums kept me awake in my bed till late into the night. My cabin, in the heart of Savane Mulet, had turned into a sort of huge stoup filled with the broken lives of collective na- tions. A small patch of illusory peace in the very midst of the war.

I didn't get mixed up in any of it.

When that Sunday suddenly came unhinged, I was absolutely convinced that one could live like that, sitting atop a heap of nightmares.

Rosan, my neighbor, wasn't a ruffian. Never beat on anyone. Wasn't looking for a fight. Was up and away every blessed morning before the sun came up. Put food on the table in his cabin. Talked big like all the males around here, especially about nonsense. Didn't like the same kind of music as Rosette. Bickered with her sometimes about the Bob Marley records and the dream she had about going back to Des-Ramiers. Didn't mingle with the folks from Ti-Ghetto much.

Rosette was my fine neighbor friend. Praise the Lord, her great-uncle Edmond Alexander left her the cabin he'd built back in the days of Renélien. After the death of the old man, it hadn't stayed shut up long. Rosette arrived one morning with Angela on one hip and Rosan following three steps behind, pushing part of their belongings in a borrowed wheelbarrow. She greeted me before even asking about the cabin. Rosette didn't come to Savane like someone entering a conquered land. Didn't want to bruise anyone. I right liked her ways. It ruffled her to hear the silence coming from my cabin. She didn't say it out loud, but I knew that she was always thinking that death could just up and carry me away any minute, surely before it would her. She made up tales and predicted that I still had fifty lives to live. She dreamt of a kingdom free from cruelty. She didn't like

Savane, said that people killed dreams there, forced herself to live there. She had two sides, Rosette did. One that hated the world and was waiting for better days, sitting and listening to 'No woman no cry!' all day long. And the other that saw good everywhere, even to the point of being blind. Sometimes Rosette would come and sit down in my cabin to dust off the loneliness, as she put it.

In truth, Eliette was never alone. Voices drifted up from Quartier-Mélo. In the very thick of the night, there were little puffs of breath that slipped under her closed door, breaths that condensed in the silence. She could hardly tell where they came from. They seemed to drift in from very nearby and yet at the same time from far away too, like an old fear that cropped back up at the witching hour. Some nights she could have sworn that a beast had lost its way and was standing right behind her door, trying to decide whether to come in and rip her throat open or just wait for her heart to go amiss and stop beating. At certain times she could hear very clearly two breaths struggling and arguing wordlessly with each other. And her room filled with the clamor of all the nations of Savane Mulet, supporting one or the other of the two breaths. Countless times the night had been slashed open with a cutlass, riddled with screams. In the morning, one of the paths that went through to Quartier-Mélo was stained with black blood. In the beginning, before they called this place Ti-Ghetto, Eliette would take on everyone's sorrow. And then she stopped doing anything but listening and waiting, not letting her heart jump around. Though she distinctly felt the longings of the people around her – who were all on some sort of a tragic and exalted quest – she herself was no longer in search of anything. Not one thing . . . And she left the others to flail around with dreams of riches, love, fame, and dignity. She herself was no longer in search of anything when that Sunday suddenly came unhinged.

Rosan sitting in the police car . . .

Angela, Robert, and Rita, she'd never met such well-behaved children in Ti-Ghetto. Especially Angela, the eldest, the one Rosette was carrying on her hip when she came to Savane.

Eliette finished her lunch. The crumbs of some thoughts had fallen onto her fork, but she didn't give them time to ensnare her. It was late in the afternoon when the first killing in Ti-Ghetto came to her mind. What had they called the man that had hacked poor Hortense into six and some pieces? . . . Régis, that was it. Thought she'd lent her body out to another. The unfortunate girl didn't have time to run from the blows of the cutlass, unlike her friend. He was a blues singer, and folks say they passed him running like crazy down the highway with no trousers on. Régis cut the girl up. And then he arranged all the pieces in batches on the tamped earth in his kitchen. The two titties that he'd sliced off quivered on a banana leaf, next to the head – eyes wide with stupefaction – and the gaping, bloody *coucoune*.

For some time now Eliette had stopped going to view the dead, or ask about the befores and afters of a killing, or run around with the others and listen to those that swore it spelled the malediction of black people. Joab's paradise was nothing but desolation now.

She wanted to sleep her nap just so the vision of Rosan sitting in the police car would stop nagging at her. But the sounds from outside barged in. Four men were playing dominos in Quartier-Mélo. You could hear them shouting. Not far away, a child was jumping up and down and screaming too, chased by a belt that must be leaving welts on his back. The dishes were being washed at Rosette's, the radio was playing 'Ti Ninon mwen,' a beguine from way back when. The only thing else you could hear was the water rushing onto the clattering plates.

The day after the second killing in Ti-Ghetto, the folks from Ravine-Guinée had declared, 'It's Chicago over that way! Call the Untouchables!' The second killing . . . You never know which thread to pull to start that kind of story.

It was in the last days of the dry season of 1973. Esabelle, a local girl and a real hot number, had brought back a strapping Indian from Grande-Terre by the name of Marius. The Indian didn't know what he was getting into, poor man. He walked around the whole blessed day in khaki shorts with his open shirt blowing in the wind displaying a large belly with three folds. You could hear him coming from a long way off because of his broken tongs flapping on the path. Marius stirred up a lot of air when he went by Eliette's door, and he got short of breath as if he were always off on important maneuvers. He repaired bicycle tires. One evening one-two words from Esabelle drifted over to Eliette on the silence. The mulatta-*chabine* was whining for an eighteen-karat necklace and a pair of filigree earrings that a Syrian jeweler selling his wares door to door had shown her. That floozy had put fifty francs down for the jewelry, fifty measly francs out of two thousand three hundred and forty-seven francs and fifty centimes . . . To take her mind off their misery and the merchant's gold, Marius gave her some loving and a few healthy thrusts of the pelvis that don't cost a thing and can be exchanged with no down payment. He swore to her that one day he would cover her with gold. Then, feeling confident, he revealed to her – shshsh! – that he had a fortune coming to him. Since he was in diapers. He had been promised a jar that was buried somewhere, a big earthenware jar overflowing with gold, jewels, coins, and bullion. Each night he went to sleep hoping for the dream that would indicate the day, the time, and the place that he should start digging. A good hundred years ago, a black slave had visited his great-grandfather in a dream. He was an Indian from Karikal, who'd come to Guadeloupe to cut sugar cane and sweat blood in the fields after slavery had been abolished. The black man had said, 'All the gold is for Marius.' The old man bolted upright on his bamboo cot, turned around, saw no Marius anywhere; his only son was a widower and his name was Marcellin, his grandson was named Melchior. And so, as he lay on his deathbed, en route for everlasting India, the grandfather told Melchior the secret of the slave and repeated to his very last gasp, 'All the gold is for Marius! Take a wife. Give her a son and name him Marius. All the gold is for Marius!' And that is what Melchior did, in compliance with the last wishes of the old man. That's why the Indian lay waiting every night for the long-hoped-for dream that would lend weight to his useless existence.

Marius was nearing fifty when he first set foot in Ti-Ghetto. After he confided his secret to her – patience – Esabelle waited a bit, asking each morning, 'Alos, Nèg, la vini?' He sighed, 'No, dear! Maybe tonight, or tomorrow . . .' From having strained his mind for so long, his sleep was now filled with nightmares. He, the great strapping Indian, who had never known the shackles of slavery, found himself tied fast, whipped, and maimed alongside Negro slaves from Africa who spoke in tongues like the apostles. Alas, try as he might to prick up his ears, not one of those bare-naked black men gave him a translation: the time, the day, and the place that the jar full of gold had made its burrow, the jar that would cover Esabelle with all of the treasures of the Old and the New World combined.

Christopher, a blue-skinned man from Quartier-Mélo, was an apprentice at the bakery and made the evening bread delivery. He fell passionately in love with the *chabine*, who had started to fill out. Tired of waiting for opulence, of imagining herself digging in with both hands and bringing up fistfuls of gold, of pawing furiously at wealth's door, she'd become a nibbler and was slowly swelling. Christopher loved her generous titties and heavy bottom. Since the revelation, Esabelle spent every day fanning herself on her bit of gallery, eating hot bread and sweet cocoa sticks, waiting for the fateful night that would open the gates to riches. Every time she saw the gold merchant walk by – he still had her fifty francs – the *chabine* became so embittered about the Indian that she hauled in Christopher and the evening baked goods and devoured them, while trumpeting her misfortunes to the man. The delivery man, who had an even greater appetite, scraped his account clean at the Banque des Îles Françaises and paid cash for the necklace and filigree earrings, which he offered to Esabelle one fine morning. Madness . . . The very moment the girl put the chain around her neck, the air over Savane grew heavy, got trapped between the sheets of tin roofing, clung to the branches of the last trees, cracked and then split open like the sky in a cyclone.

That was how the story of Christopher and Esabelle began, the story of the second killing in Ti-Ghetto. At night, while Marius opened the squeaky gates of his dreams, descended the marble staircase of his forty winks, so that the slave with the jarful of gold would consent to pay him a visit, Esabelle and Christopher straddled a Solex to make it over to Pointe-à-Pitre, go dancing and watch karate films at the Renaissance Theater. When they came back, Christopher would take her standing up at the foot of the only ilang-ilang that had been spared by the cutlasses. They howled so in lovemaking, it made Eliette's head spin. Queen Esabelle and the beast Christopher were kicking up their heels in the exaltation of their maiden voyages. Their bodies rubbed together without really knowing each other, fresh-smitten with the discovery of unexplored lands upon which to build the brightest tomorrows. When did they get carried away? People say they should have been happy with that bit of sunshine instead of asking for second helpings of fair weather. Marius certainly gave them no umbrage since, at nightfall, he was braving the great depths of sleep. By day he was so busy with his inner tubes and rubber patches, he didn't even notice the gold swinging from his sweetheart's ears . . . Maybe it was Christopher who wanted her all for his own pecker; men are possessors. For sure, the *chabine* could have gone on living like that, splitting her heart in two and keeping one eye on the jar of gold that had been promised to Marius alone.

Alas, after the intoxication of love's songs, Christopher started jabbering louder and louder at the foot of the ilang-ilang. Raving with jealousy. Couldn't stand the thought of Marius visiting Esabelle. Yet the girl swore she didn't hear him come in or go out and that he didn't stir up much of a wind, that she only felt the weight of his three-fold belly on her. So what difference did the jab of a make-believe blade make? But the black man insisted. The cherished heart had to lean one way or the other, right then and there, and even for eternity. One night he proved to her that the Indian's dreams carried no weight at all. If he, Christopher, hadn't appeared with his signed and serial-numbered bank notes, surely Esabelle would still be sitting on her veranda sweating and eating bread and cocoa, watching the Syrian as he passed in the distance, or else promising another fifty francs for the following week. Would an Indian's dream come true in a hot stuffy cabin in Savane? . . . 'You got to wake up, Esabelle! As long as your Indian don't go before the ninety-nine arms of the goddess Maliémin and make an offering of three young goats, nine roosters, thirty hens, fifty baskets of rice, and twelve pots of colombo curry powder, no Negro slave is about to give a jar full of gold to an Indian! Wealth don't come with sleep! I worked hard to get all the gold hanging at your ears and neck, Esabelle! Sweat and dirt, the bread from the Sonel bakery! I not making fun! Don't spend my time sleeping! I no dreamer!'

Despite Christopher's levelheaded words, Esabelle refused to give up hope. Marius swore that he was beginning to understand one-two words of the obscure conversations between the slaves. His slave was beginning to send him signs. His dreams were now filled with gold dust. Three centuries to travel! It was no round trip to Pointe-à-Pitre–Basse-Terre, any idiot could understand that. So the Indian explained to the girl that what was needed was a bit of patience – which black people had always lacked. Sometimes, in the mornings, a fine golden dust dancing in a ray of sunshine drifted down onto the eyelids of the determined dreamer. So then, even though her fingers weren't digging into authentic riches, Esabelle, who passionately coveted the no-sweat-gold, felt it was near, could hear its promises and said, 'I believe, Marius, I believe!' Every day she made fine resolutions, swore to herself she would reject the other man, who had nothing to offer her but his warm, hard-earned bread, the sweat of his brow, the grime of his toil, the malediction of the black people, a destiny of running afoul.

In the meantime, Christopher fulminated. He began walking up and down the dirt tracks in Savane, talking to himself. Strode over Nèfles Bridge. Ruminated criminal thoughts. Let the bread burn in Sonel's oven. Walked up and down without whistling or singing, passed bitterly by the chabine's door, who stayed shut up in her cabin, sweltering under the gray tin roof. One morning, not being able to stand it any longer, Christopher went scratching at his queen's window; she wasn't able to turn him away. She was wearing all her gold on a flouncy yellow dress. He hauled her over to the foot of the ilang-ilang. And they talked for a long time – shshsh – before sharing a treacherous kiss. At one point he held her two wrists fast, she nodded yes at everything he said. Then they went off in separate directions.

It was early in the morning on the next day that Marius's body was found hanging from a blooming branch of the mango tree that Sidonise had planted the year of the earthquake. The tree didn't have time to produce a single mango. After they'd unstrung Marius, Sisi lost no time in having it cut down. She was always seeing the Indian's body swinging back and forth, his long blue tongue hanging out, his belly exposed, and his stiffened toes in the cheap tongs. Esabelle mourned over the suicide of her Marius, grimaced in disbelief. Cried all day. And then, in the darkness that settled over the hot tin roof, she opened her door to Christopher, who entered the cabin victoriously. They say that on that night he toured the banks of the chab-ine three full times. Possessed her entirely, marked his territory. How many days dawned after that night of feasting? Who can say? . . . The air over Savane seemed to grow lighter, leaving only a few gaudy tatters: the memory of Marius hanging from the blooming mango tree, a fine golden dust raining down heavily on Esabelle's cabin.

When Christopher's eyes grew accustomed to the shape of his beloved, he brought his manly possessions over, and his boxer shorts began flapping in the wind on a line strung between Esabelle's cabin and a newly planted electric pole. The man would swagger down the path, trailing the smell of the bakery mingled with the fragrance of lovemaking after him. There was a period with no fighting or cursing. Then, on the far side of Ravine-Guinée, in Trois-Coulées, appeared a little woman who always gave her titties to the baby just when Christopher came to deliver his warm bread. Christopher had already baptized her Santa Maria when the Syrian came back to fondle his gold in front of the women of Ti-Ghetto. A fine gold dust from the coolie-Indian's unfinished dreams kicked up at his heels. That particular day, Esabelle was out on her gallery for a breath of fresh air. This time she fell for the slave chain that wrapped three times around her neck. She paid two hundred francs down – her meat money for the month. When Christopher came home that evening, he counted the bottoms of seven *canari*-stewpots hanging from their nails. He undoubtedly thought of Marius and shuddered, for his cooked-hot-and-ready dinner was usually waiting for him on the stove. Esabelle was sitting on the bed, rocking to and fro. A thick oxen chain was wrapped around her neck; she clutched a bunch of used rubber patches in her hand as if they were pieces of gold from a pirate treasure. Her big pale titties with pink tips bobbled before her, like two sacks of dried coco beaten by rollers. As soon as she saw Christopher, she started yelling bloody murder, and all Savane crowded into her veranda.

That's how we learned that the bread man had looped the rope around poor Marius's neck three times, how he and she had struggled to string him up on a branch of the mango tree, and how the Indian had carried his secret of gold to his death. Esabelle opened the wardrobe and showed everyone gathered there the necklace and earrings that Christopher had bought so she would give Marius up. Nothing but that! It was really all that long-winded black man had given her! Yes, she confessed. They had plotted to send Marius out of this world, whereas if she'd just shown a little patience, maybe the dream would have come, and the slave would have revealed the day, the time, and the place to dig and unearth the jar of prosperity.

When the gendarmes took them off to stick them in some remote jail of no return, Eliette thought to herself that evil was taking root right there in Savane Mulet. Everyone lived in the same silent com- plicity. And yet, behind the planks and the infernal sheets of tin, bits of phrases put end to end had solved the mystery of the coolie's death long ago. Everyone knew. They all kept quiet. And if those two hadn't put an end to Marius's days, he could have lived out his entire life in hopeful dreams: he didn't really mind losing so many nights to get only a glimpse of gold dust; the man was gay at heart.

No, I didn't want to weigh my heart down. And even if the glimmer of Marius's shadow and that wispy puff of breath continued to slip in and out under my door, I didn't really want to take on his sorrows and mourn over his body. I had already stopped counting the deaths in Savane. I went to all the old people's funerals, those that nature carted off when their time had come. They never hung back to prowl the earth. Heaven hauled them straight up to eternal life. But the others, all the others taken by cutlasses, poison, ropes, beatings, plumb, water, and fire, always drifted around on the edges, watching the living, playing with minds, corrupting destiny.

That Sunday, I didn't have the strength to run over to Rosette's place to ask about Rosan. I didn't want to know. Just remember his good deeds. How he had worked so hard at fixing up the cabin Rosette had inherited from her old uncle. Four Saturdays in a row he had gotten together a half dozen friends, men of the trade, masons, house painters, carpenters. Those folks would come at five o'clock in the morning and leave exhausted at sunset. They got the cabin back on its feet. Changed the rotten boards. Patched the roof. Saved some rafters that were infested with termites. Greased the hinges on the doors. And drove away the old rats. The last Saturday, the painter matched up his colors, and that very afternoon Rosan unrolled a black-and-white lino, just like a checkerboard. People came in batches to applaud, the house stood out so remarkably from the rest of Savane, it simply shone. Someone said that you could even eat off the imitation tile floor. And Rosette had fixed up potted plants along the whole length of her veranda. She'd planted other, thorny ones, around the edges, to set off her little plot of land from the neighbors. In the back, only a flat separated us. Her great-uncle had stood some old sheets of tin roofing on end between our two courtyards. He didn't like to catch peoples' eyes hanging on his place.

Rosette had left them there. Every single morning, when she went out to throw some corn at her chickens, she would say it was high time to take those barricades down. One day in September of 1981, a cyclone came through to lay the three coconut trees and the bread-fruit tree that her uncle had planted flat on the ground: not a single sheet of old roofing was uprooted. That was when Rosan measured the land and its scope.

No more than a month later, he was out there alone digging the foundations for an extra room to be added on to the cabin, which had only two.

11

Stringy clouds, long blue fingers, writhed in the already dark sky. The moon slept in its last quarter. And Savane sat brooding on a frail silence punctuated with the cries and rustling wings of night creatures.

Eliette had not gotten much rest at nap time. As if they'd crawled out of the wadding in her mattress, Hector and Renélien popped up again, more sprightly than in real life, irritating, quarreling. Those two men always found something to argue about. Without paying any attention, she'd let them babble on all afternoon. That's exactly what they were waiting for, her to open her mouth. Then the jealousy that brought them together in shared rage became a part of their little game. Renélien upbraided her as if he still had some rightful claim to her, as if he were still made of flesh and blood and brought her back the money from his bus every day. He reproached her for breaking her promise and even wept sometimes over how bitter he felt, or else he affected a commanding tone between fits of shrill laughter. Hector, her second, the perpetually inoperative, had regained his broad shoulders since his death. The big lug demonstrated his strength by sending his fists flying about in all directions without ever so much as grazing anyone.

Eliette craned her neck out from between the double doors and examined the blue patterns in the sky. She hoped it would rain that evening, simply to give her a good excuse. For not going over to see Rosette. For not asking how she was, for not facing an ugly reality. At the tail end of this long day spent resuscitating the dead, sleep wouldn't come easily. Night would dig up another fifty-some crimes committed in Savane. And maybe the demon that came to breathe behind her door would seize the opportunity to show his face. Was it absolutely necessary for her to be a good neighbor, lean over Rosette, show some interest in Rosan's troubles? She'd rather slump docilely into ignorance, be satisfied with a bunch of assumptions. But she promised herself to go the next day, with her heart safely barricaded: tuck away her feelings, listen detachedly, just as Mademoiselle Meredith had taught her, ward off the horrific visions that Rosette's every word would project. A bundle of painful secrets, a chorus of tears . . . Who could say what awaited her there?

When Glawdys, the gray-eyed girl, flung her child to the foot of Nèfles Bridge, Rosette wept over the accursement of the black people, the calamity of misery, and the dead dreams on this earth. And then she hauled Eliette over to the very place the little body had landed to show her the two rocks that opened their deadly arms and the dried blood that the river refused to wash away yet. Rosan carried the child, lying in his outstretched arms, down all the tracks in Savane, his eyes filled with silent accusation, in the face of which the inhabitants looked down and stepped aside.

Eliette knew the story better than anyone around here, better than Rosette, and from the very beginning too, the day that Hermancia, poor Glawdys's mother landed in Savane with her swollen belly stretched under her dress, her young-communicant smile, scaly legs, gray face, and those eyes, drawn back behind the thin crack of the eyelids. Hermancia came on foot, followed by a one-room cabin teetering atop a pushcart. That's the way a lot of folks came. They brought the shoddy ruins salvaged from the last cyclone, semblances of cabins that they set down on four rocks from the river. After a little while, those who landed yesterday considered themselves to be as native-born as anyone else. They took root prolifically, wildly, authoritatively, and proudly, as if to show that they answered to no God or master, and that only the fate that led them here was worthy of respect, could lay a yoke upon them. They owed nothing to anyone. The river provided them with water, the sun with light. True, poverty made them go barefoot, but it didn't keep their heads plunged in the drink of humiliation. On the contrary, each day they took to the tiller with wide-open eyes. Whenever you ran into them on the paths they were always busy, lugging a few heaven-sent boards, rush-rushed carting bucketfuls of water on their heads, running behind hand trucks loaded with old salt meat tins filled to the brim with water from the fountain. Those people crowded up next to one another. Rubbed shoulders with one another. Eyed one another suspiciously. Marked off their plots of land. Smiles and good morning–good evenings weren't freely exchanged around here. Eyes always spoke before mouths did, harboring a fundamental mistrust. Words rang high. Everyone seemed to be waiting to flare up at some disparaging remark and shower down flaming insults upon all the souls in the universe. They demanded respect, would have fought to the death for that one word . . . Respect!

Everyone understood that Hermancia with her swollen belly was simple-minded. A poor deranged soul, taken advantage of by a group of plotting dirty dogs, natives of Sainte-Angèle. The story of her life unfurled in a droning chant from the shelter of her cabin, ran over the corrugated roofing, and bounded up the steps of Savane land two at a time. Her chanting enveloped the hills, crept into the thick leafy darkness, and then drifted off on the air to join a patch of blue sky. Her voice was irritating, too gentle, a mixture of crystalline spring and harmonium. And it was pitiful to think of the dispossessed creature that embodied it.

But Hermancia was a very happy half-wit. She lived on her glorious song, the beauty of each new day, a little water, and the charity of the people from Savane Mulet, who were no more charitable than a dog in the manger. In the morning her refrains took flight right behind the crowing cock, which fell immediately silent when she began deploring her motherless childhood, the hardships of her father, who caught crabs in Grande-Terre. Sitting alone in her cabin, she sang in broken French, but she had a gift for putting incongruous words into powerful, resonant, and sparkling rhymes that melted everyone's hearts, even those grown callous from age-old misery. When her song rose, an innocent sun greeting the ordinary day, people stopped to catch a wisp of her story cradled on a wing of wind. The air grew less heavy. Fingers ran more lightly through young girls' tresses. People's hearts were suddenly filled with another era, before Savane Mulet. Then, deeply stirred souls forgave themselves one-two venial sins. Enemies soured with nearly murderous rancor suddenly found they were reconciled. Because of that chanting, Eliette once even caught herself believing that the evil spirits confined on the other side of Nèfles Bridge had gone to heaven and left this world where everything is merely doomed to dust, ruin, and tears, just like her mama Séraphine said. Hermancia chanted the misery of her life, but her mind, which could weigh neither good nor evil, gave a joyous ring to her song, full of universal hope, that people were delighted to get a free taste of.

She sang of her humiliated father. When he realized she was pregnant, the poor man started shaking her furiously like a plum tree, to bring down the name of the man or the animal ─ that utterly evil bastard who had deflowered her. After a little while Hermancia figured out what he wanted. So she smiled at him, took his hand, and led him straight to the slaughterhouse. It happened to be a Friday evening, the biggest day for butchering beef. As soon as they arrived, the innocent child extended her finger toward all the men gathered there. Seven ugly buggers . . .

That memory had Eliette in tow, it oppressed her, and she shuddered. In the sky over the distant town, a coconut tree shook its heavy head of dreadlocks. In the old days, back in Joab's time, at least three hundred coconut trees could be counted between Savane Mulet and the town of Ravine-Guinée. The cutlass had felled far and wide, opening the way for men and their cabins.

The cutlass also released the rage that swelled in the heart of Hermancia's papa when she pointed to a table scarred with the marks of knife blades, stained with old humors, encrusted with animal hair and the acrid smell of sacrifice. Black man, Indian, mulatto, white man, chabin, Carib, and coolie-bastard – there were seven of them – not one was spared. That Friday evening, the blood of the heathens that laid Hermancia on the block to take her one after the other splattered on the freshly cut meat, stained the dirty walls, and grieved six families in Mahault. The seventh hireling came from nowhere, or from some vague elsewhere. No one claimed his body. And maybe that was best, people could judge him with easy minds. Someone threw the first stone, and the whole town, its hills, its shores, its remotest corners lapidated his memory, seeing the sole and original root of evil in the uprooted man. Honest to God, his companions had simply been sheep, everyone said. If they succumbed to Hermancia's physical charms, it was merely because they lived in a state of sin, due to everlasting temptation. The innocent child smiled at them with her eyes. And her whole body bore the same smile that said, 'Take me! Take me!' Hidden under her skirt was a little heart-shaped raspberry mouth that smiled, too, and sang out just like a gurgling spring in the woods.

While her father was out gathering the crabs that had been coaxed into his rattraps and philosophically reflecting upon his simple-minded daughter, telling himself that life was a deep dungeon and black people were mere crabs tossed into a barrel with no hope of redemption, the seven males were finishing up the slaughtering. Then they took Hermancia. Every Friday night. With gentle gestures. And her flesh was as tender as the filets they cut away from the backbones of beef. She smiled with her two mouths, and they penetrated her in a never ending renewal of ecstasy. No, they didn't strike her. Didn't force any doors. And they were satiated when they left her, with something hard and sweet inside of them like a piece of polished courbaril wood where their names were engraved amongst the list of the chosen few. After the service, they washed her with ritual solemnity, in a basin scrubbed especially for the purpose. Then, satisfied, they went back to their everyday men's lives, to their cabins filled with kids, to their toothless, fat, and disillusioned wives whom they straddled when night came, still partaking, in dream, of the smiling lips of the half-wit's body.

It was after the massacre, when she landed in Savane, that Hermancia began to sing her life. Day after day, folks gleaned her story from the miserable verses she sent coiling out around Savane. The words hardly ever changed, and some women suddenly fell quiet, their arms frozen as they hung out a piece of wash, feeling something like a warm balm rising within them, delivering their tormented souls and lifting them into the air, out of their bodies. Other women, weakened for a moment, shook themselves vigorously, not to let the spell take hold. You'd see them fuming along, faces fixed in unfounded rage, soured at having caught themselves taking up Hermancia's haunting refrains . . .

You give me joy, O Lord
I does not fear love's face
And you seen into my heart
And I smile, I smile
And love come to the slaughterhouse
And I smile, I smile
O, O, O my Lord! You send the seven wise men
You give me joy
Peace be on the earth
Goodwill toward men
And I smile, I smile
And the seven wise men come to the slaughterhouse
They shut up the cattle
And the blood spattered all around
O, O, O my Lord!

The seven wise men find the star
O, O, O my Lord!
The blood spattered all around
The father and the sons, thy will be done!
And I smile, I smile
At the slaughterhouse, the slaughterhouse, the slaughterhouse!
O, O, O my Lord! . . .

Eliette recalled those songs of no tomorrows. Drifting down the length of Savane like a fine mist, they lulled the days and nights of the child growing in Hermancia's belly. They also accompanied her during the deathwatch for Renélien, Eliette's first man who died suddenly in '59, his heart worn out too early.

We noticed that Hermancia had disappeared three days after Renélien's funeral. She'd given birth alone and abandoned her child in a breadbasket. She was gone, along with her sweet chanting, no one knew where, sowing her innocence, her smiles, and her joy. Set down right smack in the center of the cabin, the child did not cry but was already babbling in a voice that could have been imagined in bright colors; that's what prompted people to look into Hermancia's cabin. Dazzled, everyone in Savane wanted to reap the fruit that Mancia had left, even the men and women who lacked bread five days out of three, even single women crushed and broken by life, those who sold their bodies to put a little meat in the *canari*-stewpot, those who shuffled their feet listlessly, already walking out in front of nine-ten kids, even the stingy-hearted, slobs, heathens, renegades, fellaghas, muscle men, even the old, thick-blooded women with milkless titties, bitter *coucounes*, like Eliette . . .

Hermancia's little girl was baptized Glawdys. Her beauty was peculiar and magical, that girl had inherited nothing from her mama, except for the smile. Some said that the seven wise men from the slaughterhouse had mixed their blood so that she would take on equal parts of each of them, the best parts. Black Negress with green eyes, straight nose, thick, purple lips, and long, curly, straw-colored hair, Glawdys baffled everyone who tried to pinpoint her race.

Eliette could have stepped up and adopted her right away, but she went back to her cabin to think it over indefinitely and escape from the clutches of reason – wondering if she would know how to care for her, if this was really the child destiny had sent her. The Haitian fortuneteller had predicted a niece; Eliette could see no relation here.

When she finally made up her mind, too late, the church bells of Ravine-Guinée were chiming furiously, and Eloise was walking away, overjoyed, the breadbasket under her arm like a prize won at a raffle. Eliette barely had time to see the green eyes of Hermancia's child disappear. She stood there planted in the middle of the path. How long? Nobody could've said. People bumped into her. She swung around, pirouette. A full basket of mullet struck her in the lower leg. The fishy smell attracted a flea-bitten dog that came and pissed on her feet. She didn't budge, was as unshakeable as an ancient tree. But inside, the feeling that she'd missed her chance to be a mother raised her up on the end of its point like a pike. Exposing her for all the world to see that she really had been born for naught.

Eloise belonged to the worst breed of voracious creatures. Yearning for everything she laid eyes on. She had one foot swollen with elephantiasis, a dirty dress, a flabby gut, and sniveling, wispy words. She spent her time prostrated in front of her mama's tiled grave, pleading for favors and miraculous remedies for the twelve children she'd borne. Twelve of an abominable progeny that had all gone adrift. Some in rum. One-two in ganja. Three girls had trailed after males with small minds and big peckers that raked in welfare checks from female bellies and then beat their chests and cried they were men before women and God. Two of her sons had disappeared in a murky mystery, some said they were rotting in prison . . . Not one made up for another. After so much damage, ruin, and shipwreck, Eloise had still been the first to jump at the radiant, babbling baby in its breadbasket. People let her do it. No one stopped her. She carried it away, the great gobbler! Just when Eliette had convinced her reason and come bearing her brand-new motherly heart to be inaugurated, her hands held out in front of her as if she were carrying holy water in a golden chalice, alas!

Voracious put Glawdys to bed in one of her dresser drawers on a sweater brought back from France and forgotten there by one of the offspring with aborted futures. She gave her some sour milk from her wilted titties and never took her out to walk in the early morning light. After that she was only seen at dusk, her shapeless shadow slipping over the horizon of vague cabins. She laughed, Eloise did, and the child laughed too. Yet, the golden color of her curls was already fading. For lack of sunshine, her hair now shone like pinchbeck. From staying shut up in the dark cabin, her green eyes took on the glaucous color of the marshes in Grande-Terre. From purple, her lips turned the disquieting blue of the high seas. Even the ebony black of her skin became dull and ashen, lost its lovely sheen.

For as long as Glawdys remained in her breadbasket with wobbly legs and milk dribbling from the corners of her mouth, Eloise cared for her in an acceptable fashion. But as soon as the child could stand up, the old lady wrapped a rope around her waist, leaving only three yards of slack for her to move around in near the cabin. The madwoman said it was to keep the child from going adrift like all the other children she'd so cherished. In the beginning she untied her at night to bed her down close against her big titties. And then, as time went by, she denied her even that last favor and kept her tied up night and day, telling everyone that the child had teeth like a wild beast and bit the charitable hand that fed her.

It's true that each day the little creature awoke a bit madder, just like the vicious battered dogs with bare-chafed necks, tethered in penitence throughout the sweltering days of the dry season and winter's driving rains. Pulling on her chain, pawing at the ground, drooling, she envied all the freedoms that came and went before her eyes: a leaf lifted on the wind, emancipated toads, women's skirts flouncing up in their stride, feet pattering on the paths of indepen-

dence. Eloise tied her to one of the corner posts of her cabin in order
to, she said, save her from the evil world teeming beyond the three
yards of chain. Keep her from slipping into rum, which shells out
three days of paradise up front and then runs up the rest on credit.
Preserve her from men. Deliver her body from misery . . .
   That's how Glawdys slowly wasted away.
   Like everyone else in Savane Mulet, Eliette heard her yapping all
day long. Of course, she could have stepped up, chided the cruel
stepmother, and freed the innocent child, whose nails were broken
and bleeding from scraping at the rocky earth. One day Eliette even
asked the Good Lord to guide her straight to Eloise's cabin. But she
lacked the necessary strength and courage. She was always putting
off D-day till tomorrow. So many times she had prepared for the
great debarkation, rehearsing the three stages of liberation in front
of the mirror . . . Hands at her sides, two furrows on her brow, in her
dreams, she saw herself marching on Eloise, shouting at her like a
male calls another male to join in fatal combat, 'Oh! Oh! Eloise! Si ou
sé on fenm, soti on fwa menm!' If you a woman, show yourself now!
Evidently, inside the dark cabin, the madwoman shook as she knelt
before a candle burning to the Holy Virgin. Then, just like a cowboy
in the movies, Eliette whipped out from between her titties the wood
chisel and the hammer that had belonged to Joab, her defunct stepfather. She struck the shackle of slavery with a single blow and carried Glawdys away without even looking back. Alas, the scenario
was lived out only in Eliette's imagination. In her cowardice, she
merely eyed the other contemptuously, turned up the volume on her
radio to cover the child's yapping, joined the circle of those who saw
and heard what went on but didn't get mixed up in the neighbor's
business.
   That's how the little girl came to be six-seven years old. One day

a woman from Child Welfare came and untied her. There were some people standing around – petty souls who'd just landed, who hadn't known the innocent child in the beginning – who said that Voracious was admirable for having fed a creature of that breed and that the Good Lord had rid her of the girl through the intercession of Child Welfare. But those who knew kept their distance, hiding behind their double doors, peeking out through the slats of their shutters, choking back the remorse that curdled their blood. The child fought, bit, moaned. They had to gag her, bind her hands and feet, give her a sedative to calm her rage.

Seeing her go by, thrashing around like a piglet having its throat cut, Eliette made herself believe that maybe it wasn't too late and that surely – she hoped with all her soul – the child would learn how to dream, smile, and babble again. She thought again of the Haitian woman that had predicted a daughter for her. Then, when her eyes met the gray gaze of the little creature, the vision of the child yapping at the end of her rope stuck fast in her mind and stayed there.

When Child Welfare gave Glawdys her walking papers, she came back pronto to roam the paths of Savane Mulet. Thank God, Eloise had already done seven full rounds of hell. Her old legs, devastated with elephantiasis, had carried her one last time as far as the cemetery, where she'd crumpled up, panting on her mama's tiled grave. How old was Glawdys? Seventeen, eighteen . . . For at least ten years, Child Welfare had kept her far from the everyday thoughts of folks in Savane. In truth, no one sought to dig up her memory. And those who inadvertently let her name drop, like a blob of ink onto neat lines of words spread over a white page, quickly understood from the ensuing silence that other words must be put in place, the story that ultimately came to haunt even the lowliest scoundrels had to be killed. Eliette still thought of the child in a painful way. Time had never helped her forget the gray eyes, the yapping, the bruised flesh that the rope bit into, her own glaring cowardice that so shamed her. It was to rid herself of the shame that she'd married Hector in '65, to square away and steer for the headlands of her childbearing dreams. At over forty-five years of age! Just to give herself one last chance, to drive away the remorse and regrets lashing at her insides. With Hector's sickness, and later his death, she'd relapsed into her endless questions, was tortured by the memories of her mama all whirled round by the Cyclone of '28, shattered at the thought she'd missed the boat of her destiny, endlessly tormented. When she thought of Glawdys then, she didn't picture her as being a grown-up, pretty young woman, only saw those gray eyes, dagger blades gleaming in the setting sun that pursued her all-long, all-long.

Down there at Child Welfare, they'd done their best to free the poor child of the rope that she still felt tied around her entire body. For a time, every night her nails scratched, ripped off the fresh scabs formed by day. But her wounds ended up healing anyway, wrapping her waist in a puffy belt of flesh. At times her complexion regained a bit of the shimmering ebony black sheen. A golden streak spread through her hair. And on some full-moon nights, the green of her eyes seemed closer to the color they were in her babyhood. But those throwbacks hardly lasted. When she came back to Savane, Glawdys was gray from head to foot.

Eliette recognized her immediately. Gray, recognizable amongst all women. A black suitcase was her only possession. Ten years of being shut up indoors at Child Welfare, she thought. Did the poor girl remember all the faces from the past who lived in freedom yet had grown accustomed to seeing her chained up, hearing her yapping at her stepmama's door?

As if they feared the light, the gray eyes stayed closed up in Eloise's cabin two-three-five days. People passed at a distance, driven from behind by the memory of the child who whimpered there long ago, scowling in the sun and the rain. They went by with their brows knit, lips tight, prepared to fight back in a battle that they intuitively felt was imminent. Just to rile everyone up more, some mean folks spread around that Glawdys was a mad-dog woman and that people should take up rifles and shoot her. Others, fearing neither God nor man, related what the adoptive mother had said: that Glawdys was a wild beast with long sharp teeth whose bite caused sudden death. And that if Eloise had been found dead right there in the cemetery, maybe it was no accident. Undoubtedly a pack of dogs, friends of Glawdys, had attacked her. Dog-demons that left no marks . . .

No one knows the exact length of time Glawdys stayed shut up alone in the cabin. In any case, when she finally came out, everyone felt relieved. They preferred to see her out in the open rather than imagine her plotting some dark revenge, ruminating a collective punishment for yesterday's deaf-dumb-blind. Ashen shadow, her waist girded with an ancient rope, she roamed the paths of Savane for three days. Three days without eating or drinking, armed with a stick that she held in her fingers like a divining rod. When she came and planted herself in front of her true mama Hermancia's cabin, all the radios started crackling with interference at the same time. And two-three bicycle tires exploded right in a row, which caused Marga's next-door neighbor, Odilon, to have a heart attack.

Dense, luxuriant foliage had completely covered the tin roof and the old gray planks of the cabin. Christophines, like big white titties, bulged on the rooftop. Others, twisting into the holes in the tin roof, dangled inside the shack. Despite hunger and voracity, no one ever stretched out a hand to pick one, not even the biggest thieves in God's creation. The place was shrouded in too much mystery. The curse of the seven wise men hung over it. It was said that sometimes the ghost of Hermancia, Glawdys's innocent mama, could be heard wailing plaintively inside. And breaths arose. Moaning slipped out through the door, which was always left ajar. One day, a neighbor even thought she heard Eloise's cracked voice asking Hermancia for another child, to try to put things right again. Then the ripe christophines fell into the center of the cabin, rolled out to the corners, rotted, and germinated on the tamped earth, producing countless plants and leaves and flowers and fruit that no one ate. Evenings, Eliette recognized every sound that came from Hermancia's cabin. And when a dog gave the death howl, she had visions of Glawdys straining at the rope, screaming at the Grim Reaper to take her, Eliette, before all the other shameless cowards around.

The gray-eyed girl didn't say anything to anyone. Her hands began ripping away the tendrils that clung to the tin roof, and the creeping, leafy vines came tumbling down under the weight of the ripe christophines. And then she kicked open the door and disappeared inside, snatched into the darkness. No one knew what she read during that time: an ancient and musty witchcraft gramarye, a manual of white magic, the Gospel according to St. John . . . In any case, the parasitic sounds that used to come from the cabin faded away one after the other. Everyone immediately thought that the mamsell had turned herself to right thinking. And when she unrolled three gunny sacks on the ground in front of her door, stacked christophines into three pyramids, and stuck up her price: three francs a kilo, folks crowded around her merchandise, holding out *koui*-calabashes and baskets for her to fill, wordlessly, with the tender white titties.

Savane Mulet ate christophines from Easter to Pentecost. Prepared them every which way, raw, cooked, in salads, casseroles, stuffed with corned beef or conch, in white sauce, curried, crystallized. Each cabin nursed its bowl of christophines, conscientiously ingesting them till they came out everyone's ears. On the Monday after Pentecost, since the gunny sacks had nothing left to offer, Glawdys folded them back up under her arm, counted her francs, and struck out on the road to Ravine-Guinée. People thought that the christophine season was over with for good. And everyone felt like new, cleansed, relieved, shiny, as if the penitence of the christophines had redeemed the faults of past sinners. Some spoke up and said she wasn't so much of a she-dog after all and maybe her life was worth more than a two-cent candle. Even predicted she'd end up saving her soul. When she walked away, a green flash streaked through her gray eyes. A golden curl, fleeting flame, shone out from the thicket of ashen hair. And even her dull skin took on the warm glow of ebony once again. A fortuneteller insisted that the christophines, which were God's medicine, had healed her.

I wouldn't have recollected those days – Glawdys and her lovely matching colors – if I hadn't seen Rosan's eyes that Sunday, I would have continued to peer at myself through the visions that hung in my soul, poorly scoured stewpots with smoke-blackened bottoms, straying memories. I would have allowed my shriveled heart to beat on, despite the misery on all sides, the blood on the paths, the waltz of cutlasses, the children in front of the church, the crimes of she-devils, and the titties of a black woman, laid out on a banana leaf.

I would have walked away from my door, which was closed to the screaming silence over Rosette's way.

I didn't try to run to her side. I promised myself I'd go the next day, first thing in the morning. I wanted to wait out the night because I already knew that sleep wouldn't have me after what she was going to tell me. Another tale of crime! I said to myself, 'People are truly animals! . . . Nice face, demonic soul. Nice how de do, devilish tongue.' I didn't want to hear any of it. Just promise her a bit of soup for the children. Just slip a coin into her hand.

  I didn't want to get mixed up in it all . . .

Glawdys hadn't flinched when she dropped her live baby. She was in her right mind. Her gray eyes were dry. No, there were no crazed thoughts darting about under that smooth brow. The thoughts in her mind lined up patiently, not crowding each other, or else they just sat waiting for their turn, like at the doctor's office. She must have thought it all out beforehand, weighed, gauged, measured the pointlessness of keeping him alive. She'd passed her judgment and thrown the baby over. They found Glawdys with her two hands glued to the iron railing of the bridge, her gray eyes staring down at the small mangled body that had landed between two elongated black rocks like the arms of those kindhearted black maidservants that serve as children's nannies. When people leaned over her shoulder to see the object of her contemplation, they pulled back in horror, as if a fist had punched them right in the middle of the stomach. Only Rosan had mustered enough courage to go down and scoop up the poor little bloodstained body. He walked through Quartier-Mélo, strode through every gully, trampled down the grass on all of the paths, displaying the martyred lamb to all so that it would not be forgotten. As he passed, people hastened their pace, their hearts filled with shame and rage. Some old women fell to their knees, ate dirt, pulled out their hair, implored the Lord God to grant a soul and feelings to black people. 'Woe be upon us! Viperess!' the women kept repeating, not understanding why they gave birth and continued to carry life and found the strength to laugh and dream in a world whose path was paved with death alone. And all Savane was filled with vain words and imprecations, with silences and cries that slowly gave way to the rhythm of hands beating furiously on a drum on some distant hill. A woman wiped the sweat from Rosan's forehead. Another wet his lips. He walked for more than three hours and stopped in the setting sun, his bare foot sliced in two from a broken bottle of Malta beer.

No one knew what to do with old fridges and dented-up stoves, so, after the baby, people started throwing them under Nèfles Bridge. Two-three was all right. Everyone thought that someday a heavy rain would come and the river would wash them down to the sea. They no longer saw the white enamel shining in the sun, the rusty doors, the pockmarked burners, the rats in the recesses of ovens. People were already getting used to them, they were sort of like extra rocks on the banks of the river. And then there got to be more than the eye could count or bear.

All of that began after they brought electricity to Ti-Ghetto. And it got worse after Glawdys threw her baby down to the foot of the bridge. Maybe the folks around here thought that if you could throw a baby down there, then anything went, there was nothing wrong with flinging refrigerators and incinerators, fans and tin cans, washing machines, canteens, jars, bars, cars.

That's how it all started, and the river became a garbage dump. When Beloved and her band of Rastas crossed the bridge to found their nation on the other side, they cleaned up part of it, pushed the rubbish into a gully where it was no longer an eyesore. They built their paradise. And the whole time they were there, no one ventured to dump garbage down there. But as soon as they left, it began all over again.

.   .   .   .

Tomorrow, early Monday morning, Rosette said to herself, I'll go over there too and throw out the old stove that's rotting in the courtyard. Rosan gave her a new one last Mother's Day, with five burners, that browns and roasts things in no time.

Out there under Nèfles Bridge had become a great garbage heap. People hadn't foreseen that when they were striving to get the mayor to plant electricity everywhere in Savane. It first came to Ti-Ghetto in 1975, like a miracle, after the election of the communist candidate, Juste Clément. The people in Quartier-Mélo looked on passionately as it glowed in the cabins of the folks in Ti-Ghetto, whom they envied. They didn't understand why all the electric poles stuck in the ground over on their side didn't string out the same wires and were as useless as greased poles after a fair. Their hearts just couldn't warm up to the lights that shone in others' cabins, to the humming of fans, to the endless cackling of TV's. In 1978, the very same year that Glawdys flung her child down to the bottom of Nèfles Bridge, the light ran out as far as Quartier-Mélo and finally crossed the age-old gloom of Savane from one end to the other. In barely a year, each tin-roofed board cabin harbored an electric fridge, a stove, a washing machine, TV set, fan, and so on. Back in the old days, during the dry season, Marga used to peddle ice at exorbitant prices in her store. She built concrete cabins in Grande-Terre with the money of poverty-stricken folks sweating in the Savane sun. That woman, who'd accumulated a neat little fortune from selling the blocks of ice she made with her kerosene refrigerator, almost went broke.

Rosette had always heard Angela speak of what they were doing to the river as a crime. In the room that Rosan had built with his own two hands, Angela filled her little sister Rita's head with her enraged ranting about the river having become a garbage dump because of the people in Savane, murderers who polluted out of spite or even just for pleasure. Not a clean spot left on the banks. No way to walk along with your nose in the air and jump from rock to rock. Broken bottles lay in wait for barefoot soles. Bags full of garbage and worms covered the carpet of dead leaves and ferns. Razor-sharp pieces of rusty tin roofing. Batteries, mufflers, puddles of thick black oil. Cans, casks, crates.

Rosette came to Ti-Ghetto in '75, along with the electricity. In '78, when the girl had thrown her child to the bottom of Nèfles Bridge, Angela had just turned five. Rosan hadn't planned on enlarging his cabin. Angela didn't even have her cozy corner yet and still slept on a little mattress on the floor that Rosette rolled up under her bed in the morning. In those days she went down to the river on Saturdays to do her washing and she loved it. She had electricity, yet didn't see any point in a washing machine. The river flowing under the bridge was clear, not the running sore it was now.

Angela talked about the crime against the river, of killing, with the air of an offended lady. But if the mayor had a mind to, Rosette thought, three-four days would be enough for the sanitation department to collect all the garbage under the bridge. And the rats that nested down there would be gone too. The rocks could be put back in place. The banks could be mended and freshed up even more. The river would keep on flowing and washing clothes just like in the old days. Dear God, the baby's blood on the rocks had been washed away long ago . . . Maybe one day people would get fed up with tearing down the signs No Dumping, Violators Will Be Prosecuted. And the tin roofing, the city garbage bags, the old fan blades, and even the washing machine drums would stop rolling down to the bottom of Nèfles Bridge. Killing . . . With those filthy words of hers, she did a good job of killing all of us.

She was almost twelve years old then, my girl, my little Angela, Rosette said to herself. When she had her first blood, I couldn't believe it. I sat down in the kitchen. She was standing in front of me, her fingers locked around a mango she was sucking on. I explained to her that she was almost a real woman. And that all around there were animals with men's faces – that those beasts hid their sharp teeth in sweet smiles and masked their lust with innocent airs. I told her, 'Don't let them come close, Angela! On the road to Ravine-Guinée, you got no idea what you might run into. You have a treasure to guard, moons to count . . .' Angela nodded her head and said yes to everything, like someone who already knows all the answers. I warned her, 'If you listen to them men, follow them into the darkness of some room, or the perdition of some cane field, it's bad. The blood might disappear because of a seed planted in your belly. The fruit of sin bears mongrels with a great legacy of malediction and shortbread destinies.' Yes, I taught her how to preserve herself. Never let your eyes rest upon a male, look through him, don't smile, don't swing your hips in a certain way, leave that to the Negresses in heat that peddle their bodies, laugh in the daytime, and cry at night in their cold beds. I told her she'd find an honest man, someone like her father Rosan. She just had to wait. If she deserved it, the Good Lord would send her some righteous man. She sucked the seed of her mango right down to its white heart. Afterward I made up a story for her about a cyclone grieving for its eye, which had dropped into the sea. She never lifted her eyes.

The day that poor Glawdys flung her child to the bottom of Nèfles Bridge, I thought, 'My God, protect me from such a lot!' What Angela has gone and done is like throwing us all down to the foot of the bridge: her brother, her little sister, her papa Rosan, and me. She didn't even flinch . . .

I saw them, wailed Rosette, all the murderers in Savane Mulet, they were staring at me as if I were the biggest criminal in all Creation. Rogues! Flea-bitten curs! Heathens! Beggarers! Bare-assed *manawa*-whores! Ratbags!

I'm just waiting till I get a little strength back. I'll go and sit by Angela's bed. Lord, keep me from raising my voice! Let her look me in the eye so I can see the lie. Hold back my hand, Jesus, keep me from beating her! Hold back my hand, ah!

Tomorrow I'm going to throw out the old stove. It's cluttering up the courtyard. Will I be able to load it into a wheelbarrow by myself? Rosan won't be here tomorrow morning. He's spending the night in jail. Good God, if I had any sense, I'd start screaming and beating her right now. A good thrashing, that's what she needs. Save me, sweet Jesus! It's my fault! Every bit my fault!

Rosan worked hard at building the extension on the cabin. Counting and recounting the money. Putting the savings aside. Collecting iron bars, roofing, cement. And no one came to lend him a hand. He was alone with his two hands to mix the mortar and set the bricks. Alone, entrepreneur, mason, carpenter . . .

Rosan carried the little lamb all the way over here while the law was carting Glawdys away, her hands tied together in front with a sort of leash. She was completely gray and no other color. Everything had been snuffed out in her, as if forever. Eliette was trembling and weeping dry-eyed, staring at the small crushed body at the bottom of the bridge. She has a lot of compassion, Eliette does. With those usually expressionless gray eyes, Glawdys stared at her in such a contemptuous way that she was stripped raw.

My daughter Angela looked at me that same way when she came home. I could have beaten her on the spot. Taken the strap and marked her back. Kicked her right in that lying mouth with my shoes. Twisted her arms and let my feet fly at her backside. Ripped her skin off . . . Ah! Hold back my hand! Tomorrow I'll send her to Aunt Fanotte's in Beauséjour. I won't see her face anymore. I don't ever want to see her again or know that she's within arm's reach. I'm holding back, Lord!

It's true I, Rosette, called for Glawdys's death along with the others, I screamed for her to be thrown down from Nèfles Bridge too, so she'd understand that human life can't be trifled with. I prayed that she'd rise up from the rocks, crippled for life. So that she'd spend the rest of her days ruminating her crime and dragging around a lame leg, paralyzed arm, broken teeth, twisted face, blind eye. I judged her, just like all the others. Today, I too could kill my own flesh and blood. Angela . . .

On the other side of the flats, Eliette resolved to go visit Rosette early the next day. She'd closed her door on the night. Just too bad if the devil came and tweaked her toes. Just too bad if the sounds from outside came in without knocking to tell her about all the shenanigans in Savane Mulet. She didn't want to get mixed up in it all. She had nothing to say against Rosan, who wasn't a bad sort deep down, even if he had committed a crime. Maybe he'd lost his head. Can you judge and condemn a man for getting angry? That Rosette was a good neighbor. And those children of hers, Angela, Rita, and Robert, were so well-behaved, Eliette just couldn't believe that their papa was spending the night in jail for something serious, not a crime of the same magnitude as the ones that had already shamed Savane Mulet.

When the christophine season drew to an end, Glawdys left with her loot. No one thought that she'd be back anytime soon. Some folks made a clean sweep of her in their minds, as if they'd paid their debts and owed nothing more. And even if she'd never forgiven them with her mouth, they all absolved themselves double-quick without making any acts of contrition. Eliette even thought that the Lord might well have spared her a heavy burden by giving the child to Eloise. That's how the regrets and remorse in her heart fell silent for a while. At times, when a dog barked, the vision of the child on her chain came back, just like a recollection hanging on a single thread of memory that unravels with thought. Eliette was halfway saved.

Two-three years went by in that way. Savane lived out its moratorium with the impertinence of the foolhardy. And then Glawdys came back with the baby that she soon flung down to the bottom of Nèfles Bridge. Before that, she played out the same old scene, took up her role as christophine vendor again. She spread out the three gunny sacks on the ground just as before, set up three pyramids of christophines, and stuck up her price: five francs per kilo. The first time folks had willingly done penance. They'd breakfasted, dined, and supped on christophines. Alas, nobody wanted to pay the ransom of remorse again. Everyone ignored her, the gray eyes that pierced consciences, the heavy, ivory-colored christophines, the baby asleep on her shoulder, the thin face and dirty feet in the old stained tennis shoes. 'What that gray girl thinking?' people said. 'Will she take advantage of people's kindness all her life? I swear she taking us for the biggest jackasses in Creation! No, by God, there are sinners in these parts sure enough, but no one got the right to tread down the wretched of the earth! Christophine! Christophine! No, the Almighty never told black folks to eat christophines every blessed day! . . .' Amongst the bunch of hardhearted souls there were of course some kind ones, housewives and mothers who would gladly have forked out five francs for a kilo of christophines, but empathizing was abdicating, admitting one was a sinner for eternity. And so everyone spied on the neighbor, preventing anyone from taking part in the girl's masquerade.

Glawdys, alone against the town, stood her ground: as long as the bland season of christophines lasted, she never brought down her price. All around her, the pale titties wilted, rotted, and germinated. The child on her shoulder didn't cry, no, but anyone could see that hunger was twisting his insides. His mama's caresses nourished him no more than her milkless teats did. She could have used a few five-franc coins to buy some milk. But folks stuck stubbornly to their guns. Maybe if she'd said, 'Please, thank you!', they would have given her money and more – roofing, boards, woolens, bed, table, wardrobe, spoon, fork, yams, beef, pigtails, bananas, jam . . . Alas, the gray eyes held too much contempt, too much pride too, even if one admitted she was simply begging for a little love, just running after one-two kisses, a little flattery, small, pointless, yet marvelous gestures that bring joy and serenity to one's life. One morning Glawdys found ten francs that a traitor or a renegade had left on a half tumbled-down pyramid of christophines. She didn't try to find out where the money came from. Maybe she knew . . . And that's the way it went every morning, for forty days. The gray-eyed girl threw the coin into a little sooty koui-calabash on the ground next to the christophines.

.   .   .   .

Would she have bought milk for her baby if I'd said, 'Here, child!' and put the coin in her hand? Would she have given the baby a chance to grow up in the world? Eliette wondered.

The day that Glawdys hurled her baby down to the foot of Nèfles Bridge, Rosette hauled me out so I'd come see. I had the feeling that I was personally responsible for all of these cataclysms. I told myself that maybe, if I'd picked up the breadbasket before Eloise, Glawdys would have held on to all her colors, wouldn't have become the woman that everyone called murderess! She-devil! Cursed bitch! . . . I didn't say anything, found no excuses for her. Didn't want to get mixed up in it all, didn't want to see or hear anything.

When that Sunday suddenly came unhinged, I no longer dreamt of taking anyone under my motherly wing.

III

Sleep just wouldn't have me. The ordinary sounds of night crowded one behind the other at the foot of my bed. And a great unbroken silence, risen from the very heart of darkness, spurred the visions that always preyed upon my mind. Thoughts came to me one after another, and I said to myself, 'Dear God! Why was I sent down to live upon this earth? All my life I've been nothing better than a stale flower bearing no promise of fruit, and now that I'm completely dried up and the time draws near for you to take me from the world, my mind can find no rest anywhere.'

I don't know how, but suddenly I found myself sitting up on the bed, all in a turmoil about my own insignificance. I lifted my opened palms before me and repeated three times: 'Lord, I am your servant! Deliver me! Show me the way!' Sweat was pouring from my face. A long shudder ran up and down the length of my body, and the dark memory of the Cyclone of 1928 completely engulfed me.

Hearing the sounds from outside, the haggard breaths, gave me a bit of a start, and I was sorry not to have a man lying by my side. I'd shake him so he'd go out and face the chaos-filled night. He'd get up and I'd wait for him under the sheets, keeping very still. Neither Renélien nor Hector (in the days when he could still stand on his feet) would have prayed for morning and hidden like a coward inside the cabin. They'd have stridden into the shadows, torn through the gloom, scattered the evil breaths. I didn't want to look or listen any more than I already had. Alas, confused cries chasing after each other filled my room. At Rosette's place the doors were closed, but you could see the light was on inside because of the yellow beams scoring the front of the cabin through the poorly fit boards. Before Cyclone, all the human sinfulness in Savane Mulet that people kept more less in leash by day was loosed at nightfall. The cutlass spoke bluntly in the darkness. Driven by hate and rage, poor sinners changed into demons. Then Bleed, Hack, Kill stepped up as the three allies of emancipation, righteously defending the cause of justice in the absence of public prosecutors or lawyers.

In 1969 it was on a night just like this that Régis chopped up his Hortense, the woman he had not married before God or man. Shacked her up just like that, like you mark an animal that you push into a cage for a life of servility. Just shacked her up, all for himself, under the shelter of the tin roof and the boards. Surely she didn't think he'd end up cutting her up and putting all the pieces on the tamped earth in the kitchen and laying her two titties quivering like almond-milk jelly on a banana leaf between her head – eyes wide with stupefaction – and the gaping, bloody *coucoune*. The first crime in Ti-Ghetto . . .

Everyone heard Régis beating Hortense, sometimes with an old conch shell that rang hollow, clonk, clonk, clonk on the poor girl's head. Blood often spurted all over the floor, spattered two-three pots, and turned the water in the bucket pink. In the beginning of their union, Hortense dreamt of another life; not that she envied the gold or the silver of possessors, but she dreamt of a glorious life at Governor Régis's side, with caresses, consideration and sweet words, flowers, sherbets, and green water coconuts. She was no pretentious damozel. But when she begged for love in all its majesty, its preludes, its climax, it's epilogue, the dumb clod knocked her out with a punch of his fist and then took her savagely on the floor because a female who asks for those kinds of things is just too hot-blooded. Got to damp her flames before she catches fire and tries to put it out by rubbing her body up against the first male she runs into. The more submissive she became, the harder he hit her.

One day Hortense ran into Eusèbe, whom everyone cried Zébio from his early childhood. She was coming back from the river, a basket of laundry on her head. Zébio was a little man with gentle eyes who sang and whistled from morning to night. On Sundays he began the day with spirituals and Te Deums, bloomed into romances, and finished up with tra-la-las and poignant serenades that filled the night, drowning out the whoop-de-do, the sounds of the tambour-kas, all the tears and the sighs in Savane. Other days he left early in the morning to stand at his post by the side of the highway. His boss came from Fonds-Abîmes in his tarpaulined pickup truck to collect them – him and some others – and drive them to a construction site in Pointe-à-Pitre. Zébio said he was a housepainter, but when work was scarce in his field, he proposed his services as a mason and even a tile layer at times. Painting and singing coincided well with his personality until the day he saw Hortense. The woman's face was already entirely demolished and disjointed from the blows of the conch shell, yet Zébio noticed the flame of a color he'd never seen before burning in her still undamaged eyes.

The approach was difficult. Zébio walked close on her heels until she turned and glared at him. Along the path he explained to her that he was a house painter, a regular singing-whistling guy, but suddenly, seeing her, his heart had been stricken with a violent desire to become an artist. With the help of God and her mysterious eyes, he felt he could capture the original and eternal color – mother of all colors – on canvas. He'd become famous the world over. People would say, 'A black! Can you believe it? A black!' If he succeeded in immortalizing that recalcitrant color, he could finally pull his feet out of the clodhoppers that always brought him back to Savane. He could say goodbye once and for all to the hard licks, lead brick he'd been dragging around since his mother had cut the umbilical cord with her teeth. Hard licks that weighed upon him every day. It was to shake off that weight that he had learned to sing, all by himself. It gave him courage. It helped him hold up his head that sometimes bowed under a heavy sorrow that fell upon him – blip! – like a sudden rain shower no one was expecting. Singing had only been a last resort for him. And don't let his cheerful airs, his flamboyant repertoire fool you; deep down inside something was steadily eating away at him. When he saw the color appear in Hortense's eyes, he understood that up to that day his life had been nothing but one long wait.

First the girl smiled behind her scars. Hortense was a dreamer, for sure, but not naïve. She'd already been hurt by more than one male with suave words coming straight from some purportedly bona fide paradise. Régis, her mate, had turned out to be the most perfidious, and the most pitiless too. Like all the others, he'd cast his seine of fine talk and newly mended promises. She had believed in him. Now, she nabbed each day as it came along, refraining from exerting her mind with empty considerations that offered no escape. Wilted, ugly, covered with scars, she figured that only death could tear her from the brutal clutches of her oppressor . . . The thug kept beating on Hortense to cool her hypothetical fiery passions. Accused her of flirting with every black man on the paths from Savane to Ravine-

Guinée. For Hortense, those days were long past, and no matter what she did, the man whipped her almost automatically. Already entirely banged up, the girl didn't wish to have any more dealings with the male species. The earth bore her along apathetically and, like the old women that have reached the last leg of life, her body promised nothing but bitterness and the shades of death. Because of that, undoubtedly, the men in Savane didn't covet her, saving their lust for other, not yet disembodied women. And also, in Savane there were no foolhardy souls, madmen from another planet, prepared to stand up to Régis, whom night alone had seen part company with his cutlass.

Zébio sang while Régis followed in the prodigious shadow of his reputation as governor of Savane Mulet.

Zébio sang for dreams and for sorrow. His repertoire included blues, cantilenas, serenades, polkas, mazurkas. Zébio sang without taking time to categorize people, pick out the mean ones, separate the wheat from the chaff.

Zébio sang well, it should have been enough to brighten his days. Alas, no sooner had he seen the original color in the eyes of that poor girl, than he knew he was born to endure the notoriety of great discoverers.

Zébio lost his voice, his love of song and, blinded, galloped off in single-hearted quest of the primal color. His passion gave him a way with words, the girl succumbed double-quick. Yes, she'd allow him to put her face on canvas and wood, to mix his gouaches to immortalize her, blessed icon, repository of the color, sanctuary and tabernacle, Holy Grail of the original essence . . . And a lot of other wise and lofty words that he later spun out with great eloquence. When he spoke in that way, he could no longer control his hands – all aflutter with future renown. And then he fell silent, feverishly clutching imaginary paintbrushes, eyes lost in his highfaluting horn tooting. And that's how he conquered the damozel. His sweet talk rekindled a small flame in Hortense's heart. And suddenly her life, which she thought was burned out, opened onto a new, unexplored, undreamt-of dimension. Yet not the slightest dream had been revealed to her in the last few nights. No sign had materialized when she was washing her sheets at the river. And even when her eyes had met those of that black man Zébio, she hadn't felt a thing, neither warning nor premonition.

For love of art and in his quest for the color, Zébio had to break her in gradually, teach her how to talk and smile and even laugh, for the mere thought of Governor Régis left her petrified with terror. Far from prying eyes, they sat down together on the same rock at the foot of the last silk-cotton tree in Savane, which had borne countless she-devils, and worked out an infallible stratagem.

At the peep of dawn, Zébio left as usual, whistling along his way. But he didn't climb into the back of the tarpaulined pickup with the others anymore. He came back to Savane, hunching down, incognito, taking a long detour to keep from treading in his morning footsteps. You could make out his elongated shadow on the sheet metal, slipping over the boards, melting into the brush. He went off hatless and with his head held high and came slinking back, with a wide-brimmed straw hat clamped down on his head like an American cowboy, Django of the Wild West.

Obviously everyone recognized our man. Posted near Marga's shop deep in some heated discussion, standing watch in the dark cabins without seeming to be, people everywhere kept an eye on him. And while he thought he was endowed with heaven-sent invisibility, everyone saw him slip secretly into the back of Hortense's cabin, carrying a large bag at calculated times when Massa Régis wasn't there. No one went looking for any long explanations having to do with love of art and a certain Holy Grail, or with a sudden painturesque vocation promising a passel of laurels. People smiled wryly at Régis's hard luck. Everyone imagined the lovers one on top of the other, in unorthodox positions learned in books Zébio pulled from his bag, which surely contained a pistol and three grenades, because you either had to be a major general or a raving lunatic to dare take the governor of Savane's woman, risk your soul in the arms of Hortense, that scarred and stitched woman, who wasn't worth the trouble.

And everyone swore, without really knowing, that once he'd disappeared into the dark cabin, Zébio spent his time trying to soothe the ardors that consumed Hortense. No one would have believed that a man with sheep's eyes, and a singing fool to boot – an expert in American spirituals and blues – had found his platonic and mystical path in the eyes of old withered-up Hortense. Alas, people were burdened only with the weight of their own miserable failures, were crushed between the walls of their personal jails. They saw and sized everything up in a narrow-minded way, without the slightest hint of magnanimity. Who in Savane could understand that the only thing that consumed those two were their dreams? She, the battered Negress, found herself beautiful in Zébio's eyes, like a magical jar bulging with gold of a color that had not yet been invented. He touched her only with his eyes. And she posed in her original nudity for kind words, honey-words, free smiles, and sometimes a green water coconut, a stick of barley sugar. She asked for nothing more. And Zébio, dazed, utterly spellbound with his art and his fantastic notions of pioneering, stuck fast in the joy of colors that sprang from his hand inspired by Hortense's smiles and curves, spent hours ruining canvases, gouaches, and paintbrushes so she would confer upon him, over and over again, just one-two sparks of the fire she held within. They spoke very little in truth, two sealed words, four hushed exchanges, suffocated laughter. He no longer singing, she smiling silently. In fact, not a sound came from the cabin, not a cry or a sigh, not the slightest murmur. And that was the only disturbing part about the whole affair for those who stood watch outside and were forever bumping up against the thick silence laden with mystery and the whiff of some presumed depravity.

One day at the bar in Ravine-Guinée some faceless person, reeking of rum, came up and whispered in Governor Régis's ear that the Negress he'd put up in his cabin, all for himself, was compromising herself with a big-bagged black man sporting a low-fitting American cowboy hat. And that people everywhere in Savane were beginning to laugh behind his back and make up songs that defiled his name. Hadn't he heard the refrain that was so popular of late? Hadn't he remarked that people had developed a tendency to whistle, sing in English? And anyway, it was clear as day, hadn't it surprised him to see folks in Savane take up the odd habit of suddenly drawing pistols hastily whittled from wood crates? Hadn't he noticed any changes back in his cabin, where the scene was unfolding at that very moment? Maybe if he cut himself some slack, if he didn't get home after midnight as he usually did, he could even make it back to Savane in time to catch them red-handed: those two knew his schedule . . . The brute just had time to snip off that nasty bunch and chew on each grape. By the time he crossed Savane, he was all worked up, beside himself with rage, prepared to kill, hack up Hortense and that low Django gigolo of hers.

Régis always took his cutlass with him, even after the hard erect cane stalks had been harvested, even when there wasn't a blade of grass to cut or a yam to dig up. His cutlass was the only weapon that could fend off desperados and evil spirits thirsting after folks who ventured out solo, soused, and in scattered soliloquy in the middle of the night.

The governor reached Savane around seven. People saw him come charging up at full speed just as Marga was closing the heavy doors of her corner store.

The sweltering heat weighed heavily on the tin roof. Inside the hushed cabin, Zébio was sweating so profusely that Hortense, out of mere compassion, stood up nude to wipe the brow of her painter friend. She told him to take off his shirt, his pants. He could just keep his shorts on, no offense taken. In that same instant, as if by some miracle, the mother color, divine and primary essence he'd sought after for so long, came out of Zébio's paintbrush. Dumbfounded, the man undressed, docile-like. And then with a somewhat irritated gesture, he ordered his model to return to the carpet from Isfahan, take up her pose again before the color vanished. In the fine shafts of light pouring in from the holes in the roof, Hortense sat back down, and the color allowed Zébio to capture it.

Régis walked past Eliette's cabin. Slaver was foaming at a corner of his mouth. His mop of hair stuck up in furious spikes, cocking his hat to one side of his head. Puffs of white smoke protruded from his nostrils. And his two square hands had multiplied; there were six-eight-ten of them, each holding a cutlass from hell. That is how Josia described it afterward. As for Eliette, she barely had time to hear his rasping breath slicing through the night that was settling gently over Savane. Murderous vapors of tafia. The vision of blood that he was going to spill filled her veranda. She was suddenly stricken with a headache. She fell into the rocking chair and stayed there, didn't call out. Closed up in the darkness of her cabin. Waiting silently. Her heart stampeding wildly as the cutlass slashed through the night on its preliminary maneuvers.

When Zébio told her that it was finished, he'd finally snared the primary color, Hortense unstiffened on her carpet and wordlessly went to light a candle in a corner of the cabin. The poor man was trembling, staggered at the genius born of his patient mixing, dazzled by the intensity of color bursting from the canvas. Finally, it was there, had been invented, found again, in all of its majesty, just like an ancient treasure dragged up from the depths of the ocean. Though the girl with the stitched-up face didn't see anything spectacular, sought in vain the lights or shadows of a virgin color like a newfound continent suddenly looming on the horizon of the Old World, she still felt somewhat moved as she squinted at the variegated mishmash, that macadam of dreams. And so she smiled at Zébio's smile. And, while he was already beginning to have cryptic visions of his glorious future, she brought the candle closer, examined the canvas that depicted neither her eyes nor her body, only a stunningly florid composition that left the man in speechless wonder. Thinking of the number of days she'd spent posing naked on the oriental carpet, all those stiff hours dedicated to art and its mysteries, Hortense allowed little pinpoints of joy to prick through here and there, as if she'd been the heroine of a divine epic and now that its color had been rescued, she could bow out. His lips broadening in a calculated smile, Zébio pulled from his bag a coconut patty, a stick of barley sugar and granted her two-three honey-words. His faded shorts nearly hung down over his knees. She would have liked for him to hug her too. But, all-a-doo-dah, he remained planted in front of his easel, his eyes lost in the depths of color. Hortense wasn't experiencing the same ecstasy, and a shudder ran through her body when, in a lightning flash, she saw her man Régis suddenly spring from the center of the canvas, slashing madly at the unique color with his sharp cutlass. Petrified, she took a step backward. Let out a little cry. And bumped into Zébio who looked at her sternly and signaled her to keep quiet.

Ruminating on his misfortune, Régis slowed his pace as he neared the cabin. He wanted to surprise the traitors. According to the information he had been entrusted with, the American cowboy who was taking his woman – that bitch Hortense! – always dragged around a bagful of rifles, pistols, bullets, grenades, and bombs. The governor would therefore have to knock the door down, take them by surprise, madly whirl his cutlass around, paying no heed to what he hit. Slice, hack, cut, he would repeat those three words to himself in the heat of action. And if the other man had time to shoot him, he would die a brave man, his disgrace expiated with the blood of honor. Slice, hack, cut . . .

Turning her eyes from the canvas, Hortense hastily rolled herself up in the oriental carpet, her nudity suddenly struck her as a hanging crime. Seized with a vague premonition, she handed Zébio's clothes to him. Entranced, eyes still glued to his masterpiece, he slipped on his shirt and dropped his pants, which fell in a heap on the gouache-spattered mud floor.

'You have to go, Eusèbe!' she said.

He didn't listen to her. Trembling, Hortense went to find a dress to cover herself, rummaged around in an old suitcase, a clothes basket. And then, once again, she felt the desire for him to take her in his arms, give her a bit of the wonder she saw in his eyes. A little love, and then she'd be prepared to die, with caresses and sweet words. She threw the carpet from Isfahan into a corner and went to rub her thighs up against Zébio's shorts. Her breasts were all aquiver, she suddenly took him in her arms as if inviting him to dance a tango.

And then she fell limp, laying down her womanly defenses. The man lifted her titties in his two pink and yellow and blue gouache-stained hands, carried her over to the bed, where sleep instantly swept her away to another land.

Slice, hack, cut! Régis repeated to himself when he was only a stone's throw from his cabin. The lover could deploy his whole arsenal, artillery, explosives – he, Régis, armed with his cutlass alone, would get the better of the American and the whole swindling, usurping, domineering, tantalizing, daring land of America. He'd show America that there were blacks and then there were blacks and that he, Régis, governor of Savane, was of the race of black men that stood tall and straight, that bowed with the tempest but did not break. Slice! Hack! Cut!

But flukes of fortune do happen . . . Missed appointments . . . Good old providence . . . While Régis was kicking in the front door, Zébio, his hat pushed down low on his head, was quietly bending out the sheet metal in the back that led to the courtyard. The painter left Hortense sleeping naked on the bed sheets speckled with fresh gouache. He walked happily away, promising the night to rescue the girl from her misery. With the money he would make from his patent as an inventor, he imagined himself illustrious, auctioning off samples of his color in Paris, London, New York, and Calcutta. He saw himself being liberated from the demons of his race, emancipated by fame and fortune . . .

In the dim candlelight, Régis saw a blissful smile on Hortense's face. The woman was sleeping, her body curled like a large Z that seemed to mark the end of a story. Yes, surely the American had come to soothe her still fevered flesh. He'd taken Hortense from A to Z. And she was smiling, satisfied. It was because of that smile that Régis lifted his cutlass – 'She never smiled for me!' he accused later in court. Stripped of his title of governor, dazed, suited, tied, they say he whimpered in the dock. And then, twisting a borrowed beret, he told of how much he loved the girl, how he'd been unable to control his murderous hand. At the time, his rum-muddled mind was obsessed with his mission – slice, hack, cut. Régis had lifted his cutlass and began to officiate. Hortense just had time to open her eyes but never close them again.

The poor woman didn't scream or cry. She just watched the cutlass rise and then fall. When Régis neatly arranged her flesh in lots on banana leaves, maybe a part of her spirit still dreamt of Zébio who'd gone off with the captive color. When you think about it, her death wasn't really a sad one. Zébio had given her more than the love she dreamt of. He'd turned her body into a chalice filled with dormant magic. When he laid her down naked on the bed, he promised to come back soon. Because of his artist's soul, he didn't want to take her in a dishonest fashion, under Régis's roof. He spoke to her of satin sheets, quilts filled with swan down, silk nightgowns. She was floating in that dream when the cutlass came down smack in the middle of her belly . . .

I remember, I jumped, shook my head to dislodge the memory of Hortense, push her far from my thoughts. A scream pierced the night. This time it was happening right next door. It was Angela. Eliette recognized her voice and that of her mama Rosette too. Angela was pleading for pardon pity and swearing to God and the Virgin that she wasn't lying, that she hadn't lied. Rita and Robert were crying and screaming too, begging, clinging to their mama to keep her from adding another crime to Savane's long list. Angela was running around the cabin, chased by Rosette's strap, blows, and curses. She called her serpent, poison, Judas Iscariot, Satan, *manawa*-whore, bitch in heat, sow, cow, vermin . . . and lots of other names of devils and animals that, in offending Eliette's ears, stuck in her brain like sharp nails. Would she once again remain shut up in her house praying the Lord that she herself would die of natural causes, even when people all around fell to and were felled by the cutlass, the rope, and bullets? . . . Even when they flung innocent beings, bags of garbage, to the bottom of Nèfles Bridge? . . . Even when she had to lift her feet to step over pools of blood, plug up her ears, turn her head to avoid seeing the petty dealers in ganja and crack? She straightened up in her rocker, testing her strength. Old, she was old.

From the noises she heard, Eliette knew that Angela had turned on her mother and was hitting back at her. At one point, the shouting stopped, and there was only the sound of chairs being thrown, tables overturning, dishes breaking, blows thudding, cudgeling, dreadful pummeling that was most definitely hitting home. Eliette imagined the mother and daughter wrestling, tearing out each other's hair, biting, sweating, snarling, scratching.

There was a lull, and then the howl of a wounded beast rose upon the night: weeping and gleeful incantations punctuated with hysterical laughter, more terrifying than any invectives that had been flung out before. Eliette strained to listen.

Foukan a kaz an mwen	Get the hell out my cabin!
Soti douvan zyé an mwen	Out my sight!
Foukan on fwa	Beat it, now!
En pa vlé vwé-w ankò	I don't want see you no more!
Pati pati pati	Out out out!
Foukan ti moun	Get the hell out child!
Foukan	
Foukan	
Foukan!!!	

Next there was the sound of a key being turned. A door opened, slammed. Eliette stood up, slipped over to the window on her tiptoes. She unfastened the bar, lifted the hook, and pushed open one window, just a little, to see without being seen. She was exposing herself. You never knew what was prowling around the cabins of Savane at night. Sometimes midnight brought the gallop of a three-legged horse, the laughter of carousing she-devils, the yapping of a man turned dog, or else the formidable shadow of a *soucougnan* fresh from a bamboche. Eliette's heart was hopping madly about in her chest, as if it were in the middle of a Reggae Dub straight from King Tubby's sound system, on a dance night in Morant Bay, Jamaica.

When a shadow slipped away from Rosette's veranda, the old woman quickly pulled her head back into the dark cabin. She was going to put the bar back and hurriedly hook the window, but a beam of moonlight suddenly projected the scene of the gray-eyed girl being dragged away on that same path. Then all of the cowardly fears that had piled up like garbage in the great pigsty inside her mind – where memory sometimes came to scratch around, rummage through, salvage something – filled her with a foul stench. The gray eyes kept looking her up and down and she just stood there, frozen with shame, her two arms spread wide, stuck to the window flung open on the night. Cowardice, that's right. Fears. Contriving too. Cowering, collywobbles, and cold feet. She saw the blue tongue again and Marius hanging in Sidonie's mango tree, and then the baby in its breadbasket with green eyes the color of dreams, and the other, mangled in the arms of death at the bottom of Nèfles Bridge. The gray creature straining at the end of her rope. The proud young vendor watching over her three pyramids of rotten christophines.

Again she saw Hortense, the poor woman with three hundred and sixty-five scars . . .

If I had a mind to, I might have helped keep those lives going for a while, take a turn for the better. Up until this Sunday, I always turned my head away to avoid getting mixed up in it all. Averted my eyes. Pulled the door shut after me to keep the thousand wars in Savane from entering the peace of my cabin. Then a voice I didn't recognize came out of my gut to cry to Angela, who was walking away alone into the night sounds.

Never, no never, had Rosette thought that one day she'd utter the same words her mama spat at her fifteen years earlier . . . Foukan a kaz an mwen . . . Foukan . . . And those words had come to her naturally, as if it were simply a matter of spelling them out, a history lesson on a big blackboard beginning all over again. Foukan, pati, pa viré, pa viré! Get the hell out, out, and don't come back!

Pati, pa viré! . . .

The same words that had just been waiting to come from her very own mouth.

Foukan! Foukan!

Rosette lay down on the floor, blocking the door to the veranda with her body. Rosan in jail, Angela gone, all she had left now were Robert and Rita. She laughed, laughed until she cried, cried with laughter; she moved to stifle the tears that she felt rising in her throat, and a sharp pang stabbed her shoulder. Struck by a chair, a fist, she couldn't remember, just grimaced with pain.

When she'd started beating Angela, in the dark room, it was only to ease the despair that was splitting her skull, only to knock the lie out of her child's mouth. Angela had curled up under the sheet, right up against the raw cement wall, crying . . . , 'No, Mama, no! Pity pardon! I didn't lie, I didn't lie!' And then she'd run from the blows. The belt was flying, whistling at her back, and sometimes it went whipping around her neck. For a long time Rosette pursued her with her insults, her fists, all of her rage. If the girl had kept running around the cabin without ever turning around, maybe she would have killed her, crushed her coldly like a roach with her heel. But Angela tripped over the bench and ended up on the floor. A whip of the belt lashed her face. Pain and tears blurred her eyes.

Angela heaved a chair first and then the sand-filled china vase with pink and yellow plastic flowers. She hurled shoes, broom, pans, kettle, bag of rice, swearing she hadn't lied. She sunk her nails into her mama's flesh pleading for pardon pity, she'd told the truth and Rosette had to believe her, and only her. When Rosette also fell down, wasted, in a corner of the kitchen near the gas canister, Angela stood over her with a clay pot in her hands. That's when Rosette started her hushed song, stark voice, dark words to lull her despair and drive her daughter far away . . .

Foukan
Foukan
Foukan a kaz an mwen
Pati
Pati é pa viré janmè!

A second later, lying motionless on the floor, Rosette told herself that Angela had been right to fight back. Yes, she would have killed her. She could still feel the blind urge within her. Would have beaten her till she felt her go limp, saw her body come undone and her soul take flight. Would have made her swallow her lies. Made her understand that you can't destroy a lifetime of struggle just like that. She stared at her devastated living room. On the wall, the archangel Gabriel eviscerated in his black frame. The trampled painting of the King of Kings, negus of Ethiopia, on his white horse. Watercolors askew. Flower pots and plants thrown about. Tablecloth torn. Table overturned that she hadn't even finished paying off at Paradise Furniture. Plates, glasses, bowls shattered. Yes, she'd been feeding a Judas for all those years. Angela, her angel . . .

She told her Foukan! Pati on fwa! And Angela dropped the pot, turned her back on Rosette as if that was exactly what she'd been waiting for. Rosette kicked the door closed and then turned the key, to show that she was mistress in her home and that there'd be no turning back. Regrets would not come seeking her out, no indeed.

Foukan a kaz an mwen
Pati!

She thought about the next day, Monday. She'd have to face the town and the looks of the people from Ravine-Guinée. She'd go to the jailhouse to see her Rosan. Console him. Ask him why destiny had been cruel to them, they who didn't rub elbows with sorcerers. Tell him that she'd beaten Angela and all the marks that he could see right there on her own face were Angela's work. So much sacrifice! Everything they'd done for that child! And this is how she thanked them! Her papa sent to jail and her mama all beaten and bruised. No, children these days weren't children. Just ungrateful brats!!! Tomorrow she'd go see Rosan. They'd find a way to get out of this mess together. Together, just like in the old days when they were young, been thrown out of the house, her pregnant, him without a cabin, without a cent . . .

Rosette was sixteen back then. Lived with her mama. Never knew her papa. She and Rosan were neighbors. He lived with his maternal grandmama. She was an old woman. Straight-laced black woman, who was unsparing with him. She whipped him with a switch of thorns. She said he had bad blood in his veins because of his papa, an old geezer who was more rakish than he was run-down. Once a woman cut off his ear so he'd never forget the damage he'd done. He always wore a floppy hat and walked with his head down, hunched over, shifty-eyed. The grandmother swore the man was packed with malediction. He was at least forty years older than Rosan's mama. And it was disgraceful to see the two of them, him so worn-out, her so new that you would have thought she was his daughter. Rosan looked like the young man his old papa had once been. His grandmama tried to love him but, when she looked at him, she saw the cursed man with his sly eyes. Rosan this! Rosan that! The whole blessed day she yelled at him to fetch the water, weed and hoe the garden, feed the livestock, light the lamp, cook the dinner. Blows rained down on him for no reason at all.

His papa and mama came to visit once every hundred years. No one ever expected them. They had to struggle to survive, you could tell from their sunken eyes and the way they walked, all brokenlike, whisked along on the wind. Sometimes the mama got the yen to reach out her hand and touch, caress her son Rosan, but he always slipped between the poor woman's fingers. Every now and again the papa was shaken by sudden outbursts of authority. He raised his voice, gave orders, imposed his will. Alas, a mere look from Rosan floored him. While his parents, whom he considered to be worse than enemies, sat there staring hard at him as if they were trying to decipher his future or read his thoughts, Rosan didn't speak three consecutive words to them. He sought neither their eyes nor their love. And when those two went back to the vacuum of their existence, he'd start whistling in a special kind of way, infuriated and heartbroken. Rosette ran to his side. Took him in her arms. Swore to him that one day, for sure, they'd be married, have beautiful children, start a family, build a big concrete cabin and tra-la-la. Then all the rage that was built up inside of Rosan slowly dissolved, leaving him limp and all churned up inside – easy prey to Rosette's romantic tales. Patting him on the back, the girl murmured sweet things, all frilled with assurances of wonderful tomorrows. She began putting words together in an unusual way, invented incredible tales, told of a time when Lady Dreams ruled the world . . . 'Lady Dreams wasn't the same as she is now, just a word in the mouth with no shape or form. She had powerful wings, a head full of hope and a pure heart . . . ,' she told Rosan, assuring him that one day everything would be exactly like that again, just for them. Sometimes she sang the refrain of an ad for American cigarettes that announced: 'Happiness is at the tip of your lips!' And to make him laugh, she started smoking imaginary cigarettes, blowing out a mirage of smoke. Eyes closed, lips curling, cracked slightly open, head thrown back, she mimed happiness – American-style.

Rosette wasn't even sixteen when she began consoling Rosan by giving him her body to caress, explore, and devour. One day their lips had met, pure accident. Embarrassed, they'd laughed. But Rosan had suddenly found himself in a man's body and Rosette had felt a strange fluttering deep in her belly.

As soon as she saw the change in the way those two looked at each other, her mama Gilda warned Rosette. She didn't like Rosan, only allowed him in her courtyard to avoid breaking old ties between neighbors. But things were taking an ugly turn. Whickering at the door, Rosan wheeled, pivoted, pawed the ground like a hunger-stricken horse from some diabolical carousel. According to Gilda, who had never been able to tell Rosette her father's name or rank, a woman's life was an accursement. She didn't like Rosan, his downcast eyes, which made him look like a hypocrite, the way he had of whistling for Rosette and pretending to believe her stories . . .

'A woman's words don't make no sense to a man,' she said. 'Child, my little Rose, your papa groomed purebred horses at some white Creoles' house. He was an aggravating, secretive nigger who swore to high heaven and never promised nothing to the damozels he let climb up on the back of his horse. You hardly ever saw him on foot. Maybe that's why everyone called him king of kings. When he wanted a woman, he just made as if he was listening to her, and it paid off every time. In Mont-Bazin, all the women wanted to get a rope around his neck, nail him down in a cabin. Rosa, that man was as fickle as the wind. The first time he laid eyes on me, I had no idea what was happening. I just stood stock still in the same spot, but it was like the inside of me was turning all upside down. Next day he was leaning up against an old shack that been closed up since time out of mind. Stiff, arms crossed over his open shirt, he stared at me without smiling or saying a word. If they'd been torches, his eyes alone could have set flame to three savannah, seven cabins, and a thousand and some souls. Yet I walked by proud as can be, my stomach all churned up and my heart capsizing. It was when his horse snorted that I turned around. I didn't mean to. Rose, I can't say that man put a spell on me. I don't think he paid no attention to sorcerers' recipes, conjurors, woman charmers. He was too vain to bow down to anyone, pay for the service, and say please or thank you. He just waited for women to come to him. Marriageable women, widows, wives or mistresses, virgins or already visited girls, old women, confident ones, brave ones, every female he coveted saw a prophecy of hope in his eyes that never promised a thing. He never stayed with one woman long.

'But you know how we is, always thinking that the man we want will prefer us over all the others, even the prettier ones. It didn't take me long to climb up on his horse. We took off at a brisk gallop, straightaway. The king of kings listened to me for a two-hour spell. His eyes showed real concern and feeling. I lay down in the grass and that's how he took me. After that, my mama told me to take to the main road since I already knew the shortcuts. I wound up in Des-Ramiers, where I rented myself out as a maid. When I went down to Mont-Bazin, I saw him sometimes, the king of kings. Strutting around on his horse, and always had some quivering girl body at his back, glued right up against him . . . Rose honey, let Rosan fight his own battles. That man never had no loving, no one ever gave him so much as a pinch of it. You can't heal all the wounds bleeding in him. He won't listen to you more than three days. He'll get weary. And in no time you'll find yourself big-bellied and talking to yourself. Bide your time! Wait for another man to show up! Rosan won't do nothing but take and leave you in torment and tears. I saw the king of kings ride off on his horse with all sorts of women. Not a one of them ever put a leash on him.'

When Rosette's belly rounded out, nice and happy, like a ripe calabash, Gilda couldn't sleep or speak for three days. Rosan and Rosette already envisioned her joining sides with them, prepared to mother, diaper, and coddle. They laughed in secret, whispered prophetic proverbs to each other that alleviated their fears . . . , 'Silence gives consent . . . Speech is silver but silence is golden . . . Patience drives a snail to Jerusalem . . . All's well that ends well . . .'

Alas, they too lost their words when they saw the mama haul a tin trunk covered with dust fluff out from under her bed. Gilda wiped it off without uttering a word, thinking of the interval in her life when dreams had carried her off on the ocean liner *Antilles* to conquer France. The spell of nostalgia passed, the woman opened the trunk that contained not the slightest article of baby linens that Rosette was already picturing. Nothing, no diapers, or lace undershirts, or christening dress, or booties with mixed moss and stocking stitches. Nothing but a lot of old newspapers and centipedes that Rosan squashed with the heel of his shoe. And then, while she filled the footlocker with Rosette's belongings, Gilda began softly singing some words that went to the tune of a very firm resolution . . .

Foukan a kaz an mwen	Get the hell out my cabin
Foukan on fwa	Beat it, now
Pa viré	And don't come back
Janmè	Ever
Foukan épi nonm a-w	Get out and take your man too
Soti douvant zyé an mwen	Out my sight
Foukan!	Get the hell out!

Gilda did not strike her, but she booted Rosette out of the cabin, told her she was carrying misfortune itself in her belly and that, God willing, she, Gilda, wouldn't have her name mixed up in the tragic business. She hurled insults at Rosan and cursed those who created and begat him. She blurted out words in long strings for a long time, a long time after Rosette and Rosan had vanished from her sight. They went off in desperate search of a place in which to lay down their love. He walked up ahead. She followed, lumbering along with her belly, pushing her mama Gilda's curses and evil omens out of her mind.

Ever since then, their life had been a constant struggle, every day, together. Rosan had not behaved unworthily. All the while she was carrying Angela, her angel, Rosan always found a way to put food and drink on the table. First they stayed in Beauséjour, at Rosette's great-aunt Fanotte's house. Fanotte was a person whose only aim in life was to give-share. Rosan, who in those days was a jack-of-all-trades, learned to be a professional bricklayer with time. He consolidated the chicken coops that had been built in some olden-day era when the wings of *soucougnans* snagged on the thorns of bitterorange trees. He built rooms onto cabins, kitchens off verandas. He never refused work. But jobs were rare in Beauséjour. They had to leave, follow on the heels of a prospective building site in Côte-sousle vent. Work didn't scare Rosan, and as soon as he got wind of a new site, he opened the tin trunk, which Rosette immediately filled with their meager belongings.

Even Angela's birth didn't come between them. While she was pushing the child out of her body, an invisible bubble, stone egg, had slipped out from between her thighs. It was then that Rosette felt true delivery, as if all her mama's maleficent predictions had broken away from her entrails. She thanked the Lord and made a vow, promised never to leave her Rosan. Though Aunt Fanotte repeated time and again a thousand tales about the tribulations of women who had irrespected the forty days confinement after birthing, Rosette preferred the discomfort of the road and the chains of love.

In discovering the baby, the little clenched hands, the so very soft skin, the fleshy gums, Rosan exclaimed that the Good Lord had sent them an angel, and Rosette named the child Angela. In those days, Rosette still dazzled Rosan. Their thoughts always seemed to concur. Without saying so in words, they had the same visions, wandered the same dreams. At times a great sadness came over the man, a terrible feeling of discouragement caused him to lose his words and bits of his laughter at the same time. Then, when Rosette was preparing to tell him a romantic tale, he pushed her away. But those lapses were rare, for he seemed to draw his life force from Angela's laughter . . .

They left Beauséjour.

When Aunt Fanotte's brother Edmond Alexander died, she put a message for Rosette on the air with Radio Guadeloupe. No one was very friendly with Edmond, who was a rather rebellious and antisocial man. Everyone knew he lived near Ravine-Guinée – to be more precise, in a disreputable district called Savane Mulet. Neither Gilda nor Fanotte had ever been there, but on September 10 of the year 1975, the day their brother Edmond died, the two sisters took the road to Savane as naturally as you please, as if they were in the habit of going there to visit on the tenth of every month. Eliette, who'd hardly been neighborly with Edmond, motioned toward the cabin with a simple jerk of her chin.

At the time, Rosan worked all the way out at Grande-Anse in Saintes' country, people from Guadeloupe with flaxen hair, old folks whose voices quavered in a faltering Creole from under *bakoua* straw-hats. With a still unbaptized child, they cast up their bile in a canoe cleaving through the high waves in the Saintes Channel teeming with the jaws of voracious sharks. In the Saintes Islands, a rich fisherman had drawn up the blueprints for a dream house in the shape of a ship facing out to sea, so that his soul would find its way back to Côtes-du-Nord, somewhere in Brittany, he said. Three months that he'd been looking for an adventurous mason, just to do the form work for his concrete vessel. Rosan was no more skilled than the next man, but his grandmama's thorny switch had taught him not to fear hard work. The Saintes man was offering a million francs to the person who could build his ship. That's what Rosan heard one morning on a small construction site in Desbonnes, Lamentin. A million francs . . . When he returned to Guadeloupe, he could rent a cabin, buy a bedroom and a living-room suite, gas stove, refrigerator . . . He imagined the million piled high as a cathedral, ready to answer all the prayers in the world . . . The million would open every door for him and would also bring him all the caresses that Rosette still held back. All of Rosette's love and caresses that neither his mama nor his grandmama had given him. He'd show Gilda that he too knew how to give love, even if he'd never received any. With that million, he'd become a man. And never again could anyone say that all he was good for was taking a woman, not even able to put a roof over her head . . .

When they left Grande-Anse three months later, the million francs lined their small trunk. Rosan had sunk iron rods into the rock and planted the concrete hull facing the sea just as the fisherman wanted; he'd always lived in a cabin made of boards and sheet metal with no foundations. The fisherman paid the million without quibbling, he'd given his word, but they later learned that he never slept in his concrete craft. Every time he set foot in it, he was overwhelmed with sadness. He felt as if he were being buried alive in there. Roots sprang from his ankles. Worms slithered over his body. The shores of Brittany were too distant.

It was only upon their return from the Saintes Islands that Rosan and Rosette learned that Aunt Fanotte had been sending out missing person announcements on Radio Guadeloupe for three months. All sorts of rumors about them were already flying. People said that they'd gone to France. That, maybe, Rosan killed Rosette and Gilda had been right to warn her about that man who had no love, no family, or next of kin, or feelings. When people saw them reappear, looking cheerful, blest with their hidden million, everyone said that, no indeed, this time around misfortune just wouldn't have them. And they ran lightheartedly to Aunt Fanotte's to learn that Uncle Edmond was safely laid to rest six foot under and that his boarded-up cabin awaited them, Rosan, Rosette, and Angela. But where? In Ravine-Guinée, Savane Mulet district. And if they didn't want it – that very day, Gilda had a list of homeless folks that were hot on her heels, counting, recounting their pennies to pay the paltry sum of rent.

Rosette remembered every detail. She was clutching the big key in her hand when she walked into Savane. My word, the cabin seemed sturdy enough. She rapped, knock-knock-knock, on the boards and beams; the wood sounded solid. Several times she kissed the big smooth green-colored key that seemed almost polished, worn between the fingers of her dead uncle. Eliette was standing on her doorstep, looking pleasant. Rosette told herself that she'd know how to get on the good side of her with Angela's ringing laughter and little ailments. She thought that – just maybe – life would be gentle in this place, already visited in the fancies of her storytelling. Savane seemed like a Garden of Eden, even if the cabins were crowded around a potholed road that frayed out, farther down, into a multitude of thin corridors snaking through the chaos of sheet metal and boards. The uncle had blocked off his land with old sheets of corrugated metal. In the sleepy courtyard behind the cabin, three coconut trees nodded in the shade of a gigantic breadfruit tree with heavy branches. A roof over their heads and food in their bellies, that's what was waiting for them in Savane, she thought. The two-room cabin with a kitchen and a small built-on veranda pleased Rosan too. There was no bathroom, but the Lord himself hadn't created the earth in a single day.

Rosan laughed, took Angela from Rosette's arms, and then tossed her up in the air. How many times? . . . The child squealed, hiccupped. Rosette clapped her hands.

IV

Angela!
  Angela!
  Over here!
  Come here, child, come!
  Maybe Angela hadn't heard. Didn't turn around. Her silhouette was already fading into the shadows. So then Eliette had to fling open her door and go out into the night herself, hound her for a long time with her calls before the young girl stopped.
  It was the first time that she'd ever run after anyone like that, be it a woman, man, or animal. She'd only run after dreams of child-bearing and scattered bits of her memory. Not even run after the men who married her. She cajoled Angela, pleaded with her to wait a minute, to just listen to the couple of words she had to say. An old woman without a family, she'd never given bits of her heart, only curt hellos, words exchanged, hollow greetings. The words came out arid.
  Angela!
  Come here, don't run away like that . . .
  Come see Eliette!

. . . .

No, Eliette no longer expected a thing from the world before that Sunday. Up until that day, human beastliness had always confirmed that she'd spared herself by retreating into solitude. Thieves, liars, murderers, she'd seen them all at work, folks from Savane and elsewhere. Yet, there she was outside, running after Angela like she should have gone after those other girls too, Esabelle, Hortense, Glawdys, and all the shadows that – in passing her door – had entered her cabin and left a little of their sour smells and a lot of their bitter thoughts. No, she couldn't recall having chased after a single soul, either to save them from death that she heard approaching in the distance like the thundering hooves of an earthquake or to stay the hand of the assassin. She'd always remained safe within the peace of her cabin, consenting to all the conspiracies, wordless witness, counting the stabs of the cutlass, the blows of the conch shell clonk clonk clonk, the punches, rifle shots, and also sounding out the heavy breathing of bodies in close combat. Always thanking God in advance for preserving her from violent death of that sort. So many had perished in that way, drunken with the glimmer of love, the dazzle of fame and fortune, burning with jealousy, strangled with nameless avidity.

Angela!

Wait for me!

Wait for old Eliette!

When Angela lifted her tormented face, her swollen, tear-filled eyes, Eliette felt all the sheet-metal and board barriers that she'd put up between her and the world crumble.

She was a coward.

Since when?

A long time already. Ever since she was eight . . . How had it all started?

With the Cyclone of 1928, so bad that she'd been unable to speak for three full years, it had wounded her in the head and the belly, had dispossessed her of all faith in herself. They'd lifted her from the blood, her black skin darkened down to the knees with a thick humor sticking to her in plaques, shiny as lacquer. All she could do was tremble, her teeth chattering out phenomenal fear.

Once again, she saw herself watching her mama Séraphine rolling up sheets and then stuffing them hastily into a basket in the bottom of the busted up wardrobe that the cyclone had thrown to the ground. Days and days later Eliette came upon her again, nursing a fire of dry branches and leaves in which those same sheets were burning. Séraphine was sitting there stiffly, arms crossed, bronze circles around her eyes.

Eliette was eight years old. The cyclone had made her like this, cowardly, indifferent, weak, and inactive. She still had a few scattered memories of the events that took place. With time . . .

No, the truth is, Eliette didn't remember a thing. It was her mama who had always told her about the night when Guadeloupe had capsized in the cyclone and been smashed to bits. She called that nightmare the Passage of the Beast. And to better burn the story into Eliette's mind, she was constantly rehashing the memory of the head and belly wound, the bloodstained sheets, the big beam that fell and nearly cut Eliette in two, the cruel wind penetrating, buffeting, lashing.

From these terrifying stories, Eliette knew of all the hardships and indignities endured by Guadeloupe, its dependencies, its neighboring and distant islands: Haiti, Puerto Rico, the Bahamas . . .

For a long time – to back up her tales and also to keep the memory of Cyclone from being distorted and disfigured – her mama kept an old trunk full of dry yellow newspapers with accounts of the number of dead, wounded, missing, crippled, victims of fevers and tetanus. For the rest of her life, right up until the day before she died years later, every afternoon Séraphine sat down in front of the cabin on a little bench. With an issue of *Nouvelliste* dating back to that era open on her lap, the poor woman – probably mad from having endlessly gone over those same sequences of the night Cyclone passed – sat staring out at some other world far beyond the horizon. She seemed to always be on her guard, prepared to affront the Beast again.

When Eliette quizzed her too much, Séraphine got lost in her accounts of that tormented night. The old woman seemed to have so much to say – jarred boiled memories spilling over – that Eliette was always left with the feeling that something was lacking, as if, without ever being able to really break through, her questions circled vainly around the eye of Cyclone. Even when she forced herself, Eliette could bring nothing back from the ruins of her memory on her own. All that remained, murky, barely perceptible traces, was blood-curdling terror, the vague feeling of imminent death, the recollection of her jaw stiffened with pain, being unable to speak, and her fingers clutching at the burning pain in her lower abdomen. Only once, the day that Renélien proposed, did she see shadows stirring behind the shrouds. Later on, during and after her two marriages, she tried so many times to make herself recall the night of Cyclone when she was eight, probed her belly to find the old, eloquent, and reassuring scars. But time had drawn its curtains, and only the voice of her dead mama arose, covering all the other elusive sounds that her memory was trying to drag out into the light . . .

She said, 'Eliette girl, on that night when the Beast came by, Lord, nobody was expecting it! Such a mean cyclone, no, there was no imagining. After that, as hard as you prayed, saying, 'Thank you,

Lord, for your grace, thank the Virgin for having left me alive on this devastated-trampled land . . . ,' another voice rose up in your soul and swore, 'No, the Good Lord don't love black people, would never do them the slightest good turn in heaven or on earth, and all those stories of Paradise and eternal life are just so much nonsense dished out by white possessors, who're only trying to pull the wool over black folks eyes . . .' People prayed all the same, in every church in Guadeloupe, to save themselves from still greater torments. People asked the Lord's forgiveness for not listening to him . . . All that viciousness been rooted in us blacks from the seventh day of Creation till the curse pronounced for et cetera generations to come. We begged for divine mercy, comfort from the Holy Virgin, protection from the loyal apostles, the arrival of rescue teams from the French Corps of Engineers, and for the fine words of the French ambassador in Washington – a poet by the name of Paul Claudel – to be realized pronto.

'The man debarked, puffed up with importance, from an armored cruiser of the French navy. Ambassador of all of France's maternal affection, he fell to his knees on the bare tiles of the cathedral, and everyone saw he was a first-rate Christian. Alas, his pale hands remained empty and his tongue thick with a coat of promises and kind condolences that were no use to nobody. Everywhere you turned, ruin and sorrow, girl. Starvation, disease, fevers . . . And you, Eliette child, you'd forgotten how to speak. By the grace of God, he fixed things so that Cyclone didn't up and blow you away . . .

'Eliette girl, you have no remembrance of the Beast's passage because – to my way of thinking – your memory couldn't keep that demon locked up in your little noggin. Thanks be to merciful Heaven that it all faded away. Yes, the All Merciful . . . Miserere mei, Deus! The Beast ran you right down as if it come just for you. That's the honest truth, Eliette. Sure thing, all around was wheeling, reeling, head-over-heeling. Sometimes I can still feel the foul blast of that Apocalypse on my skin, the fetid breath of the Beast. All over again, I see sheet metal being torn off, rafters crashing down one after the other like matchsticks, boards being ripped apart – fragile as tissue paper in the mighty clutches of the wind . . . Oh no, no! Don't ask to live that night again!

'Eliette girl, thank the Lord, we were spared. Between one and two thousand poor souls met their deaths in atrocious suffering. And just as many others missing. They found arms and legs with no bodies, stuck in the broken palms of cocnut trees. When the river started raging and rumbling, swollen with its burden of trees and rocks, I thought it would wash our cabin away too. The Beast had blown the roof off early on. You were sleeping innocently. Me, I was frantic, couldn't do a thing but watch that sky, as black as mortal sin. The wind had whisked all of the stars off to some blessed land. And I swear to God, standing there looking up at the sky, I despised this land of disillusions where, on a whim of chance, life's mast is broken, the Beast wreaks havoc, the river floods, and the earth opens under a body's feet. Just then, as if in response, the cabin shook blogodo, blogodo. The earth quaked. I bowed my head and joined my hands.'

She asked, 'Who can say where the rope that saved us came from? Thrown out by Providence, for sure. The hank of rope rolled nice as can be across what was left of the floor, just like someone had throwed it on purpose to help us. I picked it up, feeling confident, I knew from that sign that our misfortunes would come unraveled. Death wasn't ready to have us on that day. Then I felt the presence of friendly spirits on the wing that were guiding me. With that rope I dragged, piled together, tied up splintegrated pieces of wood, a sliver of tin roofing, split rafters, the door of the buffet, the pearwood wardrobe that Godmother Anoncia had given me, and some branches that had landed smack-dab in the middle of the cabin too. Even the deluge at the break of day didn't make a crack in our little nest.

'Eliette, we were as good as saved. In the morning, thunder shook the sky, but you could tell that most of the bets had been placed during the night. Through the branches I watched lightning bolts snaking across the heavens, cracking them open from one end to the other till they seemed like they were about to cave in. In the distant sky I saw drunken flocks of big-bloated black sheep prodded on by a breathless wind. They were off to darken the skies of some other nation, bleating faithfully after an old ram that was fiercely butting his horns into the black-veined rising sun. I thought it was over with, especially since all around an immense silence had risen after the thunder. We were up to our navels in water. Everywhere the deluge had left ponds, marshes, and even seas that hadn't existed before. Our nest was about one quarter submerged. I saw cadavers floating by amongst tin roof peelings, fowl plucked clean, telegraph wires strangling already swollen cows, and even whole trees going by – startled, roots tousled, bare-broken branches. I saw sheets of black oil, cracked brooms, carpetbags, hatboxes, et cetera et cetera . . . Far, far away, the breadfruit tree that used to spread its branches a few feet from our cabin was motioning us to come back, waving three leaves hanging from a crippled branch. The Beast had pushed our cabin over fifty feet at least. I lifted a wing of board, just to get a better look. And it was at that very instant that the tail of the cyclone launched a mama-rafter that came and struck you right smack in the middle of your belly, poor child . . .

'I told you already that your father left us the day before the Passage of the Beast. We were destined to struggle through that torment alone. And see, even if you lost your tongue and your memory, there is a God in heaven, yes, there is a God. Not far from our place, the bridge at Grande-Rivière was washed away. All they found was a piece of the roadway at the foot of the wharves in Jissac. The country was in dire straits, and no one would have thought, Eliette girl, that it would get back on its feet after the Passage of the Beast. You might well have died, but God saved you. I didn't have no idea which way to run. There was no hospital in Jissac. And no more church either. Collapsed. Ravaged. Dismantled. I saw Father Jean drifting around through the tumbled cabins, like an orphaned zombie. Soaked through. The head of the Blessed Virgin tucked under his arm, shouting, 'My God, my God, why hast thou forsaken me? This is worse than the retreat from Moscow, send me back to Douarenez!' Lost soul amidst lost souls, he slogged through the pestilential refuse scattered along the roads – gutted to the bone. He questioned everyone about his things from the church. 'Did anyone happen to see a breviary, my cassock, my ordo, the holy oils, my little red velvet canopy, a single member of the Holy Family?' I followed him for a time, thinking that maybe divine providence would lead him to a safe place. Alas, he stopped short in front of a large bell split down its middle and just stayed there, petrified for eternity. All around, people were pleading for help with the wounded, for water, bread, linens and then shovels, picks to bury the dying who moaned, suppurated, expired . . .'

She said, 'Liette, heaven set that woman down on my path. Ethéna . . . A midwife from Bois-Ramée. She saved you. I was walking around aimlessly, with mud up to my thighs. When she saw what the Beast done to you, poor child, she snatched you out of my arms.

She spent three days sewing you up. And if there aren't no traces or scars on your belly from the Passage of the Beast, maybe she really was a saint, and people were telling the truth when they said that a guardian angel had put her on my path. At the time, I was too upset to realize how kind she was, but I never forget her in my prayers. Remember her name: Ethéna . . . If you need to know more one day, go asking after her at Godmother Anoncia's.

'We stayed under her roof in Bois-Ramée for two moons. The cyclone spared her and her cabin. As for you, you'd forgotten how to talk. One day, Ethéna stood up, gave me a hundred sous, and then said, 'Go now! Don't go thanking me! Just curse the Beast that rent your child . . . Don't go back to Jissac, go to Ravine-Guinée. Find Madame Estelica and tell her I sent you. She's counting on you to fill a job as a servant. Stop crying, I not throwing you out. Is time for you to go back into the world. And don't worry about Liette, she'll find her tongue again.' Before going to Ravine-Guinée, I detoured by way of Jissac to set fire to some old possessions that Cyclone had piled up. And then I said goodbye to that rock-laden land seeded with such nasty memories.

'After Jissac, Ravine-Guinée seemed like a blessed place to me. Joab started courting me. He had to wait a full year. You know, when your papa went away, I promised I would never sleep under the same roof with no man again. Something inside me just set to bristling as soon as a man came near. My heart blackballed every aspect of that entire species. My blood boiled and confused words started to scuffling in my mind worse than at the very heart of Babel.

'Joab was a honey-sweet-syrup man. He died too soon . . . All the other folks said he was of the female type: soft-spoken, I-believe-in-God, and high-flown sentiments. I listened to him because he loved animals, all the animals in Creation – *yenyen*-flies the same as young goats, little red spiders as much as hogfish, crayfish and *gemme*-hens, blackbirds, ringdoves, raccoons, and even the dogs that everyone shooed off, throwing stones. He worshiped the tiniest blade of grass and thanked the heavens each day for the fruit, flowers, peas, grains, and roots that he harvested. He was a loner, said he lived in a paradise not far from Ravine-Guinée, off the beaten path, on a piece of land that he just called Savane. Joab knew that folks around there called his paradise Savane Mulet, because they thought he was as hardheaded as a mule. But he didn't pay no mind.

'Madame Estelica convinced me to accept his advances. She was going away to France. We spent all afternoon sitting knee-to-knee talking about Joab. She kept saying that she could tell just from his eyes that he was a rare make of black man, a fine fellar. I had nowhere to run aground. Joab opened the cabin he'd set down in Savane to me. That's how we came here . . .'

She said, 'Joab was a decent man, but his paradise was really a sort of hell. Wasn't a single cabin anywhere around. Savane had been abandoned, turned over to spirits of all calibers that drifted in the tall trees, rose and fell, came up from Grande-Terre and the uncharted islands of the Caribbean Sea for a change of air, to lick their wounds and set their bones down somewhere on this earth. She-devils slept in the silk-cotton trees, rubbed their bodies up against the branches of the ilang-ilangs all day long in order to, later, fuddle up and slay the fool men that sought life in the arms of an unearthly woman. Behind each dragon tree rearing its wild head hid an evil shadow, a creature turned dog, a zombie fallen from his bed. Sometimes a horse galloped at full speed through the cabin. Right in the middle of the night, *soucougnans* in heat came to romp just over my head. Their wings beat on the thin tin roof, plakatak plakatak. And their mingled breathing gave me the jitters. Joab always said, 'Séraphine! As long as I'm here, you don't need to fear the pinions of those birds!'

'Joab ate no flesh, no chicken or pork; he fed himself on his crops and on leaves and wild fruit that he found in Savane. We lived as brother and sister, child. And sometimes I wondered what he expected of me, why he had wanted me under his roof, seeing as how he never touched me, not even with his eyes. The folks in Ravine-Guinée took us for man and wife, but Joab didn't poke or seed nothing but the land of his paradise. There was not a wicked bone in that man's body. Only every now and again he pulled a panatela out of his jacket and smoked it, gazing up at the sky.

'I told you already that your papa left not long before Cyclone came. Joab never asked me no questions about him. He always thought of you as his child, his younger sister. Thanks to him, you started talking again when you were eleven, but you were still a little backward, probably due to the trials of your childhood, the Passage of the Beast . . . You didn't want to see a soul but us two, and it was real torture for you to go to town in Ravine-Guinée where there were so many eyes that fell on your body. You wanted to disappear from their sight, you told me they pierced through you and stripped you. With the animals in his paradise, Joab showed you each day that, by God, you couldn't remain a prisoner to old fears and that life here on earth also had its advantages and kind turns . . . He died in 1936, at the age of thirty-three, run over by a wagon in L'Anse-Laborde, where his family lived. You'd just turned sixteen. You mustn't forget Joab! Ever . . .'

Séraphine also said, 'Sure, I got the yen to leave Savane at that time, but I felt bound to the memory of Joab, to all the good things he done for us. And, anyway, where could I go? That's when, curious as can be, we weren't alone no more. Folks started filtering into Savane, as if someone had said: 'Be fruitful and multiply and replenish these lands where Joab lived.' The spirits slunk back to the other side of the river. And the name of Savane Mulet was always associated with Joab's paradise.'

Eliette caught her breath, passed her hand over Angela's face. Her voice became firmer.

Angela!

Angela!

The living memory of Joab suddenly filled the night, making her calm and confident, ridding her of old fears and demons. He breathed courage into the old woman that Eliette had become.

'You got to stay here, Angela. Can't go running off and disappear when the house is on fire!' she said.

Angela followed her without a word, docile as her little cat that ran away rebellious and came back all conciliatory to snuggle up in the cabin, rub up against her legs, begging for caresses, milk, and stale bread. In the blackness of Savane, Eliette mistook Angela's young body for that of gray-eyed Glawdys. She pushed the vision from her mind. Yes, she could have saved her too. She'd been given the opportunity three times over. And Eliette had denied her three times, averted her eyes. How old was Glawdys now? Hadn't she already turned into an animal in that jail where hate and indifference had thrown her? How old was Angela now anyway? Fifteen, sixteen years old . . .

Eliette had once been sixteen too . . . At that age, she already walked half broken, as though she'd carried a heavy burden on her back forever, a basketful of worries on her head just like those old women from the back country that emerge from the waning night to sell their roots in the marketplaces of the cities. As far back as she could remember, Eliette had never pictured herself running after the slightest dream. Nothing, not gold, or glory, or love, or ideals, she'd never coveted anything. The desire to bear children had held her attention for some time. But that rope stretched tight inside of her had ended up going slack too. And she abandoned the family she'd started in the meanderings of her mind. Had she at least loved Renélien and Hector? She wondered, walking behind Angela, seized in a turmoil of confused feelings she'd never felt before. When the Beast had taken her belly, her head, and her tongue, had it dried up her heart too?

She'd been sixteen. Remembered that morning when her body had risen from the bedclothes, completely changed, like a garden in full bud, promising apples, plums, flowers, and myriads of birds in the branches of the trees. It was as if in a single night she'd ripened in her sleep. When she ran to cry to her mama that her body had been changed, Séraphine threw out a few small coins of her crazed jingling laughter and turned her back on the girl, declaring that it had been quite some time that her body had become part of the female race and that unless she was careful, it would soon be gushing blood, a fine-divine oil, and even milk if she got a hankering to get speared by some male creature. And then, seeing the terror that came over Eliette from feeling so small in that big woman body, Séraphine gave her three kisses and, to make her laugh and cry at the same time, told her that, who knows, maybe, surely, some she-devil, some flying soucougnaning creature in Savane had wanted to try on the envelope of a youngster, just for fun, or maybe, in coming back down to the world of mortals, she'd simply donned the wrong body and the next night she'd take back her own skin that had fallen on Eliette's shoulders.

Eliette still recalled how at sixteen years of age she sniveled at the slightest thing, balked at everything that pushed her into the world of adults. How she trembled before the puny young fellars that whistled, hooted, used their French words when she passed. How she ran far out ahead of men. They chased her, played the banjo for her, saw no difference between her and the women heated up so many times over in the love caldrons of Ravine-Guinée. Everything about them repelled Eliette, unlike the other mamsells in those parts who dropped their rosary in the heat of love or else left their panties in the underbrush around Last Ditch Savane. It was as if some sort of a harpoon kept Eliette hooked in her mama's cabin.

She went out only to go to mass or run errands. Never accompanied her mama, who sold coconut sherbet in the town square. Never went sashaying past the young blacks leaning nonchalantly against those tree friends of theirs. She was terribly tormented by her rare outings. She didn't want any man staring at her. So, with her knees shaking and her eyes hidden in the shade of a panama hat that Joab had given her, she walked past them, gazing off into the distance. Once she picked up a newspaper that her mama Séraphine had brought back from town – she got the idea one day when she went up to Pointe-à-Pitre to visit Godmother Anoncia and saw blacks and whites strolling down the streets holding open newspapers in front of their faces. On the front page of this newspaper was an article about the new governor of the Colonies. It was 1936. A large portrait of the man spread across the page. A certain Mister Félix Eboué. 'One Hundred Percent Black Man Named Governor of the Colonies,' declared the headline. Eliette walked past a small group of young men talking in hushed voices about a choice piece of tail or two and trading genuine magical formulas for hooking any specimen of the race of mamsells. The huge, black face of Félix Eboué, one hundred percent black man, was all crumpled, and one of his ears on the paper was torn, hanging halfway off. Behind her newspaper and under her hat, Eliette thought she'd slipped into the world of the invisible. But no one could see anything but her: latania straw-hat, womanly body in a long white dress, with lace petticoat. Her slim-fingered hands with neat knuckles clutched the two pages of the old newspaper, framing the hundred percent black man's face that smiled out at the people. Alas, a rock appeared on her path. A little innocent rock that she stubbed her big toe on. Eliette stumbled in front of a *bata*-Calcutta, one of those baseborn coolies, who snatched the paper from her hands and, quick as a wink, recited over her head a funeral oration of little import and great insignificance, followed by an insolent Magnificat dedicated to all the governors of the French colonies.

That's how the story got started that Eliette kept her legs closed tight because the male sex from Ravine-Guinée, from Savane Mulet to Deadend-Coco-Shell, wasn't good enough for her. She had to have no less than a governor. A hundred percent black man. A man from Cayenne, the very place where gold grew in bunches on the trees, nuggeted in thundering cascades, and rolled endlessly down the mountainsides to fill the bed of the Maroni River. A man sent specially by the French government to show how the black people could become civilized nations, salute parading armies, and profess with a pure heart, 'We must love one another.'

Up until her marriage with Renélien, almost twenty years later, Eliette was followed night and day, closer than a shadow, by that reputation of being a one hundred percent aristocratic Negress with fancy la-di-da, panama, and regalia tastes. For a long time, certain people called her Hundred Percent, without even having the slightest suspicion that the nickname dated back to the mid-thirties, Governor Eboué's era of glory and acclaim.

It wasn't until the end of the Second World War, thanks to coconut sherbet and Mademoiselle Meredith's social skills, that Eliette was able to endure having men's eyes on her body. After her mama's death in '43 she found herself alone in the cabin in Savane, alone with her fear of cyclones, of men and of she-devils, alone with her desire to crawl into a hole and disappear from the face of the earth. She was twenty-three years old. Even so, a body had to eat, earn honest money, and not be reduced to begging. And even if Papa De Gaulle had eradicated the word colony from the maps of the world, elevated Guadeloupe and its dependencies to the rank of a French overseas *département*, she understood quite clearly that this gratification alone could not fill one's belly. She had to work. And so she took on her mother's small business, gradually forcing herself to get used to the outside world, selling her sherbets on Saturday afternoons in the town square. Head bowed, sparing of words, people accepted her as she was, one hundred percent skittish, until she broke herself into all the eyes being on her. During the week she hired herself out to Mademoiselle Meredith, an old certified schoolteacher, lonely, leathery black woman, dancing to the beat of the French metropolis. As much a stickler about dust fluffs gathering under the edges of her mosquito net as she was about the rules of grammar, she coached Eliette in the proper use of the French language and various points of etiquette – guaranteed to be universal and immutable. With her discipline, her ironclad sense of ethics and straight-laced set of principles, she clamped a heavy lid of silence over Eliette's old fears, and a little more of the young woman's wildness disappeared behind monkey-antics, phony smiles and salutations, forced how-de-dos, and skillfully put on airs. Thanks to this savvy instruction, Eliette found herself a husband at thirty-five. In August of 1955, the same year that – three times – cyclones with women's names raised the roofs in the Northern Islands, she said yes to Renélien in the church in Ravine-Guinée. Mademoiselle Meredith, who had no descendants, gave her a fine trousseau, marvelous treasures to fill up the old cabin in Savane where Joab used to say he'd found Paradise on earth . . . A complete canteen of cutlery, a seventy-two-piece set of china dinnerware, and an assortment of tablecloths, napkins, sheets, embroidered pillowcases, et cetera doilies, table runners, coasters.

When Renélien showed up in Eliette's life, it was as if he'd been heaven sent. And she told herself that after the Passage of the Beast, the war in France, and the death of her mama, who'd been lost to madness at such a young age, barely forty, maybe Joab was right after all: life on earth did have its advantages and kind turns . . .

Renélien, he was a good person, even if he did run his first wife off with a rousing series of kicks in the backside one day when he caught her, mouth between two doors, busily yakking with a neighbor while his dinner – dasheen and pig meat – was burning on the hot plate. He told his perfect Eliette several times how he thought his cabin was on fire all the way out on the road. According to his long-winded explanations, tongues of flames leapt from every hole in the kitchen. Black smoke had already made a hole in the blue sky. And the smell was so acrid he had to cover his nose and eyes. He found Zouzou deep in conversation. The neighbors were sniggering about his botched meal and the hard-earned money that had made it possible to buy the pig meat and the sweat of his brow wasted yesterday and today on the roads of Guadeloupe, going back and forth between Pointe-à-Pitre and Basse-Terre. For nothing! How many days of work behind the wheel of his bus had he lost? While he toiled away, Madame Renélien was engaging in discussions, babbling, philosophizing, tongue wagging to beat the band, advising manless women, and shaking out her contempt on Miss so-and-so, who weighed with both hands the mystery of her waddling fate in her fatherless nine-month belly. And all round everyone was already gloating gleefully as they saw the man approaching.

First off, Renélien said, 'Good evening dear!' as if nothing was amiss. Then, 'What are we having for dinner, Zouzou?' From that feigned cheerful tone of Mr. Bus Driver, the woman realized that – oh dear! – today that black man wasn't kidding around. She usually showered him with charming words that augured another flesh-meat meal – guaranteed feasting, merrymaking, and delectation. Ofttimes he'd forgiven her the charred meal, teasing her about being a scatterbrain, about that devil time scuttling away with its crafty tricks that she was unable to grasp or even assess. How often had he watched her, his guts twisting, as she threw out helpings of burned meat that he'd earned with his hard work? At times like that his heart felt like one of those black, shriveled bits she scraped off the bottom of the *canari*-stewpots, smoldering with suppressed anger, consumed with rage. Renélien abhorred waste, which was the least of his faults. Knowing he had dragged Zouzou away from her mama's house, it was his duty to educate her. 'A woman is a man's work', an old French white had told him one day – a philosopher he'd happened to meet who had settled in Du Canon in the tracks of a blue-skinned Negress from overseas. Alas, despite all of his efforts to educate her, Zouzou did not change. And he was always half starved, fed up with playacting, tired of trick playing. Never again did he want to have to dine on patience and dessert on Zouzou's body alone.

Quick-melting into the darkness of the kitchen, in a flash the damozel threw three green bananas on the fire and laid over them a very meager slice of salted cod that had been forgotten in a corner of her larder. The first time, Renélien said to her coolheadedly, 'Zouzou, your man is hungry!' She murmured three sweet quivering words. But the sauce didn't take. She could tell from the silence that he was climbing the boards of the cabin. Stroke of bad luck, the kerosene ran out under the hot plate and the flame grew dimmer-dimmer until it gave a last dying puff that brought tears to Zouzou's eyes. The cod didn't even have time to brown; the stiff, pale green bananas, lying like stones in the bottom of the *canari*, eyed the woman who stood wringing the neck of an empty kerosene bottle to make it weep another drop, just one little drop, please!

'Zouzou, I'm hungry, goddammit!' When Renélien's voice rang out a second time, the poor woman felt like pissing in her pants right in the middle of the kitchen where she stood. Already, a nerve-wracking drumming was coming from the heart of the cabin, like someone beating time, light on patience and hard on thumping the staff in the Offertory. Zouzou shuddered in her kitchen where the smoke-blackened tin roof overhead brought home to her the number of meals sacrificed to gossip, slurs, and rumors with the neighbors.

While the water in the *canari* grew obligingly cold and the piece of cod flopped diabolically under Zouzou's fascinated gaze, Renélien's voice rose a third time, 'An fen, sakré bourèl! Ban mwen manjé an mwen on fwa!' Dammit, you mean old crow! Bring my food now! In abandoning the French he had always promised to use with his legitimate wife, Renélien immediately fell into his old uneducated, insensitive black man's ways again. His fiery breath singed Zouzou's back, who, in turning around, got slammed right in the face with the leather bag filled with rolls of pierced copper chinks and nickel coins and wads of Guadeloupe bills, the ransom from Pointe-à-Pitre–Basse-Terre round trips. Zouzou babbled one-two sweet words, wept as she cooed out some story of candied sweet potatoes, promised a pot of chicken soup, mutton stew, and then bolted and ran for it with the man's swift kicks hot on her tail.

Renélien spent some time alone, didn't get used to it. Every eve- ning when he left his bus, he realized that he'd rather find a talkative woman scrubbing charred pots than the coldness of his empty bed. He tried to make amends, went and confessed to Zouzou's mama, admitted that, yes, it was his fault, he'd been hungry that day, and a hungry black man is like an animal: his belly remembers the old slave days, the lack of bread, and rage wells up from the pit of his stomach. Poor Renélien! The old woman sent him packing right back to his ancestral brutality. And he never saw Zouzou again. One day she filed for divorce. He learned that she'd married a Mr. so-and-so, who carried her off to France on a transatlantic ocean liner . . .

That was how Renélien told it as he drove his bus along the road that led to La Pointe. The first time Eliette heard his story, she was on her way to visit Godmother Anoncia. The tale distracted her. She wasn't looking for a man, honest truth. Her life stretched before her with no dips or bumps, smooth as the flat of your hand. As for love, she set no store by it, since every day she observed Mademoiselle Meredith painlessly surviving her single status, calm and composed, yet keen-minded. Eliette had a full thirty-five years under her belt and wasn't asking for a single thing, not from the Blessed Virgin or even from Sacré-Coeur. When the wind suddenly changed, tipping the scales of her destiny, she'd simply been on her way to visit her godmother Anoncia.

Renélien wasn't looking for a new woman either. He'd been living alone for a good seven years, finding a certain satisfaction in rehashing the tales of his misfortune. He used his time alone to meditate on philosophical subjects concerning the madness of the world and its creatures. When he came back to his cabin, he flopped onto the bed and, eyes closed, dined on memories of Zouzou's desserts. He always ended up puzzling over human brutality, feared the unknown forces that dwelled within him, the thoughts that took on form, that could overpower him at any time and compel him to commit the irremediable. Ever since he'd allowed his wild side to swoop down upon Zouzou, he saw the human species through different eyes. Believed that within each living being there were forces engaged in pitched battle. He always expected the unpredictable, lived in constant doubt. Since any minute tremors could start shaking the earth, cyclones could tumble mountains to the ground and the ocean whisk one's life away, he knew that beyond appearances, pretty faces, and sweet words, raging elements lay dormant, ready to be unleashed.

When Eliette stepped down from the bus, she thought it only proper to slip him one-two words with no depth or substance, learned from Mademoiselle Meredith – just to show a touch of compassion, a pinch of education, and distinguish herself from the folks who smiled openly at the driver's troubles. This is what she recited: 'Life is rough, Monsieur, but good hard work will make you successful in your undertakings, and maybe one day the burden of the pain you now feel will be alleviated.' Renélien jumped with surprise. Found himself completely dazzled and eyed from head to foot the gracious person who had gone to so much trouble to listen to his tragedy. He'd never been talked to like that before. The man was more in the habit of feeling the laughter and snickering of his passengers poking him in the back. In truth, Eliette couldn't care less about the driver's petty problems. As she was gratifying him with appropriate words, she was thinking about her sick godmother Anoncia, who had sent for her in order to make some revelations.

Eliette stayed in Pointe-à-Pitre for three days, holding the hand of

Godmother Anoncia, whom death was endlessly putting off. As for Renélien, he remained sitting behind the wheel of his bus for three days, thinking, waiting for the lovely lady who had warmed his heart and proved that there was always hope in this world; life, with its torments and its bag of nasty tricks, always held ineffable surprises. And he was filled with wonder when he realized that – incognito – kind souls of a different fiber than others could, in a single breath, check the brutality of the human race. Eliette was just such a soul. Zouzou had put the ocean between her and him. He thought to himself, Good riddance!

Three days of waiting during which Renélien never stopped smiling. He was cursed-upbraided by the passengers, who didn't understand why the driver – hang it all! – refused to go anywhere when they had business to take care of in Basse-Terre, goods that were already rotting on the roof of the bus, why that dumbstruck fool head was deaf to everything, kept his eyes trained in only one direction, and lifted his backside from the seat only to wash up in the early morning, clean his teeth, and grease his hair down into a Creole-style pompadour.

On the morning of the fourth day of petrifaction, fed up with Renélien's behavior, the passengers ended up unloading their affairs, gunny sacks, crates and baskets, chickens, vegetables and roots. Only Bishop, the porter, stayed, stretched out on the back seat waiting to see what would come of his boss's dreams. Thinking he was on strike, other bus drivers came filing past to ask their colleague what he was protesting, but the man explained to them that it was an affair of the heart.

Our friend Renélien rehearsed to himself the words he would whisper when Eliette finally reappeared. When Eliette put her foot on the first step of the bus, the radio was announcing the death of the former French ambassador, Mr. Paul Claudel, who came to kneel in the cathedral after the Cyclone of '28. Renélien's heart dropped down into the pit of his stomach, and the blood started rushing fiercely through the blue veins running along his arms. Eliette said, 'Good afternoon to you, Sir!' and then asked if there was a seat available. The bus was empty. Faced with the dilemma of picking one seat out of so many, she moved slowly down the aisle, inspecting the empty places, calculating the shade, the path of the sun along the route to Ravine-Guinée. She sat down next to a window, cradling her chin in her hand in order to think more comfortably about Godmother Anoncia. The old woman had said that one day soon she would tell her a secret and that she needed to make sure she was moored down good and fast. Disconcerted, Eliette wanted to question her further, but Hermine, the servant, intervened.

As soon as she was sitting down, three rows behind his seat, Renélien – who'd been watching her in the rearview mirror – turned the key and drove off as quick as if his life depended on it. The vehicle lurched forward, belching out a thick cloud of black smoke. At the back of the bus, Bishop awoke with a start and cried, 'Patron, Ka ou ka fè! Le patron, ka-ka ou ka fè la!' Boss, what you doing! What oh what that boss man doing! A bit shaken, Eliette asked if the bus was stopping in Ravine-Guinée. In response Bishop simply shrugged one shoulder and curled his lips and looked mystified. She couldn't remember the driver's face, and the rearview mirror only reflected the lower part of a nose and two handsome rows of slap-happy teeth grinning at the road that opened out between the cane fields. She soon noticed she was the only passenger. A vague fear moistened her brow and temples. And for a second, distant images drifted slowly up, dogeared black-and-white photographs, taking her back to when she was eight . . . The Cyclone of '28. The Passage of the Beast.

The wooden rafter rending her. And then the blood in the sheets that her mother hid in the wardrobe. A shudder ran through her body, and she touched her belly through the nylon dress, trying to feel some trace of the wound. She wiped her face with a handkerchief and called out, 'Monsieur bus driver! Monsieur, please, I'm getting off in Ravine-Guinée!' Renélien couldn't care less where she was going. He had an urgent proposal to submit to her, and even if he had to drive all the way around Grande-Terre three times, she was going to listen to him. Only afterward, if she refused him, would he drop her off in Ravine-Guinée and then go and drive himself and his bus off a cliff in Anse-Bertrand. At those words, a flutter of veils revealed the shadow of a past that Eliette had thought dead and buried along with her mama Séraphine. She saw herself as a child again, in her bed, panting. From its open mouth, the Beast was blowing a powerful and murderous gale. She saw the rafter again. The blood. And then her mama crying, carrying her in her arms. The tumbled-down world all around. And the marvelous hands of Ethéna sewing up her belly . . .

Renélien started out telling everything – from the very first to the very last stroke – all of the heartburn Zouzou had left him with, his hungry belly, and the fleshy fruits of Zouzou's desserts. Sincere, he told her again of his anger on the last day of their relationship, the Creole coming back to his lips, the serenade of kicks in the backside, and the loneliness of the present. He admitted to her the dormant forces that inhabited him. And then he asked her if she knew how to cook, how many meals she'd already burnt, did she enjoy chewing the fat with the neighbors, and who had taught her to use the French language in such a beautiful way? . . . He knew nothing about her, so little. He exulted when she announced she wasn't engaged or promised to anyone. He asked her to put his name at the top of the list, just so he could dream a bit and feel a little joy, nothing more. He wasn't in such a bad position since he was a bus driver, owned two acres of land in Maubrun, a three-room cabin on the said land, two steers, a cow in calf, and a mama who'd owned and cultivated three vegetable gardens in the hills above Plessy for over thirty years. Despite the unfortunate pant-kicking episode, Renélien swore he was not a natural beater, and he pledged that very day to cut off his hand if he caught himself indulging in that kind of brutality again.

When the bus drove past the church in Abymes for the fifth time, Renélien finally fell silent. Sitting in the back, huddled up in his seat, Bishop was crying quietly. Disconsolate, thinking of his mama left behind on the island of Dominica, he watched the rooftops gradually melting into the evening darkness. Eliette asked Renélien to give her two days. Two days to weigh her destiny was nothing at all. Afterward, he would know yes or no whether he should drive himself off a cliff in Anse-Bertrand. So he took her back to Ravine-Guinée. Confident, lighthearted, satisfied with himself for having put his life on the line for the love of a woman, he felt as if he'd conquered the savage forces that inhabited him. With Eliette, he would make amends for the kicks dispensed to Zouzou's backside. If Eliette – Eliette! What a charming name she'd left him as a keepsake – if Eliette accepted . . .

Eliette wiped away the smile that came naturally to her lips whenever she thought of her dead Renélien. He'd proven himself to be upright, hard-working, and passionate all through the years they shared. At his side, she'd been nothing but a sham, never cherished him in an honest way. Sure, she fixed him fine meals inspired by recipes in True French Cooking given to her by Mademoiselle Meredith. Renélien always found a hot dinner waiting for him, the table set, a clean napkin lying next to his plate. Even though he was sometimes quite late in coming home, detained by a delivery in Côte-sous-le-Vent, she sat down next to him, watched him eat, talked friendly with him. He loved her, you could tell by the way his eyes shone with gratitude that she didn't deserve.

On their marriage night she provided him with her mended belly. He'd loved it blindly, licking the invisible scars, groping his way along. She told him to go gently, repeating Mademoiselle Meredith's warnings. As she'd never practiced love before, her flesh was tough and the approach was difficult. But he caressed her so well and so long that she softened up naturally, finding the act of lovemaking beautiful. He'd taken her in a sigh. Nothing inside of her had been torn. He asked her if she'd known other men and made her swear, even if he died tomorrow, never to remarry. She laughed and promised. For her, he sold all of his belongings in Mauburn, demolished Joab's old shack, and built in its place a nice cabin of red wood, solid as a rock. For her, he slaved away till he died of fatigue on the road to Basse-Terre at the wheel of the yellow truck he bought for transporting materials, sand, gravel, boards, cinder blocks. He dreamt of making a fortune for her. In the early sixties people everywhere started building houses out of concrete. So he said they shouldn't miss the boat, it was now or never. Went running after money, and death was what he found.

She didn't cry at the funeral, just regretted that he'd not left her a child to love and dote over. She hadn't cried since the death of her mama in 1943. But that Sunday, with compassion knotting her throat, she finally understood the meaning of the high-flown sentiments that Renélien was always harping about. She lit a lamp, and Angela's face brought two small hot tears to her eyes that came straight down the road from her heart.

The only thing I sought after was the peace of my cabin, she thought to herself.

Not let my mind color the sounds . . .

V

Jah! Jah! Rosette exclaimed as she climbed onto the dingy bus.

When Bob – Bob Marley – died, I nearly went off into the mountains
with Edith and her group of Rastas who'd set up their bamboo
cabins in Savane on the other side of Nèfles Bridge, near a spring
they discovered by the grace of Jah! They'd arrived just one year earlier, in 1980. Never really mixed with other folks. They pitched their
camp far from the eaters of pig meat, domino players, and rum
drinkers of Quartier-Mélo.

I don't know how – out of that whole bunch – I ever spotted Edith,
whom the others called Sister Beloved, God's chosen one, because
she'd received the divine word. When I first saw her, I felt sad –
she was so different from the lovely black girl I used to play with
in elementary school at Des-Ramiers. In those days she called me
Rosanna the Highest in Heaven, just for fun!

She was wearing a red-yellow-green knit cap that was all lumpy
because of the dreadlocks pushed up underneath it, a faded pink ba-
tik tee shirt over a rumpled full skirt of discolored African material.
Her toes snuck out past her muddy thongs. Two six-seven-year-old
children were hopping around at her side, carrying big koui-cala-

bashes that held other smaller calabashes and ladles, spoons, bowls carved out of dry coconut shells, bamboo, or wood. Edith was holding a baby with an incipient Rasta hairdo on her hip. She walked straight and tall, just like a queen in a parade, and asked for no one's sympathy. I remember thinking she had the self-satisfied look of someone who 'knew,' someone who had dreamt they'd seen themselves amongst the Lord God's chosen few. You could tell from her eyes that she thought she was the repository of something close to the supreme truth: the path to Paradise or the key to eternal life . . . Her emaciated face beamed with self-confidence.

How many were they? Ten, twenty . . . Mature men with long beards, dreadlocks, and coarse cotton trousers, equipped with shovels, picks, bamboo sticks. Young males carrying bunches of bananas on their shoulders, clusters of green coconuts, infinitely long poles. Women – hair tied high upon their heads – long and bony, loaded down with baskets, pushing ox carts. Children hanging from titties, dragging rolled-up grass mats, calabashes, and gunnysacks full of Rasta mystery.

Despite the tatters that covered her thin back, her blackened fingernails, and her ragged tee shirt, Edith smiled like someone who feasted on heavenly food. I was jealous of that smile. I sensed she was a free spirit amongst the brothers and sisters. Free to walk proudly in her rags past the folks that hurried up to gawk at the 'Israel Tribe' – that's what people called them – as they went by.

Sitting at the window of the bus that brought her back from the jail house in Basse-Terre, Rosette wondered what prayer she should recite to take her back in time, years away from the trials and tribulations she was experiencing now. She missed the days when she used to share the same bed with her mama Gilda in Des-Ramiers, the days when – without knowing a thing about life – she consoled Rosan, predicted he would have a bright future, invented tales for him, and repeated, managing to keep a straight face while she puffed on imaginary American cigarettes, 'Happiness is at the tips of your lips!'

When Edith–Sister Beloved and her group arrived in Savane, how old was Rosette? Twenty-two, twenty-three years old, and already two children: Angela and Robert. She'd tucked her brightest dreams away in the drawers of the impossible long ago. When they returned from the Saintes Islands, rich with the million in Guadeloupe bank notes lining the bottom of their trunk, they believed they were saved. With the cabin they inherited from Uncle Edmond, they'd declared themselves blessed by the gods. Alas, the million did not produce a single offspring. They even had to borrow from Aunt Fanotte to replace the sheet metal and buy the black-and-white lino. And they discovered soon afterward that life in Savane was rough.

Night always came to life shot with the cries of women being beaten, cavorting crazily, fleeing before evil spirits. Dogs yapped in chain reaction. Rumors of killings sprouted up and down the paths. Earthly creatures around there ran amok with an excess of brutal words, vowing they'd marked a bullet for their neighbor, promising the slash of a cutlass, the noose of a rope, the final hour of life. All day long insults and curses ran from one end to the other of the cabins, boomed through the air like all hell let loose, mucking up the ears of newborns that lay in fish crates scavenged from behind Marga's corner store. Folks kept an eye on each other, waiting for just one word, one look, to pounce upon the enemy, strangle him, slash him with a razor, chop him to pieces with a cutlass. Life in Des-Ramiers wasn't like that, and Rosette wondered why it had been her fate to land in Savane, where misery changed human beings into wild beasts in no time. And she'd remarked so many times that folks only stuck together when they were joining forces against the law and its inquisitive gendarmes. At times like those no one had ever heard a thing, nothing but the rain beating on the tin roof. Everyone clammed up, became suddenly blind, and developed a stutter, was innocent in every way. The dead wandered Savane as if they had arrived before the gates of hell, multitudes pacing around in close quarters, each waiting his turn to be called for the last judgment.

Rosette, who wanted to distinguish herself from the lost nations of those parts, only neighbored in a friendly way with Eliette. She soon began to dream of leaving Savane, the run-down neighborhoods, the chaotic outskirts that she feared would corrupt her children. When Rosan added on the room in concrete, after Cyclone toppled the trees in the courtyard, she didn't like the idea. She begged him to save his money to buy a piece of land in Des-Ramiers, where life wasn't a daily battle. He said that the Good Lord had brought them to Savane and there was nothing awaiting them over that way. She was constantly trying to butter him up so that they could go back to Des-Ramiers. He didn't want to hear anything about it. And even when she made up with her mama Gilda, just before Rita's baptism, he never considered changing his mind.

So Rosette gradually resigned herself. Folks saw her plant more rows of yuccas and cactuses around her cabin to make up for the missing fence, and she reinforced the sheet metal in back. To forget the ugliness outside, she borrowed money to buy a green vinyl living-room suite and a dining-room set – Empire style, Seoud assured her. She laid lace doilies down everywhere, set out china vases filled with plastic roses, hung up portraits of saints, a painting of a white horse, etchings: autumnal landscapes, and still lives, bouquets of flowers and fruit from the metropolis. Often, to avoid thinking of the thousand wars in Savane, she climbed up on the back of the white horse and – munching on apples or pears – rode off into the landscapes and disappeared.

Visiting with other women in Savane had always disconcerted her. Rosette put them into three different categories. There was the vagabond-floozy, *manawa*-whore, bare-assed under her skirt, a resentful sort of body that swore and drank with the men that mounted her quick-rushed behind a cabin for ten francs. There was the cringing-floozy, walking crooked, her body broken by a lone brute – a sorry, contemptible oppressor that worked off his bitterness with thrusts of the pelvis and kicks in the pants and gloried in being a true man. That kind didn't flinch at fate's smacks in the face; she lay low, disfigured-demolished, dry-eyed in the winds of her destiny. And then you ran into one-two women who'd been saved, who'd gotten back on their feet, proudly showing their bumps and scars like medals from the last war. They walked alone in life, managed their household without males, and raised their children strictly. They might well have served as models, but it was disheartening to remain in their shadow. Their drooping eyelids attested to how little they believed in anymore. All the words that poured from their mouths, as they beat themselves on the breast, flowed out in streams of painful bitterness, frightful evocations, warnings that gave you the jitters. All about how men were animals and you had to watch their every move or they'd get their own daughters in the family way. About how the Good Lord had put woman on earth just so man would have someone to beat on when he couldn't kill his neighbor. About how women were struck with a curse that nothing would erase, ever. In the hell of Savane, Rosette had a husband who didn't beat her and two not-so-wild children. She hardly believed in happiness that came easy anymore. But she could see well enough that she had it better than others, even if she still believed in a much better someplace where men and women intertwined and cutlasses had clear consciences, where spirits didn't come back from the valley of death. In Des-Ramiers, probably . . .

Folks in Ravine-Guinée denigrated people from Savane, but they were no different themselves, so Rosette didn't have anyone to talk with. Sometimes, just to ward off the loneliness and get a dose of reality, she opened her door and exchanged two-three words with her old neighbor, Eliette, who also lived shut up in her house. When Rosan went off to the work site and she found herself alone in the cabin, she closed all the doors and listened to reggae albums – it was the only thing that could make her forget Des-Ramiers. Without understanding a word of English, Rosette sang the songs, learning the lyrics of Tosh, Isaacs, and Marley by heart. Reggae music spoke to her very soul, and she often sat there for hours playing the same tune over and over, repeating the words that throbbed heavily inside of her – 'I'll rule my destiny . . . One love . . . Revolution . . .' In a trance, she stood up and walked into the sea of colorful living notes swelling through the cabin. At first she went in on her tiptoes, fearing the notes would disappear, or that she'd make the dream bubbles burst. Her body started swaying in cadence, calculating the effect of the music. No, Rosette was no longer in control of her gestures! The reggae music penetrated her in a male and vigorous way. Left its burning charge with her. Eyes closed, she was suddenly lifted into the air. No, her feet no longer touched the floor! She drifted up, began running, walking, pedaling in the air, moving forward, forever forward. Suddenly, she was far from Savane and all of its misery. Free, despite the battles she fought to put food on the plates. No, the winds blowing over her body no longer lashed at her! Her mama had run her out, but she shouldn't cry about that anymore, 'No woman no cry . . .' She was a woman, by God! A Negress that stood tall. There was nothing left to fear. The eyes of the Almighty were upon her! Glory be to Jah-God! Yes, justice would be done in Babylon! One day there would not be the slightest recollection of a crime in Savane. And the macadam dreams in these parts would give way to a dream never before seen in this world. The Lord would send water, electricity, and toilets to all corners of Savane. There would be no more water or power cutoffs, no more wars, no more starving children walking in the gutter – 'No woman no cry . . .' She slipped into another dimension. On all sides of her, crowded Africans who had died in the holds of slave boats, at the hand of the whip, torn to shreds by dogs, vomited up by the so-called masters of the world. She heard the moaning of women and the cries of orphans, but also the grumbling of Negro-Maroons who'd escaped into the hills. And the music shook in her guts. 'No woman no cry . . .' Just rock back and forth. Console the deep sorrows of the black people. And then start walking again. Run. Jump and be reborn, fly toward the victorious tomorrows that Pope Marley prophesied. She arrived at a place – a savanna where the descendants of slaves were tending their wounds. Their blood mingled with the open sores of the earth, with the movements of the reggae music beating like a heart, fluttering, rending, bounding. She repeated, 'Revolution! . . . Zimbabwe! . . .' Tears blurred her vision. So then she closed her eyes and said to herself that one day, yes, Lord, her people would finally rise up, free themselves from the mire of the ancient curse and that, yes, Lord, blacks would be seen as men on this earth. For a moment she forgot the child thrown to the bottom of Nèfles Bridge, the three pyramids of rotten christophines, Glawdys's gray eyes looking contemptuously at Eliette – poor Glawdys who was only asking for a little love. 'No woman, no cry . . . no cry . . .'

She no longer saw the mangled baby in Rosan's arms. She walked-danced, raising her knees up high, for the path was steep and the road long. But she was no longer alone in the darkness of her cabin; a throng of people surrounded her. Crippled, blind, paralyzed black people, zombies of the universe, walked too, resuscitated in Bob Marley's music. She walked along in time, Lord, and men and women rose up in her wake, one after another: even criminals lugging consciences stained with hate, even the victims of Savane, whose story she'd heard fifty times over – like Hortense, found carved up on a banana leaf because of a glorious smile and poor Marius, hanged in a mango tree for a jar of gold lost in the secret folds of his dreams.

She hadn't known them, no, but their spirits still lived in Savane; they too must stand up to escape eternal sorrow – 'Revolution! . . .' – and be reborn far from macadam dreams . . .

What in God's name was she doing on this bus? In all of her childhood plans, her life had never taken this turn. There was Rosan, Rosette, and Love, a fairy-tale happy family. Jail hadn't been part of the deal. The dirty window reflecting her face was telling her that all this wasn't happening to her, not to Rosette. Behind the grill, Rosan hadn't spoken to her. Had sat there with his head down, thighs hugging his clasped hands. Hadn't even looked at her twice. Hair not combed. The collar of his white shirt was black. She'd hated him. Didn't have the strength to ask him for his dirty laundry, his shorts. Hadn't given him the fruit in her basket either. And all the fine words that she'd rehearsed when leaving Savane had been left at the entrance to the jail, trampled upon by the tough women who'd grown used to the jingling keys, the long corridors, the guards' looks. Since she didn't want to be looked at in the same way as those floozies that were crowding to see their criminal husbands, Rosette mumbled that she came to visit a prisoner for a work of charity in her parish. But she had to show her I D card. They saw her name, the same as Rosan's. Offended by the look the guards gave her, she started shouting they had to let the father of her children loose . . . If he were a white man, they would never have put him in jail on the mere say-so of a child . . . She'd see the district attorney, the judge, the director of the prison, the prefect if necessary. They escorted her into an office where a woman told her to cry as much as she wanted, to talk about it all, to get it off her chest. Had she seen or heard anything? Rosette hadn't seen or heard a thing. No, Rosan didn't get up in the night; she couldn't recall his doing so. No, he didn't beat her, not her or the children, not even Robert, who didn't like school. She answered all the questions docilely while her mind rambled in an autumnal landscape, munching on apples, pears.

Back in those days, Lady Dreams wasn't just a word in the mouth to suck on and then spit out. She walked around in a three-piece suit. Was accompanied by five bodyguards, night and day, day and night. But Lady Dreams felt lonely, wanted to meet other folks, get to know more about life: its five senses, its forbidden fruits, and its madness. One day, she opened the window and saw the world below with all of its lights, its grand carnival music, its top hats. And Lady Dreams jumped. Landed on a rock. And was killed instantly . . .

When Sister Beloved Edith and her group of Rastas crossed Savane to set up their camp on the other side of Nèfles Bridge, it was the year before Bob's death. It wasn't quite two years since Glawdys had thrown her child down to the bottom of the bridge. The place hadn't turned into a huge garbage dump yet. But with the electricity that came that same year, folks started buying more, everything they set eyes on, with a kind of franticness. They surrounded themselves with new things bought on credit. They were trying to make up for lost time. So they had to have everything, right away, and they vied with one another. First they got rid of the transistor radios and the kerosene refrigerators. And then, since the old things didn't go well sitting by the brand-new ones, they threw out the caned chairs and rusty wrought-iron beds while they were at it, filled their cabins with heavy vinyl armchairs, Formica wardrobes, plywood buffets. People sighted one-two rats that came prospecting around by the river. No one worried much about it. Even when they grew so numerous that there was no way to go down to wash clothes or fish for *ouassou*-crawdads.

Yes, I was jealous of Edith's smile and her free ways, her eyes that said, 'I have seen. I know. Look at me! There is a way to live a life of love in this world.' In the evening, when Rosan came home, I told him that a group of Rastas had crossed Savane to set up camp on the other side of Nèfles Bridge. Rosan shook his head and said that there were enough vermin in Savane as it was, and he wasn't going down to scoop up another broken baby from the rocks in the river. That night we talked till it was late, sitting out on the gallery, looking up at the moon. I thought he was going to decide to leave Savane and go back to Des-Ramiers. But he didn't want to hear a word of what I had to say. He just kept repeating that he had no intention of going backward. For him, life here wasn't all that bad. Just had to live next to people without getting mixed up in anything, not talk about your problems. He hoped things would get better with time. It'd been a good two years since there'd been a killing – ever since the tragedy at Nèfles Bridge. All things told, maybe folks had learned something from his long walk with the mangled baby in his arms.

When I told him that I'd recognized a girl from Des-Ramiers,

Edith, who used to play hopscotch with me in fifth grade, he exclaimed that, of all things, I shouldn't go seeing if she remembered me, those *rastacouère* folks smoked weed, were the worst sort of loafers, confirmed liars, and hypocrites. I assured him that no, she didn't interest me in the least. The poor girl must have gone mad. He should just see her raggedy tee shirt, her wrinkled skirt, that heap of uncombed hair of hers under the knit cap. I added that, no, it'd never crossed my mind to go tagging after her. He didn't answer right away. He was picking his teeth with a matchstick and watching the bats flitting around the papaya tree. And then, looking at me in an odd way, he said, 'They just like you, all they good for is lugging around a bunch of silly parodies that don't go nowhere. They waking up and going back to sleep in fairy tales and pipedreams . . .' I couldn't answer back. I just thought about how we'd stopped laughing together, how his features had hardened since we were married. Savane had drawn the two of us apart, and now I couldn't console him as I used to with my stories of happiness at the tips of your lips. After a few minutes, he waited for a backfiring moped to go by before adding, 'A body never knows what he'll run up against in this world . . . But you'd best stop listening to that Rasta music of yours before it busts your head wide open.' He got up and went to bed at those words.

The next day I cleaned the cabin early. I took the kids to school, Angela to first grade, Robert to kindergarten. And then I crossed Nèfles Bridge. The radio announced fine weather. That morning Rosan had left before daybreak, off to a work site in Vieux-Habitants. He wouldn't get off till late because of a concrete slab that had to be poured. The kids ate lunch at the cafeteria. We figured that it cost us less, and at least those two would have some meat – flesh or fish – on their plates every day. All of a sudden, being outside, I felt free. Liberated from the life that wasn't going according to my dreams. Free, just like when I danced to Bob's records. I didn't think about my 123 mama Gilda anymore, about how she'd been right . . . Could Rosan really give love? From the outside, it seemed as if they had a good life. But he never laughed. It was as if all his childhood wounds were slowly opening back up, making even deeper marks as they surfaced. At times I felt as if I were being sucked into his silence, and I wanted only one thing – for him to leave soon, so that I could put on my reggae albums. In crossing the bridge, I had the feeling that I'd broken one of the ties that chained me to the good and proper Rosette of the past. Free . . .

They met their death in the mountains; after they had attempted to leave Babylon, go back to their roots, just the day after Bob died. But the first time I went to meet them, none of that had been written anywhere yet. I saw Paradise on that day, love and a living God laying his hand on men, women, and children that were the color of the earth. The place had changed. They had cleaned up the banks of the river, pushed the litter into a hidden corner, built huts, gathered rocks, and tilled the land to plant a garden.

Edith was sitting on a mat, a baby in her arms. She'd taken off her knit cap and her hair fell down thickly onto her bony shoulders. She was dangling a piece of string in front of the child, who kept trying to grab it. From time to time she put down the little cord, dipped her fingers into a calabash, and brought a bit greenish mush to the mouth of the child, who gazed at her thankfully. In response Edith flashed one of her wide smiles. I was standing off to one side. One of the sisters – Sister Judy – motioned for me to come closer, there was nothing to be afraid of, I was welcome. Yes, I really thought I'd gone to heaven. Everyone greeted me respectfully. And their eyes said, 'You're one of the family. Everything we have is yours. Come forward, for this is the garden you have been waiting for.'

Edith called, 'Hey Rose, you lost your crown of thorns! When I saw you among your people, I prayed that your heart had not yet wilted, Rosanna the Highest in Heaven, Jah is great!'

Sister Judy repeated, 'Yes, Jah is great!'

I began, 'Edith . . .'

She said, 'No, Edith is no longer of this world, speak to Sister Beloved, which means the Chosen One. And I will name you Rose, for Rosette is a small ornament that falls apart with the first breath of wind. From now on, Rose, you will belong to the creatures of the Almighty Jah. We say rose water, rosewood, Rose of Jericho, wind Rose, gypsum rose . . . In you there is water, air, fire, earth, glory, saintliness, and many other elements that mean Jah created you as One so that you might carry out his will. Sister Rose, the Lord is our shepherd, we shall not want. He maketh us lie down in green pastures and leadeth us beside the still waters and limpid springs. You are here beside me today, Sister Rose. Tell me about your life . . .'

That day Rosette told Sister Beloved of the many battles she'd fought since leaving Des-Ramiers. She opened her soul, laid bare all of her disappointments.

'Two children, yes. A girl and a ti-male. Six and three years of age. Rosan works as a mason . . .'

'And you, what do you do in life, Sister Rose? You walk through the valley of the shadow of death in Babylon, the very place in which sin thrives,' Sister Beloved exclaimed, letting her smile fall. 'Meditate on these verses of Psalms, Sister Rose: 'Who shall ascend into the hill of the Lord? And who shall stand in his holy place? He that hath clean hands and a pure heart, who hath not lifted up his soul unto vanity, nor sworn deceitfully.' You are far from the path that leads to the mountain, Sister. But take heart. The Lord Jah is your shepherd.'

'I pray, Edith, I pray every day . . . ,' Rosette protested.

'What do you pray for, Sister? A concrete cabin, a new refrigerator, a color TV, a four-burner gas stove, silk dresses, and stylish shoes. You pray and you eat pig meat and blood sausage, honey. You pray, Sister, and your thoughts are unclean, your soul is sick and your eyes are blind.'

That first day Rosette winced and wept at Sister Beloved's words. She was flogged, bludgeoned, and blackballed with hard words. But the mortification made her feel happy. She endured all the beating. Sister Beloved, who sometimes flashed a smile at her, spoke candidly and directly, because, she said, Truth is written in letters of fire and the Word is a sword that will pierce an impure heart.

'Not everyone that saith, Lord, Lord, shall enter into the kingdom of heaven, Sister Rose. Only those who believe in the power of the Trinity – the Father, the Son, and the Holy Ghost – will be asked to the Lord's table.

'Hope is for this world, Paradise for this earth, and you have soiled the earth. For behold, the day comes, burning like an oven, when all arrogant and all evildoers will be stubble; the day that comes shall burn them up, says the Lord of the hosts, so that it will leave them neither root nor branch.

'Sister Rose, I need nothing but the love of Jah, no pretty dresses or new shoes or handbags or golden chokers, pendants, or pearls.

'The wolves have clothed themselves in sheepskins and penetrated the sheepfold to sully it.'

'And why the weed?' Rose asked.

'Sister Rose, God said, 'Let the earth put forth vegetation, plants yielding seed. And God saw that it was good.' And you, my little impure rosette, do you wish to tell him that Ganja isn't good? Know that it brings Wisdom, Reasoning, and the Patience to await the realization of the prophecy of the Great Return, as the Lord promised our ancestor Abraham. The smoke is not good, but Ganja tea heals the soul . . .'

Words mingled with biblical parables in that way until the church in Ravine-Guinée struck noon. Sister Beloved gathered her hair up under her cap and laid the child, who had fallen asleep on her shoulder, down in the grass. She looked up at the sky as if something would surely fall from it, and Brother Delroy came with a calabash of fine ash. Sister Beloved rubbed her hands with it, thanking Jah; Rosette imitated her. Another brother brought some mats and bamboo serving trays upon which two coconut shells filled with water and two calabashes danced, half full of mashed breadfruit and avocado seasoned with coconut oil. Rosette ate with her fingers, like Edith and Sister Zauditu, who had joined them. The pure, vegetal Ital food lacked salt, and the slightly rancid coconut oil made her a little nauseous, but Rosette felt as if she were tasting the very substance of happiness; she felt privileged.

In the afternoon she bathed naked in a little pool of the river, far from the eyes of the men in the tribe. With infinite patience, Beloved continued the purification of her mind, which had been cluttered with the refuse of Babylon, scrubbed her with a mixture of leaves – wild sweetsop and witch-grass stalks – and then held her in her arms like a mother. Beloved's raw bones were a pitiful sight, her flaccid breasts hung down pathetically on her stomach, but she incarnated nevertheless the path to hope, and Rosette drank in all of the fine words to her heart's content.

The sun had disappeared behind Morne Caraïbe when she got back home. She could have stayed longer in that Eden, feeding on the precepts and truths of Sister Beloved. Sitting on a rock, the tips of her toes ruffling the water in the river.
Just sitting there without stirring up much wind. Listening. Just simply breathing. Feeling life all around. Praising the Lord for the fruits and the flowers, the water, the wind . . . Never had Rosette felt so blissful. Bliss and perfection, she repeated to herself on her way home. Time had slipped quickly by in that happy state. And she was coming back filled with joy, her flesh tingling, stirred with the same intensity that had torn and penetrated her the first time she and Rosan had allowed their bodies to intertwine.

After crossing the bridge, she began to run. She ran to get back to her narrow little life, but she was full of dreams. Yes, the day would come when the accursement would end – four hundred years! Yes, the black people would come out of this battle victorious. She ran down the tracks of Savane barefoot, to feel the earth that bore her – the black earth that the Lord had used as clay to shape his creatures – under her feet. She ran, raising her knees up high, because life was reggae, a long forced march, a road to Calvary. She ran, light with liberating knowledge. And the darkness in which Savane was already cloaked no longer frightened her. She was a descendant of Abraham. Everything was written in the Old Testament. Sister Beloved truly 'knew.' She took the Bible, Genesis, chapter 15, verses 13–16 . . . 'And he said unto Abram, Know of a surety that thy seed shall be a stranger in a land that is not theirs, and shall serve them; and they shall afflict them four hundred years . . . But in the fourth generation they shall come hither again . . .' Rose was no longer blind. She saw through the shadows of Savane. She was no longer . . .

.   .   .   .

Blind! Rosette repeated to herself as she stepped down from the bus. All through the visit Rosan had avoided looking at her, bowing his head and keeping his hands clasped between his knees. He had wordlessly confessed his crime. At first she'd felt like taking him in her arms, consoling him, like in the old days, and then getting him out of jail. Thank God the wire grate had prevented her. Her eyes remained dry, but tears started flowing inside of her. Blind! No, she'd seen nothing, heard nothing. No, she hadn't noticed. Rosan didn't get up in the night. Maybe when she was sleeping, maybe . . . She'd run Angela, her angel, out of the house because of the man to whom she'd given her love and all the colors of her dreams. Blind!

The evening that she left Beloved and raced across Savane, all lit up with the light of the living Jah, Rosette found no one at her door. Rosan wasn't home yet, and the children had knocked at the door of friend Eliette, who'd given them a snack – bread and guava jelly. Rosette sent Angela to Marga's to pick up two turkey wings, a half pound of corn flour, and a can of Nestle's milk. When he got home, Rosan ate heartily, talked to her a little in a disjointed way, and then started teasing and tickling Angela. Rosette wasn't at all hungry. She listened to him distractedly, telling herself that it was so simple to escape the pattern that made life into servitude, brought new trials every day. You simply had to cross the bridge and enter the inherited paradise. That night, haunted by the members of the tribe, she had a hard time going to sleep.

The very next day Rosette went back across Nèfles Bridge. A storm warning had been issued, but the tempest had died out in the middle of the Atlantic. She raised her eyes to heaven and thanked Jah. That day Moses and Eddy – two boys from Savane who were also thirsting after dreams – came across the bridge. They had an arrogant way of holding themselves, but you could tell that they were nothing but lumps of clay ready to be molded, minds that could be easily carried away with a cortège of noble sentiments. They lived in Quartier- Mélo, but they'd come to stay, to find their homeland, rediscover their roots going all the way back to the beginnings of time.

Sister Beloved taught them the history of Haile Selassie I, two hundred and twenty-fifth descendant of King Solomon and the Queen of Sheba – Ras Tafari, Negus, King of Kings, Lord of Lords, Victorious Lion of the Tribe of Judah, Chosen by God, Emperor of Ethiopia, emancipator of the black people . . . She read them the page of the Apocalypse that says: 'Weep not: behold, the Lion of the tribe of Juda, the Root of David, hath prevailed to open the book, and to loose the seven seals thereof . . . And I saw the beast, and the kings of the earth, and their armies, gathered together to make war against him that sat on the horse, and against his army.'

Sister Rose ate her koui-calabash of pure, vegetal Ital food, drank some coconut water, rested her body, and sang Jamma songs, passed down from African ancestors, along with the brothers and the sisters. Later Beloved told her of her travels since she'd left Des-Ramiers: France, England, London, her life in the shadow of the white people. And then Africa – the Motherland, the Cradle of Humanity, with Brother Delroy who had saved her from the fires of Babylon – Jamaica, and encounters with the brothers of the West Kingston ghettos, Trench Town, and Denham Town. Her pilgrimage in the footsteps of the prophet Marcus Garvey. Her friendship with Sister Small Axe who was now praying – for long years to come – in a jail in Jamaica because she killed a cop on Nyahbinghi day in 1975. She and Delroy had lived for a while with a brother in Savannah la Mar. And then Beloved had received the Call. Jah revealed to her that she would be the shepherdess who would bring his dispersed tribe back after four hundred years of slavery. But first, she had to go back to Guadeloupe, to a place called Savane, where she should stay for twelve moons – the time to reunite the twelve tribes of Israel. Only then should she ascend the mountain for purification before the Great Return.

Rosette felt the weight of people's eyes following her steps as she crossed the town of Ravine-Guinée. The bus didn't go any farther, and she had to walk a good mile and a half before the first roofs of Savane appeared. Everyone knew what had happened at her place. Maybe they knew about it before she did. Maybe Angela had started walking differently, surely her face and her eyes were no longer those of a virgin. Tonight Rosan would spend the night in jail again. She wouldn't have the strength to go back there. Didn't want to see him again after what he'd done . . .

Would she throw him out if they ever set him free?

Would she remain under the same roof?

Sleep in the same bed?

She'd go away, hole herself up in Des-Ramiers far from people's prying eyes.

She'd hide her shame in her mama Gilda's cabin.

No, she'd heard nothing. And, no, her daughter had never told her anything either.

When Rosan built Angela's room single-handedly and then bought that big bed at Seoud's, even before windows were set in the walls, Rosette had chalked it up to man-foolishness. Such a big bed for a child of ten . . .

Had it been going on since Angela was ten? Rosette shuddered. Good Lord, no!

Recently?

When?

Angela wouldn't have waited so long before talking. Even she, Rosette, would have had time to see and realize certain things were going on under her roof. Dirty gestures. Wouldn't have been able look her angel in the face, straight in the eye. She'd have been like Rosan, keeping her head down and her hands clasped between her knees.

Angela hadn't gone very far Sunday evening. Rosette heard friend Eliette's door squeak. She saw the two shadows slip into the cabin. No, Lord, she hadn't wanted to beat her or kick her out either. But she just couldn't help it; all her fine resolutions had abandoned her. No, Lord, she wouldn't have killed her just to keep from hearing the truth. It was all the images that came to mind that she'd wanted to break-crush-smash. She didn't want to hurt her child, just silence the voice of her mama Gilda, who'd told her that Rosan was no good, that he was a sly fellar with a venomous heart and vile thoughts. She didn't want to thrash her angel, just break the wave of words that were going to splash on her and dirty her, she who always stood apart from the folks in Savane, she who preferred the company of Rastas to that of all the nations in Ti-Ghetto.

How many times had she gone across the bridge to see the tribe of Israel? How many times had Sister Beloved scrubbed her back in the river? How many times had she accepted the pure, vegetal Ital meal seasoned with that rancid coconut oil that gave her stomach cramps and caused those serious upheavals that she believed were purifying? And just when had Rosette gradually begun to go there less often? Maybe when the mirage of the alleged wisdom suddenly led to a vast emptiness, and she saw that Edith was as lost as she was, hiding behind the prophetic sermons of the grand shepherdess. A poor forlorn Sister Beloved, beyond the wise I-know-all smile and the mouthful of recited psalms that barely masked vast zones of ignorance. Sobered, suddenly seeing the shoddy imitation of paradise that was thrown up each day on the other side of the bridge, Rosette gradually shied away, believing she'd been put under a spell, bewitched by the long string of citations from the Gospel, the rancid coconut oil, and the infusions of ganja tea.

She only crossed the bridge on rare occasions, didn't allow herself to be rubbed in the river, refused the Ital food, and disagreed with every word that came from the mouth of Edith, whom she no longer called Sister Beloved. The day she found the said sister fleeing before Brother Delroy's hand, the mass of dreadlocks bobbing on her back, Rosette understood that the paradise they had presumably inherited was nowhere near Savane. As if they were used to that sort of outburst, none of the other Rastas tried to come between the man and the woman. Sister Judith and Ras Gong were having a few words, sitting up on a rock and drinking Ital tea. The children were eating with their mouths stuck right down in the coconut shells, as Sister Zauditu looked on, glassy-eyed.

'Though I walk through the valley of the shadow of death, I will fear no evil, for thou art with me . . .' shouted Edith.

'Jah!' screamed Delroy, cracking a whip at his companion's back.

'O Jah!' repeated Ras Gong and Judith.

Bob's death had been announced on the radio two days after that. I listened to his albums all day long. The next afternoon Edith was on my veranda. She was smiling just like she used to in her heyday. She wanted me to come with them into the mountains for the period of purification, before carrying out the prophecy of the Great Return to the Motherland.

'Jah came to see me, far from the eyes of the sun, Sister Rose. He said, 'Pope Bob is dead and been laid out for viewing. The twelve tribes of Israel will soon be ready for the Return Journey. The house of the Lord will open its doors to a chosen few. Gather the pure souls together, Beloved! Gather together and unite the brothers and sisters of the Great Tribulation of slavery!' I don't want to leave you in Babylon, Sister Rose. It's time for you to determine your destiny. Many have already chosen the path. Brothers Eddy and Moses and so many others have joined us. The tribe is waiting for you, Sister Rose . . .'

Again I felt the spell of her words like a balm for both my body and soul, holding the promise of the familiar dream. I remembered the way she had of rubbing my back. I saw Sister Judith bathing the children, preparing the mush of breadfruit, Brother Delroy offering the purifying ashes. One-two Jamma songs came to my mind, and even one of those old-time sunbeams that used to bounce so gaily off the tribe's bamboo huts, suddenly came shining down upon me. But other memories brought home the whole mockery of Beloved's paradise: the hungry children, the rancid oil, the garden of the early days – abandoned, the laziness of Ras Gong, the useless words, the contempt of Delroy, the madness of Zauditu, who saw life only through ganja tea . . .

Beloved continued, 'Don't let the Beast blind you, Sister Rose. What you have seen with your eyes is merely an artifice of old Satan. You must see through your heart, let it speak, and you will assuredly go to heaven where our Father awaits you.' She smiled.

For a moment I was afraid that she was speaking the truth and that my blindness would prevent me from going beyond the merely visible, to the very place where the Lord gathers the faithful. I was grieving Bob's death, and I was tempted to go up into the mountains and be amongst the chosen few. But I thought of Rosan and my two children, and a pain stabbed at my heart. Angela was eight years old that year, she looked at me as if she felt I might go away, leave her alone, disappear and never come back.

So I said, 'No, Edith, my thoughts alone go with you. I pray God to stay at your side.'

Beloved was still smiling, but her lips were trembling. She answered, 'Jah is always at our side, we have been anointed, Sister. He doesn't await your prayer before coming to guide us. Is that what you think, Rosette? You dwell in the Kingdom of Darkness. You're nothing but a little rosette pinned to the side of Babylon. Be careful not to come apart at the first wind that blows. For the wrath of the Lord is great for the half-hearted, the blind, the cowardly, and the fools that accumulate material wealth and are more tied to human beings then to their Master.'

I pleaded with my eyes for her not to give in to anger.

She looked intently at Angela, ran her hand through the girl's hair, and whispered to her, 'Your mama hasn't seen the length of the rope tying her to this world yet . . . Poor, poor little Rosette! . . . Rosanna the Highest in Heaven!'

The tribe took some young folks from Ravine-Guinée who had quickly converted to the dream of the Great Return. Sister Beloved had cleansed their souls, recited the Psalms, and showed them the paths to truth that they'd found nowhere else along the tracks of Savane. Droves had arrived after Rosette, Eddy, and Moses. They never turned back. Without saying goodbye to their families, they crossed Nèfles Bridge and ascended the mountain, singing the Jamma songs. They lost their way in the dark woods of Morne Caraïbe.

Only Ras Eddy and Ras Moses survived the purification of the Great Return. They came back broken, emaciated, ragged, nearly jumping out of their skins when anyone asked what had become of the tribe. They were given water, Sultana biscuits, tiny portions of mashed guava. Their own mamas didn't recognize the young men. Their eyes darted about like those of hunted animals. They told the story hurriedly. And then suddenly fell silent. Gruff-voiced, Eddy spoke of sheer hell up there in the mountains. He gobbled up biscuits voraciously, kissing the hands of his saviors. The bones jutted out on his torso, and his face, lengthened by a sagging beard, made him look like the black Christ in a primitive Haitian painting that hung in the parish house. At first Moses merely repeated the words of Ras Eddy, raising his eyes to the mountain every now and again. But when he started talking for himself, his revelations shook all of Savane, and a terrible gloom fell over the land that spread all the way out to Ravine-Guinée. No, people could hardly believe they'd lived so close to a world so different from their own without ever realizing that something was amiss, without ever imagining that events would unfold so rapidly, so violently and take on such importance in the minds of Savane's children. Eddy also spoke of the death of a nation, and everyone felt vulnerable, fragile, and miserable as they listened to him, as if life really could suddenly turn upside down, as if it could all happen to them at any time.

First the tribe ate the leaves of tall trees, the unfamiliar seeds that secreted bitter and poisonous milk, and then the fuzzy green wild buds. One after the other, Brother Delroy experimented with bark, moss, bitter roots. He believed he was on the verge of discovering the tree of knowledge and its fruit. He tasted everything hungrily, going into ecstasies over ordinary twigs, and encouraged the others to do likewise. With his pole, Ras Gong brought down the nests of bats and turtledoves, boasting he would bring back eggs. They were all still thrilling with excitement because they were the appointed pilgrims, legitimized by the Lord Jah. They were free. And, far from the laws of Babylon, they walked in the footsteps of Abraham along the fertile paths of the Bible. They were the history of the world and the future of the people of Jah.

Even when they fell ill with terrible fits of colic, the brothers and sisters never ceased giving thanks to Jah and never lost faith. So they fed on fervent prayers. Eyes gleaming, ablaze with fever, Sister Zauditu was the first to die, exhausted. Beloved gave a long sermon, declaring that Jah had not chosen this sister for the Return Journey and that – may she rest in peace – God's hand was swift to punish the impure.

Then Beloved announced that Jah had revealed the path to her. To return to the state of original purity, they – the Lord's anointed, the earth-colored brothers and sisters – must eat the earth itself, the earth whence they came. They all ate earth, for seven days, all of them – Ras, princes, brothers, and sisters – fed on the earth, wearing their teeth down on the rocks of Creation.

On the seventh day a deluge of rain beat down upon the mountain. The river swelled and carried off Sister Judy and five little Ras first. Eyes lost in a vision of Apocalypse, Eddy told of how he saw ancient trees fall one after the other upon the Chosen Tribe. He heard someone shouting and moaning. He fled before iron horsemen mounted on black steeds that leapt from the entrails of the earth. Tall rocks pursued him, threatening certain death. Red men's arrows transpierced his body. Beloved threw off her dress, uncovered the skin stretched taut over her bones. Through the branches of the trees, she looked up at the tortured sky filled with dark gray clouds in perdition. And then, with her hands on her hips, she shouted defiantly:

'Jah! The woman was naked and was not ashamed. Jah, I have returned to the Garden of Eden! Take me! Take me, just once! For the day of baptism has arrived.'

And then she began singing one of Prince Jazzbo's tunes softly:

For now is the time that black people should look into
themselves and see that their backs are against the wall
That is what the man Marcus Garvey ah prophesies, you know.
Step forward, youth, and let I tell you the truth
Step forward, youth, for the Babylon ah brute
Ah say they take an oath upon their mother
And they take a gun to use upon their son
Say it dread in a Jamdown . . .

According to Eddy, Beloved didn't have time to finish her song. She was lifted from the earth and flung into a pool of furious waters. As he and Moses were being swept away in the current, he heard her cry out the name of Sister Small Axe twice.

An investigation was conducted. The white gendarmes from Ravine-Guinée traipsed around up in the mountains for seven days, being dragged along after dogs trained to sniff out life or death. They say that they interrogated every tree, sounded out the branches and foliage, catalogued the rare birds and long-armed *ouassou*-crawdads. At night the deep barking of the animals drew out unbearably, echoing around in the mountains, rolling down the slopes, and knocking up against the sheet-metal cabins that brooded in silence. Just like the folks in Savane, the mountains had seen nothing, heard nothing, only the rain up in the sky. So then the gendarmes came down to search the families of the survivors – Princes Eddy and Moses – the two who now spent their days lying on the benches in front of the church, maybe as a means of thanking Jah for having spared them, maybe because they were haunted by the

memory of Beloved.

When she opened the door to her cabin, Rosette told herself she should have followed Edith into the mountains. It would all be over with now. No funeral oration or coffin or death notice, she would simply have put an abrupt end to her life on earth, as Beloved did. She wouldn't have had time to see Rosan behind bars. She wouldn't have run Angela off. She would be a free, liberated woman today. For sure, by this time God would have already let her taste the apples and pears from the vast garden where she would have never been forced to imagine Rosan pulling down Angela's panties.

VI

Bob's voice drifted over from the other side of the yard, singing 'No woman no cry.' Awakening to the reggae incantation, Angela immediately pulled the sheet embroidered with Eliette's initials up over her head. She'd slept in the little room that had gradually faded along with the hope of a desired child. The room that Eliette had never seen occupied, except during the time she laid her body down there to rest in the evenings because Hector was in such pain, was suffering so, that he couldn't stand her by his side in the double bed.

Angela had slept. She hadn't lain there waiting for the first paling of the sky to peep through the holes in the old scrap of sheet metal replacing the missing door. No, she hadn't spent the night lying in wait for the shadow that oppressed her, battling her nightmares.

The night before friend Eliette had kissed her on the forehead and, after excusing herself, sat the girl down on a varnished wood chair. While Eliette was making up the bed with sheets taken from a tall, intricately carved wardrobe, Angela was overcome with the feeling that she was finally in a truly safe haven. Though the noises from outside came in without asking, Eliette's cabin still seemed invulnerable. On every piece of massive, broad furniture – like so many bodyguards – lay sparkling white, starched doilies. Thick layers of crocheted coverlets fluffed on the beds. Heavy curtains, which contrasted awkwardly with the frail wood cabin, barred every window. Tall, imposing plants with polished leaves seemed to conceal beasts waiting to pounce upon intruders. Yes, everything here-there made it evident that the place was inviolable. Then, as she stared at a copper-and-wood ceiling fixture whose electric light shone through plastic candles, Angela made a wish for each candle. She asked for truth to triumph, for justice, for prison, for the love of her mama, and for Rita's innocence to be preserved.

On Sunday night, when Rosette had come into her room, Angela thought for a moment that the shadow was back. But it was only her mama, who hadn't spoken to her since Saturday. Rosette didn't turn on the light. Shook her. Wanted Angela to follow her into the kitchen. Angela curled up under the sheet. Rosette pinched her. Started cudgeling the girl with her fists, biting her, without saying a word, to avoid awakening Rita who was sleeping nearby in her little bed. Understanding perfectly well that Rosette was simply letting out the pain that was too much for her heart to bear, Angela took all the blows. 'Pity! Pardon! I didn't lie!' That is all she could say to keep from hurting her mama even more. But Rosette didn't want to hear the truth. Pulled the belt out of the jeans draped over the foot of her angel's bed. Started lashing her, just to make her keep quiet. Just to blot out the visions that filled the room. And then Angela had bolted from the blows; Rosette wasn't her mama anymore. Even she, Angela, felt excluded from the world, just like those lost young folks that slept their lives away in front of the church in Ravine-Guinée. Good Lord, she had caused something as devastating as a cyclone to appear in her mother's skies. She should have kept quiet, or else run away, abandoning Rita. No . . .

.   .   .   .

'I didn't lie, I didn't lie!' Angela repeated, trying to catch Eliette's eye.

'Put on this nightgown. Mademoiselle Meredith gave it to me when I wasn't even twenty-five . . . My body hasn't changed in all this time. Nowadays you don't find that quality of cotton no more. Take it!' Eliette said, gently nudging the little cat that was meowing against her legs away with her foot.

'I didn't lie . . . It's true. He wanted Rita too,' whispered Angela as she undressed. Her black skin, struck by the light of the candles, was covered with belt marks. On her legs, skinned in two places, dried blood left dark flaky streaks. Her right eyelid was swollen but, praise the Lord, the eye was not damaged. Eliette silently took inventory of the wounds as she passed a damp washcloth over Angela's pain-filled body. The last time her mama had beaten her, because of a Rasta woman, was long before Rita's birth . . .

Sister Beloved wore a long, old, faded-out dress. Her feet, stuck into mended plastic shoes threw out muddy toes with black, clawlike nails. An illuminated smile, a piercing gaze, and a rainbow-colored cap over extraordinarily thick hair gave her an aura of magnificent grace and beauty. Angela was eight years old; it was on a day in the month of May. The day before, when Rosette had heard the radio announce the death of Bob Marley, she hadn't even blinked. But the day after, as soon as Rosan left for the construction site, she sat down and played his reggae records over and over again, especially 'No woman no cry . . .' and 'Zion Train,' which she'd just secretly bought. She didn't fix lunch that day. Robert and Angela ate bananas, eggs, and bread. When the Rasta woman showed up in the afternoon, Rosette was giving Angela a dictation of her own invention that was as long as a fairy tale. She was still in the habit of expounding upon her dreams. And Angela wrote docilely, on loose pages that her mama later put away in the wardrobe, without ever re-reading them.

Once there was a magical and magnificent garden on the other side of the bridge. Folks who lived there said it was paradise. Nowhere in the world were more beautiful colors to be found. Each and every morning the trees gave thanks to the skies. The birds sang in English, and the men, women, and children cultivated the land. But their work did not resemble slavery, because the rain and the sun loved Lady Dreams.

Lady Dreams wasn't the same as she is now, just a word in the mouth with no shape or form. She had powerful wings, a head full of hope, and a pure heart. She gave to all according to their needs and lived in a little cabin smack-dab in the middle of a savanna where folks worked a field bearing fruit that was the seven colors of the rainbow. Each piece of fruit was precious to Lady Dreams, and she ate them every morning to maintain her marvelously colored wings, her head full of hope, and her pure heart. One day, out of spite, Suffering, who was napping not far away in a culvert in town, went to see the mountain and asked for just one small favor . . . When the clouds carrying water to God passed overhead, she could hold one back for Lady Dreams, snag it so it would sprinkle water on her fields, which were so tired of seeing black folks breaking their backs lugging buckets of water from the river. The mountain was a kindly woman who enjoyed being of service to others, but she saw no further than the end of her nose due to the tall woods blocking her view.

Alas, the cloud was pierced; the rain poured down so heavily that all the colors in the fields of Lady Dreams were washed away. The poor lady died of hunger and went to heaven. But ever since that day, when Lady Dreams ceased ruling the earth, folks have been blind. And Suffering has spread far and wide in the world. Rain has turned to tears and Sun to a celestial fire.

Sister Beloved called several times before Rosette looked out the window. There were always people calling outdoors, and since she didn't neighbor with anyone but friend Eliette, Rosette didn't notice the voice mixed in with the all the others that drifted up from the road. When she heard, 'Sister Rose! Sister Rose!' her face changed. She closed her eyes, took the fairy tale from Angela's hands and, as usual, walked over and put it away in the wardrobe.

Standing tall and straight on the veranda, Edith-Beloved had the same smile as Mademoiselle Estelle, who taught Sunday school in Ravine-Guinée. It was the first and the last time that Angela would see Sister Beloved. Despite her resemblance to Mademoiselle Estelle, Beloved didn't appear to be an ordinary person to her. So, without understanding why, Angela extended two fingers to touch the hem of Beloved's ugly dress as she conversed with her mama. The Rasta woman jumped back as if Angela had burnt her. She remained quiet for a moment, without smiling. Then she recited a sort of parable to her, a story about a cord and a little rosette . . .

That evening, when Rosan came home, Angela ran to his arms so that he'd pick her up and swing her around in the air until she grew dizzy, limp, and hiccupped with laughter. He kissed her on the ears, nose, mouth, and then on her cheeks. He lifted her blouse, closed his eyes, and ran his rough hand over her titties to see if the seeds had grown. It was a game, one they'd always played. Everyone laughed, even Rosette. Angela didn't have titties yet, and he swore that he'd been taught that titties sprung up overnight, and he wanted to make sure. He asked Angela how her day had gone. Drunk with laughter, Angela forgot her promise not to say anything about the Rasta woman. And she began to relate that afternoon's visit, stammering more and more as she saw Rosette's smile fade. Rosan got angry, went off to the bedroom, and didn't speak to them for several days. The next morning, as soon and he'd left the cabin, Rosette called Angela.

'How old are you, Angela?'

'Eight years old, Mama.'

'Why is it you refuse to listen to me when I talk to you? Why'd you have to go and tell your papa about the lady that came? You don't know that he don't want to see them people?'

'I forgot . . .'

'You know how they call people like you, Angela?'

'No, Mama.'

'Folks that don't keep their word are called Judas. Did you see how your papa got vexed? It hurt him. And it's your fault. And it hurt me too. Now go and get the belt so you can learn to keep your mouth shut when nobody asking you nothing.'

Angela recalls that beating because there had never been another until last night. No, Rosette wasn't a bad mama. She didn't enjoy beating her children. On the contrary, she was always looking to console them. To make up stories that lent a little color to their lives. But when her heart was packed full of grief, she felt somehow defenseless. The day after that first beating, she called Angela again and asked her forgiveness. So many things had made her unhappy in such a short a time . . . the death of Bob Marley, Edith-Beloved gone into the mountains to die too. One thing was certain, the prophesy of the Great Return would never come true. And Rosan, who never wanted to listen to a reggae tune . . . Rosette begged Angela not to hold it against her.

'We only got one mama, one papa in life. I don't even know if my papa is dead or alive. A stranger. I know they called him the King of Kings, he was such a handsome black Negro. He rode a white horse,

just like the negus of Ethiopia who's pictured in that little image Beloved gave me. Look at me; I'm no Rasta like she is . . .

Rosette smoothed down her straightened hair, showed her clean
dress, her feet with trimmed toenails. No, Rosette was no Rasta
dread, but that music went straight to her blood and stirred her to
the very quick, gave her hope.

That was the day Angela learned how to keep her mouth shut,
remain silent to keep from hurting her mama, her papa. So they
wouldn't call her Judas anymore.

It was morning. Angela had slept. Woke up all clean in the nightgown Eliette wore when she was twenty-five . . . A smile of gratitude
flashed across her face when she saw the old woman – head thrown
backward – asleep in an armchair beside her.

'No woman no cry . . .'

When Angela tried to sit up in bed, a pain in her elbow wrenched
a cry from her. Eliette opened her eyes, jumped up, agile as a young
girl.

'There, there, it'll be all right! I'll rub it in a little while. But tell
me, what'll you have with breakfast, coffee or milk? Are you hungry,
child? What time is it? My goodness, eight o'clock! The bread truck's
already gone by. But I got some bread from yesterday, I'll warm it up.'

Angela didn't feel hungry. All she wanted was to remain lying
there between the sheets . . . 'Just a little water, please.' Eliette said
no, that just wasn't possible, she had to eat to get her strength back.
She went straight to the kitchen, and soon a clatter of dishes and
pots and pans drifted from that direction.

Sounds from outside filled the cabin. Angela slipped further
down under the sheets and closed her eyes to lose herself in the
smell of lavender they emitted. The shrill bleating of mopeds rose

and fell amidst the cries and the pounding of hammers, the strum of reggae chords from a guitar, a husky voice singing, 'You must have done something you don't want somebody to know about . . .' In the distance, roosters sang out too, and dogs tied fast behind the cabins yapped with genuine rage at children who threw stones at the half tumbled-down shack, still overgrown with wild christophine vines whose fruit no one dared pick. People said it wasn't natural, and whoever ate it would be cursed with the same malediction as the older folks in Savane. Some women were chattering near Marga's, who, like every other morning, was dragging her benches out in front of the heavy doors to her shop. A broom was chasing a cat that was squawking bloody murder. Outside, Savane seethed dangerously.

When Eliette set the tray down on the night stand, one static-filled radio began blaring out death notices as if to drown out still another set resounding with *tambour-kas* and Eugene Mona's flute . . . The funeral procession will begin at Bel-Air . . . Lago ka monté o Sénat . . . Cars will be provided at Bel-Air . . . La rivyé pa ni bèl pawol . . . Attila Ka monté o Sénat . . .

'Eat, child! Hot chocolate, bread, and butter. Eat just to humor friend Eliette who never had no child to coddle. Eat to keep from falling sick.'

Angela would have liked to kiss Eliette, thank her for everything she was doing, but she didn't move. Everything inside of her was so churned up that her eyes started leaking a bit of water, clear words that spoke her despair and trickled down drop by drop to dampen the lace on her nightgown.

'I didn't lie,' she began.

But Eliette stopped her, telling her to eat so she'd get her strength back, so she'd fill out and grow taller . . . Eliette didn't want to hear the truth she held. She just wanted Angela to stuff her mouth and bury the words that were coming up like vomit, put bread and butter and hot chocolate on all the wounds, on Angela's memory that kept hashing over the dread of those nights when her papa Rosan became a stranger, coveting Rita already.

'Eat!' Eliette repeated.

So Angela dunked the bread into the bowl of hot chocolate.

It was after Rita's birth that the idea of an extra room began to take shape. Rita came the year after Bob Marley's death. No one was expecting her. Angela, who had just turned nine, heard her mama tell Aunt Fanotte that Rita had been an accident. In the beginning Rosette wanted to call her Beloved, but Rosan refused, insisting that his daughter was neither a Dominican nor a Jamaican. So Rosette thought of Rita, Bob's widow. When Rosan wasn't home, she called her baby Bien-aimée or, sometimes, Beloved.

Nights, Rosette put Rita down in the bed between her and Rosan till the child was one. It was no solution, but money was always too scarce to start any projects. With Angela in her cozy corner under the window, there was room for the four of them in the room. Robert, who was already seven, slept between the buffet and the dining room table on a foam rubber mattress that Rosette rolled up and stuck behind the wardrobe in the morning.

When the Cyclone of 1981 blew down the three coconut trees and the breadfruit tree that grew in the courtyard, it made Rosan's job easier; a space had been cleared for Angela's new bedroom. He started mixing the mortar and fitting the cinder blocks hurriedly, as if he suddenly felt the house was cramped and urgently needed enlarging. It was all he ever talked about with the children: the new room, the new bed that they'd put in there . . .

If Rosette had been asked her opinion, how she felt about it, they wouldn't have started or built anything new in Savane. For a long time she continued to evoke Des-Ramiers, where she said life hadn't degenerated. She spoke of it with longing, and sometimes tears welled in her eyes. Late at night, lying by Rosan's side, she tried to discuss the matter. She talked to him of the old days, the days of romantic fairy tales, but he rebuffed her. She tried to soften him up, bring him around to her way of thinking, whispering that Savane was a place filled with accursement. Had he forgotten all the crimes committed here-there? But no matter what she said or did, Rosan always answered that he hadn't lost anything in Des-Ramiers. Then he fell silent. Rosette kept talking for a little while, but her words became frayed, or else she'd watch as they went smashing up against Rosan's muscular back one after the other.

The new room didn't even have its tin roof yet when Rosan took to sitting down excitedly smack in its center, with Angela or Rita on his knees. Contemplating the walls he had built, planning already – as soon as he'd finished this room, he'd add on another one so that Robert would also have a room, a wardrobe, and a bed to himself. It hadn't been all that difficult after all. The plastering and painting could come later; in the meantime Angela could move in. They'd find two pieces of sheet metal to pull up in the evening in place of the missing door and window.

Rita left her parents' bed and replaced Angela in the cozy corner under the window. Then – five years later – when Rosette saw neither door nor window appear and had grown used to pulling up the pieces of sheet metal every evening, she gave up and dragged the cozy corner into the unfinished room herself.

Even when the radio warned of high winds, Rosan seemed in no hurry to close up the room. He merely nailed boards in an X across the openings. Rosette still mentioned buying a door and a window; he answered that money was short and that if she found a way of bringing in a few bucks, to please let him know about it. Sometimes he'd remain silent for a whole day before answering a question she'd asked him in the morning. Picking his teeth with a matchstick, he'd mention to her the old happiness at the tips of your lips. Send her off to shake one of those silver pillars shoring up all of her tales to see if riches would come tumbling from it. So then Rosette would keep quiet; she continued to take down and put up the sheet metal every morning, every evening. Rosan was certainly no chatterbox, but he never talked for very long at all. His words were curt, his laughter brief, and his silences so profound that the poor woman even stopped trying to find the Rosan of her youth in the man who now shared her life. At times – very rare times – his eyes lit up with interest, and Rosette imagined she could still dazzle him. Alas, the fairy tales had lost all of their power. Rosan spent his time scolding her about money, saying that she was wasteful. When he got angry with her, he didn't shout. He simply said, 'No one ever drew blood from a stone. And you think money grows by the roadside! You been dreaming long enough, girl . . .'

He laughed with his children all right, he loved tossing them up into the air and catching them in his arms, carrying, caressing, and tucking them into bed. Angela was his favorite. When he came home in the evening, he always exclaimed: 'Sweet Jesus, now there's my little Angel, my joy, my dreams!' and Angela would come running to him. Rosette sensed that Rosan had changed toward her, but she loved to see him with the children. She firmly believed it was because of the rough life in these parts. In truth, the only thing she could really complain about were the relatively hard words, the silence that he allowed to come between them, and his hatred of Rastas who, according to him, smoked poisonous herbs, were immoral, lazy, and stole from their neighbors with the blessing of their black Jah. Rosette wasn't all that foolish, she knew quite well how lucky she was: all the other men around beat their wives, ran after other women, and shamelessly got them in the family way. And friend Eliette, all long repeating that Rosan was the only well-mannered black man she'd run into since her dearly departed Renélien.

So Rosette watched him laughing and sitting Angela on his knees, telling herself that she too must become a true woman because Rosan had become a real man. Men didn't seek consolation in dreams and stories of happiness at the tips of your lips. They built on solid foundations. And when she observed him – brow furrowed, lost in reflections – she thought that he'd matured quickly, whereas she'd remained a child who told lies, bought records in secret, and made up fairy tales in which life wasn't life but simply a fabrication built upon dreams. At times like that, she told the children, 'Don't grieve your papa. Got to love him with all your heart. He slaves at earning money and bringing home food. And everything in this cabin is thanks to his hard work.'

Before she was alone in her big bed, Rosan already enjoyed kissing Angela in her little cozy corner under the window in his room. While Rosette was finishing up the dishes, he ran his hands over the child's titties. Just for fun. To see if they'd sprung up come nightfall, like those flowers that only open after sunset. And then his fingers walked up and down on Angela's belly, galloped in a comical way, skirted her belly button, and went to paw gently around the small mound of her *coucoune*. Rosan put one finger to his lips and Angela stopped laughing, all of a sudden. She just breathed in very heavily through her mouth. While her papa's hand pierced her body, she was gripped with the fear that her own heart would open up like a wooden chest. She always wanted to stop, hold her father's fingers back or pull them away, but she didn't recognize him anymore. His whole face became foreign to her. Yes, he smiled, but with a doglike smile. His teeth seemed to grow longer. He stared at her wildly. His jaws stiffened with a pain she could not name. He seemed to be suddenly angry with her. So she began to caress his hand so that he would forgive her, would love her again, and turn back into her nice papa Rosan. As long as he heard the dishes clinking in the background, he said good night to Angela, letting his tongue go down the same forbidden paths his fingers had taken, licking, sucking his child's little body. The game of the old days had changed, just like one of those antique merry-go-rounds with rusty parts that, instead of tinkling along sweetly, resound with an infernal clanking and creaking.

Rosan came back every evening. Good night, my little angel, good night. Every evening. His rough finger hardened from cement. Every evening groping in her panties, searching, wounding, sucking. Eyes crazed, one finger on his lips, shsh! Heart racing. Fear. Dear God . . . Mama Rosette . . .

To find an excuse for him, Angela sometimes imagined that an evil spirit had taken possession of her papa and that he had no idea how the demon used his fleshly envelope to abuse her. Its face resembled her father's, but it was always in the darkness. The same voice, but he spoke so softly . . . 'Good night, my little angel! Say good night to Papa!' How could she know if it was really her papa? Her nice papa Rosan? In the daytime he didn't touch her titties anymore, not even for fun. He barely even looked at her, or else he shot glances at her as if she stood for some evil and powerful world.

All of these changes happened one right after the other. And then speeded up when she moved into the room with no door or window.

She was ten years old. She slept there alone in a double bed that he had bought at Seoud's. Alone . . . The first time he came to say good night to her in her room, he promised to come back later and show her a secret. In those days the seeds of Angela's titties were growing, and when Rosan ran his hand over the budding breasts, he was seized with a fit of trembling, and he started breathing harder. He pressed the seeds, made them roll between his fingers as if to soften them up, like brush cherries. When she complained, he apologized and swore it wasn't his fault, said he'd be careful, and then brought his lips immediately to her stomach.

The first evening, when he promised to come back to her new room, Angela thought her papa Rosan planned on explaining to her how to combat the demon while it was sleeping. She thought a good angel would give her at least one supreme prayer to drive the beast off to some distant place of no return and come to the rescue of her papa's soul that was locked in some dark garret room. At Sunday school Mademoiselle Estelle taught her that visible and invisible fiends and instruments of the devil could be felled with the glaive of a single prayer wielded by a faithful and vibrant voice. Angela also knew that evil spirits lived everywhere on earth and that they could easily take possession of anyone's body.

'Shsh! Don't say nothing to your mama. Ever . . . Don't betray our secret!'

That was all he'd said before he lay down on top of her. He was so heavy. His big body completely hard. He put one hand over her mouth. And then he kissed her on the neck. Trying to catch her breath, she saw his eyes, his quivering nostrils, his lips curled back, and fear fell upon her soul. No, it wasn't her papa Rosan, a demon, Lord Almighty, a demon . . . With all of the strength of her young faith, she recited, 'I believe in God,' but the beast did not whoosh away in a cloud of steam, did not explode into a puff of dust, did not leave the envelope of her papa Rosan and go back to Beelzebub's world of darkness.

When the beast tore her panties off, Angela wanted to call to her mama, but a voice called her Judas, so she kept the call locked in her throat. No it wasn't her papa. She closed her eyes to keep from seeing him. The devil had the power of taking on any form. She knew that. No, it wasn't her papa . . .

That night he didn't make his fingers walk over her belly. No, Lord, he shoved them between her thighs in such a brutal way that she lost her breath, only had the strength to weep silently. He didn't kiss her titties, didn't ask her forgiveness. Crazed, in search of some secret booty, he spread her legs as if to tear her apart. She let out a gasp that did not stop him. He smashed in her mouth. When she felt that he was jamming a rod into her little well-knit *coucoune*, she wanted to push him away, far from her belly that was splitting open. She wanted to cry out again, but she'd lost her voice. She wanted to struggle too, but the beast had already forced open the gate, staved it in, pillaged. Was already inside her. Deep in her entrails. Slithering through her belly. Slipping up into her throat. The beast was rooting around inside of her, burning. Yes, fire. There was a fire burning between her legs. Don't move, so you won't turn to ash. Fire! Bite your lips. Fire, Lord, fire everywhere! In her little ravaged *coucoune*, in her belly, in all of the veins in her body, all the way up to her head that she could feel was completely ablaze, like the savanna in dry season. She began to cry as he held her tighter, swelled within her, sought to push still further along the paths of her flesh, gripped her, groaned. Then she wept small tears of blood that one might have mistaken for ordinary, transparent salt tears. But it was really blood. Little tears of death, since she would surely die that night in her room. How could it be otherwise . . . Wordless weeping, so as not to hurt her papa, her mama Rosette. He was clutching the two buns of her buttocks, smashing her forcefully against him so that the beast could go in all the way up to the hilt, slice and rend her. She was filled with the long beast that she could neither vomit nor tear away from. She thought of Mademoiselle Estelle, who always said that young people today no longer sought God's promise, and so Christ left them to their fate. Little tears of blood and death. Wordless tears shed over that fire.

'I didn't lie!' repeated Angela that afternoon.

'I know,' answered Eliette, who was standing behind her combing her heavy mane of hair.

'I didn't lie, I just wanted to spare Rita . . .'

'Life can be pretty ugly, Angela. No one can even count the number of crimes and misfortunes that have already marked Savane. I myself saw my mama go mad here after the death of my stepfather Joab who believed he lived in paradise on earth. My poor mama, who talked about the Cyclone of 1928 every day of her life . . . I might well have died back then. A rafter fell on me, almost went right through me. My belly was ripped open according to what my mama said. She always called Cyclone the Passage of the Beast, as if a beast had actually passed over me.'

'The police didn't want to believe me either. It's when I told them I'd write the district attorney that they invited me to sit down in an office. It was already late. Mama had just sent me out for a can of corn. I was on my way. I hadn't decided nothing yet when I started out for Ravine-Guinée. But as I made my way, I kept telling myself it weren't no papa I had, just a demon, a beast hungering after Rita's flesh, Rita's little seven-year-old body. He promised me not to touch her. And I promised him not to say nothing to anyone. Ever . . .'

'He had a nice face, your papa did. He never gave himself away. That's when you see how powerful evil is on this earth. Do you pray God, Angela? You know, it was prayer that saved me from despair when I realized I couldn't have children. I don't know if it's because of the rafter that went through me on the day of the cyclone . . . Or because I never knew a man before I was thirty-five. When I met Renélien, my first husband, it was already too late. You never met him, but I listened to the advice of a certain Demoiselle Meredith, a schoolteacher, who taught me good French, good manners, and the art of conversation. I went to see her, and she told me not to worry about that, to simply pray to God that I would receive according to my needs . . . I hoped. For a long time . . .'

'I asked the Good Lord not to let him find the way to my room no more. The prayers didn't help. He went around back. Went through the courtyard. All he had to do was pull a piece of sheet metal away . . .'

Eliette shook her head. She'd heard all of that. Yes, she must have. The footsteps in the courtyard, the piece of sheet metal being pulled out and then the mingled breaths . . . 'Forget all of that! . . .' she hissed at Angela.

The girl fell silent and then closed her eyes as she stroked the little cat that had just jumped onto her knees. The teeth of the horn comb being pulled through her hair scratched her head deliciously, forcing her to really relax, while the fingers of the old lady separated, picked, plaited.

Sixteen years old! Eliette thought. She too had been sixteen. A timid creature, never wanting to see anyone. Talk to anyone. Afraid of every single body. Afraid of men and cyclones, their evil eyes. Walked around with a panama hat on so no one would notice her. Walked around with a newspaper opened out in front of her face. Borne along through life on the crazed voice of her mama Séraphine, who couldn't forget Cyclone '28, had kept all the old newspapers that bore witness to its singular and genuine wickedness. Even she, Eliette, couldn't forget. And she was asking Angela to forget . . .

The words had been torn violently from her mouth. No one ever forgot. Even if there was no trace of scars on her belly. Even if another set of memories had come along and helped her pile up other recollections to distract herself with on lonely days and thank the Lord for having allowed her to come through such a raging cyclone alive. Lord, even if death came for her right here and now, somewhere, buried deep down, part of her would always remember the Passage of the Beast on her body, in her belly. It all suddenly dawned upon her with such violence that she needed to find a chair and sit down. And there, mind shaken, body limp, and eyes lost in the fog of images, a name appeared: Ethéna! The very lady that had sewn her up . . . She was surely dead today. Sixty years ago now . . . Ethéna who saved her with her own two hands. 'Ethéna, remember that name,' her mama Séraphine had said. Sixty years ago now . . . Then Eliette saw the rafter coming straight down toward her, coming to ram into her. A living rafter with a face, two eyes, long teeth, nostrils quivering with rage. She was eight years old . . .

'Friend Eliette, are you ailing? What's wrong? You want some water?' asked Angela.

'Yes, a little water, please. Take the carafe on the stove. My cup is right next to it. And thank you, dear,' she whispered at the girl's back who was already disappearing into the kitchen. 'And thank you, dear . . .'

Who could have revived days that were dead and buried long ago? Sixty years spent in blindness. Godmother Anoncia might be able to tell her a little something about those forgotten days that had made her into this miserable old cowardly woman with a desiccated heart and body. Sixty years ago now . . .

Going back and digging up the distant and hidden past like that made her feel nauseous, as if she were sticking her head into a slimy quagmire, searching its depths in order to dredge up the real truth, corked in a bottle of strong spirits that had aged for sixty years.

'Forget all of that!' she repeated to Angela.

When her periods started, Rosette made Angela sit down so she could tell her there was a breed of animals with men's faces, savage beasts in truth that hid their long teeth behind sweet smiles. Angela was just barely twelve years old, but her mama hadn't the slightest idea that her panties held the gaping *coucoune* of a woman. If the fire of the first times had died down, it didn't change the fact that Angela felt herself blazing like a hot ember when the sun went down. Morning found her – like a cabin set afire and ravaged in the night – in sputtering flames, taking stock of damaged timbers. She'd gotten into the habit of keeping a basin of water under her bed. To bathe first thing in the morning. Wash herself inside. Free herself of the impatient hands that she could still feel pressing at her body. Strip away the traces that her papa Rosan's long beast had left. Cleanse. Scrub. Send great splashes of water to wash away the sweat and the vile humors that impregnated her whole being. Just barely twelve years old . . . and even before the very first blood ran between her legs, she was already burdened with that wide-open *coucoune* that she bore like an irremediable scar.

What more could her mama teach her about men . . . They shared the same male. Rosette in her sweet ignorance; Angela struggling through the leaden mire of silence. Rosette, who saw her pretty little family as all smooth and clean – smiles, nice clothes, and attractive poses – just like the portrait they'd taken after Rita's birth. It was before Angela had her own room, in the days of little innocent good nights lost in tickling and laughing. Rosette, always dreaming of finding happiness at a discount. At the tips of your fingers. Hardly a stone's throw from Savane, in Des-Ramiers, where her mama Gilda lost all of her prickles the first time she set eyes on Rita. Rosette, who experienced the great reconciliation as a healing process and stopped seeking a mama in the Rasta Beloved woman, stopped seeking her father in Haile, the King of Kings, perched upon his horse. She felt only happiness all around, especially since Savane seemed to have calmed down. Apart from some occasional beatings, a violent death or killing had not been deplored since the unfortunate fate of the Rastas in the mountains.

When Rosan saw Angela's first blood, he threw everything into reverse gear and, without so much as a word or a good night, stopped his visits altogether. Angela thought he'd been set free, believed her prayers had been answered. At the dinner table they sat facing one another, their hearts weighed down with the same visions. Their eyes met only by accident. Rosette was talkative. She was always trying to draw them into conversation but never obtained more than a few sparing words between forkfuls. Rosan answered her questions all right, but in a detached way that desperately deepened the ensuing silence. Deleterious secrets stuck in the throat, cold shifty glances. Bitter thoughts. Angela never had anything to say, nothing to relate about her days; she barely spoke to anyone but Rita, who at the time was cloaked in her three-year-old's innocence. Rosette admonished her about it every day, chalked it up to heredity: like father, like daughter.

For Angela's thirteenth birthday, to sweeten her up a little, Rosette pressed him to buy a small gold medallion and chain, which he went and laid out on her pillow. Rosette stood off at a distance, clapping happily, begging a smile, a kiss. Angela simply granted a sullen thank you and Rosette got irritated, told her: 'You're not a nice girl, Angela! You lucky to have your papa . . .'

That same evening Rosan pushed the piece of sheet metal aside again and came to take Angela's body once more. It had been a year since he'd lost the way to her room. He came holding a finger to his lips . . . 'Shshsh! Let your papa give you something more . . .'

She said no. Struggled furiously and desperately against him. Kicked. Punched. But he was too strong, too heavy. Already climbing atop her, prying her legs apart with strong jabs of his knees. Her arms and legs pinned down, she wanted to bite the hand he was mashing down on her mouth, keep him from jamming the long beast into her body. Only thirteen years old, and she had to fight against three mountains, five cyclones, and a thousand demons.

'I your papa,' he whispered to her, 'I your papa! Every day I put food on the table in this cabin so you can stand on your two legs. I got the right to mount my filly before others do! I your papa, Angela! When you find another man to give you this, you won't be thinking of your papa no more. So I'm clearing the path for others. And don't you go saying a word to your mama or anybody if you don't want to see some big trouble stirred up around here.'

Could she have cried out anyway? . . . Yes. What kind of trouble? Maybe it wasn't her papa. Maybe Rosan was actually sleeping innocently by Rosette's side, not saying anything. Maybe this big demon would reduce her to dust if she resisted, set fire to the cabin, use its blade like that black man in the old days of Savane who carved up a poor girl named Hortense . . .

'I won't get you pregnant . . . ,' he let out in a gasp, 'just let me taste a bit of your flesh again. I won't . . .'

So then Angela closed her fingers around the bars of her headboard. Stopped fighting. Opened her legs more. And then clenched her teeth when the fire started burning again between her legs. Let him come all the way in, until she felt her stomach pushing up into her throat. Don't scream. Just close your eyelids like a corpse in a coffin. Just bite your lips. Endure the other bucking body, horse from hell. And quiet the voice of your mama Rosette rising within you, reciting a fairy tale in the form of a dictation . . .

In those days, Laugh and Cry were good parents. They weren't of the same breed, but they lived together as a family. Laugh owned all the land, hills, mountains, woods, fields, savannas. Cry ruled the seas, the oceans, the deepest depths. If Laugh ran out of salt, Cry dug some out for her from the large sacks that he brought back by the cartload from his homeland. 'Whatever will I do with all this salt! Take some! Please!' he said to Laugh and her children, who showed their appreciation by breaking out in sparkling bursts of precious stone, falling stars, and golden spider silk. If Cry asked for a few seeds to hold him over till the next season, Laugh sailed out and dumped fifty tons of corn, wheat flour, yams, boukoussou-peas, custard apples, breadfruit, and God knows what else smack-dab in the middle of the sea . . . Alas, the day came when man landed on one of the shores. No one knew where he'd come from. But wherever he went, the man said, 'I come from the dust of the earth. All of the riches in this world belong to me. The gold in the rivers, the most precious woods, the water, the fires of glory, love and its torments, its strings of gold necklaces, the pointed titties of black women and their pearl white teeth. I will master the glassy sea, the choppy ocean, its golden salt, its flying fish. I will go beyond these horizons to conquer more and more lands. And then when I've had my fill of gold, I'll cross the sky to test my greatness and find the path to eternal life. The man, who was quite irresponsible, wanted to start a war between Laugh and Cry. The lands and the seas were all drawn into the conflict. The war lasted seven centuries. And that's why, ever since that day, because of the man who wished to rule all, the descendants of Laugh and Cry have forgotten who their parents were. But, nevertheless, some traces still remain . . . little salty tears that well up in the midst of great bursts of laughter. Or, sometimes, a tiny laugh, a flicker of hope that glimmers in the very depth of fear or the muddle of tears.

Rosan explained to her that this is the way it was, everywhere. Under all the tin roofs in Savane, behind the wooden planks, in the darkness of the cabins of Ravine-Guinée, and elsewhere there were fathers who sought light between the legs of their children. No one ever spoke of it, but it was neither wrong nor a sin. He told her he had the right to mount her like a young filly because he had created her. He promised her there would be big trouble if she ever spoke of their secret. His eyes rolled crazily in his head. Once he asked Angela to hold him, body against body, sweat mingling, breaths battling. And he told her that Rita's turn would come too, that he had the right, every right . . .

Bob's voice came floating across the courtyard again. Running one hand over her forehead, Angela shut out the memory of Rosan looking for Rita's budding breasts. Rita's laughter. The hiccup that made her whole body arch because she laughed so hard in the arms of her papa Rosan, who was throwing her up and swinging her around in the air, around and around, just like he used to swing her.

'No woman no cry . . .'

VII

I didn't want to get mixed up in all that.

Only open my door to Angela, poor girl.

Just make up for the wrong I'd done to Glawdys.

Just stop the wretched thoughts that, no matter how hard I tried to blot them out, always brought back the memory of the men and women of Savane who'd been murdered.

I thought especially of Glawdys, whom – by being too reasonable – I'd missed the chance to take in. I was never able to forget those eyes that turned gray and all of the colors she lost because she had no love. Yes, I heard her yapping. I saw her tied up. I was convinced I was better than that Eloise woman, whom I allowed myself to judge. I called her voracious and looked down on her. I thought her eyes were bigger than her heart. In fact, it was her heart that was too big, three times bigger than mine. Life had not given her a chance to show it. The high winds outside had taken all of her beloved children from her.

For a long time I thought that Glawdys was the daughter I'd been promised. But I still didn't move – stayed closed up in my cabin when I heard her crying. I wanted to rescue her, break the chains, snatch her from the clutches of her stepmother, but I always lacked just a touch of courage, just a shade of willpower. I waited for the cries to stop, melt away into the night, be drowned in sleep. Yes, I stepped over pools of blood. I averted my eyes some fifty times to avoid seeing the signs of death and human savagery. It's surely my fault that Glawdys threw her baby down to the foot of Nèfles Bridge, it's my fault, dear God. When she came back from Child Welfare and started selling her christophines, I could still have taken her in. Even if the marks of the rope around her waist hadn't disappeared, it wasn't too late. No. It's my fault. Instead of just giving her a few coins to ease my conscience, I should have walked up in broad daylight and bought all of her rotten christophines. Maybe she would have felt a small wave of love run through her heart. Wouldn't have ended up going to such extremes. By this time she's either dead or half rotten, like the christophines she tried to sell to people in Savane. She was just asking for a little love after all the folks around here had ignored her so long with their cold looks.

I knew too when Christopher and Esabelle started plotting against poor Marius because of the jars and baskets full of gold that he was hauling around in his dreams. I heard Christopher promise his queen Esabelle gold and riches in a new life. There was nothing to it; the girl went wild for a few grains of gold. The smell of murder might even have crept under my door the night before. But I kept all of that to myself. I didn't want my name mixed up in any crime. I saw Marius walk by in the afternoon, light as a feather – unaware of his destiny. Walking so lightly, fine particles of gold swirled about his heels. He greeted me. And I didn't say nothing. Dazzled as I was by the gold dust that his old thongs were stirring up, I looked at him without saying a word. I already knew he'd never find that jarful of gold; that he'd already been tried, sentenced, hanged. I let him go by. I might even have heard Christopher and Esabelle dragging his body and hanging it from a branch in Sidonie's mango tree. I didn't say nothing to the law. Two days later, when Christopher brought his things over to Esabelle's, no one said a word. Everyone knew they'd murdered the poor Indian. Everyone knew . . .

I remember the evening when Régis crossed Savane with his long cutlass slashing the air, already hacking poor Hortense to pieces. Could I have stopped his hand? I always heard when Hortense cried out under the blows of the conch shell. I heard clonk-clonk clonk-clonk. I'd see her walk by all stitched up, broken, bruised. I never called out to her. I pretended I didn't see. As if her skin was untouched, smooth and transparent, with no bruises or bumps. Soon as I saw Zébio walking after her, I knew in advance that the whole business would go wrong. Just like everyone else, I figured those two were having a good time together. I didn't say nothing to the police, didn't say nothing to Hector on his deathbed either. Maybe Zébio really would have taken Hortense far from the misery in Savane. That's what he said later in court. But he was mostly seeking after fame and its laurels. He was blind to everything else, even the sharp blade of Régis's cutlass hanging over Hortense's head.

Did I hear the heavy breathing coming from Angela's room? No, I didn't know. I wouldn't have just sat here . . . I thought Rosan belonged to a fine breed of people that they just didn't make anymore. To my mind, Rosette was a kind girl. She walked a straight path, dreamt of a better world – a sort of paradise. She'd never liked Savane, because of its ugliness, its crimes, the apathy that pervaded everything like in a conquered land. Did her dreams and her skill with fairy tales keep her from seeing Rosan abuse Angela?

.   .   .   .

Eliette gathered her skirts and pulled herself up from the rocker. She was just going to have to face all of her fears, step resolutely forward, and banish the frightened little girl who had never grown up, who shook like a leaf and couldn't stand for people to set eyes on her for long. Though Eliette kept telling herself she was now an old woman who'd been through hell and high water, all of the fears she'd stored up inside kept her a prisoner in the dark corridors of her childhood. With Angela's story, glimmering torches had been lit that attempted to bring the murderous rafter to life, give it a terrifying face. The Passage of the Beast . . .

Wielding that same rafter, Cyclone '28 came back to rend her again during the night – sixty years later . . . She cried out in her sleep, awakening her little cat, which came bounding up to lick a salty tear on her cheek. Tears, how many years had it been since she'd shed a tear for anyone, either living or dead? Like from a fountain, water gushed from her usually dry eyes, sweeping along in its course the dregs of secret suffering buried in the darkest recess of her memory. That's the reason she'd never wanted to hear about the torments and sorrows of the world. Just live on the sidelines. Exist, without trying to raise the flaming veils of earthly passions. Protect herself from the burns that high-flown sentiments could cause. Not put her heart on the line.

She promised herself to look Rosette straight in the eye, just to see if they were of the same breed – cowardly, fearsome, and blind. Just to peer into the depths of her heart and see if the woman did or didn't know what Rosan was doing, see if she'd been a party to it.

Sixty-eight years old – no, Lord, it still wasn't too late to walk out of fear's prisons, just get one foot out in the world where all of life's truth was laid bare. No, she wasn't all that old. The heart of a child still beat and leapt deep within her. Though time had wrinkled and shrunk her body, it had passed over her without disturbing the old inquiline fears that had made of her life a great cowardly masquerade, nothing but window dressing; a tissue of lies.

It was thanks to her stepfather Joab that she'd started speaking again. How old was she then? Eleven. Three years after the Passage of the Beast.

'What good will it do to drag all that out in the open? That was sixty years ago!' whispered her dead mama. 'Forget those days! Forget, child!'

'No, your memory bled you dry for years – make it reveal its secrets!' taunted another voice. 'Dig up the past! Go back in time! Rip the veils away at last!'

'No! Eliette, get yourself out of this trap!' Séraphine begged.

'It's too late to back down. Go on, open your eyes!' the other faceless voice urged.

Then a piece of Eliette's memory slowly tore away from the reef of oblivion, floated up before her eyes like a bit of sponge being tossed about in the waves, and – quivering with life – finally washed up on the beach.

First she saw a skinny child running and jumping after a tall black man who walked bare-chested through the sun-filled savanna. The man wore a straw-hat, white shorts tied around his waist with a rope that hung down in front like a monk's sash and bobbed against his thighs when he walked. Birds flitted about his head, and he spoke to them like everlasting friends. Three young goats bounded out in front of his long strides. And the man alternately whistled, sang, or talked, spreading joy around him as if he were sowing good seed in all parts of the savanna. The skinny little girl followed so closely on his heels that you would have thought he'd tied her to his steps with an invisible string. Sometimes he would stop to caress the wings of a butterfly or say hello to a dragon tree swinging its leaves in the warm breeze. Joab, whom folks from Ravine-Guinée called the Mule, was a king in his savanna. A truly benevolent king. Once Eliette had even heard the leaves of a tree name him the King of Kings. He ruled with neither severity nor tithes of any sort. But everyone bowed down to the man, who was respected by all: the smallest branches on the trees, the pinhead *yen-yen* flies, the fruits, the flowers, the peas, the seeds. He ruled over all living things on land, in water, and in the vast freedom of the sky that opened onto other, unknown worlds. Ruled with no cutlass, no rod or kicks. Ruled with his heart alone that cast long lifelines into the depths where Eliette lay. His heart that scattered feathers she could one day gather and sew together to make a large set of wings and fly far away if she felt like it. Far away from the world of silence into which the Passage of the Beast had cast her. Fly away, out beyond the impossible, reach dizzying heights.

The skinny child walked behind the man, slipping into and following every dirt path that was cleared in Savane. Back then, days dawned in a very well-behaved manner. All of the devils, she-devils, spirits drifting far and wide, zombies, incredible flying creatures and petty *soucougnans* lived peacefully by Joab's side. As demoniacal as they were, these creatures – cousins to Beelzebub – became as gentle as lambs when they encountered Joab, the King of Kings, and the two women he'd taken from the world. And even if Séraphine saw hell every blessed morning, those maleficent creatures had no real influence on Savane. They slept the whole day through. They talked of the damages they incurred in a ruthless, unforgiving other world, in close combat with human beings. In her mama's eyes, Eliette could see demons pursuing them on the afternoons when they had to go down to the river. She could hear the pounding of the hoofs of she-devils, the cavalcade of squadrons of dragons. She felt her back blistering at the lick of flaming tongues that the evil spirits sent after her. Eliette hadn't started talking again yet. So she hiked up her skirts like her mother and ran wildly down to the river to throw herself amid the abnormally long rocks that resembled the arms of the living. At eleven-twelve years old, Eliette already knew that there was evil everywhere in the world, that you had to protect yourself, flee the danger to keep from being stuck with an arrow of accursement, stricken dead by a rafter from the cyclone. Hide your body. Spare your soul. Barricade the entrance to your heart to keep from crying and suffering and getting yourself all worked up.

'Tell her about the Beast!' snapped the voice.

So Séraphine told Eliette how she'd loved her papa – handsome face, promises, and caresses – an angel come down to earth. And then the Beast got into him. He'd done that. She almost killed him for it. She'd only had time to lop off one of his ears. Only had time to leave him that souvenir of what he'd done, the rake, the heathen, the killer . . .

'What? What, Mama Séraphine? What'd he do?'

'No, he wasn't really a man . . . The way he won my heart was no natural thing. I should have seen it from the way he looked at my poor crucified Jesus over the bed. I should've thrown him out the day he closed the Bible that I always kept lying open by the lamp. That's how my life fell into Darkness. I might have gone crazy . . . Did I go down in that ditch, Lord? Did I lose my mind because of what he done?'

'What? What? What'd he do?'

'All those newspapers from the time the Beast passed – rent you in two – I got them all,' Séraphine cried. 'I keep them all. It came just for you. I was completely broken. The foul Beast wanted it all. Cursed Cyclone! Wanted it all: the tall trees, the fruit, the flowers, the young saplings, the buds, and even the seeds that had just been put in the ground. Everything, the voracious killer! Wanted to destroy it all. Crush, trample, tear everything up. We never seen a cyclone like that since. Came just for you. I carried you, didn't know which way to go. I walked for a long time, lost, frantic. You all bloody. With your blood running down your legs, down the front of my dress. Black blood. I only had time to lop one of his ears off. If I could have, I'd have run him through with a cutlass. But I didn't have the strength left. My arms were all weak. Just one ear. Cyclone '28, Eliette, no, don't ask to bring it back . . .'

'Go on, what else? Tell me what else!' Eliette begged.

'Is all in the papers. You don't remember nothing . . . Haiti, Puerto Rico, the neighbor islands, the dependencies. Bad wind! Wind from hell! Wind of the Apocalypse! Just one ear that I cut off him. When I ran across him, his devil eyes were going crazed. He didn't know when I grabbed the knife to lop his ear off. Maybe he still running, his hand on the side of his head, blood running over it like a glove. Cyclone '28 was desolation, spoliation incorporated. Tin roofing yanked off, rafters fallen in one after another, boards ripped apart in the mighty clutches of the wind. Don't ask to go back to that night! The river swollen with its burden of trees, the black sky, the deluge. And then them corpses drifting past, plucked chickens, strangled cattle, uprooted trees . . . The Passage of the Beast, Eliette, the rafter that split your belly open. Yes, might be he's still running, the rake, if Cyclone '28 didn't decapitate him for eternity. Didn't send a sharp piece of sheet metal flying into his legs to cut him down. Didn't chop him up in pieces to wipe out his kind forever.

Lord! I walked around lost, in the mud up to my thighs. I thought of Anoncia who so loved her Ti-Cyclone . . . And look what he went and done! Yes, heaven set Ethéna down on my path. A midwife from Bois-Ramée. Ethéna, remember that name! When she saw what Cyclone had done to you, poor child, she tore you from my arms. Ethéna everyone called her. She put your organs back in their nest, and then she sewed you up from one end to the other. I recall how sure her fingers were, pulling at that needle. While I was praying God to save you, she swore there'd be no marks or scars left on your body, that forgetting would cover all the suffering you'd been through. You lost your speech and your memory at the same time, poor child. You turned a little dimwitted, cowardly, shrinking, 'fraid of the slightest little thing.'

'Tin roofing yanked off, rafters fallen in, boards ripped apart in the mighty clutches of the wind . . . The black sky, the deluge,' Eliette repeated, stunned by the words that were slowly taking on meaning. 'The rafter split your belly open. Yes, maybe he's still running,' she moaned, 'that rake who's been hiding behind Cyclone '28 for sixty years . . . Was that my papa?' she asked.

'We stayed at that kind woman Ethéna's place for next to three months. Time enough for your flesh to mend. Time enough for the ashes of forgetting to settle over the burning embers. When we had to leave, Ethéna gave me a hundred sous, and then she whispered, 'Go now! Don't go thanking me! Just curse the Beast that rent your child . . .' She sent me right straight to Ravine-Guinée to snatch up a job as a servant on her recommendation. But I went through Jissac on the way, I had to burn the bloody sheets hidden in the wardrobe I'd left behind . . . Godmother Anoncia didn't want to believe me when I told her what her Ti-Cyclone had done. She just loved him too much, she said. Talked about how she'd brought him up, saved his life time and again, and how he could never have done a thing like that. After that he never went back to see her. He never tried to find out what Cyclone had torn up around her place in La Pointe. He disappeared. So she ended up believing me. But she always felt ashamed and sorry, as if she were responsible. One day she ran into him in Victory Square, hat pulled down low over his missing ear. Something she'd never done in her whole life: she spat in his face . . .

For two days Rosette had been sitting on the floor in the middle of her room reading Angela's dictations. Two days that she'd been fondling, reading, and rereading the loose white sheets covered with blue writing. Soft, rippling lines like little waves on a smooth sea. Two days that she'd been rocking back and forth, lulling her pain. A small boat on the sea, that's what she was. A boat that was leaking and would surely end up sinking, touching bottom, and going through the floor. Paradise, flowers, fruit, frills – the world of dictation described a blessed world, painted rainbows of hope. Lord, how beautiful her dream world was! Colonies of love, saintly families, innocence, and candor. At times she shed a tear on the lost dreams, and the lines of ink blurred, blossomed on the paper, spreading out in pale splotches of pastel blue. Mawkish stories, silly fables, old-fashioned tales. Life outside of those pages roared with violence. And every day was a cyclone. Every single day that God brought for the sorrow of women and men in Savane.

There once was a time when Cyclone's path passed far from Earth. He simply looked at it from a distance with both eyes and went on his way. Earth hardly seemed interesting to him in comparison with all the stars he used to set dancing with a mere huff of his breath. Earth seemed inanimate, dull, bleak. But one day, as he was blowing quick-rushed after a falling star, Cyclone noticed little bits of land right smack in the middle of the sea. He turned around and saw islands, specks of dust. He leaned over so far that he lost his balance and fell. Cyclone was able to catch himself on a cloud, but his right eye fell. Half blind, Cyclone tried to fish the lost eye from the sea. Alas, the waters had closed over it forever. And that is why, for ages and ages, Cyclone has only had one eye with which to see the world. The fallen eye never lost hope. It struggled and still struggles to get back up into the sky. Every time La Soufrière growls and weeps ashes and spits rocks, the other eye hanging in the firmament knows that one day, maybe, after trying for so long, the fallen eye will find its old place in the sky again. And, maybe, Cyclone will stop throwing itself so furiously upon Earth.

Every day, thought Rosette, the shame and wounds came up from the farthest reaches of the past to smirch the present, its mirages, its promises of fabulous tomorrows. No, nothing had changed since the first blacks from Africa had been unloaded in this land that breeds nothing but cyclones, this violent land where so much malediction weighs upon the men and women of all nations. Nothing had changed, cutlass, rope, chains . . . Jah! And the very same demons hovering over the fold, inspiring greed, wickedness, crime, incest . . . No, Lord, nothing had changed, and Sister Beloved was right to go up to the mountains, go far away from the system of Babylon, the works of Babylon, the Babylon hell . . .

One line of the dictation caught her eye and rekindled her interest; she read:

Lady Dreams wasn't the same as she is now, just a word in the mouth with no shape or form. She had powerful wings, a head full of hope, and a pure heart . . . Suffering, who was napping not far away in a culvert in town . . .

Jealous, Rosette repeated out loud. Jealousy, that's the key. They were too good, that's it! A hard-working man, Rosan. Three pretty children that didn't tag along after ganja peddlers and crack smok- ers. Children who were going somewhere in school. Jealousy . . . She'd always told Rosan that this place, this place they called Savane – respect! – was the last bastion of accursement, it was Beelzebub and Lucifer in cahoots. Rosan, she'd always told him that in Des-Ramiers they'd find their paradise, brotherly love, and happiness at the tips of their lips.

Rosette broke out in a fit of cackling laughter at those last words that had cropped up again, all festooned with the certitudes of her youth. Happiness at the tips of your lips.

Glawdys, the girl who threw her baby down to the bottom of Nèfles Bridge had never believed in happiness. She was just like the black women on the first boats who killed their newborn babies so they wouldn't be born into slavery, wouldn't fall into the hands of slave traders. The girl had simply torn her child from the claws of Babylon, from its lies, its tinsel hopes, its macadam dreams and its resurrections, its official indictments, its laws, its lights, its grants, its welfare benefits, its subventions . . . People said that her body once sported colors just like flowers, confetti, garlands, and the rest, just like folks put out for the grand celebration on Corpus Christi Day. The shadows of Savane made her turn gray, disillusioned, treacherous. Glawdys knew what happened to the children given over to Babylon. How many escaped its temptations, its vice, its paths leading straight to jail, to the benches in front of the church, to the sidewalks of Bas de la Source in La Pointe, to the world of zombies pacing the deadly halls of crack? Jealousy! We were too good for them, isn't that right? Too good for the folks around here. Too fine a family for all the damozels that opened their fate to passing men. Too good for the whores that lay down on their bellies or backs and let four-five drunken fellars take them at once, for a hundred-franc note. Too good for the women that were beaten day and night, burned, boned, bashed, and picked clean. We were too good. Fine family.

With Rita, who came along when I wasn't expecting anyone else . . . Rita, who showed up the year after the death of Beloved and Marley. Rita, an accident. Just an accident, I told Aunt Fanotte several times. But Rosan was happy, and he started talking to me again just like in the old days. He liked girls. He called Angela his angel. 'Come say good night to Papa, my little angel!' he used to say. 'Let's see if the titties ripened today while I was mixing cement in the sun to bring home your bread! Come kiss Papa, my own little angel!' And Angela would throw herself into his arms. They swung around, swung around. And their laughter swung around too. Bursts of sunshine on the black boards. And at times like that I didn't think about the paradise waiting for me in Des-Ramiers. I didn't think about my papa, King of Kings, conqueror, riding on his white steed. I laughed too. And my laughter rang false in the light of their joy like someone who hasn't followed the gist of the story, but who laughs anyway just to be included. He didn't laugh so much with me, Rosan didn't. He no longer found consolation in the fairy tales I invented, but he didn't neglect his duties as a father, and that was enough for me.

It was after the birth of Rita, right at the hind end of the Cyclone of 1981, that he decided to build on an extra room to the cabin for Angela, who was still sleeping under the window in our room when she was eight or nine.

He loved to kiss the smooth skin of his baby girls. I saw no harm in that.

I don't recall exactly when Angela stopped laughing, like one stops talking. Closed up in silence. Nothing to say. Never anything to relate. Always . . .

Rosette closed her eyes to try and piece together all the signs she hadn't understood, the silences, the looks . . .

. . . Alas, the day came when man landed on one of the shores. No one knew where he'd come from. But wherever he went, the man said, 'I come from the dust of the earth. All of the riches in this world belong to me . . .

How long ago had she given Angela that dictation? The ink on the written page had turned violet, the paper had yellowed more than the others, as if the words were too heavy to bear and had aged it prematurely. Rosette continued:

. . . And that's why, ever since that day, because of the man who wished to rule all, the descendants of Laugh and Cry have forgotten who their parents were. But, nevertheless, some traces still remain . . . little salty tears that well up in the midst of great bursts of laughter. Or, sometimes, a tiny laugh, a flicker of hope that glimmers in the very depth of fear or the muddle of tears.

Cursed dreams! grumbled Rosette. She'd sacrificed Angela to those cheap dreams. Her eyes drifted far away, far beyond Savane, far from the black people and their accursement. Far from the wooden cabin that her dead uncle Edmond Alexander had built. Too far from her kin, to an imagined carnival, day of the Mardi Gras parade. Fine family all right. Had she ever really seen Angela? What did the silences, the downcast eyes mean? The way she protected Rita like a mother hen. The way she'd never say good morning or good night to anyone anymore. And Rosan saying, 'Let her be, Rosette! Let her take care of her own business!'

He knew what her business was, Rosette thought.

When did he give it to Angela?

When had he started his business?

At the same time as the room with no door . . . No, Angela was ten then. She couldn't have kept that tormented secret in her heart for six years.

Maybe he'd just tried one time – day before yesterday.

Just tried.

And Angela had turned him in right away.

He hadn't had time to really accomplish his crime . . . Lord, please don't let him have had the time!

Rosette hadn't seen a thing, hadn't heard a thing.

Maybe all that time she'd been exalting in her paradise, busily hanging stars in the sky. Walking back up the slopes of the valley of tears to enter the kingdom of the ancestors, return to Mother Africa with Beloved. Surely her eyes had been elsewhere, picking flowers in Eden, stroking lions, and speaking with birds. Or maybe she was dancing to reggae music, lifting her knees high – one of Bob's numbers, a Gregory Isaacs or Prince Jazzbo tune.

Step forward, youth, and let I tell you the truth
Step forward, youth . . .

Seen nothing, heard nothing in the vast night silence, only the creaking of boards, the rain of rocks that the black children lofted at the cabin covered with those cursed cristophines that no one picked. Women screaming under the blows. The fury of a *tambour-ka*. A boisterous *zouk* tune braving the demons of the night. The return of rumdums. Seen nothing, heard nothing.

Seen nothing, heard nothing, just like all the folks in Savane, witnesses to murders, that never saw or heard nothing, nothing but the rain on the tin roof, the mopeds backfiring, the yapping of homeless dogs.

Rosette, far from everything. In exile, sitting in the middle of her room on the termite-eaten floor covered with the black-and-white lino they'd bought with Aunt Fanotte's money. Sitting there within the four walls. With only the thin tin roof between her and the sky bearing down on the other side. Weighing down on the tin roofing that was already rusting and full of holes. Sitting amidst the fine white pages of her paper dreams. Happiness is at the tips of your lips, Rosette said to herself while the radio announced Cyclone Hugo. '. . . Will arrive tomorrow, sometime on Saturday night,' claimed a voice on the radio. 'Hugo, worse, stronger than Cyclone '28!'

Rain came suddenly spitting down on the roof full of holes. Drops started weeping on the loose sheets of Angela's dictations. Rosette was weeping too. Outside, the wind rose. The sound of hammers pounding furiously at the night to fix bars across the doors and windows of Savane's flimsy cabins. Voices drifted up from the dirt path. Folks were running barefoot behind creaking wheelbarrows. Women calling to one another, crying that the Apocalypse was coming to fall upon the earth. Cyclone! Cyclone!! . . .

There were four of them. Two blacks, one *chabin*, riddled with tics, and a big red fellar. Four men, stretched out on two sets of bunk beds with a narrow space running between leading to a sink that had undoubtedly once been white and a toilet filled with stinking, greenish water. The flush mechanism was broken. Every now and again someone threw a bucket of water in the bowl to wash down the pissy smell that filled the place. As soon as he flopped down on his cot, the *chabin* set about ruining his eyesight by contemplating a color photograph of a woman he'd torn from a magazine and tacked to the wall, level with his eyes. One of those plump white women with big titties, hair in a tight-curled permanent, red lips, and pink tongue sticking out. He'd given her a name – Diana. All she wore was a skimpy pair of unbuttoned denim shorts that she promised to take off soon. The *chabin* fell asleep and woke up under the gaze of that girl who gradually puckered along with the paper. Maybe the smile, the tacit invitation, the dreams of good times were enough for him. He never talked about his desire to have a woman as most did. Desire for a warm wet *coucoune* that smelled so sweet it made your head spin with desire. Desire to squeeze a woman's body. To jam the blade in. To cut. To bang, Lord! Bang a woman!

At night the *chabin* called out to a woman: 'Elisa! Elisa! Elisa!' The women who came to see him in the visitors' room all had other names. There was Hermina, his mother, Marie-Claude and Francine, his sisters. The woman he'd killed with a shotgun was named Myriam. That's what the prisoners said between themselves. 'Badass *chabin*!' they said behind his back. 'Badass *chabin*!' He didn't have such a mean face on him, except that he had those tics. The corner of his mouth twitched upward fifty times a second, which made his eye blink shut automatically. He also had the bad habit of touching his private parts, fondling them to make sure everything was in place, still alive, hadn't vanished.

No one really knew the whole story, why he'd emptied his shotgun into the Myriam woman. But for a time a copy of *France-Antilles* had circulated in the jail. It related the crime in all aspects of its horror. The word 'savagery' was repeated every three lines. He'd gotten twenty years. He had already paid years to society and swore – as soon as he was out – he'd get a shotgun to blast that mama of Myriam's off the face of the earth. According to what he said it was all the fault of that woman, who'd unscrewed his girl's head so she'd leave him. Yes, everything was just hunky-dory between the two of them until the day the girl said she couldn't stay with him any longer, she had to go. Something was pushing her far away from him. Far, far, far away! No sooner said than done, she dragged all her possessions over to her mama's right quick. Chabin wasn't allowed to see her or speak to her again. He'd been condemned without a trial. And what had he done to Myriam, eh? Nothing at all . . . Nothing but good – love and its trappings. Praise be to God that he'd found a good friend to give him moral support the day after his life had been ship-wrecked. To keep him from slipping into eternal grief, his friend came to sit in the womanless cabin every day. He shook his head and – his only attempt at consolation – repeated, 'Sé fenm-la sé dé isalop, mon chè! Sé fisi yo mérité! Pas plis ki sa!' Them kinda women is bitches, friend! They not worth nothing but some buckshot from your gun!

So one day Chabin had unhooked a neighbor's hunting rifle. He posted himself behind a cabin not far from his Myriam's house. And he just waited for her to come by, wondering why she'd left him, re-peating his friends righteous words: 'A good shotgun what women deserve, the bitches! A good shotgun!!' Myriam hadn't seen him point the gun. Hadn't seen him behind the cabin with a mouthful of 'isalop.' He'd said to himself that with her high-heeled shoes, her slit skirt, and the flowered blouse he didn't recognize she must be coming back from La Pointe, the very place where a man can buy love in the arms of a woman-isalop, sansculotte, regular cocotte . . . The thought that she gave herself to others crossed his mind and he pulled the trigger. Once. Twice. Myriam fled death, with blood on her blouse. Three times. She fell to the ground, begged for mercy, her arms stretching toward help that did not come. And then she didn't move anymore.

.   .   .   .

When the voice on the radio announced the approaching cyclone, Chabin turned toward Rosan, asked him if he had a sturdy cabin, nails, and boards so that his wife wouldn't be in danger and could board up the doors and windows. Rosan answered yes with a mere jerk of his chin and went back to the spectacle of the rust stains on the old mattress over his head. Lying on his back, he watched the winding marks that the springs of the bed frame had left on the canvas mattress. An infinity of intertwining scrolls. Great sweeping whorls, small arabesques, rusty scribbles and dribbles, rusty droppings. Scalloped burns on the torn canvas that sometimes opened, showing wads of foam resembling repulsive rolls of flesh. Wicked spirals and paths of perdition in which he wandered, wishing he could slip off and disappear into the shame and the pain knotting in his throat. Cyclone . . . So many times he had thrown himself more violently than a cyclone on Angela's body. Wild beast! And it could have gone on for a long time. He couldn't stop himself. There was a machine inside of him, diabolical mechanism that always pushed him into Angela's room. His angel, his redeemer . . . There was a voice that called to him from deep down inside of Angela. And when he entered that corridor, he ended up in heaven. Paradise! So light and soft, warm and fragrant. He remembered how much pleasure he'd always felt in taking his baby Angela in his arms. Simply touching her soft skin, his whole body was filled with electricity. The desire to eat, to slip inside, like into a hiding place where the demons of his childhood could not penetrate. A secure and secret niche, more real than all of Rosette's tales, which could never relieve him from life's burdens for very long. So perfectly tender, Angela's flesh. Damnably tender. No, he didn't mean to hurt her. Ever . . .

In the beginning, she liked it when he touched her all over. Voracious and insidious caresses that galloped over her soft skin. While

Rosette was making dishwashing noises, his fingers pranced up and pawed at the entrance to the corridor. Pawed and drummed until they forced the locked mesh door open. Such a fine veil of mesh for such a vast paradise awaiting him on the other side. He'd pushed on to the farthest extreme. To the ends of paradise. In the very depths of Angela's *coucoune*. And it had all happened naturally. Came after the caresses and kisses. Like a series of beautiful ideas follows a logical course, the verses of a Gratien Midonet song.

Van-an lévè, ka hélé, ka hélé	The wind a rising, is calling, calling
Ka mandé lé répondè	It asking for an answer
Van-an lévé, manman . . .	The wind a rising, Mama

She laughed so hard when he swung her around. She always got the hiccups. And she fell on his chest, came and sat on his thigh, and it churned everything up inside of him. He felt like throwing her on the floor, getting inside her to see the world she hid in her belly. A better world, in which laughter cascaded so lightly. Where there were no torments, or wounds, or bumps. Only innocence and love . . .

His grandmama had been entirely right to whip him with that thorny switch, Rosan thought. The old woman knew all the accursement he carried within. He'd inherited that from his old papa with the missing ear. That old monkey under his circus hat.

Up above Rosan, the red fellar shifted his weight and then sat up on the edge of his bunk, making the intricate patterns of rust on his mattress bounce and ripple. He sat there for a moment, saying, 'Cyclone! Cyclone!' Over and over again as if it were an alarm to wake everyone up. His long legs with tufts of red hair dangled in the air right in front of Rosan's face. He turned his head toward the marred wall covered with old scribbling. The man yawned, loosened up, scratched himself under the arms. He was a Rasta from Sainte-Anne. His hair was gathered into two clumps of frizzy plaits, one that fell onto his forehead, the other tied back into a ponytail.

'For the day will come when Jah will destroy Babylon, its faithless men, its work, and its war machines, see!' he exclaimed.

'Pé gèl a-w!' Shut up! Chabin answered.

'The era of Babylon has come to an end, see. Everything will be destroyed, and only the Chosen Ones will inherit the New World . . . Jah Rastafari! Glory be to you! Lord of Lords! King of Kings . . .

'Enough bullshit now!' the *chabin* cut in. 'What you know about anything, 'cept selling ganja and crack?'

'Damn fool!' hissed the Rasta before pulling his legs back up on his cot and lying back down to show everyone how cool and collected he was as he awaited Doomsday.

Once, when they'd been younger, in Des-Ramiers, Rosette had told Rosan that she thought of him as her knight in shining armor, just like the kind you find in French fairy tales. Lancelot of the Lake, Du Guesclin, Roland de Roncevaux, Prince Charming . . . She sometimes dreamt that he abducted her from her mama's house, rode off with her on his horse. They galloped for days until they reached God's blessed land where everything was so easy – there were no problems, no wars, or jealousy. Yes, Rosan had believed in it. When they'd walked along the potholed roads, he still believed. And even when he'd had to work so hard on the concrete vessel for the man from Saintes – the million francs dangling there at the end of his labor – he still thought she was right and that happiness really was at the tips of your lips. But the million hadn't lasted. It had gone into the tin roofing and the boards for Uncle Edmond's cabin. The million with which they had built castles had been sucked up by nails, boards, and thin sheet metal, the thinnest, the cheapest, the gray kind that gets rusty right away. The million that seemed so fat in the bottom of their trunk vanished in a thin, glittering mist . . .

Another day he'd made Rosette hush up right in the middle of a tale in which she was opening up a vast and fabulous world for him. He'd already stopped believing by the time Angela was two. He could never reach the shores of Rosette's dream worlds. There was always something like high waves that pushed him back out to sea. And he had to row and struggle against the current, bail out the water to keep from sinking, bail out the water to avoid scuttling his life. On rare occasions he sailed into Rosette's stories, but he quickly found himself – damn fool – clinging to a thin fin of fancy. So then he plugged up his ears and thought about the tender flesh of his angel, who came straight from heaven. Who had real, soft, tender flesh that he could touch any time, caress, and take in his arms to make the laughter and hiccups come tumbling out. It was after the girl threw her baby down to the bottom of Nèfles Bridge that he'd thought that his angel could die too. And that idea had filled him with terror. She was five years old that year, Angela was. He'd carried the mangled baby through all the tracks of Savane so that everyone could judge and weigh the hell of the world, it's damnation. And even if he had thrown his shovel, his pick, and his trowel over on the other side of the high waves to build a concrete cabin in Rosette's paradise, he already knew there was no paradise on this earth, not in Savane or in Des-Ramiers. Not anywhere. There was just a small voice that called to him from inside Angela. Just a corridor of mesh to cross . . .

'Hugo! Did you hear that, men? They already named it: Cyclone Hugo, worse than Cyclone '28, Lord!' The fellar talking was a black man, taller than Rosan, older too. He was standing in front of the toilet bowl pissing with his legs spread apart, holding up the wall he was facing with one hand.

'I don't give a shit about anyone outside . . . ,' he said as he walked back to his cot.

'Ou pa ni fanmi! Ou pa ni on vyé manman adan on kaz, vou!' You got no family. You got no old mama in a cabin! the *chabin* cried.

'An pa ni pon moun!' I got no one. No one pray for me. I don't give a shit about nobody. They can all drop dead!

'Too late for prayers . . . The time has come. The fires of Jah will fall upon the earth. They will sweep away the towers of Babylon. And claim all who do not recognize the blessed herb of knowledge!' the Rasta predicted.

'The blessed herb!' the man repeated, his voice sneering. 'They say you were selling crack . . .'

'Shouldn't heed everything you hear . . . See, the cyclone that's coming, its name is Hugo, see. Its name is Apocalypse. Apocalypse, brother. And it's been coming for a long time, not just since day before yesterday, see. You didn't know yet if you'd be born in China or in Africa or Australia. You were nothing at all, not even a fart, and folks were already talking about Apocalypse, see.'

The tall black man turned over on his belly and started grinding his hips as if he were penetrating a woman's body.

'Yeh!' he said. 'Send that Apocalypse on over! I asking only one favor, that they send me a woman first. A pretty woman with a bottom as big as that, hard titties, and a gold chain around her ankle. A woman that lifts her legs up high and isn't 'fraid of a stiff rod. Yeh, let it kill everyone outside! They can drop dead with they tongues hanging out . . .'

Did Rosette know that a cyclone was coming? Rosan wondered.

The tin roof of the cabin was so thin, already full of holes. If he'd been back there in Savane, he would have carried sacks of sand up onto the roof, rocks, cinder blocks too. He had at least fifteen cinder blocks left over from Angela's room. Fifteen cinder blocks . . . He would have nailed bars up in the doorways, boards over the sheet metal. He would have nailed down the piece of sheet metal that closed off the entrance to Angela's room. And maybe afterward he would never have unnailed it, never gone back in.

He could see well enough that there was hate in Angela's eyes. There was nothing he could do about it. He had to go in, go all the way in. He'd threatened her with terrible trouble. And it's true there would have been bad trouble if the gendarmes hadn't taken him away immediately. He'd sworn not to touch Rita . . .

The man lying in the jail house because he'd stabbed some fellar with a knife on one of his drinking nights started whistling to show the others that, cyclone or no cyclone, his heart wasn't beating any faster, either from fear or compassion. 'They can all drop dead!' he repeated again.

All the patterns of rust, twisted up together, that's what the coming cyclone would bring. There'd probably be nothing left of Savane. Rosan counted the number of concrete cabins he'd built in all of Guadeloupe. Emptying out the sacks of cement. Breaking them open with a stroke of the shovel. Mixing the mortar, pouring the concrete slabs, and laying the cinder blocks one on top of the other. Building up the walls of cinder blocks all around him. But when the sun beat down too hard and he felt like needles were sticking in his back, he dreamt of the honey that he'd left at the other end of the corridor, behind the mesh, in Angela's room.

VIII

Five days that Angela had been sleeping at Eliette's.

The sky was so calm on that Saturday, so calm, even though the night before a nasty rain had beat down on the tin roof, instilling an age-old fear in Savane.

Wherever you went, that's all you heard: 'Cyclone! Cyclone! Worse than Cyclone '28!'

Ever since Cyclone had been announced, folks hadn't stopped running from one emergency to the next, cursing the days that they'd put off a job till later or turned away from two pieces of tin roofing that needed rejoining. They grumbled about time being against them, about not having enough money or energy. The money they'd gambled away in the hopes that a million from a lottery would drop into their laps, the money they'd drunk up in the tin mugs at Marga's bar, the money splurged on a gold ring, the money sunk into a yard of silk for a fancy blouse . . . But it was too late for moaning. Lord, every single one of them was in danger of perishing in the rage of the great winds that the sky was bringing their way. Sinners, yes, they were terrible sinners, and they repented that same day. And promised to burn a candle, put a necklace around the neck of the Jarry Virgin, donate some money for the priest and the Blessed

Church of Guadeloupe. How many Sundays had the church in Ravine-Guinée missed seeing certain folks? Not surprising if calamities came bowling down on Savane.

Now fear was on everyone's face. And you couldn't take their outbursts of laughter or the way they had of mocking Cyclone seriously. Everyone was thinking bitterly of their flimsy cabins sitting precariously on four rocks on the land that they'd squatted on one day, with no title or legal papers. Driven by a chance encounter, they didn't know at the time how many years they'd see go by there. They had followed the pointing finger and the word saying that there was a place where the poor could dream, out there in Savane Mulet. Had to go quick! Still some plots of land to be snatched up. They ran, lugged their bundles along with them. And ever since then the years hadn't changed a thing about the miserable cabins thrown up hastily to settle a plot of land. Sheet metal nailed down in haste, thin boards of pine wood, and fish crates. Time standing still.

And they also thought about all the crimes of Savane, about all their cowardice, about all the times they might have shown a bit of courage, just a little bit, Lord! They thought about their eyes being deliberately closed, their averted looks. And all of the effort they'd put into hate, jealousy, contempt, and witchcraft came back to them too. So much energy wasted . . . And they tried to be reborn as brothers and sisters in a new fellowship that amazed them, yes, deeply moved them. In their shared misfortune, they discovered they were vulnerable, helpless in the face of the wild hounds loosed by the cyclone. But they didn't have time to be amazed for long, to be joyful, to hold each other's hand, to hug one another. No, the doors and windows had to be nailed shut. They just had time to resurrect the words of the old folks: 'Neighbor! I got three nails left! Take them! And here's a board too . . . Here, I'll put the handle back on your hammer!' They found the strength to wheel the handcarts all the way to the river and lug the elongated rocks shaped like arms back and distribute them along the tracks of Savane, lay them on the roofs to keep the sheet metal from being ripped off, Lord have mercy! Run here-there with boards on their heads. Fill gunnysacks with sand and throw them up on the roofs to keep the sheet metal in place – easy, easy, stay in place, Lord!

If Joab had still been of this world on that day of September 16, 1989, Cyclone day, for sure he would have smiled and applauded Savane, his paradise, the fraternity and friendship that folks demonstrated. As long as one didn't consider the shabbiness of the cabins they were patching up . . . Squalid cabins brimming with misery. Narrow shanties housing penniless families. Seedy hovels in which the only light came from a color TV plugged into a mysterious maze of extension cords strung up like clotheslines to another cabin that proudly housed a certified E D F electricity meter. Temporary sheets of tin roofing, fixed forever for lack of funds, concrete extensions built onto wood shacks that were slowly but surely rotting away . . . In truth, if one didn't take too close a look – jaded with the arrogance of affluence – one might have thought that a new town was being built here, with heartfelt hope, the vigor of youth and all its built-in dreams. One might have thought that all those folks hadn't taken life's licks and that their skin was soft, their hands free of calluses . . .

Siklòn!	Cyclone!
Nou ka atann vou	We waitin on you
Siklòn!	Cyclone!
Nou pas pè-w	You doesn't scare us
Sé dyab ki voyé-w	Is the devil sent you

Nou ka atann vou	We waitin on you
Woy woy!	Oh me, oh my!
Ti moun ja ka pléré	Them children is crying already
Siklòn!	Cyclone!
Ou pa ni santiman	You ain't got no heart

When the lone voice of the *tanbouyè*-drummer arose, borne aloft by the hands beating on the skin of the *tambour-ka*, it drowned out all the other sounds that had been filling Savane since the night before. It was coming from a cabin near Nèfles Bridge. From a man's throat gruff with tobacco. Came from a fellar's throat that had surely never said 'I love you' to a woman, even if he had known and loved more than one. A man that made hearts beat by pounding on the taut skin of the *tambour-ka*. And the wind scattered his words through all the defiant minds of the gathered nations. His voice challenged the coming cyclone. It left peoples' souls ajar, and even Eliette, who had never wanted to hear or understand that black-man music, stopped her hands in midair as they were smoothening her pleated skirt. The voice, the sound of the drum, and the words of that man strangely touched her; she was alone facing the drum. She caught herself thinking that she might have danced if she'd been younger. Wag her hips, spread her legs, and let the sounds of the *ka* enter her whole body and help her find the movement, just like those Negresses she hated for allowing themselves be possessed by the music that spoke to the lower levels of the body, to unknown instincts hidden behind tall trees on inner hills, buried under layers of dirt sown with bitter rancor. Now she too felt shaken, called upon to dance to shore up her courage and stand tall in the face of the cyclone. Chosen, she felt she'd been chosen at last.

Siklòn!	Cyclone!
Nou pas pè-w	We not fraid
Non!	No!
Woy woy!	Oh me, oh my

Yes, she had the right to let the music into her body. Because she was made of flesh and blood. And dance until she fell to her knees before the *tanbouyè* straddling his *ka* like a wild horse. Listen to the pulsing of her flesh and give herself entirely to it, sway, dip, swing and thrust her hips to suck in the music. And make a cyclone of her belly and spin all around in the strong winds, arms and legs whipping out, broken-necked. Haul in the nets of her life, drag her insides out to see what was there, root out the beast cringing in there. She danced, the old weak-kneed Negress, before man and cyclone. And it wasn't because she'd been married twice to angel-cake men that she felt she was saved, delivered from her fears. She danced all right, lifting up her skirts for the very first time. And at last she flung herself open to let in the music of the *tambour-ka* that spoke to her from afar.

Siklòn!	Cyclone!
Ou ké pasé pasé a-w	You coming all right
Mé nou tout ké rilévé	But we'll all stand again
Siklòn!	Cyclone!
Pon moun pa pè-w ankò	Nobody 'fraid of you now

Fall to her knees and offer her body to the *tanbouyè* who was telling the tale of the black man's bravery off in the distance.

.   .   .   .

'Are we going to leave, friend Eliette? I'm ready now,' sighed Angela as she put her hand on the old lady's shoulder.

'Huh? Huh?'

'Oh, you were sleeping? Are we leaving? I finished my breakfast.'

'Oh, yes!' answered Eliette. 'Here, come here, my little angel, let me give you a kiss on the forehead. Sure enough, you're my angel. The Good Lord sent you to me. Come along now, come on! And don't forget the cat either!'

The day before, like every day since Sunday, Eliette had gone to see Rosette, who talked about her life again, told of her misfortunes . . . Her mama Gilda, her papa – King of Kings – on his white horse, the concrete vessel for a million, Rosan's old papa, and Bob's dreams . . . She didn't eat a bit of what Eliette brought and spent her time sitting smack-dab in the middle of her cabin, crying, reading the pages of dictation, and rocking back and forth. When Eliette came back, she told Angela that her poor mama didn't deserve to be abandoned. The miserable woman had only sinned out of blindness. Seen nothing. Heard nothing but the voices on the reggae albums.

'Thoughts of beating you have left her mind, Angela. Go and give her a kiss. I told her we were going to La Pointe. If she wanted to come with us . . . She said no. She knows Cyclone is coming. She's waiting for it . . . I informed the firemen in Ravine-Guinée. Go ask her once more if she doesn't want to come with us!'

Angela answered that she didn't want to go back, ever . . .

'Not now. Keep me close to you, friend Eliette! I don't want to see her, please! And what if he comes back . . .'

Eliette had insisted, repeating to Angela that above all she must look deep into her mama's eyes, see that she was just a woman who'd stopped dreaming. It wasn't her fault if all these misfortunes had come bowling along. Some folks were like that, they saw great and faraway things: no changing them, just couldn't bring themselves to look at the little pain-filled lives struggling all around them.

'You'll have to talk to her,' Eliette pursued. 'You two will be alone at last. Robert and Rita went to take shelter from the cyclone at Great-Aunt Fanotte's. There'll be just the two of you. Mother and daughter, two women looking each other in the eye. Heal and bury the whole business. Forget . . .'

Angela had promised, 'After . . . after the cyclone . . . After the trip to Pointe-à-Pitre. Afterward, please . . .'

Had Séraphine opened the same eyes as Rosette when she realized what had been done to her daughter? Eliette wondered. Shame had stuck black knives into Rosette's eyes. And the looks people gave her were unbearably hurtful.

'Seen nothing, heard nothing,' she swore to Eliette. 'How can it be possible. All these years sharing the same man, just like two rivals. Taking on the same rod and living in the same cabin. And I didn't see nothing in the sheets, nothing on his forever closed face. I didn't hear nothing. When did he do it, good God? What time of day or night did he climb up on her? Maybe it was on the days I went to Des-Ramiers when my mama Gilda was out of sorts. And why didn't she tell me about it? Lord, why didn't she scream? Seen nothing. Heard nothing. I swear, friend Eliette. I swear. Can you believe me? And why is this happening to me? My mama Gilda warned me that one day I wouldn't have enough tears in my soul to cry with. She said that nigger everyone called Rosan, the one I called my prince, didn't have no love in him. It's true, he hadn't been given any love. His papa was already an old sinner, a heap of things to be reproached for, a load of accursement that he stuck under his floppy felt hat. Old scoundrel, dirty dog of a man, who dirtied God knows how many women before starting to walk with his tail between his legs, hauling his misery around with Rosan's mama. Old black monkey man who – after serving Satan with all his soul – struck Virgin Mary poses, scolded or played the role of the indulgent father when he came for a Sunday visit, one sorry Sunday in all of the et cetera days one can count in the length of a year. And Rosan's mama, who was a child compared to that old black man, treated Rosan like an animal to be petted. My poor mama Gilda warned me. She probably already knows that Rosan is spending his nights in jail. She knows what he done right under my nose. Aunt Fanotte too. I told Robert and Rita not to say nothing, just that they didn't know nothing about the whole business. I'll never go back to Des-Ramiers. Never set foot there again. When Rita was born, I thought that my mama's predictions couldn't come true anymore. The day of the baptism she even talked to Rosan a little. We could never go back to live in Des-Ramiers. Seen nothing, heard nothing, friend Eliette . . .'

Eliette had left her alone in the dark room. Alone with the words that she kept rattling on and on. Heavy words that made the air grow slowly thicker. Five days that Rosette had been rocking back and forth, sitting cross-legged on the floor. Drifting along on a stray current, waves of white loose-leaf pages that held Angela's writing and her, Rosette's, fairy tales. The same iron had branded them both . . . Lives of lies. Lives to be thrown down to the bottom of Nèfles Bridge, to be lost at sea. Had Séraphine wanted to disappear too, slip into the deep waters, drown in a gush of words to stave off the vision of the tall man rooting around in the child's body?

Rosette looked at Eliette without seeing her. Hollow eyes, shimmering with troubled waters in the bottom of a well of terror. Trapped eyes, crazed reflections, saber blades, anger, and death. She hadn't eaten, hadn't combed her hair in God knows how many days. She smelled. And her odor filled the room, lingered on the words that brought up the past, Rosan's youth. Stench that stated the filthy shame, revealed the stain, the carrion smell of rape, the putrescent horror, the pestilential depths of remorse, decomposition. Eliette closed the door, thinking to herself that her mama Séraphine had surely felt the same way when she'd thrown herself at the demon with a will to kill. Alas, she'd lacked the strength. Felt so nauseous her knees buckled beneath her. Only one ear slashed off, a little blood running down his neck, and that was it. No, the demon hadn't even seen the inside of a jail!

Godmother Anoncia knew all about that cyclone. Had run into him once, with his low-fitting hat. She'd spat in his face for what he'd done. How could she have kept quiet all those years? Godmother had looked after herself, kept herself alive. Death had tugged at her many a time, but the old lady had never lain down to really die, agonize, rant, and rave on her big boat-bed. Even though she was born before the turn of the century, Eliette thought, the Good Lord would never let her go to heaven as long as she hadn't told the secret that made her a party to the acts of the Beast. A secret that tarnished her soul and rekindled dark recollections. A saintly woman had predicted she would live to be a hundred. Said there would be two horrific cyclones in her life. She would never be in want of food or drink. She would know when to invest her money and turn a profit. But – the prophetess had assured – she would always feel something gnawing inside of her, due to an incalculable sorrow that could only be assuaged by unburdening herself of the secret.

Oftentimes Eliettte had felt the low whisper of words pushing imperceptibly at her ears. But Anoncia always held them back, knotted her tongue, winced at the biting teeth gnawing inside of her, always swallowed the words in her mouth. The day that Renélien had declared his love for her in the bus, Godmother was recuperating from heart failure that had almost flattened her for good. On that occasion Eliette thought once again that she would start talking and reveal parts of the great secret. Alas, as soon as she'd been relieved of her suffering, the old woman buttoned her lip and stowed her secret back away.

La Pointe, she had to get to La Pointe before the cyclone. People said the one that was coming – Hugo – was the master cyclone, the king of cyclones, a roaring lion, the scourge of God, the helmsman of hell, general of the armies of Satan, wind of the Apocalypse, and end of the world. She had to see Godmother Anoncia. Godmother must talk. Before the cyclone. Eliette wanted to hear, from Godmother Anoncia's lips, what she already knew. Everything, she wanted to hear it all from the lips of a living being. She was entitled to that much. Relive it all, so she might finally get out from under that rafter that had crushed her life.

So she asked the Lord to guide her steps until she reached La Pointe, found Ethéna, who was surely still alive, the old caretaker of a garden of ancestral medicines. That kind of wise woman didn't up and leave the earth in a hurry as ordinary creatures did. They always lent credibility to their lives. Ethéna – because of her, because of the forgetting Ethéna had breathed into her, Eliette hadn't been branded for eternity with the mark of the Beast. She'd known men that had loved her, had given her joy. Hadn't seen too much sorrow. Except for the missing child. Eliette wanted to see the face of the woman that had mended her, sewn hidden stitches so tight that forgetting had made an empty envelope of her, useless, left lying around with no destination or return address. She would have liked to be a beautiful love letter, quivering with the kind of words that speak and tell of interesting things, a tumult of passion, outbursts of emotion, dense, fragile experiences that fill the soul and make one aware of being alive, standing on one's feet in this world. Instead of that, she'd led her life in a bland way. Had Ethéna snuffed her out when she saved her? All the flames that had danced within her, smothered. All the flames that lit the way to the sound of the drum, snuffed out. She'd known only the darkness of forgetting, for which falling mute and being left with a dulled mind were the dues she'd had to pay. Her heart was a wasteland. No, Eliette, she said to herself, the Beast alone snuffed you out, broke and bruised you . . . Respect Ethéna who put your body back together and laid forgetting over you like an unguent on your burns.

She'd give Angela some time. She hadn't known the miraculous hands of Ethéna. Angela didn't know what forgetting was like. Would probably never know. No more than she'd know the peace of the hard shell that had made a fool of Eliette for sixty long years.

Unsteady peace
Macadam peace
Illusory peace . . .

'After the cyclone we'll come back here and you'll go see your mama . . .'

'But you'll still let me stay with you, huh?'

'Yes, if you want to!'

Just before leaving Savane, Eliette went back to get Angela's clothes. She didn't forget the bluejeans and the little flowered blouse that she just had to bring back. Rosette was weeping tearlessly, smoothing out the pages that the rain had washed clean. Eliette found her sitting on the floor in the same position. Drowned roaches floated in the bowl of soup she'd brought over the night before.

'You'll go say goodbye to your mama all the same, Angela!'

'When we come back from Pointe-à-Pitre, maybe I'll go and say hello to her.'

'During the cyclone we'll be staying in Pointe-à-Pitre, where Godmother Anoncia has a concrete house.'

'Ah! Is she your godmother?'

'No, angel! She's my mama's godmother!'

'Ah!'

'It's time to go now! Come along!'

It was the morning of the day of the cyclone. Two hours before midday. Marga had already taken her benches inside and nailed the doors to the shop closed. She'd sold everything: the sugar and candles, the oil, the transistor batteries, the flour for the dankit-bakes for the days following the cyclone, the bottles of Capés Dolé water, the cans of Sovaco butter, the ten-liter canisters of gas, the cod, the herring, the pickled pigs' tails . . . Yet, she wasn't smiling as she packed up her account books in plastic bags in order to bring them back out three days after the cyclone. If the wind was as strong as they said, the banana plantations would be devastated in no time, crops lost, and money would be hard to come by under Savane's roof. And how were folks going to pay her what they owed, how?

There were still buses running in Ravine-Guinée, but it was said they'd be scarce after noon. All parked till Cyclone had given its last blast. Eliette was holding Angela by the hand, as if she were walking with a two-year-old child that she was afraid might dart out under the wheels of a car. By the hand. So proud to be with her girl Angela. And the looks people gave them didn't wound or offend her. She was already thinking about the day after the cyclone when they would walk around arm in arm. That's what the Haitian fortuneteller had predicted.

In town the name of the cyclone was on everyone's lips like a popular word, flippant and promiscuous, handsome, pleasing to the tongue, spicy, and bitter: Hugo! In front of the church, Moses and Eddy – the two brothers who had survived the mountain – were crossing themselves as they watched people fleeing. Right in the middle of the general upheaval that made the situation all the more tense, those two stood cloaked in grim Rastafarianism. They were filthy, their hair gummed up, their nails scratching at invisible creatures burrowing in the caked grime and the rank hair on their bodies.

'Go back to Savane! Folks are waiting for you back there! Go back to your birthplace and join all the others who are barricading and nailing things down! Don't stay here!' Eliette told them.

Moses just lifted an eyelid to see if his brother Ras was stirring any.

'Cyclone is going to flatten everything tonight. Go wash yourself under Nèfles Bridge and then go back to Savane where there's work to do!'

'Mam Liette, everyone back there is already done gone! They all . . . condemned, already dead, zombies! Don't break your heart over them! Bab . . . Babylon be destroyed tonight.'

'Friend Eliette! Let's go! The bus is leaving . . . ,' Angela begged.

'Go back, children, go back!'

Yeh, Mam, yeh, we going back into the belly of Babylon, and we going to help the lost souls of Babylon. They all going to be washed away, and then the Good Lord going to start his kingdom on earth . . .'

'Come on! Let them look after themselves! They're as good as lost . . .'

'No one is ever really lost, Angela! No one!' Eliette answered as she walked away.

'Cyclone! Cyclone!' repeated the bus radio in the break between zouk tunes. 'Worse than Cyclone '28 – the worst ever – the one that turned all Guadeloupe upside down.' 'Pray to God!' a priest was now saying on the air. 'Make a long chain of prayers so that those who are least protected do not perish! The churches will open their doors to the congregations until six P.M.' 'City hall, the district schools, and the municipal cafeteria will be open!' chanted the mayor of Ravine-Guinée in his bleating voice. 'Needy inhabitants from Savane Mulet and surrounding areas should take their belongings to the village hall: mattresses, beds, chairs, tables, televisions . . . A guardian has been appointed to ensure their safekeeping, he is presently on site. Possible cut-off of water lines; fill containers now as a precaution! Possible electrical blackouts; have candles, matches, oil lamps on hand! Careful not to set your cabins on fire!' The voice of a specialist followed, describing beforehand the damages to come: 'Guadeloupe will be wiped off the face of the map, like after a bombing. All the plantations will be destroyed. Not a single banana tree will be left standing. Tidal waves will come and waste everything along the coast. And, considering the force of the wind, La Soufrière just might become active again – like in 1976. Earthquakes are likely. With the waterlines ruptured, epidemics could spread and . . .'

Disgruntled, the bus driver jammed a cassette into the radio and the voice of Eugène Mona swelled, swelled, swelled, until the passengers, whose eyes were hooded with fright, started beating time, entered into the mystery of the *ka*, heard and understood its call. Once again the sound penetrated Eliette, but this time she wasn't half asleep. Her eyes were wide open. And the *tanbouyè* was beating on the skin of her belly, which was taut and smooth like the skin of a young girl. And the flute carried her back to Savane, back to the days when Joab spoke to the animals, to the days when her mama Séraphine fled before invisible spirits and cried out at nightfall under the tin roof because she heard a bacchanal of *soucougnans* and zombies or saw with her own two eyes a horse gallop through the cabin. Eugène Mona's flute sang of the river in the days when folks didn't throw stoves or old broken fans into it. When rat families didn't dwell in washing machine drums. And the flute was the speech that she'd regained thanks to Joab, who spoke to animals and asked forgiveness for bending grasses under his light step. The flute told of the hope that no one is ever really lost – just gone astray in the world. Her people weren't cursed, just had a thick black skin that could endure all kinds of weather, work in the sun, walk into the fields through the razor-sharp grasses, embrace the thorns of sorrow without even shedding a tear. And that was a blessing.

Thinking of Lot's wife, Eliette left Savane without looking back. She'd put the bars up on the window shutters, hooked the doors, and turned the key in the lock, just out of habit. She had said no to all those who wanted to bring sacks of sand and big rocks to put on the roof of her cabin. 'May God's will be done! Come what may!' she said to them, without seeming to be affected by the idea that Cyclone could blow her roof away, flatten her cabin. Deep inside of her something told her that Cyclone '28 was and would always be the most horrendous she'd ever known. This one might well blow her cabin away – what of it? She was sixty-eight years old. Lived sixty years with a cyclone curled up inside of her like a snake that strangled all the babies that she could have carried, all the infants she would have liked to let suck on her breasts. A cyclone that had crushed the love in her. A long beast like an insidious tapeworm that had devoured her insides and brain. She squeezed Angela's hand tighter, her baby Angela that she'd waited on for ages and ages. As fate would have it, they had both run into the same rafter with its grimacing face, its long voracious teeth, its crazed eyes. Cyclone! A voice coming from the radio suddenly started singing 'No woman no cry,' the very same reggae music that threw Rosette into a trance and undoubtedly gave her the courage to carry on, the strength to face her life in the hell of Savane. Without understanding the words, Eliette began to sing the refrain that spoke clearly to her for the first time . . .

No woman no cry
No woman no cry
. . . When we use to sit
. . . in Trench Town

Yes, the sun up in the sky was predicting that everything would be all right. Nothing new to report, not even the finest drizzle, good strong sunshine. Treacherous sky! Eliette thought. Not the slightest breath of wind in the fronds of the coconut trees, tall, straight, hieratic, contemplating the world below, mad ants.

No woman no cry
No woman no cry

Everywhere, on every cabin by the roadside, gunnysacks swollen with sand and rocks weighting down the thin tin roofing. And people walking rush-rushed, pushing handcarts, carrying bundles on their heads, young goats, children. Lord, where to pen up the cattle?

Where to store the vinyl living-room suite and the Formica wardrobes paid for in installments that you'd been impertinent enough to covet, stick inside the cabin of rickety boards and thin tin roofing to fool yourself into believing you'd accomplished something, risen from the breed of scrawny animals under the master's thumb always begging for a pittance with their nose in the air. Lord! Where to hide your body when they say the coming cyclone is cousin to the descendants of the Apocalypse, when – knowing we are all sinners before God – you shrink away, overwhelmed at the clarity in his eyes and the clairvoyance of his spirit? Nowhere to run today: the hills are exposed to the thrashing wind, the sea all around is posting guard – prison. Condemned to hold up under the battering, the bashing, and the great buffeting of Cyclone. Suffer the angry skies. Bite your lips to keep from cursing Creation. No escape but hope, patience, and prayers. Gather up your scattered courage. Laugh and tell jokes and tales of Yé krik! Yé krak! Throw your head back and let the rum catch your blood on fire – Yé krik! Yé krak! Then join your hands and place yourself in the hands of the Almighty. The borrowed cinder blocks, the sacks of cement, the nails, the heaven-sent planks, mighty blows of the hammer, and the pounding of the *tambour-ka*, just to keep from showing the coming cyclone a distraught face . . .

No woman no cry
No woman no cry

On the hills the still, leafy green trees were waiting too, in awed calm. Tomorrow, they said amongst themselves, we'll count those who've been broken, who've been left on the ground. Tomorrow, day after tomorrow, we'll all stand again, even if we've lost our leaves, have been decapitated, mutilated. Tomorrow we'll grow new limbs, and sap like has never been seen before will flow within us, the burgeoning of the fires of heaven will burst forth upon our branches. Tomorrow . . .

The cyclone didn't terrify Angela. She was even awaiting it, figuring that it was a fury unleashed by the heavens to rid her of her papa Rosan. She thought, May it swoop down upon the earth like a great war! May its furious armies, lightning, and batteries of thundering canons storm over the land! May it turn time around and send me back to my mama's belly! May it beat down upon the jail once and for all. Ruins, dust, everything would turn back to dust. Even memories, swept away by the great winds. Blown away, scattered, dispersed.

When La Pointe appeared, on the other side of the Salée River bridge, Angela made a wish and prayed that the cyclone would thoroughly cleanse her body, put it all back together again just like before, back in the days of innocence.

La Pointe, Angela never recognized it. The town had many faces, just like her grandmama Gilda, one day joyful, another mournful, and still another worried and standoffish.

La Pointe . . . Concrete towers gazing out at the silent and treacherous arm of sea stretching before them. A multitude of dilapidated cabins thrown up among the arching mangroves, the *Babèt*-crabs, the marsh hens, the long-legged rails, the mud, and the *yen-yen* flies. No rollers heralding a tidal wave, just small sluggish waves sloshing at the shoreline. Just the fishermen's gommier canoes hauled up on the sand and, off in the distance on the wharf, shiny white motorboats, sailboats back from a trip around the world, yachts anchored nonchalantly.

La Pointe with its ups and downs. Ancient wooden houses leaning against weather-beaten and proud concrete buildings rising up three stories. Hibiscus and dwarf coconut trees leaning over delicate bronze balconies. Rusted iron gratings, miserable shops, and tinsel storefronts. Rich and poor sweating the same heat. Hot prices, good prices, friends, yes indeed! The police – blue! And the Haitian women with their large bags hastily packing up their wares. No more stands on the sidewalk. Nothing left to sell. Blue! Run breathlessly from the billy clubs of the black lawmen. Blue! Stuff the bath towels – three for a hundred francs – into the gunnysacks. Blue! Hide the empty boxes of brassieres, girdles, and women's panties. Sweet Haiti.

'Candles! Pa oublié, bouji a zot! Don't forget your candles! Flashlights at all prices! Five francs, ten francs! Wheat flour, salt cod! Rich, thick kerosene!' shouted a pistachio-nougat vendor who'd hastily converted to the heaven-sent precyclone trade. The crowds flowed through the two streets of La Pointe as if it were the day before a celebration. Moving up and down the street, up and down, along with all the others that didn't know where to hole up and were preparing for the lean days and moonless nights to come. Moving up and down the hot street. 'Don't wait till afternoon to get provisions! Putting things off brings you sadness and regrets, remorse, and exclamations of I-believe-in-God!' raved tempestuously a small black man glistening with sweat who was making a brisk fortune by dipping into a gold mine of American candles that had materialized from Sint-Maarten.

Three big-bottomed black women were walking along in single file, carrying nearly bursting, tightly bound cardboard boxes on their heads. Had it been any other day, the rebel cobbler, who was plying his trade in front of Fine Shoes, would have complimented them on their curves. But this was no time for kidding around. He still had two-three heels to nail, a sole to glue, and was in the process of beating an old piece of leather on his block. Still, he was smiling. Smiling slyly at his radio, which was announcing the force of the coming winds and the implacable determination of the elements. Smiling softly, standing behind his workbench – a barrel perched atop three cinder blocks – and thinking of the water that would flood all the way to the back of the Syrians' store. Water and mud that would seep in everywhere, mucking up and drowning millions of new pairs of shoes stored in the back room of the shop. Despite the iron gratings pulled down, the alarms and the padlocks, the water and the mud that Cyclone spit out would get the upper hand. And the fellar was smiling to himself as he put away his nails and old fabrics, his glues and soles. Soon he'd go hang his barrel up in his kitchen – made of concrete. And he would thank the Lord for having made him an itinerant tradesman, who could preserve his wares from the fury of the winds. The Syrian shoe merchants, who had tolerated his presence in front of their shop windows for a quarter of a century, were truly unfortunate – condemned to standing by and watching their merchandise be devastated. At least for one day in his lifetime the man felt he was lucky, blessed by God, one day out of the three hundred and some of this long year. Yes, he thought, the time comes when even the wealthy have to endure the whip and learn to weep, naked, their two empty hands imploring the Almighty.

Anoncia lived on a formerly pretentious street leading up to Victory Square. Wrought-iron gates, overgrown with threatening and thorny pink and mauve bougainvilleas, kept out prying eyes. Up and down the street, the houses – facades redone a hundred times, well kept and splashed with vivid paint like the powdered faces of old affluent matrons – concealed mysterious shadows behind half-closed blinds. And the exuberantly colorful gardens were like bursts of laughter in the luminous play of sunlight. A fortunate marriage with a mulatto – a doctor of tropical diseases – had made Godmother Anoncia the first black woman to be a legitimate resident in a concrete house on the said street. A squat house that lacked any real charm. Its only saving grace were the flowers protruding from a luxuriant foliage, half dissimulating the heavy molded balconies, the thick walls.

Eliette pushed open the gate, which – awakened from its sleep – creaked crossly, sending heavy boughs of large, ethereal leaves swaying to and fro. Short grasses wound their way between the worn cut-stone paving in the dark courtyard steeped in a heavy, subdued silence that shielded it from the scathing sounds – clattering and horn honking – of La Pointe. Godmother Anoncia was a tough-skinned Negress, a product of another century. Time had progressively shrunk her, but she still felt youthful in her old body. If she hadn't been obliged to keep the secret of the Beast, she might well have never known the bitterness of dark thoughts, the burden of silence. She would have lived her life in insolent lightheartedness, throwing her money away on gold necklaces and pendants. She would have enjoyed her fortune alone, behind the elaborate, rusty wrought-iron gates, behind the walls that spared her from the gaze of the poor. But she could never laugh heartily – cra-cra-cra! – or take advantage of her widowhood and go dancing, shake her hips, and get a young whelp into her bed. Bouts of a nameless sorrow kept her bedridden, feverish, on the verge of despair.

At times, believing she'd been delivered from her burden, she powdered her cheeks, put on some pink lipstick, and – strolling through Victory Square – suddenly thought she saw life differently, as if the Beast had never crossed her path. As if she'd never had that brute for a brother, that slimy creature of the depths that had split Eliette in two and thrown Séraphine's life off track . . . Lord, as if she'd never had that sweet little brother that everyone called 'Ti-Cyclone,' just for fun. 'Ti-Siklòn! Ti-moun lasa sé on Ti-Siklòn!' That child is a Ti-Cyclone! railed Mama Glorieuse when he began to walk around in the cabin, knocking into things, tearing everything apart. Ti-Cyclone, Anoncia had seen him again one-two times after he'd done it, just passed him in the street in La Pointe. She had spat in his face. She had repudiated him for what he had broken. And at times, knowing that he was of the same blood as she, the old woman felt unclean, putrid, and repulsive.

Folks from the country, old acquaintances, sometimes came scratching at her door to pay a courtesy visit. Sunken deep in the velvet armchairs of the living room, the first-rate fools – legs crossed and mouths puckered – chatted uncomfortably as they sipped on old rum. And then, with one fell swoop, they dropped the name of the Beast. Like a savage dagger, the name tore Anoncia up, so much so that she believed her entrails had been ripped out, delivering her at last from the inner gnawing. But the name pronounced did not really kill. It merely left Anoncia terror-stricken, standing stiffly amid the crumbling walls that she'd been rebuilding every day since the hell of 1928. Anoncia alone and helpless against the idiots who had violated the cathedral of forgetting, unknowingly laughed hard, and kept evoking the name of Ti-Cyclone in a jesting and carefree manner. Yet she always found the strength to laugh as well, to lie to them too, inventing wonderful news from a rose-colored France where she'd allegedly sent Ti-Cyclone.

In truth, the man never left the area or its confines. For a time he holed himself up far from the fury of Séraphine, thinking that she would be hunting for him with that knife of hers for some time. A long knife to stab him with. She'd left him with only one ear, which buzzed when the wind was up. The next day, the day of Cyclone '28, he found himself at the mercy of the elements – thrown from one place to another all night long, whipped off his feet and then slammed back to the ground, buffeted with blows, slapped up sideways, tossed topsy-turvy. And scraps of sheet metal slashing through the air whistled treacherously over his head. Ropes twisted around his neck. Branches, planks, nails, rocks rained down upon him with a hellish din. All of Séraphine's unleashed rage echoed and whirled in Cyclone '28 . . .

Years afterward he still lived with the memory of that terrifying night that had spared his life, with a buzzing in his ear and scars all over his body. If he went down to Pointe-à-Pitre, he hugged the walls, like a rat, walked along hurriedly under his floppy hat, stooped, hunching his shoulders up around his ears. When his sister Anoncia had spat in his face, he hadn't understood. No, he didn't think of himself as all that bad. And he'd even forgotten Séraphine and her little Eliette as he grew older. One day he'd gone walking after a young damozel who hadn't recoiled at his missing ear, his scars, and the trembling in his voice and fingers. He was so old he no longer dreamt of his posterity. She'd given him a son, Rosan. No, he didn't consider himself to be some kind of demon. He'd liked the child all right, even if he couldn't bring him up due to his advanced age. He and Solise struggled hard to get by.

Anoncia learned of her brother's death the day that President Giscard d'Estaing was elected. She sent Hermine out to buy a bottle of champagne and drank and cried all night long. More than once she had intended to enlighten Eliette about her mysterious father, about her mother's madness. Alas, the words stuck at the back of her throat. She was consumed with shame. The gnawing was eating her away. And her still keen memory did not even grant her the blessing of forgetting.

Hermine, the servant with no family who had been living with Anoncia for four decades, was Eliette's age. There was a sort of rivalry between the two women for the attentions of Anoncia, who sometimes indelicately confused them. Eliette criticized Hermine for being too familiar. Hermine snapped back resentfully, invoking the numerous paintings of Jesus on the walls as her witnesses, claiming that she too was Anoncia's godchild, and chanted the date of her baptism in a singsong voice till late into the night. Her life, she declared – filled with bitter jealousy – could be summed up by forty years of dedication, sacrifice, the life of a recluse! She hadn't had her fill of men, had hardly known the meaning of going to a dance and feeling its giddy vapors, didn't even have a cabin in which to lay up her old age. And who would take care of her when she grew useless? Won't be no one. Anoncia swore by Eliette alone, called to her in her sleep, and harped all day long about her godchild Eliette being a poor, unhappy body deserving the Good Lord's favors. Hermine thought of Eliette as a dried-up, mealy-mouthed soul with a heart of stone.

For the first time in her forty years of service to Godmother Anoncia, the sight of Eliette did not inspire a flood of rage in Hermine's heart. Godmother had been hearing Cyclone rumbling in the distance for three days. She didn't leave her bed and cried like a baby, saying that Cyclone was coming to get her, that she didn't have the strength to die. She was constantly calling for her two goddaughters and her mama Glorieuse. Hermine made her drink some tea made of bark from the immortelle tree, basil, and semen contra leaves. But Anoncia didn't even want to close her eyes, for fear of remaining eternally caught in the wells of sleep. The night before she had started telling the servant the whole truth about Eliette. Her father, who'd fallen upon her the night before Cyclone '28, had pitched into Guadeloupe in exactly the same way. Her mama Séraphine, who'd lost her mind. The missing ear. Eliette ripped open, rescued, and sewn back together by the Ethéna woman . . . And then Liette losing the faculty of speech, her mind grown dull, until she met with Joab and the peace of Savane. And, finally, keeping the secret with sealed lips to avoid causing any more pain, prevent the pain from welling back up in the body. The poisonous secret . . .

When the wind started banging the gate around furiously and beating on the closed shutters, the two women were sitting at Godmother's bedside. Angela had fallen asleep in one of the rooms upstairs.

'That fortuneteller who promised me two horrific cyclones wasn't lying, was she? He's been on his way for some time now. Been hearing him galloping along for days on end. Dear God, he's coming back to get me!' Anoncia whimpered. And bright golden tears from her nearly burnt-out eyes shone on her cheeks. Her flaccid fingers clutched pitifully at the white linen sheets. Outside the branches of the trees had begun to moan and knock against the shutters like beggars that no one wishes to see or hear. Cyclone was there, outside, an infuriated madman. Rushing like a fierce army through the streets of La Pointe. Breathing ruin and desolation. Mean. Murderous. And turning ancient trees to kindling, matchsticks. Ripping cabins to pieces. Sweeping clean, crushing all. And his diabolical laughter – showers of chains, volleys of gunfire, and barrages of artillery – made the stone walls quake down to their very foundations. His breath stank of absinthe.

The Beast, Eliette thought. The devil she sometimes heard behind the door to her cabin in Savane. The mad-dog Beast who gnashed and bit ruthlessly. The Beast with its long cutlass rushing through the air, blowing its funeral dirge. Spitting serpent. Savage scythe. The wind that smashed, decimated, stripped, docked, splintered, bearing along with it water and mud, life and death – all in the same demented bacchanalia.

'You want a wee bit of tea, dear Godmother?' asked Hermine.

'Ah, yes! I'd like that!' said Anoncia, suddenly in better spirits.

'Godmother, tell me, my mama, my papa . . .'

'What? Now – just leave be Eliette. Leave the cyclone go by, girl.'

'Godmother, was my papa the man that mama called the Beast? Tell me!'

Outside the town was splitting at every seam under the onslaughts of wind and flailing rain driven by the drunken cyclone as it tempered and ground its infernal tools; Outside the darkened sky looked on as tin roofing and tree trunks, tattered parasols, casseroles, and tea pots sped by. Gutted mattresses, broken dreams, new boards, and fleeing dresses. Wingless animals were also flying amidst cabins turned crazed tops, spinning dizzily, all shaken up, floors smashed in. Huge and terrifying merry-go-round. And then there was a tremendous ripping sound, flesh tearing and bones breaking, as if the earth were splitting open to let the blade of Cyclone in – humph! humph! – all the way up to the hilt. Off in the distance, somewhere out in the night, a wounded woman called out. Broken, demolished woman crying to the Almighty. Cries for help tore through the lull in the storm. Other voices rose in echo: swollen zombies spitting up the waters of the great deluge, furies gone astray in the streets filled with dead trees upon which smashed dinghies slept, daring women braving the silence that had fallen over the town.

Suddenly the wind had nothing more to say. The eye of the cyclone was directly over La Pointe, evaluating the damage, maybe searching through the debris for the other eye that had fallen to earth long ago. Deep in the darkened sky some saw the wicked face of Iscariot contemplating his treacherous kisses, others, an implacable beast with its single eye open, preparing to charge headlong into the land that lay below.

The water, which had leaked into every room in the house, dripped from the closed windows, crept under the doors, seeped in, rose around the sculpted legs of the varnished mahogany furniture. Eliette remained at Anoncia's bedside, letting Hermancia struggle with her rags and buckets. When Cyclone whirled around and rushed in for a renewed attack, she didn't hear its ransacking the shops, snapping off the electric poles, and hurling the trees that had been spared in its first passage. Her thoughts had carried her far away, to a time before Savane. And Eliette saw herself, hiccupping with laughter in the arms of her papa, who tossed her up into the sky once, twice, a hundred times.

That is how the face of the Beast appeared, first bulging up unevenly from the soft wood of the rafter, then gradually detaching itself. He was singing in a coarse voice that didn't fit with the bursts of laughter coming from his throat. His eyes – embers of desire, shiny baubles, cracked through from the stirrings in his soul – were already rooting around in Eliette, assaulting her in thought. Sad crumbs of memory . . .

From time to time Eliette came back to reality just to put a question to Godmother, who said that all those old stories were dead and buried et cetera times, she couldn't recall a thing about them. Anoncia clenched her teeth against the secret, listened to the wind, covered her head with the sheet, put off, put off the moment of truth.

In the morning, when Cyclone moved away, wagging its tail like a handkerchief to the tune of 'Adieu foulard, adieu madras,' Godmother started – God knows why – to talk freely:

'He had a boy after you. Oh my, years later. With a young gal. He was already old and homely with his ear cut off . . .'

'He was my papa, wasn't he, Godmother? I saw his face carved in the wood.'

'He been dead quite some time now . . .'

'Godmother, I saw the rafter with his face carved in it . . .'

'To me, he been dead long before his death, Eliette. And even so, he ruined my whole life.'

'Godmother, tell me about this brother!'

'I don't know anything more . . . So many people pass without leaving a single mark. Your papa was my sweet little godson . . .

'Oh! All these years . . . '

'I was consumed with shame. Shame for my people and my name.'

'Your brother, my papa.'

'A man possessed by the devil. I bore his shame all my life, Liette. A cursed man.'

'Godmother, tell me what he did that night, the night before the cyclone!'

'Eliette, girl, you already know the whole story. Leave the cyclone go its way and know that you can't go through life always looking back. There'll be other cyclones, lots of them. And no one can do nothing about that, even the great scientists in France. No one can stop them. Just predict them. And a body will just have to lie low and then stand back up again, rebuild, dress the wounds, try and look forward to tomorrow's dreams, and keep replanting, with hunger twisting in his stomach. If the Good Lord could just grant me a little extra time, I wouldn't stay locked up in here stoking the fire of my pain. I'd come out from under the chains of shame, out from under fear and its endless boggy marshes. If the Lord allowed me to stay two more days on this earth, I wouldn't let my zombie brother ruin my life; I'd lay down this infamous burden. I'd spread my wings and travel, see the other faces of the world and its scattered peoples . . .'

'Godmother, tell me about Ethéna . . .'

'No, she didn't live to be a hundred . . .'

'From what mama Séraphine said, she was a saint . . .'

'Not at all!' exclaimed Anoncia.

'Then a sorceress?'

'Just an ordinary woman, Liette. Always ready to help with her two giving hands. An unpretentious damozel, Liette, her heart torn apart by this world that had picked her dreams clean. No, she didn't have great powers. She was no healer big on words and short on medicine. No, Ethéna didn't raise the spirits. And her eyes didn't roll back in her head under the hand of Satan. She passed away last year, without suffering, in her sleep, all curled up like a baby in its mama's belly. Smooth, trusting, and new, just like a child who hadn't seen nothing of the world and its ugliness. You see, it's as if all the good she'd done on this earth had spared her the difficulties of the crossing. That's how I would like to leave this earth, with a smooth brow, a trusting soul. I'm afraid of the crossing, Liette. I'm not prepared to close my eyes. If only the Lord would grant me one small favor . . . Staying a little longer on this earth. For better or for worse, luck, love, dreams, pain, and torments. We'd go dancing, Liette. We'd go sit on Victory Square in the shade of a cabbage palm. We wouldn't talk much, but we wouldn't let bad thoughts make our hearts bleed again . . . We'd feast our eyes on the spectacle of the street and . . . I wanted to eat a coconut sherbet, Liette. Just to keep the taste on my tongue during the crossing. I'm afraid I'll have a rough time . . .'

'Godmother, Cyclone has passed.'

I know, child, I know. Horrific like its brother of '28. But maybe it's always the same one that comes back, Liette. You'll think of your old godmother sometimes, won't you? I never forgot your mama, the poor soul. And, you see how life is, I was nine when I baptized your papa. He wasn't even two months old; your mama wasn't born yet. Those two are already dead and here I am talking away. Before he was ten, he'd almost been killed three times: drowned in the river, strangled on a mango seed, laid out flat with fever, I always saved him. And what for, Lord?'

'You didn't know, Godmother.'

'Maybe I shouldn't have saved him. We wouldn't be in this fix today.'

'You didn't know. We don't know much about the days to come. We make assumptions, we dine on regrets, we wait and see. I strung a lot of ifs, one after the other, too.'

'The shame, Eliette, it was like a companion I was always leaning on. I should have opened up my house more and given from my heart. Don't make the same mistake I did, Liette . . .'

'I promise I'll . . .'

'You know that girl you brought along looks just like you when you were fifteen, after you'd learned how to speak again. Today she's got no more mama or papa, and that's a real pity. But you're here . . . You wanted a daughter if I recall . . .'

A daughter, yes, thought Eliette, old new mama who was already thinking about a roof to cover her Angela's head. What was left of her cabin in Savane?

She'd probably have to rebuild. Yes, there was still a way to get it back on its feet, old Joab's paradise of macadam dreams.